Lightning Bound

Lightning Bound Series
Book 1

Samantha Vance

To my husband, my white lightning.
Thank you for bringing light to my darkness.

Chapter One

Tree branches slashed my face and arms as I sprinted through the forest, the thicket nearly too dense for me to get through. Desperately, I ripped and clawed my way through the tangle of trees, ignoring the sting of the shallow cuts across my skin. I had to get away. I needed to get away.

I didn't know what was chasing me through these woods, but its aura was unlike anything I had ever experienced. It was a red so deep it was nearly black, and it was everywhere, a swirling mass of hunger and malice descending upon me like the plague.

Whatever it was, it was powerful and strangely integrated into the forest, the sky, even the air I breathed, and I wasn't sure I could fight it off on my own, even with my magic.

The sky overhead was black with no moon in sight, the only light twinkling down being the slight glimmer of the stars. Every muscle burned from the strain of exertion, and I wasn't sure how much longer I could keep up my pace.

I had been out for an evening walk amidst the trees, connecting with nature as so many witches often do, listening to the winds and flowers when darkness rained down from the sky, eating away the sun and casting the forest into shadow. The winds died away, leaving the air stagnant with the slight scent of iron, of blood.

That's when the growls started, surrounding me, herding me deeper into the forest. So, I ran. Sometime during the chase, I had gotten lost, unable to find the path home.

If I could just get home to Vivian, she would know what to do. She could help me escape this creature.

Dread filled me as I felt a root catch my foot, and I hit the ground so hard my teeth clicked together. My muscles ached and screamed in protest as I scrambled to my feet, stumbling slightly as my vision swam. Hot breath brushed against my neck, and I whirled around, backing up slowly.

My heart was pounding, and a cold sweat trickled down my spine, my breath shallow as I looked around frantically for my unknown attacker.

The menacing growls and screeches intensified, so loud I practically felt them vibrating in my chest. All at once, the noises stopped, and the air stilled, building up a fearsome tension that pressed against my skin.

"*You can't escape me, Blair. I am coming for you,*" a voice hissed from the center of the darkness.

I stiffened at the use of my name, but it was not a surprise that the creature hunting held knowledge of who I was. Still, the thought of this monster knowing my name filled me with unease and had me wondering what else they knew about me.

My back hit a tree behind me, and shadows sprung forward, swallowing up the entire forest and sky, trapping me in an endless void of terror. I tried to scream, but no sound escaped my lips. I flicked my fingers, willing my magic to come to my aid, only to find it blocked, giving me a glimpse as to what it would be like to be utterly human.

Tears were flowing freely now, but despite the palpable fear coursing through my veins, I balled my hands into fists before bringing them in front of me in a defensive position, and I steeled my jaw, readying for a fight.

I tried to call upon my magic, digging deep into that well of power within my soul, only to find a damn wall blocking me from accessing it.

This isn't real. It's just a nightmare.

Even those comforting words I chanted to myself failed to quell the terror burning inside me, to keep the doubt from creeping in, having me questioning the very reality around me. Not having access to my magic could happen for several reasons, this being a dream being one of them, but dreams—nightmares, they couldn't feel this real. Could they?

I felt hot breath on the top of my head rustling my wild hair, accompanied by two glowing crimson eyes staring down at me, emerging from the void like two burning coals.

"What do you want from me?" I growled, my body betraying the fear I felt, shaking as I stared into those red eyes.

A large, pale hand breached the shadows, brushing a piece of my hair out of my face. I flinched away and heard a chuckle, glancing up to see the eyes gleaming with humor.

"Well, isn't it obvious?" Red Eyes rumbled. His voice was low and thick with an English accent, but it radiated an old sort of hunger.

He lunged forward, bringing his face out of the dark abyss. His skin was pale and smooth, only further illuminating his blood-red eyes. His mouth was curled into a cruel smile, revealing two sharp fangs on each side of his front teeth.

Vampire.

I'd been fortunate enough not to have encountered a vampire before. Vivian, my adoptive mother, had elected to homeschool me, although my education was far from the normal human homeschool experience.

Mine consisted of the history of witches, stories of the gods, how to practice magic as a traditional witch, and what supernaturals to avoid. She had strictly warned me away from vampires, as well as a few other creatures, during our lessons.

Vampires craved powerful blood to feed on and wouldn't hesitate to drain me dry if they ever got a taste.

So, to make sure that never happened on the off chance that I *did* have a run-in with a vampire, or any other supernatural that meant to cause me harm, Vivian made sure that I knew how to defend myself. She helped me harness my magic, learn the control that it so desperately needed, and how to wield the number of abilities I possessed. She taught me how to fight, not only with magic, but in hand-to-hand combat, because relying solely on your magic could get you killed.

The vampire's hair was platinum-blond and shaved on the sides with long locks slicked over the top, each hair styled perfectly. He leaned down until we were at eye level and purred, "*You.*"

I screamed as he dove for my throat, his snarl sending a tremor through the world around us.

I threw a punch towards the vampire, and the force of my swing twisted my body out of my twin-sized bed and onto the floor in a tangle of sheets.

Fuck.

I managed to sit up and lean against the iron bed frame, checking my surroundings quickly. There were gray walls all around, oak wood floors beneath me, a small window to my left with a view of the surrounding red rocks, and a blue painted wooden door.

I was back in my room at St Christopher's Convent in Sedona Arizona.

Wasn't I?

I chanced a look down at my still trembling hands. My olive skin tone lacked its usual tan glow, and I had to work to suppress the shaking.

I concentrated on my connection to fire, the element I held the most power with, and brought it to the surface. Flames burst from my fingertips, dancing there beautiful and strong, bathing the simple room in an orange glow.

Thank the gods.

The nightmares were becoming more and more frequent, but

they were always the same. I was always running away from the dark creatures, always in the same forest, unable to get away, unable to use my magic, and unable to distinguish dreams from reality until I woke up. But never had I seen those red eyes before, never had I seen the creature behind the nightmares.

Regardless, a supernatural creature, or supe for short, was hunting me, out for my blood, which is exactly why I was here.

Hiding.

The residual fear faded, and in its wake left the usual empty depth in my chest. That was all I had felt during my time here: fear and emptiness.

A knock grabbed my attention, and I quickly extinguished the flames as the wooden door creaked open and the silhouette of a familiar nun gingerly walked into the room. Sister Maria flicked on the light. Her eyebrows lifted as she took me in, sitting on the floor, sweaty with sheets trapping my feet.

"What are you doing on the floor?" she quipped, leaning against the wall, her dark eyes amused at my clearly ruffled state.

Sister Maria was already dressed, her hair neatly tucked into her veil, and the rest of her black habit was clean and pristine as it always was. She was the first friend I made when I came here, having just arrived here from Rome herself. Many of the other nuns were wary of me, and the strangeness of my situation did not do me any favors, but Sister Maria never cared about any of that. She had been my lifeline during my time here.

"I thought everyone started their day like this." I smirked.

She chuckled and strode over to me, her hand outstretched. I took it and stood up, kicking the sheets away from my feet.

After I had righted myself, Sister Maria looked over my face with greater detail, a small wrinkle forming between her dark brows as she studied me. "Another nightmare?" she asked.

I shrugged before I pushed my long black hair out of my face.

She sighed, worrying her lip briefly before she spoke again,

"Maybe I could ask Mother Superior if you could be taken off kitchen duty this morning?"

I rolled my eyes and gave her a knowing look.

She sighed again, knowing how incredibly stubborn I was. "Alright, fine then, you'd better hurry and get changed. I'll meet you in the kitchen to start breakfast."

And with one more sympathetic smile, she walked out and closed the door behind her.

I let out a shaky breath and stepped over into the bathroom. I didn't even bother looking in the small mirror in front of me, knowing what I would find in my reflection. My gray t-shirt stained with sweat and purple-tinged circles splotched under my brown eyes.

I attempted to brush through my thick hair, barely managing to put it up in a messy bun before flicking my hand, turning the shower on. As I brushed my teeth, I swirled my hand to bring heat into the water with fire magic. The water pressure here was still terrible, but at least I wouldn't be freezing.

Witches were able to wield the elements: earth, wind, fire, and air. Most witches could harness all four but had a dominant element they were more drawn to. I was not most witches, as I could only control fire and air, but I had a strong affinity to them both and was able to wield them with greater intensity. In this situation, with the awfully cold water, I was grateful to Hecate, the Goddess of Magic, for giving me the gift of fire in my veins.

Small blessings.

Not that the gods ever granted me many of those. I stopped praying to them a long time ago—other than the Mother of Magic of course, the creator of witches.

I had never met my birth parents, but Vivian was able to work a small spell that would tell me which parent I had gained my witch heritage from. As I had unique abilities, Vivian knew immediately that I was not a full-blooded witch, and after the ritual we learned two things.

The first was that my mother was a witch, and the second was that she was dead.

It was a hard thing to come to terms with. I mean, how can you mourn someone you never met? But still the pain was there, as well as the longing to meet her and knowing I never would. Vivian was able to get a single photo of my mother, but not the name, as many of the records of my birth and admittance into the foster system were sealed.

Vivian was unable to gather any information on my father, something that seemed to frustrate her to no end. All we knew was that he was still alive, as those bloodlines were still connected, according to the spell.

That was a harder truth to live with. My father was alive, and he wanted nothing to do with me.

I sighed as the water gently poured over me, heated by my magic. Despite the more tolerable temperature, I missed the shower in my house. I missed my own bed, my clothes, and the quiet street on the outskirts of Cottonwood where I lived.

I let out a shaky breath at the memory and let the tears finally flow down my cheeks under the hot water. I was afraid, and it made me feel like a coward. I had no idea who this vampire was who was hunting me, and despite being in hiding for over a year, he had not given up.

It had all started with nightmares, waking me nearly every single night to the point where I was sleep deprived and barely able to function. Vivian gave me some herbs to help me sleep, though they didn't help much, and now knowing that the nightmares were magical in nature, it made sense. This went on for months. Then, out of the blue, nightmares became less frequent for a time, making me think I was in the clear, but that's when I started to notice I was being followed.

I noticed him first as I was walking downtown with Vivian. Every turn we made, a tall man in all black clothing followed. He started appearing everywhere I went, but he always kept his distance. Even when I started staying home, I felt eyes on me through the windows, just watching, and unable to breech Vivian's wards.

It wasn't until one day when I was running on a trail near my house that he tried to close that distance. I heard footsteps that weren't my own coming up behind me, and I cast a look back and saw him. I was able to keep ahead of him until I hit the main road where my best friend Sage was waiting for me in her car. I leapt in with no hesitation and she peeled away quickly, leaving the man in black behind.

"I had a vision," Sage had said as she drove away, her blue-green eyes continuously checking the rearview mirror, making sure the stranger was no longer following us.

She was a psychic and had visions, though many times they were cryptic and vague.

Sage had looked over at me, her shoulder-length golden-blonde hair shaking from the movement. *"Blair, you need to leave Cottonwood and hide. They're coming for you."*

I'd nodded, trying to catch my breath. She drove me back home, and we settled in on Vivian's couch. The warding Vivian and I had erected around our home would keep out any unwanted visitors.

"Do you know who or what they are?" I'd asked her.

She shook her head. Sometimes her visions only showed her mere glimpses, and we often had to piece together what was to come. Her eyes had been sad and full of fear as she pulled me into a hug.

"Multiple kinds of supernaturals, and none of them nice. They'll stop at nothing to take you, Blair. You need to go somewhere that no one would think to look for you. That will throw them off your trail for a while." I nodded at the information she was able to give me. *"And Blair, trust the lightning."*

I had raised a brow. Trust the lightning? Despite knowing what Sage's response would be, I opened my mouth to ask, but she raised her hand.

"Blair, you know I can't elaborate more than that. The Fates only

allow me to see so much, and telling you everything could change the future. Just trust the lightning, and be ready, okay?"

And so, that's what I would do. Trust the lightning. And for now, I'd hide out here, away from the vampire after me, for as long as I could.

Vivian taught me that I could not be caught under any circumstances by another supernatural. They would kill me for what I held inside me, a storm of power that was begging to be unleashed upon the world.

It had been so very long since I had seen Vivian and Sage, my best friend. They were the only two people in the world who cared for me, and I missed them dearly.

After my shower, I dried off and dressed in my usual attire, gray t-shirt with a blue knit cardigan and some jeans. Fashion may not be the main concern at a convent, but at least I could dress comfortably. The Reverend Mother had told the rest of the convent that I was here for volunteer work for a college course, which allowed me to stay here without raising too much suspicion. I put my high-top white shoes and slipped out the door to head towards the kitchen.

On my way to the kitchen, I passed various other nuns I knew, all finished with their morning sunrise prayer and heading off to their various jobs and tasks for the day.

The hallways were the same bright dove gray in my room, only decorated with an assortment of religious paintings and sculptures. I couldn't help but pause at a particular sculpture of the cross, adorned with various carvings and set in front of a large window that overlooked a small canyon of red rock.

Human religion held parts of the truth, but they had no idea of the true nature of the gods. Perhaps at one time the entire world knew of the true gods, but that knowledge died out long ago.

Throughout all religions and regions of the world, there is no shortage of gods and lore of the divine, which made the whole concept of a higher power seem unbelievable since there were so many different versions of gods, and some who shared seemingly identical characteristics and powers.

I learned that was the point really. A long time ago, the gods agreed that they would all go by many names in order to suit the needs and ideologies of each region and people of the world. It was unrealistic that everyone everywhere would believe in the same celestial beings. So there are many different versions of themselves known across the world, with each culture worshiping a variation of the same god. During my teenage years, I had wondered if the gods' strategy in all this was genius or arrogance.

As the years passed, I grew to believe in the latter more than the former.

A few nuns were scattered about the kitchen working on mixing batter for pancakes and waffles or chopping fruits to go with them.

I found Sister Maria quickly, washing various berries in the large sink, along with a wooden cutting board, a knife, and an assortment of bowls waiting for me.

I smiled and greeted the other nuns by name, having been here long enough to at least know the ones I worked with in the kitchens, then settled in my task of drying and cutting the fruit before placing them in the bowls to be brought to the large cafeteria where everyone would eat together.

Then there was the kitchen spirit, who blinked in and out of existence near the stove, just watching me. There were more than a few spirits within these walls, which made my heart heavy. How could you not find peace in death at your very place of worship?

This spirit wasn't aggressive or wild like some of the other spirits I had previously encountered; she was a young woman in a habit. Even though her whole form was nearly transparent, her overall figure grayish-white in color, I could tell her eyes were sad.

Seeing ghosts and spirits was just one of my unique abilities as a necromancer—an uncommon gift amongst witches, although it was one of the less creepy ones that came with the title. I have been able to see them for as long as I can remember. Various foster families I had when I was young just thought I had a very vivid imagination. It wasn't until I hit my teens that I truly understood what I was seeing.

For the most part, they never interacted, but there were some who were curious, and strong enough, to speak with me.

In addition to necromancy, Hecate, the Goddess of Magic, deemed me worthy of being a chaos witch, an extremely rare kind of witch. I can see auras, the spiritual energy around all beings, and as I grew to become more familiar with my powers, I found no limitation to what I could do. Even stopping death was not outside my reach, although I had only done it once, and I intended to never do it again.

Vivian was a witch and taught me to never reveal what I was to anyone. Chaos witches were hunted and used in rituals as sacrifices and all other kinds of truly awful things that made my stomach churn. I was always so careful, and yet here I was, in hiding.

Everything in the convent was seemingly normal, sure.

But this uneasy feeling in my gut was warning me to stay alert. I shook my head, as if I could shake away the swirling sense of dread in the room. Surely, it was just residual feelings from the nightmare...

Hopefully.

Chapter Two

Bells chimed over the intercom, and Sister Maria and I finished carrying the last of the bowls to the long line of tables where everyone could make their plates to their liking.

Having kitchen duty had its perks, as we usually got to grab our food first, however we did have to wait until every nun in the convent sat down with their food for prayer prior to eating. I was particularly hungry this morning, as I usually was after a nightmare, and it seemed my stomach would be loudly protesting until I finally got to eat.

"That's odd," Sister Maria whispered to me as Sister Louise conversed with a few other nuns at the heads of the table where the Mother Superior usually led grace before breakfast. "Mother Superior isn't leading us in morning prayer. I hope she isn't sick. You remember the last bout of flu that blew through here."

Before I could respond, Sister Louise stood before the convent and apologized for Mother Superior's absence, explaining that she was sick, and then began leading the morning prayer.

The entire cafeteria bowed their heads, myself included, as Sister

Louise spoke of God and blessings and for the Mother Superior's swift recovery. I listened, closing my eyes and letting the words wash over me. Soon enough, much to my stomach's delight, the prayer was over, and I dug into my heaping plate of pancakes and berries with extra syrup.

After eating, I helped clean the dishes from breakfast, then was able to take a quick break to sit out in the large courtyard, settled under a tree to read while Sister Maria and some other nuns went to the market to fetch a few things for both lunch and dinner that the kitchen had run out of.

During the sister's various prayer hours, I usually either read a book or stretched my legs and went for walks around the convent.

The sun had finally set after dinner, and I made my way back to my room, eager to finish my book and get some sleep—if I was lucky enough to sleep without a nightmare tonight. I had just gotten settled into my sweatpants and t-shirt when a soft knock had me sitting up in bed.

It was odd for anyone to knock on the door at this hour, as it was time for the sisters to retire to bed after their evening worship. "Come in!" I called out, and to my surprise, Sister Maria stood in my doorway, a troubled look on her face.

"The Reverend Mother would like to see you. Sister Louise sent me to fetch you for her." Sister Maria shrugged, clearly as confused as I was.

I didn't have another meeting with the Mother Superior until the end of the week, to discuss my continued stay here. She had been trying, unsuccessfully, to convince me to join the convent officially as a nun, and while I appreciated her taking me in and allowing me to stay here, only asking that I helped out, this was just a way to lie low for a while.

"Huh, weird, but okay. She must be feeling better." I got up slowly, grabbing my cardigan and wrapping it around my body as a cold chill ran down my spine.

Sister Maria only shrugged again, opening her mouth but shutting it quickly before she began guiding me down the hallways leading to the Reverend Mother's office space just behind the large hall where the convent gathered to pray.

Moonlight trickled into the courtyard and corridors, casting an eerie glow across the religious statues and paintings. It was quiet, and the absence of the sounds of baying coyotes or the buzzing of cicadas had every one of my senses on high alert. Quiet warning bells were ringing in my head, but I pushed the internal sound away, trying to convince myself that I was being paranoid, and this unease was just the after-effect of my nightmare.

I walked next to Sister Maria down the long hallway, continuing to ignore that little voice telling me to run the opposite way. She knocked, only opening the door after she heard the Reverend Mother call us in.

"I'll see you in the morning." I patted her shoulder and gave her a quick smile as I stepped into the Reverend Mother's office.

She was sitting behind her desk, hands folded neatly in front of her. Sister Maria gave me a small smile, one that didn't reach her eyes, that forehead crease making its appearance again as she looked between the Reverend Mother and me. With a nod, she bid us farewell and left.

Unlike the rest of St. Christopher's, the room was painted a deep purple color, and her desk was a rich mahogany wood. Behind her leather oversized office chair was a bookshelf filled with various religious titles and artifacts.

A few pieces of mousy brown hair had fallen out of her veil, something that was unusual for the Reverend Mother, giving her a slightly less polished look than I was used to seeing. Her cheek bones were sharp, and she had an extremely slight frame from what I could tell, her belt cinched as tight as it could go across the waistline of her habit.

As soon as the door shut behind me, the air settled around me and seemed to have a coppery smell that made it difficult to breathe.

My magic stirred inside me, immediately shifting into defensive mode. I straightened my spine and froze in front of her door.

"Is there something wrong, Blair?" she asked me with a slight smile.

I slowly shook my head and took my usual seat in one of her plum-colored chairs. Alarm bells were ringing through my head, warning me to get the hell out of here.

There was something off about her, the way she looked at me, and even her voice sounded different—colder and unfeeling. I focused on the energy around her, shocked to see her aura was a deep crimson red that swirled with bloodlust, so unlike her usual cool blue that surrounded her.

The Reverend Mother inhaled deeply, her body shaking slightly when she finished, as if she couldn't stand to sit there any longer. I kept my body forward in the chair, ready to jump up and run if I had to.

As if she could sense my discomfort, her smile deepened.

"I was thinking today we could speak about what brought you here a year ago. We haven't discussed it for a few weeks, how scared and in need of aide you were that night, and I think it would be beneficial to revisit and see why your perspective hasn't changed on joining our convent officially." She clasped her hands together tightly, her knuckles white from how hard she clenched them.

I raised an eyebrow at her. She continued to smile, and her body remained still other than the slight trembling and slow rise and fall of her shoulders. The hairs on the back of my neck were standing straight up, continuing to remind me that something was very wrong here. I slowly nodded, and she leaned in closer to her desk.

"Someone is looking for me," I stated simply, as I leaned back and casually threw one of my legs over the arm of the chair.

To most, the move would have seemed arrogant, but it was deliberate, and it gave me a better angle to leap for the door. My words were true, without diving into the whole complicated story. The

Reverend Mother had already heard this, and even though she looked and sounded like herself, I didn't trust her. Auras never lie.

Her smile faltered slightly, and her brows pinched together, cracking her whole pleasant nun façade.

"And why do you think someone is looking for you?" she asked, narrowing her eyes, making her features impossibly sharp.

I began to shift in my seat, trying to keep my limbs loose. I shrugged my shoulders, dismissing her question.

Her smile quickly thinned into a hard line, and her lips pursed. "I just want to understand, Blair. I have been far more lenient than other convents would have been. I have given you shelter, food."

I gripped the arms of the chair tightly. The woman in front of me was not the sweet, soft-spoken Reverend Mother I'd come to know during my time here. No, this woman was cold, a hollow shell only looking to inflict harm and destruction.

"What happened to generosity of spirit?" I snorted, giving her a sarcastic smile. The words fell from my mouth, and I cursed myself for my sharp tongue that would surely get me into trouble one day.

Her face was twisted in displeasure, the skin around her eyes tightening as she glared at me. I refused to drop my gaze from hers, even though my heart was pounding wildly in my chest. I willed my power to pool there, ready to use it at a moment's notice, but to my dismay it was slow-moving, like a beast trying to wake up after a long sleep.

She let out a sigh, "Blair, after all the kindness I have shown you, your silence is truly disappointing. Perhaps we will have to reassess your living situation and find you placement somewhere more appropriate."

I stiffened. I could cut open the veil and slip away, but with no recent practice, I didn't trust I wouldn't get stuck somewhere in limbo. Slipping through pockets in the veil was another strange ability of mine, but it was too risky to use right now.

I decided in that moment to tell her a small portion of the truth, hoping it would briefly satisfy her while I came up with a plan to escape.

"I began having nightmares of something chasing me. After a while, I started to feel like someone was following me around town. I felt paranoid and crazy, so I ran away from home and found my way here, hoping the church would offer me sanctuary."

Whether it was pure kindness or sympathy for a deranged girl showing up on their doorstep that caused them to take me in, I was never sure, but in that moment, I had felt safer than I had in a long time.

A slam on the desk startled me, the Mother Superior's face set in a rage. She shoved back her chair and rounded her desk to stand in front of me.

"Enough of this! You may have thrown him off your trail for a time, but it ends here. Purchasing all of those plane tickets and hotels in various states and countries was smart, I will admit, but not even you could evade him forever," she snarled at me. A fleck of spit hit me right on the cheek, and I brushed it away and glared back at her. "With you finally in his grasp, we will be stronger than ever!"

It was then I noticed the tiniest hints of red in her brown eyes and the tips of fangs peeking out from under her curled lip. Shit, she had been turned into a vampire. I willed my chaos to float to my hands, ready to fight her to get out of here. I leaned to the edge of my seat, angling myself perfectly to escape.

"Go to hell." And with that I launched a chaos-packed punch at her stomach.

She flew back into the desk and as she pushed herself back up, I quickly jabbed her nose, the crack echoing in the small office. She shrieked with rage as blood poured down her face. Pivoting around the chair, I reached out to the door with my chaos and swung it open, only for a familiar scream to greet me.

Sister Maria.

Sprinting down the hallway, I didn't even spare a glance back towards the office, heading in the direction I thought the scream came from. As I made the turn towards the courtyard, an arm stuck out and hit me square in the chest, which effectively knocked me on my ass and left me gasping for air.

A caveman-looking vampire with a bald head and dark, thick eyebrows towered over me. He was dressed in black pants and a black button-down, but the red tint to his eyes betrayed what he truly was. He bent towards me and yanked me to my feet by my arm. I could hear the Reverend Mother strutting down the hallway towards us, heels clicking on the tile floor.

I reared my head back and then swung it towards his face, the loud crack of our skulls connecting echoing in the hallway. Unfortunately, it hurt me more than it hurt him, and all I managed to do was piss him off.

I was too frustrated and dazed from my attempt at a headbutt to duck away from his fist coming at me.

It connected with my right eye, cracking something in my face, and my knees gave out. A blow like that from a human wouldn't have fazed me at all, but vampire strength nearly mirrored my own. Black spots danced in my vision, and I fought to stay conscious. The Reverend Mother walked up to us and had a cat-that-ate-the-canary grin stretched across her face.

"Let's go." The male threw me up over his shoulder. My head was still too fuzzy to fight back. They started down the hallway towards the exit through the courtyard that led towards the church parking lot and burst through the door.

The cobblestone gave way to pavement, and when I managed to look up, I saw the tall walls of the convent, the rough stone glowing in the moonlight. I hadn't so much as left the inside of those walls for almost a year, and now I was being forced out by the very creatures that had been hunting me. The surrounding red rocks and desert were quiet, the only sounds being the vampire's footsteps thundering across the parking lot.

I heard a car being unlocked, then a trunk being opened, along with the clanking of handcuffs, and my stomach dropped. I managed to angle my head to peer around the hulking vampire to see Sister Maria lying on the ground next to the sedan, unconscious and with blood pooling beneath her neck.

These fuckers were not putting us in there.

He shifted me to a cradled position in his arms as he neared the trunk. My head was clearing, and he must have noticed as I tensed my muscles to fight back. A damp towel that reeked of a powerful sleeping herb was brought to my face, but just as it was an inch away, he paused.

I held my breath, trying not to inhale the paralytic fumes. The big thug holding me snarled, dropping the cloth just as a growl erupted through the night.

"This doesn't concern you, *dog*," the male vampire spat.

I wanted to get a look at whomever he was talking to, but my instincts told me to stay limp and wait for an opportunity. Another growl rumbled, this time closer.

"Victor, get rid of him," the Reverend Mother snarled at the male vampire holding me.

Victor started to lay me down in the truck, and right when my butt hit the bottom of it, I kicked him in the jewels with all the supernatural strength I could muster and scrambled out of the black vehicle, stumbling slightly, fighting the effects of the sleeping herb.

I rounded the car and barely managed to get an arm underneath Sister Maria, but the Reverend Mother followed quickly, using her vampire speed and grabbing my hair, yanking me backwards and forcing me to drop her back to the ground. I struggled against the Reverend Mother, only to pause when I felt the cool sting of sharp metal against my neck.

My body froze, every muscle going taut. Any movement would result in my throat being slit right open. Fear chilled my blood, and I bit down on the inside of my cheek to control my shaking. She leaned forward, and out of the corner of my eye I could see a set of fangs hanging out of her mouth.

"Control your fear! Use it, dive into your natural instincts and

your magic to help get yourself out of danger." Vivian's voice pierced through my panic, reminding me of the training and teachings she had instilled in me.

"Let her go," a deep voice demanded.

In front of us was the silhouette of an impressively tall, dark-haired man. He was wearing dark wash jeans, leather boots, and a black t-shirt that stuck to his broad shoulders and defined chest. He had to be at least six-foot-five and thickly corded with muscle.

I couldn't really make out the details of his face because of the way the shadows hid his features, except that he had glowing sky-blue eyes.

The Reverend Mother let out an awful cackle, her body shaking with it. "Not a chance, dog. She's coming with us, and we're going to bring you along as a snack for the road. This one seems to be nearly tapped out." She nudged Sister Maria with her foot, who let out a slight whimper, her brows pinching together in pain.

I struggled against her hold again, only stopping at the increased pressure of the knife against my neck.

I glanced over to see her partner sidle up next to her, his fangs sticking out of his grim smile. I let my eyes scan my surroundings for a weapon to wield, all the while trying to bring my fire magic to the surface, but I must have inhaled more of the paralytic fumes than I thought. My limbs felt heavy, and my magic was sluggish.

Twin growls snapped my attention back to the stranger, and as I focused on the shadowy street behind him, I saw movement and two more sets of bright eyes. Two massive wolves emerged from the shadows, hackles raised and teeth bared.

Holy shit, werewolves were coming to my rescue.

Chapter Three

"You're outnumbered. Let her go, and your death will be quick." His voice was deep and smooth, and it reminded me of the feel of velvet against my skin. I squinted into the shadows, trying to get a better glimpse of his face.

In response to his words, the knife against my throat pressed in, breaking skin and drawing blood. I hissed at the pain. He stepped forward into the light and *oh my god*. His hair was a rich brown and tousled as if the wind itself ran its fingers through it. He had a jawline that would make the gods jealous, and it was covered with dark stubble. And his mouth was simply sinful, even as it was set into a grim line.

Not the time, Blair.

His eyes, nestled under a set of thick brows, shined through the shadow cast over his face with an impossible sapphire glow.

The moment our gazes met, flashes of white light obscured my vision, and an invisible bolt hit me straight in the chest, painful at first, but as it spread throughout my body it became a pleasant hum. As it flowed through me, I saw flashes of his vivid blue eyes, a light so bright it was almost painful to look at, a stunning black wolf running beside me in the forest, and a single black feather floating down from the night sky.

Sage's words echoed, *"Trust the lightning."* The white lightning cleared and opened my eyes to see those sinful lips curved into a cocky, lopsided grin.

The Mother Superior and her minion seemed completely unfazed by the new energy flowing through my body, so powerful I felt bolts of lightning skittering across my fingers.

What the hell just happened?

At a small flick of his fingers, the two wolves behind him snarled and broke out into a run towards Victor. The gray wolf reached him first, leaping straight for his throat. Victor caught the wolf by the shoulders, narrowly avoiding a mouth full of teeth. Meanwhile, the tan wolf circled around and went for Victor's legs while he was distracted.

A sharp tug on my hair brought me back to my current predicament, as Reverend Mother was trying to drag me back towards the trunk of the car. The wolves were still entangled with Victor, but judging by his screams, he was losing.

The Mother Superior inhaled sharply, and her eyes zeroed in on the blood that now trickled down my throat. A low hiss erupted from her lips. With fangs now on display, she moved closer to my neck, the knife pressing in harder and releasing more blood.

I looked around frantically for something, anything I could grab a hold of while wildly fighting her tight grip on me.

There.

A deep growl that seemed to shake the world erupted from behind us, stilling our movements.

I smiled. *Hello, handsome.*

The Reverend Mother snarled and spun us around. Before me was a jet-black wolf the size of a bear growling and snapping his maw at her. While she was distracted, I used my now charged power to grab the knife and throw it out of her hand before blasting her backwards.

I hissed as the blade cut me when I threw it, but I felt the wound already closing. I turned to see Mother Superior climbing to her feet, her aura a bright crimson now, pulsing with anger.

Without a second thought, I reached out towards a shovel near the garden shed just beyond the pavement with chaos, and the invisible tendrils of my power sent it sailing towards her at lightning speed, sharp end first. Her facial expression was still in an in-between state of fury and surprise as her head slid off her neck and hit the ground with a wet thud.

The black wolf spun around and looked at me, stunned, an expression I never thought I'd see on a wolf. I shrugged and smoothed out my shirt. He scoffed and trotted behind the garden shed. The other two wolves came to stand in front of me, and even with blood streaking their fur, it didn't appear they were hurt.

They briefly turned and listened to something coming from the building, and I took that as my chance to creep away. I took a few steps, keeping one eye on the wolves and one on the still unconscious Sister Maria.

These wolves may have saved my life, but I didn't trust them. No one in this world did anything without asking for something in return, especially supes.

The gray wolf quickly leapt in front of me just as I reached her, keeping his stance playful, his tail wagging quickly behind him. The tan wolf stalked over to stand next to the gray one, his ears pressed back against his head, his amber eyes studying me seriously.

I flicked my gaze between the two. I could make a run for it, but seeing as I hadn't trained properly in a year and they would likely catch me, it didn't seem like a smart idea. The only other option would be magic, but I was feeling particularly tired between the blow to the head and using a considerable amount of chaos for the first time in months, not to mention the sleeping agent still in my system. I huffed out a breath, coming to the realization that I wasn't getting out of here without seeing what they wanted.

I bent down to check Sister Maria's pulse and breathed out a sigh of relief when I felt it beating strong, despite the blood pooling beneath her. I tore off the bottom of my t-shirt and pressed the fabric into her neck to stop the blood. She groaned slightly at the contact, but her eyes remained closed.

Out of the shadows strolled the mystery man, clad once more in his dark jeans and boots, carrying his shirt, the muscles on his bare chest rippling with each step towards me. He stopped in between the two wolves and looked up and down the length of my body. Not paying any attention to the dismembered Victor not two feet to the left of him.

I eyed him curiously as I stood, the images of those entrancing blue eyes, the black wolf, and the bright flickers of light dancing across my vision once again, and I had to blink them away. He chuckled, his eyes twinkling with mischief as he took me in.

"If you're done playing modest, maybe you could let me get out of here before more of their friends show up." I looked skeptically at the man in front of me as he finished tugging his shirt on, my gaze snagging on his flexing muscles. But Sage's words rang in my head, willing me to trust that these wolves would not hurt me.

Easier said than done.

He gave me a lopsided grin. "Do you have any idea how expensive it is to constantly replace clothes if you don't strip before you shift?"

I rolled my eyes at him and made a rude gesture.

"What do you want from me, wolf?" I kept my tone bored and my limbs loose as I waited for his response. Clearly, they had known I was to be kidnapped tonight, which only made their rescue even more curious. The possibility of these wolves having knowledge of what I was, what power I held, was unsettling. Despite their help in eliminating the vampires, I didn't trust them or their motives.

"To offer my aid and bring you to safety. I thought that was obvious." He shrugged and stuck his thumbs into the pocket of his jeans. His relaxed stance only irritated me, although I had to admire the self-confidence he exuded. Not that I would tell him that.

"And I thought I made it obvious that I didn't need your help." I flicked my gaze to the Mother Superior's headless corpse on the asphalt.

His eyes followed mine, and he reached up to run his fingers through his dark hair. I stepped to the left, angling myself closer towards the tree line. Just because they didn't want the vampires kidnapping me didn't mean they were here to ensure my safety.

He tracked the movement and adjusted his own stance to block my path. "Seeing as they almost had you in their trunk, I would say that my services were completely necessary." He lifted a dark brow, and my blood boiled.

"What I did with the shovel is only a parlor trick. I could have gotten away at any moment," I snapped at him. I felt my chaos pooling at my fingertips, the effects of the drug wearing off, excitedly waiting for my command, as if it was charged up in his presence.

Ignoring my moody magic, I focused on the black sedan, and invisible tendrils of chaos covered every inch of the metal. I made a fist, and the metal groaned, glass shattered; the pressure of my magic crushed the car in on itself. Within seconds, the car was nothing more than a ball of metal.

His aloof expression faltered at my words, briefly letting his curiosity show through before that infuriating smirk reappeared. "And if they had gotten those cuffs on you? What then?" Blood drained from my face as I looked over at the cuffs lying on the ground and cursed. The ancient runes etched on the side glowed slightly orange, giving away what they were.

Witch cuffs could snuff out all my magic and render me powerless. I didn't know the extent of what they could do to me, as I was more powerful than the average witch, but the thought alone gave me the chills. I would not be chained up again.

"I would have managed. Magic is not my only skillset," I scoffed, feigning confidence.

"Hmm. Tell me, is it customary where you're from not to thank those who have aided you?"

"Is it customary where *you're* from to be such an ass?" I threw back at him. He chuckled.

"Come on, Raven, if we wanted to hurt you, we would have already. You're hurting my pride here. All I'm trying to do is help you and keep you safe. Come back to my pack territory with me, and I swear I will ensure your safety." He held his hand out to me.

I glared at him for the nickname and inched away from his outstretched hand.

He added, "My territory is located within a safe community for supernaturals, just outside of Flagstaff. If you accompany me back, you will have the protection of my pack as well as the wards that protect the city." I raised my brows at that.

A supernatural community? I had never heard of a place like that, although my knowledge of other supes was fairly limited. Vivian kept her teachings basic and simple. She told me what I needed to know about supes that posed the most threat to my life, how to defend myself, and above all not to trust anyone.

Vivian had not once mentioned supernatural communities before, so the knowledge of their existence was deeply troubling.

But knowing how protective Vivian was of me, and of anyone finding out what I was, perhaps that is why she kept it a secret. She did not want me to venture into a city where I would be surrounded by those who would kill me or use me for their own power.

Still, doubt filtered through me. How could she not have known about them? And if she had, why didn't she think it was important to teach me about them?

My mysterious savior explained that there were various supernatural towns throughout the world that were considered safe territories for supernatural beings to live without the prying eyes of humans, who were blissfully unaware of our presence on this earth. Each community had its own council, with members that were from various supernatural races who worked together to keep the peace and keep the town safe.

"How did you know the vampires were going to try and take me tonight? I find it hard to believe you just happened upon the situation." I narrowed my eyes at him, unease and distrust swirling in my gut. No matter how good his offer seemed, there was something he wasn't telling me.

He studied me for a moment, an emotion I couldn't quite place dancing within those pools of blue, and it took all my energy not to squirm under his gaze. "I understand your distrust, but I swear to you that I only wish to help you. Call it a leap of faith, divine intervention, or whatever you wish. Just come with us, and I will explain everything."

I huffed out another breath, thinking through my options and finding there weren't many.

I could run again, but in truth I had no idea where to go. I certainly couldn't go home. I ran through many possibilities, all the while Sage's damn premonition was playing on repeat in my head, and when I found no viable option, I begrudgingly looked back at the werewolf.

"Any ass sniffing that occurs will result in a neutering, do I make myself clear?" I gave a stern look to each of them to drive my point home. The two wolves let out chuffing noises and turned towards the street.

The male let out a bark of a laugh and motioned for me to follow him towards the end of the parking lot. Before I did, I snapped my fingers, and blue flames enveloped the dead vampire's bodies, burning them quickly until they were nothing but ash on the asphalt. If he was shocked at my ability, he didn't let on.

I then turned back to Sister Maria, warring emotions filtering through me as I looked down at my friend. I wished she could come with me; her presence had been a constant comfort during my time here, but she was human, and she was in more danger with me than she was here.

I sighed, bending down as I brought chaos to my fingertips. They glowed a bright silver, as I pressed them to her temples and pushed my magic into her mind.

Human minds were easier to manipulate, because they did not have magic to protect or ward their thoughts and memories. My silver magic washed away all memories of this night, leaving only the knowledge that I had to go and speak with the Mother Superior. I fabricated new memories, weaving into her mind that she had heard a noise in the courtyard, and she tripped and fell, hitting her head, explaining the weakness and possible dizziness that came with the blood loss.

I then directed my magic to the puncture wounds in her neck, where Victor had bitten her and willed the skin to close. Once it was done, my magic retreated into me, and my lip quivered slightly as I looked down at my friend. She would wake confused, but with no knowledge of the supernatural, and I would be gone.

Without asking, the male approached and lifted her into his arms with ease, and I showed him where in the courtyard to set her down gently to adhere to the memories I had placed.

"Goodbye, my friend," I whispered, trying to ignore the ache in my chest as I looked down at Sister Maria for the last time.

Together, we emerged from the courtyard, and he led me down the narrow driveway of St. Christopher's Convent towards the rest of the city. We walked side by side, with the wolves trailing slightly behind us as we made our way down the small hill. Keeping our pace quick, we made it out to a row of shops. The only lights burning were the streetlights, all the storefronts had long since been closed for the night. The city of Sedona was quiet, and the citizens had no knowledge of what had transpired just a mile up the road.

"Let's just hope there are no midnight joggers running about tonight," I mumbled, looking to my side at the gray wolf next to me. Tongue lolling out of his mouth, he gave me a wink and kept trotting along.

As we made our way down the street, a black SUV was parked near a cluster of trees near a park that broke up the shopping in this part of town, allowing for tourists to take in not only the eccentric shops but also the beautiful desert vegetation and red rocks that made this city famous. The two wolves walked ahead to the side of the car and began to shift back into their human forms. I could hear the bones cracking and see the shimmer of the magic sliding over their skin as they shifted back, leaving two very naked men in front of me.

I was no stranger to the male form, having had a few sexual partners throughout my adult years, but they had never been anything serious. Mostly, the encounters were just heated moments that were a means to release, as not having attachments was just easier. It had been hard growing up to form relationships with anyone during my years in the foster system and especially after I had been placed in Vivian's care. She was protective, to say the least, and distrustful of anyone she didn't know—which was something we had in common.

Still, I hadn't seen bodies quite as hard and toned as theirs.

All three of the males were near the same height, but each had their own striking features. The previously tan wolf had deep brown eyes, rich golden-brown skin littered with scars, and onyx hair that trailed down his back. His features were sharp and far more angular than the other males. He appeared to be the more modest of the two as he quickly opened the door and pulled on his jeans, trying to angle the front of his body away from view.

He finished dressing quickly, turning around with a scowl, distrust burning in his gaze as he watched me.

The other male had a slightly lighter shade of brown hair that hung to his chin, as well as green eyes. He was the gray wolf, and he sure took his sweet time grabbing his clothes, not bothering with shielding his body. All three males were in incredible shape, the contour of their muscles evident in the light of the moon. The first handsome stranger was by far the largest, as the other two werewolves' frames were slightly leaner.

"Now that we can all speak to one another, how about I get your names?" I looked at the three wolves. I crossed my arms in front of me; they may have saved my life, but that didn't mean I was letting my guard down. The more information I could gather on them, the better.

"My name is Dean, and this is Calian." He gestured to the grumpy onyx-haired man and then the brunet. "And Miles," Dean spoke with authority, his dominance over the other two obvious.

"Well, thank you for saving me. My name is Blair. But just so we're clear, I'm not always a damsel in distress. They just caught me by surprise is all." I sniffed.

Dean chuckled as he opened the door for me. I slipped inside, and the wolves all piled in, with Dean sliding right next to me in the back. Calian started the car and peeled out.

"So eager to get out of town, Cal?" the one named Miles joked, grabbing the handle just above the window as the car lurched forward.

"You know I do not like being away from New Haven," Calian growled, and Miles's expression turned somber. Seemed like a touchy subject that I had no business asking about.

"I still want to know how you knew I was in danger tonight," I snarked, raising an eyebrow at Dean. I didn't believe in coincidences. Everything happened for a reason, and I wanted to know how and why these werewolves decided to save me from being vampire food.

"I was... told that you would be in need of some assistance," Dean said carefully.

The way he paused and seemed to search for the right words was a dead giveaway that there was more to that story. I searched his eyes for answers, but all I discovered were two pools of ocean that I found myself wanting to drown in.

"Told by who?" I demanded quietly.

Dean's brows furrowed. His mouth opened and closed a few times before he blew out a harsh breath. "It's complicated. Do you know of the Fates?" I nodded, and he continued, "Let's just say they made it known to me that you would need saving tonight. I promise that I will explain everything when we are back in New Haven."

Hells bells. The Fates being involved only made this situation far more complicated. If he was telling the truth, that is. But I was no stranger to the Fates and their vague and meddlesome ways; having a psychic best friend will teach you that very quickly.

Despite the frustration and distrust roiling through me at his evasive answer, his eyes held me captive, ensnaring my soul with their depth, pulling me in closer. The hum in my veins grew louder, pushing my hand to reach for his, and once our hands touched, another bolt flashed in my vision. *Trust the lightning.*

"So, you can throw and crush things... with your mind? That's fucking awesome."

I nearly jumped out of my skin at his words, breaking the spell Dean's gaze had held me in. I snatched my hand back from his and shook my head to see Miles staring at me curiously.

What the hell was that all about?

"I'm a powerful witch. What can I say?" I shrugged.

I had no intention of revealing what I was to these males. They may have rescued me, but they also could turn around and sell me out to the highest bidder at the drop of a hat. Or worse.

I had never revealed what I was to anyone, and I was careful of how much of my power I showed. Luckily, the knowledge of chaos witches was uncommon, and I was banking on these three were-wolves being unable to see the truth.

Miles leaned in closer and lifted his nose to me, inhaling deeply. "Hmm. There are hints of witch coming off you. But it's different, more wild. Whatever you are, I've never met anyone with a scent like yours, supernatural or otherwise." He gave me another wink.

Dean growled at him, and he promptly turned around in his seat, chuckling.

I turned to Dean to find him staring at me, studying my face. His eyes traveled lower, and my breath hitched as his eyes stopped, lingering where the knife had been held against my throat. He reached his hand up to the spot, and I knew all he saw was a thin line of dried blood that also trailed down my throat, but otherwise smooth skin.

"You healed," he breathed. I nodded at him, and I felt all the wolves' attention on me.

I shrugged away from his touch and cast my eyes down. Werewolves could also heal very quickly after being injured, as did many supes, so it wasn't a very uncommon gift, however witches rarely held this ability. I ignored their probing stares and turned my gaze to look out the window.

The city lights eventually started to become more spaced out until there was hardly any in sight. Lining the road were tall, beautiful trees, and I finally started to relax after the encounter with the vampires. I knew trouble would have eventually caught up with me, I just hadn't expected it to be so soon. I chose St. Christopher's Convent because I needed somewhere secluded where there weren't many visitors or wandering eyes. The convent was still close to the city, however the nuns went out into the community for their duties, and it was uncommon for them to have visitors. Plus, there weren't many places that would allow you to stay without any money and did not ask many questions.

Faith is also a powerful thing, whether it was with the real gods or the god that humans worshipped, and it allowed me to hide within their walls undetected for almost a year.

I had showed up at St. Christopher's tired, wide-eyed, and full of fear on a rainy evening and without question the Mother Superior had given me a room to stay in for the night. The following morning, I gave her the barest of explanations, that I was on the run from someone who wanted to hurt me, and that I needed somewhere safe to stay for the time being.

I begged her to stay, willing to work for room and board, and she agreed, only if I considered taking my own vows and joining the convent. Even though the Reverend Mother had been corrupted by the vampires, I will forever be grateful to her for allowing me to stay for as long as I did.

I knew I couldn't stay there forever, but I thought I would have had more time to figure out my next move. As the days went on, I developed a false sense of safety, and making my plans was put on the back burner. I let myself get soft and comfortable, and that was my mistake. I shouldn't have been surprised that the vampires found me. Most humans wouldn't turn down the opportunity of being immortal and powerful, even if it cost them their morality, including a nun apparently.

I thought I was totally alone regarding my strange abilities, and then one day when I was eighteen years old, I was reading at a local coffee shop with Vivian, and Sage pulled out the chair opposite me and sat down smiling.

Vivian had been extremely distrustful at first, nearly hauling me right out of coffee shop until Sage explained that the Fates had shown her a vision leading her to me. At the mere mention of the Fates, Vivian had relaxed. The more I got to know her, I found that she was like a ray of sunlight in the dark, and I finally had a friend I could share my whole self with.

That was six years ago, and we have been best friends ever since. I really missed her friendship over this past year, and even though I knew I had to leave, I wished things could have been different. Her premonitions have saved me more than once, so I knew I had to trust her that I was doing the right thing.

Resting my head against the seat, I closed my eyes and thought more about Sage, and if she had any more insight as to what was coming next. I knew I was on the right path with the werewolves; she had predicted that much. Well... not that my rescuer was going to be a werewolf but that *he* would rescue me in the first place.

There was a sense of familiarity within my soul when I looked at Dean, and being near him gave me a sense of security. Sage was right. As soon as his blue eyes had met mine, I knew he would protect me. Which was a freaky feeling, since I rarely trusted anyone except myself when it came to my safety.

My breathing slowed, and I let my mind rest. The smells of the forest, leather, and a hint of amber filled my nose, and I barely registered I was leaning into Dean's shoulder. Vaguely in the distance, I saw a dome of sparkling magical energy, but that could have been the exhaustion making me hallucinate.

The heat from his body and the sound of his heartbeat lulled me to sleep, and for the first time in a long time, it was without a nightmare.

Chapter Four

I opened my eyes only to practically be blinded by sunshine streaming in through a window next to my bed. I groaned and rolled over, closing my eyes once more, snuggling deeper in the covers.

I sighed, relaxing further into the mattress, when last night's events slammed into my brain and my eyes snapped open. I sat up quickly and looked around the room.

The walls in the room were painted an emerald green, and on the opposite wall of the bed was a fireplace with an antique wooden mantel. There were only a few pieces of furniture, a chest of drawers, and two bedside tables that matched the wood of the mantel. The large window revealed a lush forest outside set with an abundance of greenery and beautiful pine trees. I swung my legs over to the side of the bed and rested my feet on the hardwood floor.

Stretching my arms above my head, I noticed that I was still in my clothes from the convent. I saw a bathroom connected to the room and padded over, cringing when I looked in the mirror.

I rifled through the drawers and thankfully found a hairbrush, toothbrush, and toothpaste, so I quickly went through my normal morning routine. Halfway through attempting to detangle my hair, I decided to hop into the shower, knowing my efforts were pointless. As I let the hot water run over my body, my thoughts went over the details of last night.

Vampires had been tracking me, trying to kidnap me for almost a year, and they almost succeeded last night. I had been so careful to cover my tracks when I left home, picking a near perfect spot to lay low. I had bought various tickets with my credit cards to different cities, some even out of the country, hoping to send my stalkers on a wild goose-chase after me. And in the end, I had stayed within a few hours of my home, at St. Christopher's Convent in Sedona Arizona.

Not even Sage had known what my plan was, and I trusted her with my life. I needed to figure out how the vampires found me or else they would just find me here, and I couldn't put the wolves in danger that way. They had risked their lives to save me.

I raised an eyebrow as I paused washing my hair.

Why *had* they saved me?

Once I felt like the water had sufficiently relaxed my muscles and my hair was successfully detangled, I stepped out of the shower and realized I left the towel sitting on the vanity. As I went to grab it, the bathroom door swung open. I flicked my hand, and the towel flew to me as I cursed, struggling to get it wrapped around my body.

"Fuck! You could have bloody well knocked!" Irritation flowed through me as I spun to look at whoever had decided to barge in on me. I turned to see Dean standing in the doorway with a surprised smile on his face.

"Don't cover up on my account, Raven," Dean purred, strolling into the bathroom and casually leaning against the vanity. He was wearing a similar outfit to last night, dark-washed jeans with a dark gray V-neck shirt and boots. My eyes traveled down his muscular form, and by the time I realized it, that devilish smirk had widened into a wolfish grin, his eyes set aflame as he watched me.

"Don't call me that," I snapped, securing the towel around me as I glared at him. He merely chuckled.

"I brought these for you. Although, I think I rather like what you're wearing right now." He winked and set some clothes on the white marble countertop, still casually leaning against the surface.

I narrowed my eyes at him. "You think you're funny?"

His eyes twinkled with mischief as he lazily drawled, "Among other things." And with one more heated look, he strolled out of the bathroom, laughing at the vulgar gesture I gave him as he shut the door.

I dried myself off quickly, letting out a stream of curses as I did so and walked over to the clothes, determined to give that nosey wolf a piece of my mind. I rolled my eyes as I quickly put on the black lace bra and underwear, then moved onto the skinny jeans that hugged my every curve, along with a white shirt that hung off my left shoulder.

Everything was shockingly my size, but I then remembered that werewolves were pack creatures, and he probably borrowed some clothes from anther female.

I ran the brush through my damp hair before calling upon the air around me to help dry it. Wind blew through my long dark locks and tickled my cheeks, only stopping once my hair was dry and draped down my back in lazy waves. That was by far one of my favorite parts of being a witch, not needing to use a blow dryer.

My magic felt stronger here, more than it had been in months. Like the town held some of energy that was charging my own. Power buzzed in my veins, and when I focused on it, the well of it seemed endless. I nervously checked the part inside myself where I kept the dark magic, and to my relief, it was still locked up tight.

The dark magic was the root of my ability to see and communicate with the dead, but there was so much more hidden within those inky depths. Power that felt uncontrollable, a wild beast that craved destruction and darkness, one that would not hesitate to set the world on fire.

That part of myself had been locked away for as long as I could remember, but I often felt it testing the cage for weaknesses, trying to get out.

Back in the bedroom at the foot of the bed was a pair of combat boots and socks, so I shoved them on and strode outside the room. As soon as I opened the door, the smell of bacon wafted towards me, and I followed the smell downstairs and into a huge kitchen.

Miles and Calian were sitting at the bar-top on the massive wooden island with a concrete countertop while another female with golden-brown hair tied up in a bun was busying herself in front of the large stove, cooking up breakfast. The cabinets were a rich oak color, the top ones reaching the ceiling, with antique looking black hardware. Emerald subway-tile backsplash added a sense of rustic elegance to the space, matching the color of the trees just outside these walls.

The biggest fridge I had ever seen was off to the right, and to my left was a breakfast nook with a round table and six chairs. The entire room was beautifully put together but still managed to feel homey and lived-in.

Dean was leaning against the countertop next to the coffee pot, a slow smile spreading across his lips as I paused in the entryway, suddenly unsure of myself.

Dean strode over to me, that signature cocky grin plastered on his face as his eyes roamed over me curiously. I looked over him too, offering him a shy smile as he stalked towards me. Just as he came within range, I swiped out quickly, landing a blow right in his stomach. He doubled over with a grunt and Calian sprang into action, teeth bared and growls filling the kitchen as he set his sights on me.

Dean waved him off as he righted himself, still clutching his gut as I smiled sweetly at him. "Do not walk in on me unannounced again. Or I'll aim *lower* next time."

Instead of being furious with me for striking him, a challenging look twinkled in his eye, and a grin so feral spread across his face, I nearly stepped back. Resisting the urge, I held my ground, glaring up at him as he rasped, "So quick to violence, Raven... I like it."

"Stop calling me that."

Miles merely smiled at the exchange, while Calian reluctantly sat down and went back to eating, keeping one eye on me. The woman at the stove wiped her hands on a nearby towel and walked over, shoving her way between Dean and me.

"So, this is Blair! Well, it is a pleasure to meet you, dear. I am so glad to see that you made it here unscathed. My name is Selene. Take a seat. I heard you coming down the stairs, so I went ahead and fixed you a plate. I hope you like to eat!" Selene grabbed me in a quick hug and pushed me towards a breakfast table near the island. I slipped into a chair, and Dean made quick work of grabbing me a cup of coffee before taking a seat next to me.

I muttered a thank you to him before inhaling the sweet aroma of coffee and pouring myself a generous amount of cream. I nearly moaned at the taste, having only had sub-par coffee for the past year at St. Christopher's. Dean sat next to me and scooted his chair so close our arms were nearly touching, and I gave him a sharp glare in warning.

"Back off, wolf. There's a thing called personal space, and you're invading mine." I sniffed.

He only chuckled and put his arm around the back of my chair. I shoved it off before taking another sip of coffee.

A laugh mixed with choking noises came from Miles, and as Selene made her way over to me, she smacked him upside the head. He yelped and rubbed his head but kept chuckling into his food.

Selene set a plate full of eggs, bacon, sausage, and toast down in front of me with a smile, her chocolate eyes bright with excitement. My eyes widened as I stared at the very full plate in front of me, and my mouth started to water. I quickly dug into the homemade meal, ignoring the curious looks from the werewolves in the room.

"You've met Cal and Miles already, and now Selene. They're all members of my pack." Dean pushed his knee up against mine underneath the table.

Every touch was like lightning along my skin, and I almost didn't hear his words. Despite the pleasant feeling, I knocked his knee away and gave him an irritated glance, before his words registered.

His pack. He was their alpha.

Throughout the morning, I learned that Selene was Dean's biological aunt, and Miles was his second-in-command and cousin. The house was nestled on 100 acres of land in the town of New Haven near Flagstaff, and throughout the front of the property were other cabins that the pack members stayed in. Most of the wolves lived outside the acreage, closer to town and to their jobs, but a few families lived on pack lands.

Dean explained that there were many species of supes that lived in New Haven, and any that came across or knew of the sanctuary could request entrance. The thought that any supe could enter New Haven concerned me, though Dean quickly assured me that anyone asking for entrance was heavily vetted.

The whole city had a powerful ward in place that repelled humans to steer clear of the town, unless approved by the council, which Dean held a seat in. Only humans who were mated to a supe that resided in the city were usually approved to live within the wards of New Haven.

Being mated was something Sage and Vivian had not really gone into a whole lot of detail about while they had given me lessons on the supernatural world. It was extremely rare, but it was a bonding of two souls, or rather the other half of your soul. Species didn't matter; it was simply the perfect other half to yourself, and you were bonded for life, whoever's lifespan was naturally the longest.

I sat quietly listening to the wolves chat, and I was thankful that no questions were directed my way. I didn't know what to think of my current situation, and even though I felt a strong connection to Dean, I didn't want to put his pack in danger. Eventually, the three pack members left for their own homes or duties, leaving Dean and I alone.

"Okay, spill. How did you know where I was and that vampires were going to take me?"

Not that I wasn't grateful, but my nature was to get to the bottom of things, not to mention I was naturally distrustful of strangers. Getting comfortable with someone was never easy when you were a foster kid growing up, then learning that you were a rare supernatural that was hunted for their power did not do much for my trust in others.

He smiled and leaned back, running his hand through his messy hair. "That took you a lot longer to ask than I thought it would. I was expecting you to question me as soon as you came downstairs. Instead, you just punched me."

"I'll do it again if you don't answer my question." I raised a brow. He chuckled again, and I almost did punch him out of spite.

"I was out for a run in the woods on our territory two days ago. A storm started to roll in, and I was on my way back to the house when I heard something. It was barely a whisper at first, and then it just got louder and louder. The voice called to me, and magic was thick in the air. I scented it all around me as I searched. The storm raged, and lightning struck me right in the chest, and then all I saw was you."

He paused to look at me, his hand lifting to rub a spot near his heart.

"I heard you laughing, saw you smiling, reading, just quick glimpses but I—I wanted to know you. Then it all changed." His gaze darkened. "I saw the convent, the two fangers hauling you into their car and taking you away. That same voice rang through my head as I watched, and it told me that I needed to save you. That you would be... important."

I stared at him, unable to find the words to respond.

"Important how?" I barely managed.

Dean leaned in, as if drawn to me by an invisible pull, his blue eyes brimming with possibilities. The air between us vibrated with energy, my breath catching as I inhaled his scent. It was intoxicating, and it captivated me as much as his eyes.

I had never seen a male so sinfully handsome. He opened his mouth and then abruptly shut it, and as he did, I heard loud footsteps racing down the stairs.

"DEEEEAAAN!" a girl screeched, and a mess of long dark hair flew into the kitchen.

Chapter Five

A girl, maybe to around eighteen or nineteen, stopped dead in her tracks when she saw me sitting at the table. As she pushed her dark hair away, I noticed she had similar features as Dean, but her eyes were more of a pale blue, and her jawline was softer.

"Uh, sorry. Is this her?" She motioned to me as her eyes flicked over me. Her gaze was curious, but also guarded.

"Good morning to you too, Hayley. This is Blair. She's going to be staying with us for a while." Dean turned to look at me, a slow grin spreading over his lips. We hadn't discussed how long I would be staying, but he seemed to have decided for me.

Bossy alpha wolf.

She turned her gaze back to me and gave me a shy smile. "I'm Hayley, Dean's sister. I didn't mean to interrupt whatever was going on here." She glanced between the two of us with an eyebrow raised and a smirk. "I just came down to ask if Dean had seen my necklace? I can't find it anywhere."

Panic flashed in her eyes, and she wrung her hands together. Dean shook his head, and she started pacing the kitchen.

I quickly interjected, "Can you tell me what the necklace looks like? In as much detail as possible." I motioned for Hayley to take a seat at the table with us. She slowly came over and took the seat across from Dean, her eyes wary. She raised an eyebrow at Dean, who just shrugged and gave her a quick nod.

"It has a white-gold chain, and the pendant is shaped like a crescent moon, lined with silver. It was my mother's." Her eyes cast down to look at the table, and Dean put his hand on her shoulder and gave it a gentle squeeze. The 'was' in her statement pulled at my heart, and I looked between the siblings.

I reached out for her hand and took it between my own, ignoring her raised eyebrow. I closed my eyes and envisioned the necklace in my head. Chaos lined my fingers in a silvery glow, gently coaxing Hayley's aura to make a connection. Once I grasped it, I used my connection to Hayley to search for the necklace within the house. Invisible tendrils of chaos floated about looking in every tiny space until finally, *there*.

I moved my top hand and faced my palm upwards. The chaos grabbed the necklace, and I willed open a small portal between spaces and it dropped into my open hand.

I opened my eyes and put the necklace in the palm of her hand. Both Hayley and Dean's jaws were hanging open as they looked at the necklace and then me. She carefully lifted it up and examined it, her eyes wide.

"How... how did you do that?" she whispered.

"Just a bit of magic. It was under your nightstand, by the way." I smiled at her, happy to return a piece of her mother to her.

The relief was plain on her face, and her eyes twinkled with gratitude as she whispered her thanks. She put the necklace around her neck and patted the crescent moon pendant on her chest.

I thought I saw the swirling of a spirit over her shoulder, but as soon as I focused on it, the whisps were gone. Hayley leapt from her chair and pulled me in for a hug, squeezing me tightly and whispering a thank you before she left the kitchen.

"I've never seen magic like that before," Dean said softly, his eyes still wide.

I ignored his statement with a shrug. "I never really knew my parents. My father wasn't around, and my mother died when I was a baby, so I don't have a lot of memories of her. Bringing that piece of your mother back to Hayley was a no-brainer." I didn't pry as to what happened to his mom.

The thought of my birth mother made my gut twist, the grief of not ever getting a chance to know her rising to the surface. I was promptly thrown into the foster system upon her death with nothing except a picture of her, which I kept safe in the drawer next to my bed back at home. I did have a few similar features as her, but she had long golden waves of hair and beautiful amber eyes that were nearly a brilliant orange just around the pupil. Her jawline was rounder than mine, a feature I was sure I got from my absent father, along with my dark hair and eyes.

He reached over and traced his fingers along the side of my face, gently tucking a piece of hair behind my ear. I looked down at the table, as if that could keep the heat from rising to my cheeks. I was not a very touchy-feely kind of person, but when Dean was concerned, I found I didn't really mind the contact.

"Why do I feel this unavoidable pull to be close to you?" he murmured.

Because I have this unexplainable tendency to ruin serious moments, a laugh escaped me. I couldn't help it. This whole situation was just too unbelievable. Last night I was almost kidnapped by vampires, only to be saved by werewolves, and now I was in their territory eating breakfast. I had been alone in that convent for a year, unable to communicate with my best friend or adoptive mother, let alone make sure they were safe.

To top it all off, I have a sinfully sexy alpha wolf sitting dangerously close to me, and he just told me how a voice in the woods told him to rescue me because I was *important*.

The laughing continued, and Dean sat there staring at me like I had just sprouted wings, until the laughter turned into quick, shallow breaths. It felt as if an elephant sat on my chest, weighing down my heart and crushing my lungs. I was gasping for air, shaking uncontrollably as I fought to rein in the fear and uncertainty I felt.

Understanding dawned on his face, and Dean slowly wrapped his arms around me and wordlessly began stroking my hair.

At first, I went rigid in his arms, unease filling me at the contact and intimacy of the situation. His scent filled my nostrils as I still struggled for air. I heard his heartbeat thumping steadily, and my body melted into his, my breath slowly beginning to match his own. The wild tides of my emotions calmed in his presence, at his touch, until they finally quieted to a distant rumble. My breathing slowed back to normal rhythm, and I closed my eyes.

After sitting like that for a few minutes, I finally sat up and gently pushed him away. Murmuring a thank you, I quickly put distance between us, scooting my chair away from his as I tucked my hair behind my ears, feeling exposed to him in a way that I'd never felt in front of anyone else.

"Sorry... Constant nightmares and being in hiding over a year has really done wonders for my charming personality. Plus, the vampires trying to kidnap me is just the cherry on top of this shit sundae." I huffed out a breath and rubbed my temples.

"I think you handled what I told you remarkably well. My family didn't easily come to terms with the fact that an unknown entity was sending me visions and I was willing to blindly follow them just to know the female I saw. Cal nearly blew a head gasket."

I smiled at that. "Having a psychic as a best friend made me learn not to be shocked when you hear crazy things. You learn to roll with the unexpected and cryptic."

In that moment, I realized just how much I missed her and what I wouldn't give to see her.

Sage was the girl who instantly lit up a room when she entered, possessing this unnatural pull about her, like a sun pulling everything into her orbit. It was no wonder that both Hecate, the Mother of

Magic and the Fates took a liking to her, blessing her with her psychic abilities.

I sighed; being sad wasn't going to change anything. And I couldn't return home until this vampire situation was taken care of. Sage and Vivian were my top priority, the only true family I ever had, and they would not be put in danger because of me.

Chapter Six

Dean decided to show me around his home and a bit of the surrounding territory. The main house was something straight from a magazine, beautifully modern architecture with both wooden and stone accents. The best part was the many large windows that almost allowed a panoramic view of the entire surrounding forest. The interior was a blend of masculine and modern styles, with dark furnishings and straight lines accented with pops of earth-toned colors.

To accommodate the pack, Dean's family added cabins throughout the acreage for some of the members who wished to remain close to their alpha. The rest that lived throughout the town were close enough to get to the house quickly if needed. Dean's family owned a lot of the businesses throughout New Haven, which provided jobs for his pack.

While being in a community where I didn't have to hide my nature sounded inviting, I felt more paranoid than ever. Not just because I needed to be on my guard so as to not reveal that I was a chaos witch, but also how *right* it felt that I was here. It was like a feeling of coming home, of finally being where I was destined to be.

The feeling made me wonder if this was the feeling all supes felt when living in a supernatural community like this one. Would Sage or Vivian feel the same way?

The thought of Sage teaching her yoga classes to supes brought a smile to my lips, knowing that no matter the species, they would all adore her. Vivian was a different story, as she was much more of a hermit, preferring to keep to herself. It was odd for a witch to not have a coven, and when I had questioned her about it, she gave me the simple answer that she had once belonged to a coven, and it just wasn't for her.

But still, the energy in this place was enchanting, and I don't think even she could resist. Perhaps I could bring them here once this whole vampire business was over. I smiled at the thought.

The territory was filled with mostly pine trees, but scattered throughout the green were beautiful clusters of orange, yellow, and red trees. Normally, it would be the beginning of the fall season that brought out the rich colors in the leaves of the aspen and maple trees, making them look like sunsets shining within the forest. But to my surprise, Dean told me that the trees looked like that here year-round. There was a small lake at the center of the acreage, and past that was a mountain range.

As we walked a dirt path, we saw various other werewolves who bowed their heads in greeting out of respect for Dean but cast wary looks my way. I didn't blame them. All I could offer was a soft smile and wave as we passed, hopefully conveying that I was not a threat. While we walked, Dean talked about different members of his pack and their roles.

Calian oversaw the sentinels of the pack, which consisted of a grouping of thirty wolves specifically trained to watch over and protect the pack and the city. Each species that was able contributed sentinels to help protect the city, and the council assigned shifts for each group to follow.

The sun began to set, casting golden shadows through the trees, and I couldn't help but marvel at how breathtaking this place was. It reminded me of Sage's home in Flagstaff, surrounded by the forest and nestled in close to the mountains.

Witches were drawn to nature, and most chose to live surrounded by it. I could see how witches could be happy here.

Dean led me to a barn with huge sliding doors on the front, and inside were three banquet tables. At each of the tables I saw families talking and laughing with one another, children running around and playing. He had mentioned earlier that the pack would be gathering tonight in celebration of the upcoming full moon.

Each month, the pack gathered the night before the full moon and had a huge dinner for pack bonding. Then the following night, they would run together as a pack throughout their lands.

Werewolves could shift any time they wanted, contrary to the tellings of many fictional books, but the full moon allowed them to further connect with their inner animal and allowed them a sense of total harmony. Though I had worries that I would be seen as too much of an outsider at this event, Dean insisted that I attend.

"This is nicer than I expected. It's so peaceful." A slight smile crept onto my face as the wind ruffled my hair. I meant it; I had never seen a community where there was so much love, so much kinship.

"That almost sounded like a compliment," Dean mused.

I rolled my eyes. "Just a compliment to the scenery. Don't go getting a big head about it." I waved him off, even though I knew it was a lie.

Dean's pack loved him, genuinely loved him, and I could see why. He may be the leader, the alpha, but he clearly cared about every pack member like family and treated them as such. It was how a leader should be, not some domineering asshole like I imagined a werewolf would have been.

He gave me a teasing smile and tilted his head towards the middle table. As I followed him to the head of the table, I felt eyes watching my every move. Out of the corner of my vision, I saw Selene struggling to bring in several platters of various roasted meats, which smelled of rosemary and other herbs and spices, to the serving table at the far end of the barn. I quickly turned around and made my way over to her. The stares followed me.

Selene was setting those platters down as soon as I walked up, and she was turning back towards the house.

"Do you need some help, Selene?" I tapped her on the shoulder, even though I knew she heard me coming.

She gave me a genuine smile and squeezed my arm. I actively had to make sure I didn't shy away. I was going to have to get used to how touchy these shifters were.

I had never been a touchy-feely person, and during my time with humans in various foster homes, that didn't change. I liked my personal space, and they either respected that or didn't bother with personal affections anyway.

"Oh no, dear, thank you though. I just have a few more plates to bring out." She began hustling off. I kept my pace with her and insisted on helping. We soon got back into the kitchen and there were at least ten more full plates of potatoes, roasted vegetables, and freshly baked bread. I looked at her and raised a brow.

"A few more plates, huh?" I remarked, and she gave me a cheeky grin and waved her hand dismissively. "You know, I can get all of these plates out there all at once. All I would need is for you to open the door."

I leaned up against the island counter. She looked at me curiously, then glanced back at all the plates.

"It would be a piece of cake." I gave her a wink.

"I suppose it would prevent any of the food from getting cold..." She let out a sigh and nodded at me.

I took a breath and sent out tendrils of magic all underneath the plates. They lifted one at a time and formed a line in the air above the island. Selene inhaled quickly, her eyes like saucers.

I chuckled and nodded at the door. She quickly righted herself and quickly opened the door, her eyes widening again as I strolled out of the house with the plates following behind me. She caught up to me and kept looking over her shoulder to check and see if the plates were still following. They were.

All voices immediately stopped as soon as we stepped foot into the barn. I made my way over to the serving table, praying to the gods that I wouldn't trip, and let my magic gently set the plates down where Selene had left room for them.

"Thank you for your help, Blair. Ignore them; they are just a curious lot and seem to have forgotten that it's rude to stare." Selene grabbed my hand and winked at me, her last words loud enough for the others to hear.

I glanced back to find the wolves pointedly looking anywhere but in our direction.

I looked back over to Selene, her chocolate-brown eyes shining brightly up at me, and I nodded at her with a smile. I was slightly surprised that using so much chaos hadn't exhausted me; it has been a long time since I've had to use so much of it. My magic had been recharging quickly since I had shown up here, and I seemed to feel an intense connection to the land.

Selene looked at all the wolves sitting at the tables, some of them with their mouths hanging open. "Well, go on. Dig in!" She gestured to the table.

Snapped out of their gawking, the wolves hurried to their feet and began making their way over to the food tables. Before I could go to the back of the line, Selene handed me a plate full of food. I opened my mouth to object and was about to hand the plate back when she just shook her head and shooed me towards the tables.

I slowly walked over to the center table, where Dean had been leading me before, and took a seat near the head. I took a deep breath, and the smell of the food made my stomach rumble in anticipation. I was hoping that there wasn't a werewolf custom of waiting for the alpha to eat, but then again, I wasn't a part of his pack. So, I began eating and ignored all the lingering eyes focused on me.

As I ate, I started to wonder what my next steps would be. I didn't want to put this family in danger, and my presence here would only bring trouble to these people. I wished Sage was here with one of her premonitions. She would probably just shrug and say something like *"The path will reveal itself to you in time"*. I snorted at the thought.

I knew the reason for the vampires' search for me had to do with my magic. When I was younger, I could hardly control my power; a hormonal teenager with powerful magic was not a great mix. I bounced from foster home to foster home because of *small accidents*.

That didn't excuse the hell some of those families put me through, and honestly, they should have been frightened of me.

Things got better once Vivian took me in. She had helped me control my magic as best she could. She wasn't a necromancer or a chaos witch, but she taught me the same lessons of control she had learned from her coven when she was younger. It helped, but there was still a darkness inside me that pushed and pushed to be released.

I had kept it at bay for a long time... until I didn't.

"Penny for your thoughts?" Miles sat down next to me, jostling me back into reality. He gave me a lopsided grin and then began picking at the pile of meat on his plate. Looking around, I saw the wolves had all sat as far away from me as possible. I hadn't even noticed.

"Just pondering how you all became such giants, but you've supplied me with the answer," I replied, pointedly looking down at his heaping pile of chicken and beef.

He let out a deep laugh, one of those laughs that had you laughing along with them. It felt good to find humor in something, as the past few months hadn't presented many amusing moments.

"I'm a growing boy. What can I say?" He patted his stomach and continued eating.

I chuckled and began picking at my food again. We sat in a comfortable silence, and as I finished my plate, I let my gaze wonder throughout the pack.

I spotted Dean over by the serving table and scanning the barn, watching over everyone. His eyes came to me and stopped. I couldn't help but let my gaze wander down his body. For his height, he managed to be extremely muscled with wide shoulders, defined pectorals, and thick arms and legs.

My eyes made their way back up to his, and he had a satisfied smirk on his face. I rolled my eyes, inwardly cursing myself for getting caught staring.

He started to walk over towards our table until a female caught him in his path. She was slender and short, with crimson red hair hanging just on top of her shoulders. I couldn't see her face, but she grabbed his arm and pulled him close. His eyes kept flicking from her back up to me, but I looked away.

I did not need to get swept up in any she-wolf drama. Even though I had a brief vision of snapping the redhead like a twig that had me smiling, even if I didn't understand why.

"That's Rose. She's been sniffing around Dean ever since he became alpha. I would say to steer clear of her, as she likes to pick fights with other females who even come close to Dean, but I think I'd rather like to see that show." Miles gave me a gentle elbow.

I looked back at Dean and Rose to see her raising on her tip toes to get close to his face when Hayley came barreling between them. Hayley knocked Rose to face my direction as she pulled Dean's attention towards her, and even from where I was sitting, I could see the satisfaction in her eyes at Rose's evident irritation at the interruption.

I would have let out a little chuckle if I hadn't caught the quick curl of Rose's lip when she looked at Hayley. But it was gone as quickly as it appeared, and she plastered that fake sweet smile back on her face before Dean could catch it.

"It's none of my business who Dean *interacts* with." I sniffed, looking away. "Besides, I'm here to get away from trouble, not to cause more."

I glanced back up towards Dean who, much to Rose's dismay, was walking towards where Miles and I sat. Hayley ran off towards some other teenagers, but not before she shot me a smile and a slight wave.

With Dean's back to Rose, she didn't bother to conceal her snarl directed right at me. I fought the urge to give her the finger and instead offered her a bright smile. Kill 'em with kindness and all that. Her face turned the color of her hair, and I noticed the slight lengthening of her canines before she spun towards another table and stomped away.

"Too late," Miles chuckled into his napkin.

I glared at him, and in response he pushed me lightly with his shoulder. It was no wonder Dean kept Miles close. While he was goofy and friendly, he was also observant. Not to mention built like a tree and useful in a fight, as I had already seen with the vampires.

"Too late for what?" Dean asked as he sat down across the table from us.

He raised a brow as he looked at the two of us, a slight smile playing on his lips. God help me, he was handsome. Even with the lights in the room, his blue eyes seemed to glow against his tan skin and dark hair.

"To go to the training area! Blair here wants to train with the sentinels to show us what she's got. Sure, she can kill vamps with shovels and crush cars with her mind, but I'm not convinced she could hold her own in hand-to-hand combat." Miles clapped me hard on my back, right between my shoulders.

I shot him a glare as he just smiled back at me. *Ass.*

A wicked smile spread over Dean's face as he said, "Oh, I would love to see that. I'll take you there tomorrow morning. It would be good for you, I think. Show us you're not always a *damsel in distress.*" He played my own words against me, and I lifted my chin at his challenge.

"It would be my pleasure to knock you both on your ass." I paused and looked over at Miles, who just rolled his eyes lazily and mouthed *okay sure.*

I may be a little out of practice, but I could still hold my own in a fight. And I could guarantee they'd never sparred with someone like me.

Chapter Seven

Eventually, the barn cleared out, and the two males helped Selene bring the dishes back inside. I almost used my magic to just bring the platters in the same way I brought them out, until Selene gave the three males a look and they quickly began picking up plates.

After the kitchen was clean, Dean walked me up to my room, his hand lingering on the small of my back. I nearly stumbled twice, not being able to concentrate on anything but his hand. He pretended not to notice my missteps, but I saw the slight twitching of his lips out of the corner of my eye.

"We filled the dresser with the essentials of what you might need while you're here. But if you're needing something specific, we can always have someone run into town to get it for you."

I opened my mouth to object, but he just shook his head.

"You need to lie low for a little bit. Let me help you." He grabbed my hand and gave it a gentle squeeze. Knowing he was right, and I needed to figure out my next move before I just ran off, I gave him a curt nod. I saw relief flash in his blue eyes, and we both relaxed.

Sage had told me to trust the lightning, and when I first looked into his eyes, that was all that I saw. I had felt it too, coursing through my body and electrifying some deep part within myself I had no idea was even there. I trusted Sage, and I had a feeling that this was where I was meant to be.

"Thank you. Not just for the clothes or letting me stay here, but for saving me the other night. I would have been in deep shit if you hadn't come along when those fanged asshats were right about to shove me in a trunk, and I don't take that lightly. I owe you my life." I dipped my head and peered up at him through my lashes.

"Such a way with words," he chuckled before he lifted a hand to my chin, tilting it up.

I had never felt such attraction to another male before. Everything about him drew me in, but still, Dean was a stranger, and I needed to remember that.

I took a step back away from his hand, closing myself off again, any tension between us dissipating in a blink. He watched me carefully, the predator in him coming to the surface, and his lips parted. I braced myself for whatever pretty words were about to flow from his mouth.

"Dean! Did you eat *all* the leftover pie?" Hayley's angry voice rang out up the stairs, and Dean's mouth curled into a sheepish grin as he glanced towards the staircase. I clamped my lips shut to hold my laughter in.

He ran a hand through his dark hair and chuckled, looking slightly guilty at Hayley's accusation.

"I'd better go see to that. Goodnight, Blair." Dean backed away from me towards the stairs, his eyes sparkling with humor and a longing that I didn't quite understand, but it took my breath away regardless.

I mumbled a goodnight and pivoted into my room, quickly shutting the door behind me. I leaned my head back against the door.

I could not let Dean get under my skin. The Fates may have put him in my path, but that reason was still shrouded in mystery, so I needed to remain on guard.

No matter how sinfully attractive he was.

* * *

A guttural growl came out of the trees behind me, and a cold sweat trickled down my spine. I slowly turned to see two glowing red eyes staring back at me between two trees. I began backing away, keeping close to the beach along the lake in Dean's territory.

The path back to the pack house was just behind me. The red eyes matched my every step, until a figure emerged from the trees. I stopped, dread pooling in my gut.

The vampire gave me a slow, cruel smile, and a laugh rumbled out of his throat. "My, my, you are a tough one to catch. My friends tell me you had some help evading us at St. Christopher's, and that you burned dear Victor and the delicious Mother Superior to piles of ash." The vampire took a step towards me. "Come with me willingly, and your saviors will not suffer." He lifted his hand and held it out to me.

I shifted my weight between both of my feet, waking up my muscles up for a fight. I gave him a vulgar gesture and took off towards the water's edge and away from the pack. I ran as fast as I could, heading for the mountains. I had to lead him away.

Just as I made it to shore and nearly to the tree line, he crashed into me from the side, tackling me to the ground. We rolled and landed several feet away, with his body looming over mine. Using a combination of his weight and vampire strength, he pinned me to the ground.

Despite my own otherworldly strength, I was weak from months of inactivity. His fangs hung out of his mouth, and he let out a menacing laugh that echoed across the mountains.

"Blair, I must say this is a nice little spot." He swooped in low towards my face. "The perfect spot, actually, for what I'm planning for you." He skimmed his nose along my cheek and tightened his grip around my wrists, inhaling deeply.

I jerked away from the vampire, hoping to catch him off guard to scramble away.

He tightened his hold on my wrists, and all my struggling did was expose my neck, which he took notice of. His bloodred eyes flashed, and he tilted his head, a purely predatory move. He leaned in and licked the side of my neck first, and I thrashed out with my legs but couldn't throw him off me. His fangs slid across my skin, a warning, and I stilled.

I felt it then, that dark magic I had worked to keep locked away. Its vengeful presence pressed against the barrier I had created in myself to keep it separate from my other magic. The magic whispered to me, persuading me to unlock the cage, its seductive words wrapping around my soul, offering protection.

I wanted to give in, but I couldn't. No one would be safe from me if I did.

Instead, I grasped at the silvery magic that ran freely through my veins, willing it to come to my aide and fill me up with its power.

"Get off of me, you overgrown *leech!*" I screamed as I gathered up my chaos and pooled it around the center of my body. To my surprise, the silvery glow flashed out of my chest, like a giant bolt of lightning, blasting him off my body towards the lake.

I scrambled up and saw Red Eyes walking out of the water, with smoke coming off parts of his burnt flesh where my magic had touched him. He stopped at the edge of the water, adjusted his shirt, and ran a hand through his platinum-blond hair, fucking smiling as he did so.

"That is exactly why I need you, Blair! Your power is unmatched, and I need it to help me with a little... *problem.*" He clasped his hands together and took another step towards me, his skin slowly healing over.

"Let's get something straight here. I don't give a flying fuck about your *little problem*, and my power is not yours to use." I balled my hands into fists, letting chaos fill every part of my body.

His smile dropped, and he quickly trudged out of the water and stalked towards me.

In the distance, I heard someone yelling my name. I shook my head and began twisting my hands around, following blind instinct, using chaos to create a short sword made entirely of light and power. I whispered words in a language I didn't recognize, but I knew I spelled it to be *deadly* to any who fell beneath the blade.

The iridescent light glowing from my sword was bright against my skin and illuminated the rest of my body. Red Eyes broke into a sprint, and I brought my sword up and in front of my torso, waiting to strike.

Only that moment didn't come. Time came to a near stand-still, and I briefly saw confusion flash in the vampire's eyes as his run suddenly slowed like he was underwater. A massive beam of golden light erupted directly in front of me, blocking him. The force of the blast of energy threw me back on my ass, but I hopped up quickly, lifting my sword back in front of me in a defensive position.

A male emerged, and the light spread out behind him like a huge set of wings. He stood tall in front of me, wearing dark leather pants and an armored top that covered his upper body. Metal cuffs gleamed on his forearms, and attached to his side was a sheath with a longsword.

I could hardly bear to look at his otherworldly features, which were all too sharp and perfect for any human. His eyes were fearsome gold, and his hair was a sandy brown, tied back behind his head. A sense of familiarity sparked within the recesses of my mind as I looked at the being, but I had no idea why. I kept my sword in front of me, my hand trembling slightly.

"Don't let Alistair invade your mind, Blair. You are stronger than that. Wake up," he commanded. The mountains behind me shook from his power, a power so like mine that it sent a jolt of familiarity through my body.

I heard the vampire roar behind him, then a slew of curses accompanied by the sound of burning flesh.

As soon as the words were out of his mouth, everything went black, and I sat up in bed. I was covered in sweat with the sheets sticking to my body and my feet tangled in the material. I was shocked to find the sword I created still in my hand, casting light throughout the room. Dean was staring at me wide-eyed from the side of the bed, wearing nothing but some gray sweatpants.

I sat there panting, frantically looking around the room. Just another nightmare.

Dean cautiously approached the bed, his hands outstretched, his eyes flicking between me and the sword. He sat across from me and reached out towards my blade. I tensed, but he didn't try to take it from me, only lowered my hand to the bed.

"Are you alright?" he murmured, his eyes cautious as they took in my features.

My hand shot up to my neck, checking for wounds, and I let out a breath when I felt smooth skin. Red Eyes—I guess I should say Alistair—hadn't pierced my skin. I nodded once in response, focusing on slowing my breathing.

"I-I'm sorry," I spluttered, unable to say anything else. Tears threatened to escape, and I fought that tightness in my throat.

I hated to admit it, but I was scared. Alistair's threat still rang in my head, and my heart couldn't bear it if any of these werewolves got hurt because of me. It was strange to finally have the identity of the vampire who had been after me for so long, and despite the fear still coiling within me, I felt a sense of purpose, of determination.

The winged stranger had given me an edge. Now I could focus on finding him, Alistair, before he found me.

"You have nothing to be sorry for. I heard you yelling, so I came to check on you... The whole room was shaking when I walked in, and I couldn't wake you. Then that sword appeared in your hand." He flicked his eyes over to the still-glowing sword lying on the bed.

I shakily lifted it up in between us both, marveling at how stunning it was. I couldn't believe my magic could create something so otherworldly.

Ignoring the fatigue from using so much chaos, I ran a hand down the length of the sword, and as I did, the glow faded to reveal a silver blade with an obsidian stone adorning the pommel. The hilt was covered with silver leather, and there were intricate markings down the length of the blade I didn't recognize. The sheer power coming off the sword was staggering, filled with the same magic that ran through my veins.

I sagged against the headboard as the adrenaline faded, leaving me exhausted.

"I can't stay here. I'm putting you all in danger," I whispered in between breaths. I dropped my chin to my chest, letting tears fall down my cheeks.

Dean shifted his body next to mine and pulled me against him. He wrapped his hands around my shoulder and rested his head on top of mine. I had no energy left to resist or push him away, so I leaned into his warm body and let go of the sword to hold onto him.

"I won't let anyone hurt you," he whispered softly into my hair. I felt him kiss the top of my head as he tightened his grip on me. I sobbed into his chest, his words bursting open the emotional floodgates.

I let the sobs rack my body and the tears flow freely. I cried for the fear I had held ever since the nightmares started, for how lonely I had been over the past few months, and for the danger I was now putting Dean's pack in.

"You don't need to explain anything right now. We can talk about it in the morning."

I pulled my head from his chest to look at him, my eyes stinging and no doubt now bloodshot from crying. He loosened his arms from around me and leaned his head back on the headboard.

"Thank you," I whispered. He nodded and made a move to get off the bed to leave, but I grabbed his arm and shook my head. "Stay. Please." I had a feeling I wasn't going to get back to sleep tonight, but I would still feel safer if he stayed with me, even if I knew I shouldn't.

I scooted over to make room for his large form, and he gently slid into bed next to me, pulling me close against his body, letting my head rest against his massive chest. His warmth and alluring scent wrapped around me like a protective cocoon, and I nestled further into him.

Sleep did not find me again, but I still felt safe in his embrace.

Chapter Eight

Dean fell asleep at some point during the night, and I stared up at him from where he had let me rest my head on his chest. Despite the exhaustion pulling at me, there was no way I could have fallen back asleep; the fear of Alistair entering my mind again was too great.

I replayed everything that had taken place in the nightmare over and over again in my head, trying to make sense of everything that had transpired.

Alistair said he had a problem, and my power was going to help him with it.

What sort of problem could a vampire have? They were powerful supes, blessed by their Goddess, Morana, with strength and speed, and were able to gain more strength with the more blood they consumed. Perhaps there was some vampire hierarchy he wanted to be at the top of?

Judging by the strength I had seen in my nightmares, I could tell that his supply of blood wasn't lacking, so what could he want to use my power for?

I also couldn't let the familiarity of the winged stranger's face go either, and I wracked my brain trying to figure out if I had seen or met him before only to come up blank. How did he know who I was? And why was he trying to help me?

I had far more questions than answers, and I inwardly cursed the Fates, rubbing my temples, hoping to alleviate the headache that was already starting. Dean twitched in his sleep, snapping me out of my tumultuous thoughts, and I lifted my head up to look at him.

Dean's face was peaceful as he slept, and I couldn't help but marvel at how handsome he was. He appeared so much younger, what I imagined he looked like before the responsibility of leading the pack was thrown on his shoulders. Before his parents had died, and he was no longer a parental figure but merely a brother to Hayley.

The sun rose, and I carefully pushed myself away from him and grabbed the sword I created, sitting on the edge of the bed. I had never created a weapon before, let alone one in a dream and then brought it back to the physical realm. Its energy nearly sang in my hand, and I felt it tethered to my soul and magic.

I shook my head and set the sword down underneath the bed before padding over to the bathroom. My appearance was a little disheveled, but I was slightly surprised at how much better I looked after only spending one night in New Haven. Despite the nightmare that tormented me last night, the dark circles were gone, and the deep olive color had returned to my skin. The brown and amber in my eyes was bright, and I hated to admit it, but I felt more like myself than I had in a long time.

"Don't you remember that werewolves have excellent hearing?" Dean's words nearly made me jump out of my skin. He chuckled and sat up in my bed, his hair almost as messy as mine, and I couldn't help but give him a small smile.

"You sure about that? Because you snore. *Loudly.*" I leaned against the bathroom doorframe and raised an eyebrow at him.

A bark of a laugh erupted out of him as he shifted to the edge of the bed. He stood up and stretched his arms over his head, his muscles rippling in the morning light. I bit my lip as I lazily peered over him but quickly righted myself as he turned to look at me.

"Dress for training today, Hayley picked out some clothes for you that should fit. After breakfast, you and I will talk about last night and head to the training area after that." He smirked at me and then walked for the door. At the last second, he turned. "Oh, and let's leave the sword behind today. I have a feeling there will be enough injuries without it."

He shut the door quietly behind him, and I chuckled at his fair assessment.

In the dresser, I found an assortment of workout leggings, sports bras, socks, lightweight tank tops, and t-shirts. After I located running shoes in the closet, I trotted down the stairs and followed the hallway into the kitchen.

The wolves were already eating when I strode in, not that I was shocked, and they either lifted a hand in greeting or a nod of their head. Except Miles, who gave me a goofy grin with his mouth full of food. I laughed and made my way over to grab some coffee.

I drank my morning fuel at the small breakfast table with Dean, Hayley, and Selene. The conversation was light, and in between bites of food I managed to find out that Hayley owned a small yet very popular boutique in town, passed down to her after their mother died. She not only carried clothes that humanoid supes like me would wear but attire for the less-human-looking-supes. In addition to being incredibly accurate at guessing clothing sizes, she accumulated a lot of samples from vendors and offered them to Dean to give to me while I stayed with them.

After the wolves had their fill of waffles, I gathered the pack's dishes before Selene could stop me and began washing them in the massive sink. To my surprise, Dean joined me at the sink and helped load the dishwasher and hand-dried dishes. Selene planted a kiss on both of our cheeks and excused herself to tend to her vegetable garden.

Once finished, I turned around and leaned against the counter to look at the wolves in front of me. The alpha and his beta, along with his sister, and commander of his sentinels, all stared back at me. Dean tilted his head in silent command for them all to leave, which most of them started to do, except one.

"I think we deserve an explanation, Dean." Hayley didn't take her eyes off me, and I lifted my chin, not submitting under her stare. She was an alpha in the making, strong-willed and assertive, but her words were more curious than anything else.

"You know we went to rescue Blair from vampires two nights ago. The rest is up to her if she wants to share." Dean gave a hard look to his sister, remaining unwavering at my side as he stared at his pack members.

The three wolves peered at me curiously, and I decided to give them a small portion of my story. A portion that would not get me killed.

"A little over a year ago, I started having these nightmares. It started as a few here and there, and then soon it was nearly every night. But these nightmares felt way too real, too intense. That's when I noticed someone was following m. Everywhere I went, the same person was there, watching me. I was almost abducted once, but my friend Sage saved my ass. She has visions; she can see pieces of the future and the past, whatever the Fates allow her to see. She was the one to warn me that I needed to go into hiding."

I paused, letting them soak in the new information.

"I sought out help at St. Christopher's Convent, hoping to remain hidden and out of the public eye, and I stayed there for a year. The night before you all rescued me, I finally saw the creature that was after me. It was a vampire with red eyes."

At this, Miles swore under his breath.

I crossed my arms over my chest, suddenly feeling way too exposed to all of them. I was not used to sharing, even if I left out the huge truth of why vampires would be coming after me. I didn't trust them, and I had to protect myself first, even if I did feel slightly protective of them already for the help they had given me.

"The male following you in the woods must have been one of the vampire's day servants. They have humans work for them during the day, and the bargain is usually letting them drink their blood in exchange for eventually being turned into a vampire," Miles explained, and I raised my brows at that.

"That doesn't explain what a vampire would want with you, nor why our alpha decided to risk his neck to save *you*," Cal ground out, and Hayley elbowed him before turning a questioning look to Dean.

I said nothing, giving them all a cool stare.

Dean let out a huff of a breath and offered Hayley a very short version of what happened to him out in the woods. He briefly spoke of the images of me but left out the emotion he showed while telling me about it, then went right to the vision of the vampires taking me.

Hayley's eyes widened as she listened to her brother. She spluttered out asking why he'd listened to a strange voice in the forest in the first place. And with one low, menacing growl, he shut her up.

His alpha power seeped out into the kitchen, and I was shocked at how strong it was.

"I get that it's difficult to understand, but you weren't there. Only the Fates know why I was given that vision, and besides, if the vampires want her, don't you think it's in our best interest to keep her *away from them?*" He kept his voice even, but the authority in his tone had all the wolves shrinking just a bit lower in their seats.

I raised my brows at his words. I was not some object to be tucked away from the world. I took a sidestep away from him, his eyes flicking over to me as I did so. Irritation flowed through me, and I resisted the urge to knock Dean upside his head.

Looking at anyone but him, I made eye contact with Miles, whose green eyes softened.

"So, who is this vampire that's looking for you? Any information about him could be useful," Calian asked.

I shifted my gaze to him. He was quieter than the rest of them, but as I looked into his chocolate-brown eyes, I saw cold calculation there. He observed everything, cataloging the information away to assess the threat. Whether he viewed me as one I wasn't sure, but I held his gaze despite the possible suspicion.

"Alistair. I was told his name was Alistair," I murmured. No recognition flashed in their eyes at the name.

I relayed the nightmare to the wolves, their expressions shifting from curious to grim as I described the scenery of the dream. Although New Haven was heavily warded, as was their own pack territory, that didn't stop the worry from entering their eyes, their own home at risk for harboring me.

"Did you recognize the other supe that showed up?" Dean arched a dark brow at me.

I scowled. "Don't you think I would have mentioned that if I knew who that was?" I felt the other wolves tense at my harsh tone.

Dean frowned, his eyes tracing over my face for a moment, but he eventually gave me a slight nod.

"Let's start by getting more information on this Alistair. He's the name we have, and he's also the one after Blair in the first place, so we should make knowing more about him our number one priority. Then we can worry about Ponytail." Miles clapped his hands and rubbed them together, looking to his alpha for approval.

"Agreed. Cal, reach out through our contacts and see what you can find out about a vamp named Alistair. Be discreet," Dean instructed, and Cal nodded as he whipped out his phone and shot off a few texts. "We should do some research on supes that are able to enter dreams. It wouldn't surprise me if Alistair has a dreamwalker under his control, but this *Ponytail* got there on his own. We need to figure out what he is."

The plan was set, and while they hammered out the last details, I absentmindedly began tying my hair up, readying myself for whatever training these wolves had in mind.

The four wolves began walking out of the kitchen, with Hayley heading upstairs, and I followed the three males out of the house at a distance. Dean had the sense to give me space as we made our way through the back entrance and into the forest. The insinuation that they were only protecting me to keep me out of the vampire's hands had my guard up and my blood boiling.

The worst part was, I didn't even understand why I was so angry at the notion. Dean was nothing to me, just a male who helped me when I needed it, and I had to remember that even *he* was likely to use me for my power if he knew what I truly was.

I was so lost in my thoughts that I didn't notice Miles had stopped in my path and ran right into his broad chest. Stumbling back, I scowled and gave him a shove, which he allowed but remained in front of me.

"Save it for the training ring, little witch. I just want to talk."

I peered around him to see Calian and Dean disappear into the trees without a glance back at us. I crossed my arms and lifted my chin to him, urging him to say what he needed to say.

"Dean told Calian and I the full version of what happened to him in the woods. He spared no detail, and even then, I could see that he had already made his decision. Calian thought he was out of his mind for even considering going after you and putting our pack on the vampire's radar. Vamps aren't super common here, but we've dealt with them more times causing trouble in New Haven than we can count. In the end, *you* were worth the risk." He stared intently at me and placed his hand on my shoulder.

I didn't know what to say. I still felt hurt that he felt the need to hide that emotion from his own sister, but the sting lessened knowing that Calian and Miles knew everything. "Why leave out parts of the truth? And that doesn't change the fact that he wants to keep me away from the vampires like some toy he doesn't want to share."

"He's our alpha, Blair. For one, it would make him seem vulnerable to manipulation if anything out in the woods could just slam him with a vision and essentially order him to save you, even if you could be 'important' to him or the pack. The wolves questioned his dominance enough right after his parents died. He constantly needs to show his dominance to remind the wolves who he is. Vampires are powerful enough, and if they somehow could use you to make them stronger, they could become even more dangerous to everyone, supernaturals and humans."

He shrugged, and I hated that I understood the reasoning.

"As for his sister, she would have scratched his eyes out if she knew he was risking his own ass for a female he had never met. They both are a bit more protective of each other since their parents died." His green eyes were sad as he looked to where Dean had disappeared.

I contemplated his words and couldn't deny they made sense. I didn't know a lot about the dynamic of a werewolf pack, but I did understand not wanting to show vulnerability to those around you. It didn't change the fact that I still wanted to throttle him, but I at least tried to let the anger go.

He turned and tugged on my arm to follow the path that Dean and Calian took into the forest. But just before we entered the trees, I stopped him.

"What did you advise him to do about the vision? About me?"

He gave me a lazy smile and a slight shrug of his shoulders. "He's our alpha, and we would do whatever he ordered us to, but more than that, he's our friend, and my cousin. We protect each other, and if he was going out into the human world to rescue some female he had a vision about, then we were going to, regardless of how insane it sounded."

I nodded, understanding that urge to protect those you cared about.

He continued, "It just so happened that when I saw you, I totally got his reasoning. With the hair and this whole sassy thing you've got going on? Yeah, I'd be rushing into danger to save you too if I'd seen a vision of you." He winked, flashing me a dazzling smile.

I gawked at him for a moment, then burst out laughing. It was the kind of laughter that had you doubled over, tears leaking out of your eyes. He joined me, and we continued through the trees.

"Shameless flirt." I smacked his arm, still laughing as I did.

Miles slung an arm around me as we walked. "Oh, you have no idea, little witch."

Chapter Nine

We emerged into a clearing where the ground had been cleared and leveled, and within the space were three large circles marked off and a shed with its doors open. In the circle farthest away from us, Rose and a male werewolf I didn't recognize were exchanging hits and jabs that were loud enough to hear from across the clearing.

I saw the moment Rose became aware of my presence. Her eyes darted to me, and her nostrils flared as she snarled.

Her opponent seized the opportunity and had her by the throat in a matter of seconds, slamming her into the ground. She screeched with fury and scrambled to throw the male off, but he used his weight to his advantage and held firm.

"Never let yourself become distracted. That's how you get yourself killed. You know better, Rose," Calian barked at her from the edge of the circle, his head shaking in disapproval.

She bared her teeth at him but tapped twice on the shoulder of the male above her, and he helped her to her feet. Calian's statement reminded me so much of Vivian's instruction during my own training sessions.

Miles nudged me towards the empty circle closest to us and launched into a series of stretches, and I followed suit. I had workout routines I used to do before I left for St. Christopher's, and as the soft burn of the stretches melted over my muscles, I realized just how long it had been since I trained.

I briefly let my eyes wander to where Dean stood and saw him stretching as well, his muscles rippling with each movement. As if he could feel my eyes on him, his gaze flicked to me, and I immediately looked away.

"So, are you going to keep stalling, or are we going to train?" Miles gave me a wicked grin.

Without another word, I swaggered over to the ring and beckoned him with a curl of my fingers. That wicked grin only widened, his green eyes lighting up at the challenge. I rolled my shoulders and cracked my neck to the side while he made quick work of grabbing tape and wrapping both of our wrists.

"We've been working on close quarters combat training. The goal is to pin your opponent by *any* means necessary. Stay within the circle," he instructed, taking a few steps backward and bending his knees into a slight crouch.

I smirked and did the same. My muscles ached in anticipation, and I was buzzing with excitement I hadn't felt in months.

Miles launched himself at me, far quicker than any human, and I barely had a chance to sidestep out of the way of his outstretched hands. I darted to the other end of the circle and waited for him to strike again.

He turned and slowly prowled the edge of the circle, that cocky smirk plastered on his face. I didn't move as he stalked closer to me, his features wolfish as he titled his head, trying to anticipate my plan of attack. I kept my features impassive, not giving away anything, keeping my body rigid and in a fighting stance.

I let him get close.

He swiped out, attempting to grab my arm, and I leaned my body to the side, dodging his outstretched hand and taking advantage of his open chest to swing out, summoning a pinch of my power to send him flying back to the middle of the circle.

He landed right on his ass, and the shock on his face was priceless. Silence filled the clearing, and all other sparring of the sentinels stopped.

"You said by any means necessary!" I shouted as I sprinted towards him.

He swore and barely rolled out of the way before I was on him. I was out of shape from the months at St. Christopher's, so I was slower than usual, but I was still faster than a human.

I turned to see him crouched on all fours before he sprang towards me again with animalistic agility. I slid under him as he soared over me and jumped to my feet to face him again.

Miles barely gave me time to recover before he swiped out towards me, and I narrowly dodged his hands. Panting, I threw out blows of my own, which he either took with a grunt or blocked. I didn't fully release myself upon him. I may not be as fast, and I knew my strength surpassed a werewolf's, but I couldn't let them see the extent of my abilities.

He made a move to tackle me, but before he could, I willed my chaos to open a portal beneath my feet, falling through it. Time slowed, and darkness enveloped me as I slipped into a pocket between realms, waving my hand as I fell to create the opening I needed. A slice opened, revealing the training clearing, with Miles just a few feet beneath me, still staring at the spot where I disappeared.

I slammed down into his back, and we both hit the ground hard.

Breathing heavily, I pressed my body weight into him, effectively pinning him to the ground. Stunned silence surrounded us.

Miles's back rose and fell as quickly as my own breath, and he swiveled his neck to look back at me, his eyes wide. I simply smiled back at him, and he busted out laughing, a cloud of dust skittering up from the ground with his breath. He rolled over with minimal effort, and I let him, having made my point.

I laughed along with him on the ground, and we slowly composed ourselves enough to help each other stand. I dusted dirt off my leggings and pulled a twig out of his hair. I glanced over to see Dean with a look that was a mixture of shock and awe, and Calian gave me a slight nod of approval, his eyes twinkling with guarded amusement.

"Holy gods, Blair. Your punches and combos need some work, but you held your own well. But next time, pin me on my back. I think that would have been a lot more *enjoyable* position for the both of us." He winked, and I swatted his shoulder.

"Too bad she couldn't fight without her powers. Besides, Miles was going easy on her." I heard Rose sniff as she started walking out of the clearing.

I rolled my eyes, but still sent out a small tendril of chaos, letting it wrap around her foot. The resulting thud and *oomph* sound she made as she hit the ground was like music to my ears.

Was it petty?

Maybe.

Was it worth it?

Yes.

She growled as she jumped to her feet, whirling around to face me. I kept my face neutral as she stalked over to me, shoving her face in front of mine, her teeth bared.

"Just try that again, witch, and I'll claw your eyes out," Rose snarled up at me. She was a short little thing, her head barely reaching my shoulders.

"You're a fool if you think using my powers in a fight is a weakness. It would be like you not using your wolf form to your advantage." I snorted before inching my face closer to hers, our noses nearly touching as I murmured, "And if you actually want to see how *easy* I was taking it on Miles, then by all means, step into the ring with me." I looked directly into her eyes, my gaze unwavering, challenging her.

Her fiery hair vibrated as she shook with rage, her canines lengthened, and she snarled. I brought all my chaos to the surface, preparing for a real fight.

She raised a clawed hand to slash my face, and I just as quickly began willing chaos to put an invisible shield in front of me. It was strong and would effectively knock her on her ass as soon as she touched it.

Dean's growl erupted in the clearing. Rose stopped moving but did not lower her hand, nor did she retract her claws. True fear entered those brown eyes, her breath coming in quickly as we both felt Dean's approach.

I didn't dare take my eyes off her, even with my shield up. Dean stepped in between Rose and I, forcing her to stumble back, and only then did she lower her hand.

"Blair has been brought here under my protection, and if you raise a hand to her again, you will have me to deal with." His voice was low but dripping with rage. A sense of sick satisfaction ran through my body, heating my blood as I watched him.

"She started it," Rose half whined, half growled at him.

From behind Dean's massive figure, I could barely see that her eyes were flicking between the ground and Dean's gaze, fighting the submission.

That only earned her another snarl from Dean, one so loud that I felt it in my bones. I saw his claws burst out from his fingers, and his naked torso rippled with the urge to shift. The forest went completely silent, as if it too was shrinking away from the feral beast emerging from Dean.

The power emanating from him was intense and pressed against my skin, radiating pure dominance, an ancient sort of power that demanded you to yield. To submit.

Rose immediately dropped to her knees with a whimper and tilted her head to the side, exposing her neck to him. All the wolves in the clearing dropped down into the same position. Miles silently grabbed my arm from his kneeled position and pulled me a step back. I let him, even though the force coming out of Dean did not scare me, it merely vibrated against my skin like tiny lightning bolts racing along my body.

It didn't frighten me, nor demand I kneel before him. No, it was like a lover's caress, stroking against my skin. My own power rose to meet it, the sensation dancing deep within my soul. The dark power within me raised its head in intrigue, recognizing the emotion, the rage that was flowing from Dean.

Rose was shaking again, this time from fear, the scent of it filling the air. I heard her whispering apologies to him, which he ignored.

"*Go,*" he growled.

Rose scrambled up and quickly left without a backwards glance, the other sentinels following her, with only Miles and Cal remaining.

As she left, the power slowly reeled itself in back into Dean's body, and as it disappeared, the forest came back to life. The birds began chirping again, and the plants swayed with the breeze, no longer afraid of the predator within.

No one moved, but I slowly released my chaos shield. I wanted to reach out to him and let him know I wasn't afraid, but before I could, his body erupted with light as the change reshaped his body. Dean's clothes ripped to shreds and fell in a pile beneath him. I could barely hear the bones cracking from the change, and as the light dimmed, a familiar black wolf stood with its back to me before it tore off towards the trail leading deeper into the woods.

I immediately raced towards the shed, grabbed some clothes, and then took off down the same path as the wolf.

I barely heard Miles swear and then call after me. I uttered a spell as I ran, one that would help me take the same path as Dean. I followed him, willing my legs to move faster than I had ever run before to catch up with him. Not even Miles could have kept up with me.

I was the wind, swift and fluid with the air and sky.

Only when the path took me to the edge of the lake near the base of the mountain did I slow. Uneasiness crept over me at the familiarity of the scene, the same scene from my nightmares.

I pushed those thoughts away as I caught sight of a massive black figure pacing just within the tree line. I took a deep breath, centering myself, and slowly walked towards the trees, watching the glorious creature in front of me.

When Dean saved me from the vampires, I hadn't been able to admire just how beautiful he was in his wolf form.

He was bigger than any wolf I had ever seen, muscles rippling over his lupine body, his fur a pure black, like it absorbed all light within its inky depths. His sharp claws disrupted the dirt with each powerful step he took, and his long canines nearly shined with his lips curled into a snarl. He let out growls and snarls as he paced back and forth just beyond the tree line.

I kept my steps light, not wanting to startle him. As soon as I broke the tree line, he stopped in his tracks and whirled to look at me. His eyes were more of a pale blue as a wolf, and he let out a soft growl, a warning to stay away.

I ignored it and continued towards him until I was a mere few feet in front of him. In response, he took a couple of paces back, his hackles raising, but his tail lowered, nearly sweeping the ground. He lifted his nose to the air and sniffed towards me, then his face relaxed as I stood before him, no longer drawn up into a snarl. His body was still rigid, unsure of my presence.

I took another step towards him, one hand clutching the clothes I brought for him, the other outstretched to him, my palm facing up. He side-stepped and angled his body like he was going to take off again, his ice-blue eyes darting from me to a path that led towards the mountains. I stepped again, blocking him.

"I see you, and I am not afraid." I looked into his eyes, pleading with him not to run away again. He cocked his head to the side but made no move to run. "Dean." I moved closer to him, keeping my hand in front of me.

An unknown magic filled the air, and I felt the power of it stretch between Dean and me, drawing us together like magnets.

The wolf slowly closed the remaining distance between us and paused a few feet away. He tilted his head once more, his eyes searching mine before we were nose to nose. His eyes were a pale blue to the point of almost being silver, and they looked far more human now that he had calmed.

His hot breath blew against my face, rustling the stray hairs that had fallen from my ponytail, but our eyes never left each other's as he lifted his massive paw towards my outstretched hand and white light slid over his body.

Dean's hand gripped mine as the light faded away, and he stood naked before me. He stared down at me, and I had to lift my chin to look up at him. I held his hand tightly, hoping it conveyed that I wasn't going anywhere, and nothing he could do would scare me away. That I knew what it felt like to be feared for the power you held, the power that you didn't ask for.

His other hand reached up and cupped my cheek. I leaned into his hand, letting the warmth of his calloused palm wash over me, but I kept my eyes on his.

Out in the forest, away from prying eyes, it was easy to just lean into the strange connection between us. I wanted to reach out and pull him to me; my skin was nearly vibrating with the need to do so, the magic wrapping around us like a siren song, filling all my senses until goosebumps erupted all over my skin.

"Blair, I'm sorry. The wolf inside me... it feels *protective* of you. Rose threatened you, and I snapped; it was pure instinct. I hate that you saw me like that. I-I can't control it sometimes. There is a reason other packs fear me, why I have a seat on the city council at such a young age. This power inside, the wolf, it's untamable," he murmured.

Shame and anguish burned in his eyes before he squeezed them shut and dropped his head, an exasperated sigh slipping out of him.

I wordlessly held out the clothes to him and looked away as he quickly dressed. Once he was done, he tried to take a step away from me, but I immediately stepped into his space again and reached up to place both hands on his cheeks. He froze, and even though he was wary, there was a glimmer of trust in his eyes. I felt him relax into my touch, just as I had for him.

"I need to show you something. But I won't do it unless you agree to it." I lightly rubbed my thumbs across his cheekbones, and he gave me a small, lopsided grin. I could almost see the dirty innuendo come out of his mouth, but to my surprise he held it in and merely nodded. I was relieved to see that he was already falling back into his normal self.

I needed him to understand that I knew this immense weight he felt on his shoulders. I have hurt more than I have healed, let my darkness leak out more than letting the light shine from within, all because of the wild beast of power that resided inside me.

It took years for me to reinforce the cage that kept it locked away, and even now, I felt it roiling inside me, looking for weak points, eager to be set free.

I closed my eyes and called upon my chaos, letting it fill me up, and then channeled it to open my mind to him through my touch. The sensation was much like opening a door, and I was using my physical connection to allow him to see through it. A silver glow flowed out of my hands and onto his face, and I let the memories overtake me.

I screamed, grappling for control of my magic, but it was too late.

Glassware shattered throughout the small house, shooting shards all throughout the room and slicing into my foster father, Mr. Yates and Holly, his daughter. Water burst out of the sink, and chairs and picture frames lifted into the air, vibrating against my power pressing against them. The house quaked beneath our feet, and even as their screams of terror reached my ears, I couldn't stop it.

The vision swirled away like smoke, changing before the next memory revealed itself.

I woke up to darkness all around me, and no one answered my screams for help. I banged against the locked cellar door, but of course these powers of mine didn't always work when I needed them to.

The resulting beating of that accidental flare-up of magic had been the worst I had ever received. And though I was grateful for the advanced healing ability after the fact, it only reinforced their belief that I was something spit out from the pits of hell.

I wasn't even sure of how long it had been since then, as they covered the cellar door with a tarp to block out any sort of light. I sank down against the wall, hugging my knees close to my chest and sobbing.

I needed to get out.

The doors to the cellar creaked open. I scrambled up the steps to escape, but Mr. Yates was faster, as I had no energy from the lack of food and water.

He shoved me down the steps, and I fell hard, feeling bones crack as I did. Following him was a priest clad in a black suit, a thick wooden cross hanging from his neck. Two other men I recognized from church stepped down behind him, with long chains in their hands.

"Chain her to the chair, and then we can begin the exorcism," the priest ordered.

I broke into a run, trying to use my inhuman strength to get past them, but a dizzy spell hit me as I stood. I must have been down here longer than I thought.

I didn't go down without a fight. I kicked, scratched, spit, and punched the whole time they manhandled me into the chair. But I still ended up chained to it. A sweat broke out along my brow, my breath coming out in sharp pants. The priest started reciting Latin words and sprinkling me with holy water.

Then I felt it.

That swell of power was finally creeping up and flowing through my veins, promising vengeance. I smiled, and without hesitation, I let it out. I wanted them to hurt as they had hurt me. With a flash of light, all four of the men flew back into the surrounding walls with a sickening thud, their eyes wide with fear.

I ripped out of the chains easily now, the silver power flowing through my veins, and I glowered at the trembling men before me. They were struggling now, but my power held firm.

My hatred for them all was so strong, the silver light started getting darker until it was an iridescent black, pushing against the men on the walls. I felt more power escaping me now, more than I had ever used before. I silently tried to reel the black tendrils of magic back in, panicking at its resistance.

Blood began to slip out of their noses and ears, screams tearing from their throats. I closed my eyes, desperately trying to regain control, but a small part of me reveled in their pain, wanted more of it. I could take their lives, I realized. I could rip their souls right from their bodies. They deserved it, after all, for what they had done to me.

Then I felt hands on me and a voice calling my name. My eyes peeled open to see the neighbor, Vivian, with blood streaming out of her nose and worry in her green eyes. I snapped my magic back to me, and the men fell to the ground. Broken and bloody.

The memory faded away as I shut the door and pulled my hands away from Dean's face. The silver glow faded away from my hands, and he opened his eyes to look down at me, his eyes holding a mixture of wonder and understanding.

"I see you, and I am not afraid," he repeated my words back to me. Gently, he reached for my hands and brought them back up to rest them against his cheeks.

I gave him a small smile, nodding as that same strange magic wrapped us in its song once more.

Chapter Ten

We made our way back to the training clearing in a comfortable silence. The air felt lighter, less oppressive after the moment we shared deep in the forest. He walked closer to me, his hand gently brushing against my own. I don't even think he noticed it; we were both just following a natural gravitation to one another.

Calian and Miles were arguing with each other, but they immediately hushed as we entered the clearing. They both appeared to let out a heavy breath, seeing Dean back in his human form. Calian gave me a reluctant nod of approval, and I dipped my head in response.

"I'm glad to see he didn't rip you to shreds," Miles quipped, his green eyes alight with humor.

I rolled my eyes as Dean gave him the finger. Miles merely grinned in response and pulled Calian over to one of the circles to spar.

I turned to Dean. "Well, come on then, alpha. Let's see what the *big bad wolf* can do." I gestured to the circle closest to us with a sly smirk.

His shoulders relaxed slightly, and I knew I'd made the right decision. The best way to get out some pent-up anger was physical violence. Well, one of the best ways. I didn't even let my thoughts travel down that road, not with the image of a naked Dean fresh in my mind.

"Alright, Raven. Let's start with some combinations." He winked, and I chuckled at the challenge. After feeling the power radiating off him when he wolfed out, I knew he could handle all I could give, so if he wanted to see how hard I could hit...

Wish granted.

Dean shouted out various combinations of jabs, crosses, hooks, and uppercuts. I met each call he made, my fists hitting their mark each time. Dean gave me a wild smirk as I began adding a little bit more *oomph* into my blows.

Moving all around the training circle and slowly adding in a series of kicks, it oddly felt like a dance. I hardly noticed the sweat now dripping down my body, nor the burn of my muscles as we continued that way, lost in each other.

Catching him off guard with my speed, I snapped out a kick straight to his side. He grunted but caught my foot, grasping my calf with his other hand, his thumb rubbing slightly into the muscle, holding me in that awkward position. He winked before I spun, yanking my leg out of his grip. I danced away to the other end of the circle, keeping my eyes on him as I went, his wicked smile a mirror of my own.

Dean's eyes were dancing playfully, the various hues of blue nearly glowing from across the training ring.

Gods, he was devastating. Sweat flattened parts of his dark locks to his head, the shirt I had brought him from the shed sticking against his muscled form. I could see those muscles rippling with each breath he took.

My eyes snapped back up to his, which were now dancing—no, *burning* as they traveled down my body briefly, before making their way back up to meet my gaze.

My breath caught at the pure lust gleaming in those azure depths, at the colors swirling in his aura. The first, a deep burgundy, much different than the crimson that craved violence. No, this was the color of wine, of passion, of lust. The second was a deep blue, the color so close to the outer ring of color in his eyes; it was trust. Dean trusted me and felt at peace in this moment.

Simultaneously, we both broke into a sprint towards each other. I pushed my legs to go faster, gathering up all my strength, chaos coating my skin like a shield. The surrounding trees were a blur, and I was flying towards Dean, who raced to meet me, his arms outstretched to catch me.

Our bodies clashed together in a tangle of limbs and power. My chaos mingled with Dean's alpha nature, bonding together until it was a ball of pure energy, before it blasted out into the forest. The combined force thundered and echoed throughout the trees, breaking branches and sending debris tumbling through the air.

We hit the ground hard, and much to my satisfaction, I was straddled on top with Dean flat on his back underneath me and my face barely hovering above his. His eyes were wild with delight and wonder as he took me in, resting atop his body.

A slow smile gradually took over his beautiful face until a laugh thundered from his lips. His laughter was deep and rich and instantly made me want to smile, want to laugh as well. Not being able to help myself, I threw my head back and joined him, our bodies shaking with it.

"What in the actual hell was all that?!" Hayley's voice rang out in the clearing.

Both of our heads snapped towards her, taking in her arms thrown out and wide eyes. We glanced back at each other and laughed again.

I pushed off him and stood up, dusting myself off briefly before offering him my hand. His blue eyes roved up and down my body, then flicked over to Hayley as he took my hand to stand. Dean remained in my space for a moment, peering down at me with that same look of wild delight and awe, his dimple fully on display, before turning towards his sister while still remaining at my side.

Miles and Calian had moved next to Hayley, staring at the both of us with the same shocked expression. Their hair was windblown, and I think I saw some sticks and leaves stuck in Calian's dark locks.

I continued to dust myself off, avoiding their gaze. How could I have let myself put out that much chaos? Letting loose like that was dangerous. That immense power could have easily ripped apart the wall I kept it locked behind if I was too distracted.

"Holy shit. You *were* going easy on me!" Miles blurted out.

Calian rolled his eyes and clapped him on the back of the head. I vaguely heard him mutter something about Miles's language, but I couldn't even muster up a chuckle. I cast my eyes down.

Anxiety-ridden thoughts began plowing through my mind. It was likely Dean's pack members would call to kick me out. Or worse, someone would figure out what I was and demand my death, or for me to be used or sold.

"Blair." Big hands grabbed both of my arms and gave me a little shake until I looked up. "You are far more than the power that lurks within you," Dean murmured quietly just to me, and I gave him an understanding nod. "And as far as I'm concerned, the pack should thank you. No one ever wants to spar with me when I'm like that."

He flashed a cocky smile, but his eyes shined with sincerity. There, in the depths of his eyes, our words to each other seemed to echo through me again.

I see you, and I am not afraid.

He understood me. Dean saw the darkness that lurked deep within my soul, but he didn't shy away, because they were the twin shadows of his own.

"I'll spar with you any day of the fucking week, alpha-boy!" Miles shouted playfully, but Calian cut him off.

"Miles, will you watch your mouth for once in your life? There are *ladies* present."

I scoffed at that. I hardly considered myself a lady. I was about to tell him as much when I noticed Hayley was still standing there, now with her arms crossed as she gave me a curious look.

"Selene says lunch is ready, if you're all done rolling around in the dirt," she quipped and spun around back down the path towards the main house.

Miles and Calian grabbed their shirts and started off after her. Dean's hands were still on my shoulder, his touch still vibrating along my skin, and for once I was glad my cheeks got red when I worked out, actively hiding the growing blush.

I looked at him beneath my lashes to find him still staring down at me. That easy smile began to spread across his face, and he slowly let go of my arms and nodded his head towards the path.

The others were not far ahead of us, and I could hear Miles teasing Calian about his civilized language, practically begging him to teach him how to not be such a brute. I chuckled as we followed.

I spared a glance or two over to Dean as we walked after catching up with the others. Dean was tall and extremely muscled for his height. And yes, he was an alpha, but that didn't explain why his wolf was nearly twice the size of Calian and Miles.

From what I had gathered in Vivian's lessons, alpha werewolves were only slightly bigger than the rest of the pack, not three times the size.

"What?" His hand brushed mine, and another jolt of electricity flew through my body. It wasn't unpleasant. In fact, it was warm.

"I just was wondering... why are you so much bigger than the others?" As soon as the words left my lips, I brought my palm straight to my forehead. "Get your minds out of the gutter!" The laughter and objections coming from the two males in front of me had me wanting to smack them all for having the maturity of teenage boys.

"First of all, *I am the biggest.*" Dean gave me a wink and shushed the wolves in front of us. "Alphas are naturally larger than other werewolves, so as an alpha it is expected that I would be bigger than others in the pack. But my unusually large size has something to do with my father's line. We have all been alphas, but we have also all been freakishly large. It's a rare gene, but it runs in the family." He shrugged as if it was no big deal.

"Is Hayley your size as well?" I asked, curiosity getting the better of me.

Dean's face changed, his eyes growing sad, and he opened his mouth and shut it several times.

"I haven't shifted yet." Hayley stopped walking and stood in front of me with a pleasant smile. She looked at her brother and then back to me. "Wolves usually have their first shift around their sixteenth birthday, but it isn't uncommon for there to be a few late bloomers within the pack. I was just turning sixteen when our parents died. I just... I never shifted. And three years later, still nothing. I still have the perks of being a werewolf like speed and strength and enhanced senses, just no wolf."

She shrugged and scuffed her shoes into the dirt. Dean stared down at her affectionately and patted her shoulder.

"Just because it hasn't happened yet doesn't mean it won't happen. Don't give up, Hales," Dean murmured.

She just smiled brightly and nodded up at him. But then she paused, as if contemplating something, and linked her arm with mine. I tried not to show my surprise as we began walking together the rest of the way up to the house, with Dean following behind.

"I'm not afraid of you, just so you know." Hayley turned her head to look at me. A few pieces of her dark hair fell onto her face, and she quirked an eyebrow at me. "Dean lost control of his wolf a lot when he just started shifting. Shifters in general are extremely emotionally driven creatures. Mix that with some puberty and the beginning years of physically shifting and well... let's just say more than a few fights tended to break out. My dad was the same, when he was young."

She caught herself rambling and took a deep breath.

"My point is... I've been surrounded by power like that my entire life. Just because you don't change into a furry beast doesn't mean it's more dangerous, it's just different. So don't feel bad for letting that out occasionally. You're not going to scare me into chasing you out of here with torches and pitch forks. Shifters respect power. Revere it, even."

All I could do was nod and give her an appreciative smile. There was a tightness in my chest that I hadn't felt in a long time.

We continued walking together up to the house, and once inside, she and I took seats next to each other at the breakfast table. She leaned back in her chair and stared at me with her head tilted slightly. I lifted a brow at her in question.

"I like you. Dean needs someone who can kick his ass." She smirked at me, and I laughed. This girl had some spunk, and I found that I liked her too.

"Who's kicking whose ass?" Selene shouted from the fridge. She grabbed some juices and soda and put them on the island with the rest of the lunch spread of various sandwiches and snacks.

Dean walked in. "I prefer the phrase 'lost gallantly to a beautiful female'," he joked and took his usual seat next to me, pushing his chair slightly closer to mine.

"Sure, Dean, whatever helps you sleep at night," Miles said through a mouthful of food, which earned him a look from Selene. He sheepishly smiled at his mother, and she rolled her eyes affectionately. She then came over and set down plates of food in front of each of us before taking a seat next to Hayley.

"I felt the shift in the forest earlier while I was tending to the garden. I sent Hayley out to the training grounds to make sure you were alright, Dean. Everything okay?" she asked, and there was no accusation in her voice.

"Dean threw a bit of a wolfy tantrum when Rose decided she wanted to slash Blair's face open. Blair took off after him, and when they came back, they sparred, and together they nearly blew down the entire forest." Miles popped a chip in his mouth, a teasing smile on his face.

"You can see why we are constantly shoving food in front of him, not that it stops him from running his mouth." Hayley smirked at her cousin, who gave her a rude gesture in return.

Everyone was chuckling except for Selene, who was looking at me quizzically. Her brown eyes searched my face, for what I didn't know, but I didn't shy away from her gaze. The others kept talking, but she continued to take me in, glancing between Dean and I, the closeness of our chairs, and then back to my face.

"How did you get him to come back? From being a wolf, I mean," she asked suddenly, and the others went quiet at her question. She was trying to keep her voice casual, but there was a distinct tone that led me to believe there was a reason for her question.

"I followed him and just called out his name with my hand held out to him." I shrugged. I merely chalked it up to power respecting other power.

Her mischievous smile made me think otherwise. When I asked why she wanted to know, she merely offered a non-committal response and resumed eating. Dean shrugged his shoulders and did the same.

* * *

After we finished eating, Dean and the boys had to go deal with some pack meetings, and seeing that I wasn't a part of their pack, I excused myself. Besides, I needed some time alone to mull over everything that had happened over the last couple of days. Selene graciously led me into Dean's study, which quickly became my favorite room in his home.

It had breathtaking floor-to-ceiling windows lining the far wall, which provided an amazing view of the greenery surrounding the house. The remaining walls were all lined with built-in bookshelves filled with various tomes. There were two emerald-green oversized chairs with matching ottomans on the right side of the room and an identical sofa on the other side. The whole room was tied together by the large wooden desk that was perfectly aligned with the center window and the ornate area rug.

Selene chuckled at my obvious awe of the room and started to walk out and join the others.

I stopped her. "Selene, downstairs you were shocked that I was able to calm Dean down enough to shift back. Why?" That sneaky smile of hers crossed her face again as she walked over to me and took my hands.

"It's just an old wives' tale, dear. There's a legend among the werewolf packs of the world that a wolf's bonded mate can bring them back to human form by just calling out to them. When we are in our wolf form, we don't have the same instincts we do as when we are human, and especially when we are in a rage or scared, we lash out exactly like wolves do in nature.

"Dean, being as powerful as he is, has trouble coming out of that state; his instincts are too intense and wild. To hear that you were able to pull Dean out of a state like that and show no fear, it just seems like you were fated to be here." I opened my mouth and shut it. "He has been more at peace in the short time that you have been here than I have seen him since his parents died."

Her eyes turned sad, and I remembered that she had also lost her sister when Dean and Hayley lost their parents.

Without another thought, I reached out and hugged her. She was shocked but quickly sank into the hug and patted my back. When she pulled away, she squeezed my hand and I smiled at her, which she returned before leaving the room.

I scanned the various shelves and internally freaked out at the fact that this was like a little mini library in Dean's home. A man after my own heart.

The books were separated by genre but also age. There were beautiful copies of classic novels that had to be worth a small fortune, as well as some books that were about supernatural lore. I saw several books on werewolves, including details of Dean's family lines, a few copies having to do with spirits, and various other supes.

I was insanely curious, and I hoped these weren't "pack eyes only", but I decided it was worth the consequence seeing as I had little knowledge of other supes. I pulled a thick leatherbound book off one of the shelves, its title worn off the side, and settled onto the velvet couch. I opened the book and realized it was about vampires. A shiver ran down my spine at the coincidence.

I got lost in the pages, soaking up every piece of information the book offered, and searched for anything that might tell me why Alistair was after me. The book offered some more details about vampires that I hadn't known before, but there was nothing in here as to what a vampire would want with a chaos witch.

Amid my reading, I heard a scratching and tapping against the window, so I got up and peered out of it. Looking at the forest in front of me, at first I didn't see anything or anyone, but just as I was turning away, I saw a black cat sitting next to a tree staring up at me. Its inky fur seemed to gleam like it was polished, reflecting the little rays of light that made their way through the trees. Its eyes were a striking shade of green and incredibly intelligent as they watched me.

I turned to put the book down on the desk, but when I looked back out the window for the beautiful creature, it was gone. I shook my head, wondering if I was imagining things, then grabbed the book and plopped back down onto the couch.

Chapter Eleven

Through my reading, I quickly learned a few pieces of valuable information on vampires and reviewed what I already knew through Vivian's teachings.

First and foremost: They can't walk in the sun. And not because they sparkle, either; they would literally burst into flames.

There were a few other ways to bring about their death, and they were classics. Stake to the heart, lighting them on fire, decapitation, or if you were an overachiever, a combination of the three. Although a lot of supernatural lore was made up to confuse the humans, those things held true.

Second, they survived on blood.

Obviously.

I did learn more about their day servants that the wolves had mentioned earlier. Turns out, vampires have been using humans to do their daytime dirty work for centuries. The vampires usually exchanged their services for sex, their own blood, or even turning them into a vampire, depending on their mood I supposed.

A human on vampire blood was faster and stronger than a normal human, which explained why the man in the woods was nearly keeping pace with me while out on the trail. A normal human wouldn't have been able to keep up with me, but a human all juiced up on vampire blood was a different story. The consumption of their blood would also allow a connection between the mind of the human consuming it and the vampire providing it.

While on vampire blood they would want to please the vampire and do their bidding. The blood was extremely addictive, enticing, and even the purest soul could be corrupted by the substance.

Vampires also had the power of suggestion, or compulsion. That ability came with age, but they could get humans to listen to their commands with a simple look.

I laid the book down on my chest and rubbed my temples, the information overload giving me a headache. A deep chuckle nearly had me rolling off the couch, and I shifted up onto my elbows to glare at Dean, who was leaning in the doorway with an amused look on his face.

"I'm going to put a bell on you," I grumbled as I sat up and put the book next to me on the couch.

That only made him chuckle more, the rich sound giving me a fluttering sensation in my stomach. He strolled over to the couch and sat down, reaching across me to grab the book, his hand just barely caressing my knee, and a little bolt raced towards my heart.

"Did you figure out a reason as to why Alistair might be after you?" he asked, skimming the pages, his knee inching closer to mine.

We were drawn to each other, and I had never craved anyone's touch more than I craved his; it was truly unexplainable. Although Sage's prediction played over and over in my head, nearly begging me to trust Dean, to trust this pack, I still was on guard. It all was too good to be true, and I had been burned too many times to think differently.

I shook my head. "Nothing I didn't already know. But this is quite the library you have; it might be my favorite room in the house."

I forced my eyes to look at anything but him. He was just too handsome, his dark hair all ruffled from training and curling just a bit at the ends, and his sharp jawline was begging for me to just run my lips along it.

Dean's head snapped over towards me, and he gave me a cocky, lopsided grin. Those azure eyes were nearly glowing, and he slowly draped a muscled arm across the back of the couch. His fingers delicately played with pieces of my hair as his body crowded mine, his rich scent curling around me, intoxicating me. He inhaled deeply, a slight rumble escaping his chest before he exhaled slowly, the glow fading from his eyes as he relaxed back once more.

"This room was originally my mother's. She was quite the reader and would sit up here for hours. I didn't have the heart to repurpose it after she died, so I just use it for my office." He set the book down and shifted closer to me again, every point of contact sending tingles all along my body.

"Who taught you to fight?" Dean asked, changing the subject. I looked over to see him studying me quizzically, one of his dark brows slightly lifted.

"My foster mom, Vivian, did. She was a fitness instructor and specialized in various fighting styles. After she found me, she taught me how to defend myself. Witch's magic is extremely unpredictable when it first emerges, but she made sure I knew how to fight as a human in case my powers weren't cooperating. I was a quick learner." I winked as I leaned further into the back of the couch, his hand shifting to rest gently on my shoulder.

"She was the one who rescued you in the basement?" he asked.

I nodded at him. I explained that she had been watching the way they treated me for months, saw how frail and thin I was getting, and that night she had heard my screams.

"Vivian was the closest thing to a mother I ever had. She taught me everything I needed to know about being a witch. She saved my life." I looked over to see Dean studying me again. I tilted my head, meeting his stare.

Dean looked at me as if he could see right down to my soul, and in turn, I could see his. Neither of us balked or shied away from what we saw. The rest of the room fell away, leaving only us, basking in the glow of our shared darkness. But even as Selene's words brushed the edges of my mind, I wholly ignored them.

"We should both probably go get cleaned up before the rest of the pack shows up for the full moon run. We'll keep at the research, and we should hear back from some of our outside contacts within the next few days." Dean ruffled his already messy hair before he stood, grabbing my hand and pulling me up with him.

As I reached the threshold of my door, Dean grabbed my arm as he leaned against the doorframe, one arm braced on it, his stare intense as he looked down at me. The silver essence of my chaos pushed against my skin, wanting to get closer to him, and I barely could stop myself from reaching out. He leaned down and planted a kiss on my cheek, but he lingered there, slowly moving his lips across my face.

"Quit looking at me like that, or the pack will be missing their alpha during the run tonight," he whispered huskily, his breath hot against my ear. I didn't think I was breathing; every fiber of my being was on fire, and I wanted to burn.

Without another word, he turned and strode towards his room, only to offer me a wink as he disappeared inside.

I stood there for a few minutes, trying to reboot my brain. I tried not to think about how Dean was probably in his own room right now, getting undressed and into the shower. I shook those dirty thoughts away and walked into my bathroom to turn on the shower. I wasn't sure what the dress code for a pack run was, considering the werewolves would be stripping down to shift anyway.

I quickly remembered that Hayley couldn't shift either, and I would at least have someone to talk to during the event. This presented a great opportunity to get to know her a little more, which I suddenly realized I wanted to do.

It felt strange, wanting to be close to these wolves, since I did not have many people in my life I cared for, nor who cared about me. I was lucky enough for Vivian to have saved me when she did, and then to find Sage a few years after that. Even Sister Maria, who I had only known during my time at St. Christopher's, had quickly become someone who I considered important to me. She had befriended me during a time when I had felt more alone than ever, and I would forever be grateful to her for that.

A sharp pain shot through my heart as I thought of the two people who meant the most to me in this world. I missed them both desperately, and I hoped it was safe enough to see them again soon. I knew Sage would have let Vivian know what was going on and why she hadn't heard from me, but I still had felt guilty about not telling her myself. The decision came so quickly, and I didn't want her to get involved and possibly get hurt.

The image of Sister Maria bleeding out after being attacked by vampires swirled in my mind, and I winced at the memory. I would never forgive myself for her suffering just for being close to me, and I wouldn't allow anyone else to be harmed for the same reason.

I looked up to see steam clouding the mirror in front of me, and I pushed away the thoughts away to strip down and get in the shower. The hot water ran over my body, relaxing my aching muscles. While I wasn't as strong as I was before entering the convent, I was sure to get there with how the werewolves ate and trained.

Once I was done, I stepped out, wrapping the towel around myself as I walked over to the closet to look at the clothing options that were stocked for me. Again, I was at a loss on what was appropriate to wear, but I went with what I would normally wear. Ripped jeans and an awesome vintage band t-shirt I spied in the back of the closet.

Walking back into the bathroom, I called upon air to blow my hair dry, giving my long dark hair some slight curls. I found some ankle motorcycle boots and threw them on.

Satisfied with the outfit and filled with some confidence, I opened the door to find Dean with his hand already raised about to knock. A slow smile spread across my face at the shocked look on his.

"Did someone finally teach you how to knock?" I chuckled.

His eyes traveled down the length of my body, and I felt heat pool in my core at his lust-filled expression.

As his gaze slowly came back up to meet mine, the two pools of blue were nearly glowing. A soft rumble came out of his chest, and the sound sent gooseflesh across my skin. He was wearing a black flannel rolled up to his elbows, and a pair of dark jeans with boots.

"You look..." He cleared his throat. "Angelic doesn't even begin to describe it." Dean stumbled over his words. I scoffed.

"Dean, I'm wearing a t-shirt and some jeans, not a ballgown." I tried to act like his words weren't bringing a flush to my cheeks, even though they were.

His chin dipped as he purred, "Ballgowns have too many layers and are a pain in the ass to take off."

Dean's words stirred something in me, and I reveled in the heat that bloomed in my core. I bit my lip at the images that formed in my head of him taking my clothes off and of me removing his.

"Skinny jeans aren't much better, but I guess it's a good think you have claws." I gave him a sultry grin.

Dean groaned and bit his lip, and I wished I could taste that sound on my own lips. We stood like that for a moment, his eyes brimming with possibilities, the tension in the air similar to an impending thunderstorm, charged and electric.

After a deep breath, he ran his hand through his dark, messy hair and said, "It's a little cold out, Raven, better grab a jacket."

I nodded, and I would be lying if I said I didn't sway my hips just a little more than usual as I walked back to the closet to grab a leather jacket I had spotted earlier. I met him in the doorway, and we started down the stairs. I took a deep breath at the landing and wondered what a full moon party would be like with a bunch of werewolves.

I guess I was about to find out.

Chapter Twelve

We met up with Hayley in the kitchen, and I couldn't help but admire what a female she was. Her long dark hair hung in wild waves, and her ice-blue eyes were bright against her tan skin. She wore a charcoal sweater paired with jeans and boots, a simple style, but she made it seem elegant.

She greeted me with a smile and quickly linked her arm with mine, pulling me out the door.

Dean followed close behind, and I felt his stare at my back the entire way into the woods. I could vaguely hear music playing up ahead and saw the faint glow of fire near the large barn where pack dinner was held.

"I'm super excited you're here for the full moon. Usually, it's just me left out. Dean tries to stay in his human form for as long as he can, but it's all a part of pack bonding to run together, and it would look bad if the pack's own alpha wouldn't partake in that." Hayley leaned in close, glancing back at Dean as we walked.

The laughter grew louder, and rock music was playing through outdoor speakers at the entrance to the large barn doors. Off in a nearby clearing was a roaring bonfire. A few large tables had been brought outside the doors and were nearly covered with enough pizza boxes to feed a small army. I spied some coolers and a couple of kegs off to the side with several werewolves crowding around them.

First impression: Werewolves knew how to party.

"I'm going to check in with my friends for a little bit, but I'll find you before everyone starts shifting." Hayley unlinked her arm and waved before walking off to a group of young shifters near the tables with the pizza.

I waved back and turned to Dean. "Don't feel like you need to babysit me. I can take care of myself." I crossed my arms, surveying the crowd.

Dean laughed. "I don't doubt that for a second after your little display today. I... I want to know more about you, Blair." His expression was honest as he looked down at me, the light of the fire casting shadows on the hard planes of his face.

I could only manage a shocked smile as he grabbed my hand and pulled me towards the coolers.

Little sparks were firing everywhere our skin met, and I didn't shy away from the sensation. His hand was warm and slightly calloused, and I had flickering thoughts of how they would feel roaming my body.

As we reached the coolers, I found bottles of mead and quickly poured some into a plastic cup. Dean helped himself to some beer from one of the kegs.

"So, what do you want to know?" I sipped from my cup, looking up at Dean. His responding smile was slow, and it made me weak in my damn knees.

"Everything."

* * *

Conversation with Dean was easy, and I found myself smiling so much my cheeks were beginning to hurt. Dean talked about all the shenanigans that he and Miles had gotten themselves into when his father was still alpha. I shared stories of learning to fight with Vivian, along with some of the funnier interpretations Sage and I made of a few of her visions, which had usually resulted in us getting ourselves into some sort of trouble.

I found myself totally relaxed, which was a rarity considering my past and my current predicament with the vampires, but Dean had that effect on me. I was always comfortable being around Vivian and Sage, as they were the two most important people in the world to me, but Dean took that a step further. I felt peace when I was around him.

Eventually, Miles and Calian joined us, and even though we were now talking as a group, I kept stealing glances at Dean. The bonfire cast radiant light and shadows across his skin, and his eyes glowed in the shadows.

Just as I was about to refill my drink, the music died down, and the conversations stopped, leaving only the crackling of the bonfire and sounds of the forest.

I glanced around the clearing and noticed all the wolves looking over at their alpha, waiting. The moon was at its apex in the starry sky, shining brightly down on the pack, their eyes reflecting in the light. I looked back to Dean, finding his eyes were locked on me. The intensity of his stare was overwhelming, but I was captivated, those cerulean depths capturing me in their wake, leaving me breathless.

He took a step towards me, invading my space to where our chests almost touched, I had to tip my head back to look up at him. He reached out his hand and grazed my cheek with his thumb, wholly trapping me in his gaze.

"Time to run," he murmured, offering me a wolfish smile before he threw his head back and let out a howl that pierced the very air between him and the moon. His pack followed suit, and the chorus of howls filled the forest, a melody of predators.

I kept forgetting how werewolves were not shy as far as nudity went, and suddenly I was surrounded by people stripping down to their birthday suits.

I tried to avert my eyes as best I could, and I could hear Miles laughing at my embarrassment. To my surprise, Dean had disappeared, and even though I wanted to look around for him, I didn't want to make any eye contact with any rogue body parts.

The clearing filled with the glow of the shifters changing form and the sound of cracking bones. I spotted Hayley walking towards me from the edge of the trees where she had been talking with her friends. Her eyes were downcast, her mouth set in a slight frown, and my heart went out to her. These were her people, and she couldn't share the one thing they were all supposed to have in common. She looked up and saw me, giving me a smile, although it didn't reach her eyes.

I felt a push on the back of my shoulders, and I grinned, this one genuine. I turned to see a familiar massive black werewolf standing behind me, his heavenly blue eyes staring intently at me. I had to look up at him slightly, as even in his wolf form he stood taller than me.

"Hello, handsome," I called to him, and quicker than I could react, he licked my cheek.

I squealed and pushed him away, laughing. His eyes twinkled with mischief as he pushed his head against my chest and up to my right shoulder. I threaded my fingers through the thick fur, and he leaned further into my touch, letting out a rumbling noise.

"He's marking you as his, you know." Hayley stood next to us, looking back and forth at Dean leaning into me and my outstretched hands. Dean swiveled his head towards her and gave her a quick lick, nothing like the slobbery one he blessed me with.

"What do you mean?" I asked her, as Dean rubbed his head across my chest to the other shoulder. I ran my hands through his fur again and heard him rumble in approval.

"Werewolves are territorial, just like wolves, and he just marked you with his scent in front of the entire pack." She gestured around to the surrounding wolves, who were either patiently waiting for their alpha or playing with one another.

"It's just because I'm under his protection. Rose and I had that little tiff earlier today, so he's just assuring that everyone else follows his orders."

I continued to run my hands through his fur and was rewarded with another slobbery kiss. This time, I pushed him away, still laughing, and he gave me bump with his head and then trotted off towards Miles and Calian, who were currently a tangle of tan and gray fur, wrestling on the ground. I stood up and turned to Hayley, who had a wry grin on her face.

"Yeah, keep telling yourself that, Blair." I ignored her and busied myself with pouring another drink.

A haunting howl filled the clearing, Dean's black head thrown back to the sky, singing his harrowing song. The rest of his pack joined him, and the sound sent gooseflesh across my skin. The howls died off slowly, and Dean was the last to break it off. He trotted up to Hayley and me once more, looking between the two of us.

"We're fine, Dean, go on! Stop hovering." Hayley chuckled and shooed him away, and he let her.

He glanced at me once more before he took off into the night with the entire pack behind him. The thundering of their paws faded the farther they went, the only sound remaining in the clearing the sound of the crackling fire.

"I wish I could run with them..." Hayley whispered to herself. I looked over at her to find a single tear rolling down her cheek.

A wispy white figure caught my attention behind Hayley, and I tilted my head slightly to get a better look as I grabbed her hand and gave it a comforting squeeze. The longer I looked at the nearly transparent figure, it took shape. The spirit could be Hayley's twin, just older, and I quickly realized I was looking at Dean and Hayley's mother.

She was beautiful, just like Hayley, with long flowing hair, proud cheekbones, and full lips. She gave me a sad smile and reached out with her hand, placing it on Hayley's shoulder.

Hayley shivered slightly and looked in the direction of her mother, unaware of her mother's presence. My heart clenched at the pain and love in her mother's eyes as she was trying to comfort her daughter. She opened her mouth as if to say something, but no sound came out.

Spirits had varying degrees of available energy to take form and even speak. However, only certain people or other supernatural beings had the ability to see or hear them. It took a lot of strength for a spirit to speak with the living, and even with my necromancer gifts, I could not understand what she was trying to say.

"Let's go walk the path they took. It's such a beautiful full moon; no need to waste it standing around waiting for them. We can enjoy the night together." I put my arm around Hayley's shoulder, my hand laying over the top of her mother's.

Hayley nodded and gave me a smile, leaning into me. Her mother's eyes widened at the sensation of my touch, and then she smiled and mouthed, *Thank you.* I gave her a slight nod, and Hayley and I began walking into the forest.

The light of the fire faded away and was replaced with the slivery glow of the moon, with the company of the stars in the black and purple sky. We walked in a comfortable silence, and I contemplated telling Hayley I saw her mother's spirit.

Death was an uncomfortable topic for most, let alone the knowledge of spirits and ghosts. Ever since my powers began manifesting, it became something I had to be comfortable with, although at first, I was scared. But the more contact I had with spirits, and even the occasional ghost, I wasn't afraid anymore. I had empathy for the lost souls who could not let go of their life and move on across the veil into Purgatory for judgement.

"I am thankful that you're here, you know." Hayley's words brought me out of my internal debate. Her blue eyes were forward, and her face was serious. "Dean has been more himself since he brought you here. Like he was before my parents died. And... having company on a full moon is comforting."

"I'm glad to be able to offer you company, any time you'd like it. Being alone is not an easy thing." I swallowed at the memories of the first few lonely days in St. Christopher's. The grief of leaving Sage and Vivian behind was almost too much to bear, even if it was the right thing to do. But Sister Maria took a chance and befriended me, and that friendship helped keep the loneliness at bay, which I realized was what I hoped I could do for Hayley.

"I couldn't imagine not seeing anyone I loved for a whole year, being locked up in a place like that. You are a strong female, with a strong heart." Her words sounded like they belonged to someone beyond her years. I smiled at her.

"I had very few people I cared about before hiding away in St. Christopher's. But I did it to keep them safe. I know they would have done the same for me."

We continued walking the path, following the pawprints of the pack until we reached the black lake within their territory.

"Don't discount your strengths, Blair. You have the heart of an alpha." She smiled and tossed a rock across the lake, the small stone skipping three times atop the surface.

Another haunting howl broke out, and I closed my eyes at the sound. The wolves were close, the echoes of their paws and calls to the moon amplified by the mountains around us. Rustling in the forest behind us had me quickly opening my eyes and turning around looking for the source. Hayley did the same.

"Probably just a rabbit," she muttered.

I kept my eyes peeled, although I knew she had better night vision than I did. I hated to admit it, but being on the run from Alistair had made me slightly paranoid. Being stalked, having horrific nightmares, and experiencing an attempted kidnapping will do that to a girl.

Hayley motioned for us to keep walking, and we started off around the edge of the lake heading towards the base of the mountains. I had the feeling we were being watched and kept looking in the surrounding forest for any sign of danger.

Hayley seemed quite relaxed, and I tried to calm my nerves. If the werewolf wasn't worried, I shouldn't be either.

Right?

The rustling continued, the sound coming from just inside the tree line, following alongside us. My gaze kept flickering between the path of paw prints in front of us to the trees shadowed in darkness. I muttered a curse and took a sharp turn towards the noise, my hands clenching into fists. I heard Hayley change course to follow me, jogging to catch up.

I had always found the forest comforting before the nightmares started. Now, unease settled in my chest every time I set foot in the woods after sunset. I chose my steps slowly and carefully, keeping my eyes peeled for any sort of movement. Tendrils of chaos flowed from me, searching around me.

Hayley stopped and inhaled deeply, scenting the air.

"I don't smell anything, Blair, just the forest and the pack. It's just us out here. But the others will be heading back soon. We should circle back and meet up with them near the boulders." I barely heard Hayley, and I resisted her gently pulling me away.

Crack.

I lunged through the thicket and threw my hand out to grab whoever was hiding in the darkness. Only, my hand met nothing, and I hit the ground with a loud thud. Annoyed with myself, I planted my forehead into the dirt and tried to ignore Hayley chuckling behind me.

But then I looked up to a pair of chartreuse eyes staring down at me. At first, the eyes were all I saw, but as my vision adjusted to the darkness, I realized I was looking at the same black cat I saw through the window in Dean's office. Its fur was a shiny onyx and short, the light of the moon reflecting off it, giving the cat an ethereal glow. The cat leaned in closer, scenting me, its whiskers tickling my cheeks.

"What are you doing out here all by yourself?" I asked the tiny beast.

It continued to sniff my face, and then it rewarded me with a sandpaper kiss right on the nose. I slowly pushed off my hands and sat back on my knees, trying not to startle the animal. It mirrored my movements and sat down, staring up at me with its head tilted.

Hayley came to stand behind me and gasped.

"Ohhhmyyygoodness how cute! Look at the little thing! What is it doing out here all alone?" Hayley exclaimed.

The cat's glowing eyes didn't waver from my face. There was an intelligence twinkling there that far surpassed the normal feline.

"That's not another shifter, right? I don't want my eyes scratched out if I try to pick her up."

Hayley inhaled deeply again, "She is female,"—another sniff—"and a cat,"—another sniff—"but there is something off about the way she smells. She's not a shifter, but she actually smells kind of like you. Like magic."

I shrugged and reached out to the cat to pick her up, but as soon as my arms extended, she leapt into them, and I had to scramble to catch her.

I laughed and adjusted her to a more tolerable position, until she decided she wasn't comfortable, and she climbed her way up to my shoulders and draped herself across them like a scarf. I raised an eyebrow at the cat and then Hayley. The cat just looked at her surroundings and acted as if this was totally normal, and Hayley opened her mouth and then shut it several times before shrugging.

"You're an interesting little creature, aren't you?" I lifted my hand to scratch under her chin and was quickly rewarded with the loudest purring I'd ever heard. "I guess I wouldn't be a proper witch without a black cat, right?" I joked, and Hayley laughed.

We started heading back towards the lake to meet up with the pack. The cat stayed up on my shoulders, just enjoying the view as Hayley and I walked along the shoreline. The memories of my nightmare began surfacing again as we reached the clearing where Alistair managed to tackle me to the ground before the armored stranger appeared and saved me.

I felt my heartrate pick up in nervousness, and as if she sensed my anxiety, the cat leaned into my face and rubbed her cheek across my own. Her purring was rhythmic, and her fur was soft, silky, and smelt slightly of the trees. All of it combined managed to push the memories away, and my heartbeat slowed. I looked up at her and smiled, reaching up again to scratch behind her ears, and I whispered a thank you.

The path led us to a clearing, where there were many boulders scattered about the base of the mountain. The surrounding forest was quiet, the only sounds being the gentle breeze ruffling the leaves of the trees. Hayley plopped herself down onto one of the boulders and gazed up at the bright moon, letting out a soft sigh.

"Why don't you run with them?" I asked her suddenly, while absentmindedly I was scratching behind the cat's ears as I sat on the boulder next to Hayley.

She gave me a look and then gestured down to her human body, as if that were answer enough.

I frowned. "Just because you can't shift does not mean you couldn't just run with the pack as you are. You said earlier that you still have the advantages of strength and speed of a werewolf, so why not just run along with them?" I asked.

She opened her mouth and then shut it, her brow furrowing as she considered my words. "You know, I have never once thought about that. I guess I just felt ashamed. Like I wasn't really one of the pack because I can't shift."

"Next full moon, you should run with them. You're not broken or have anything to be ashamed of. You're the sister of the alpha of this pack, and you're intentionally ostracizing yourself when there's no need to. Just consider it, but I think you would enjoy yourself."

She worried her lip and nodded at me, tucking a stray piece of her hair back around her ear.

"What about you? If I run with them at the next full moon, then you'll be by yourself." Her blue eyes swung to me, and I smiled. It warmed my heart that she cared enough to not want me to be alone. Not to mention that she clearly thought I would be here for another month. I wasn't sure if I would be, even though I didn't have any other place to go.

"Don't worry about me. I have a new friend to keep me company." I smiled and reached up to pet the purring mini panther on my shoulders.

Hayley's face softened, and she gave me a slight nod with a small smile.

The pounding of paws on the hard ground alerted us to the pack getting closer, and Hayley explained that they run through here and often stop to rest before heading back home.

I felt the cat stiffen slightly at the sound, her gaze turning watchful as she stared into the forest. I wondered how she would react to being surrounded by a pack of werewolves, but even as the sounds of the pack got closer, she stayed where she was.

The pack burst into the clearing, with Dean at the front.

Miles and Calian flanked his sides, and I noticed a small red wolf trying to sneak around them to get closer to Dean. As a unit they all slowed, then spread out to rest or play.

The red wolf finally managed to shoulder her way next to Dean, and she tried to rub herself along his side. She looked like a pup compared to Dean's massive size. I saw Dean's upper lip curl and a matching growl tear from his throat. Still, the red wolf tried again, her head lowered into a slight submission.

Dean was baring all his teeth now, and he snapped his jaws at her as a final warning. The red wolf whined and backed away, its eyes briefly meeting mine. Even at a distance, I could see the fury in them.

Dean padded over to Hayley and myself, his head tilting slightly as he took in the cat resting on my shoulder. To my surprise, she didn't move even as Dean approached.

He bumped his nose against Hayley's knee, and she gave him a pat on the head. He then walked over to me slowly, eyeballing the cat, and she met his stare with a bored look. I held back a giggle.

Dean sat right in front me and slowly lowered himself to rest on my knees. His gaze flickered between me and the cat; the question might as well have been written across his furred forehead.

"I found her in the woods when Hayley and I were making our way here. She made herself comfortable with us quickly." I shrugged, and the cat had to adjust herself to not slide down my back. Dean's ears flicked, and he closed his eyes with a huff.

In content, we sat there soaking up the light and magic of the full moon.

Chapter Thirteen

Once the wolves had rested for a while, we all made our way back to the barn, where the fire was barely a smoldering ember. I saw Dean pad towards the barn again as the rest of the wolves began shifting back and shrugging on their clothes. I averted my eyes and focused my attention on the cat still perched on my shoulder, as if she was always meant to be there.

"Well, if I'm going to keep you, I'll need to think of a name for you," I murmured to her. She rubbed her furry face across my cheek, her whiskers tickling me. My thoughts of names quickly disappeared as Dean emerged from the barn, fully clothed.

His gaze locked with mine, and he started walking over to me. There was power in his walk. His alpha energy radiated through the clearing, and my chaos was pushing against my skin to mingle with his.

Out of the corner of my eye, I saw the red wolf trotting over towards him, blocking his path, before it shifted, and Rose stood in front of him.

The irritation was plain on Dean's face as she stood naked before him. I couldn't hear what she was saying, but I saw her lean in closer, pushing up her tits, but Dean's eyes were firmly locked on me. He spoke a few words to her and then stepped around her, continuing his path to me.

I tried to hide the smug smile on my face as the she-wolf turned around with a snarl on hers. It shouldn't bring me such satisfaction to see her so riled up, as Dean and I were nothing to each other. Right?

Selene's words of bonded mates and the old wives' tale came back to me, and I couldn't help but ponder the thought.

Mates were rare, and even though doubt filled me at Selene's notion, the possibility made me nearly smile. Dean had been granted a vision of me, to save me from being captured by the vampires, and Sage spoke of him saving me as well. Perhaps that was the reason for this intense pull I felt towards him from the moment we met, not to mention the tension and sexual attraction between us.

I sighed. While the thought was nice, the odds were not in my favor, nor would I believe that the Fates or even the gods themselves would be that kind to me.

Still, there was something inside me gleaming at how Dean dismissed Rose and made his way towards me.

Dean stood in front of me with a dark brow lifted, his eyes shifting between me and the cat perched on my shoulder. "Isn't it a little cliché for a witch to have a black cat?" he teased.

I chuckled and shrugged my shoulders.

"Isn't it a little ironic that you're a werewolf who is shy with his body?" I raised my own brow at him. His responding laugh sent tingles across my skin. It was a rich, deep, and beautiful sound, one that brought a ridiculous smile to my face.

"If you want to see me naked, Blair, all you have to do is ask." His voice turned husky, his eyes smoldering as he stepped into my space. My toes curled in my boots, and I bit my bottom lip as I looked up at him.

"In case you forgot, I *have* seen you naked," I commented, my voice coming out far more like a purr than I meant it to. From what I saw, which I tried to keep to a minimum out of respect, he had no reason to be ashamed of his body.

His eyes blazed blue fire. "But you had no time to enjoy it then. And I know you'd enjoy the site of me naked before you. Just say the words, Blair, and I'll make it happen."

His challenge sent a swirling sensation low in my core.

"Cocky much?" I surprised myself with how low and smoky my voice was as I stepped closer to him. My skin was tingling, and I felt myself clench my thighs together.

A slow, devilish grin appeared on Dean's face. "Extremely."

A throat clearing brought me back to reality, and I glanced over to see Miles with a shit-eating grin on his face. I took a step back, trying to escape Dean's intoxicating scent, but he only stepped towards me, regaining the space I tried to put between us.

"I hope I'm not interrupting anything," Miles quipped, glancing between Dean and me.

"The look on your face says the exact opposite of that statement," Dean nearly growled.

"Okay, I did. But if you wouldn't mind keeping your scents to yourself, we'd all appreciate it."

Confused, I looked around at the clearing to see the rest of the pack either smirking to themselves or pretending to be really interested in the ground, minus the jealous face of Rose. Even Hayley was giggling to herself as she gave me a small wave.

Dean glanced over to me and then back at Miles before clearing his throat. "Let everyone know I wish them a goodnight." He placed his hand at the small of my back and gave me a gentle push back towards the house.

On the walk back, I focused on taking deep breaths to calm my heartrate and the inner fire burning for him. I really needed to remember that these damn wolves had heightened senses, because even Dean having his hand lightly placed on my lower back had me wondering how his hands would feel in other places.

"Are we going to talk about your new... friend?" Dean's question snapped me out of my dirty inner monologue.

I spared a glance at the cat still perched on my shoulder.

"I thought there was something in the woods following Hayley and I as we were out enjoying the full moon. I was feeling a little... paranoid after all the nightmares, and I followed the sound to make sure it wasn't—"

I broke off, shaking my head at how insane I sounded.

Clearing my throat, I added, "Turns out it was this little creature. I picked her up, and she hasn't really left this spot since then. Hayley said she wasn't a shifter or anything, so I assume she's just a cat lost in the woods."

Even as I spoke the words, I knew that it wasn't true. There was something special about her presence; I just needed time to figure out what it was.

"She's not a shifter," he confirmed after sniffing her, "but I'm not entirely sure she's just a house cat. You have similar scents. It's not the same, but there are hints that match each other." He furrowed his brow.

"Are you saying I smell like a cat?"

Dean chuckled, and the sound sent tingles along my skin. "There are a lot of elements to a person's scent, and for supernaturals you can usually tell what kind of supe someone is."

"I still feel like you're saying I smell like a cat." I raised a brow at him.

He laughed again and ran a hand through his dark hair. I pretended not to notice the curve of his muscle with the movement.

"For example, the smell of wildflowers is an extremely common smell for witches to share. You smell slightly of wildflowers, but you also smell like the air right before it's about to rain. Your cat here also smells of the air before a storm, and cats usually don't smell like that." He wrinkled his nose as if to further prove his point.

We reached the steps, and Dean opened the door for me, gesturing for me to go inside first.

He added, "I have a friend on the council that might have more information on your situation. I'm still young as far as the council members go, and she's one of the oldest, so her knowledge is extensive."

"You really trust her with all of this?" I asked.

I was nervous to reveal my situation to anyone, and an old supe may be able to identify what I was based on my abilities alone. That, and Alistair's warning chilled me to my core. I couldn't bear to see any of these wolves hurt because of me.

"She's trustworthy. One of my oldest friends and a friend to New Haven. She even has ties to Hecate." Dean gripped the countertop in the kitchen, and I couldn't help but admire him.

His shirt was just tight enough on the shoulders to see the hard lines of his muscles, even though his stance was relaxed. His dark hair was slightly curled, and his striking blue eyes stood out beneath dark lashes.

"What's her name?" I asked, trying to focus on anything but him.

"Nathara. She's one of the first creatures Hecate created, so she has a vast knowledge of all things witch-related. She can be a bit... prickly, but I think she will help us. Don't look her in the eyes for too long, though, or avoid it if possible."

I raised a brow, but before I could even ask, he waved a hand.

"Just trust me on that."

I nodded warily, wondering what kind of supe he could introducing me to that I couldn't look in the eyes.

My new feline friend leapt from my shoulders and sprinted up the stairs like she owned the place. "I can find her a new home tomorrow. I'm sorry, I should have asked if I could even bring her inside the house—" I stuttered and started to take off after the cat, but Dean grabbed my arm.

"It's fine, Blair, I'm not worried about the cat. She can stay." He rubbed idle circles along my arm as he looked down at me. With those baby blues so focused on me, I couldn't think of a response other than a whispered thanks.

He walked me up to my room, and we found the cat sitting in front of the door, barely visible in the dark hallway other than her glowing green eyes. I rolled my eyes as she pawed at the door upon our arrival. I quickly opened it for her and turned to Dean.

"Why do you shift where no one can see you?" I blurted out, needing to fill the silence. Aside from the other day at the training ring, Dean had always stepped out of sight before shifting.

Surprise flashed briefly in his eyes, probably due to the randomness of the question, but he gave me a lazy shrug. "Honestly, I don't normally, but I thought it would make you feel more comfortable if I did."

My eyes widened. "But you shifted in front of me before."

"You had caught me... off guard. I wasn't in control of myself." I opened my mouth to respond, but he cut me off, "I'm *really* starting to think you just want to see me naked, Blair."

I rolled my eyes at him. "I was just curious. All the other wolves are free with their bodies. I didn't know if it was a custom for alphas or something."

"If anything, other alphas rather enjoy showing off their bodies. Displaying their body is a show of dominance. But my father, and now me, never really played into that. There are other ways of showing dominance and earning loyalty other than sheer displays of power or arrogance."

I was taken aback at his words. All this responsibility had been thrust upon him after his parents died, but here he was, leading with the grace of someone who has held the role for many years.

"How do you manage to be so smug in one sentence and then completely honorable in the next?" I leaned against the door frame, looking up at him.

He smiled, and I caught sight of a dimple appearing.

"It's one of my many talents," he replied with a smug grin.

I rolled my eyes and chuckled. "Goodnight, Dean."

I gave him a little shove as I turned to enter my room, but he caught my hand and pulled me back. We were now only inches away from each other, his depthless eyes gazing into my very soul.

"Thank you for spending time with Hayley tonight. I know she gets lonely during full moons, and I think it meant a lot to her to have someone to roam the forest with. I know it meant a lot to me." His eyes roamed over my face, and I felt my breaths become shallow as I inhaled his woodsy scent.

"It was nothing. I rather enjoyed her company." I let myself say the words I had been holding back since I got to New Haven. "I enjoy all your company, as it happens. So, thank you. For saving me." I looked down, feeling vulnerable under his intense gaze.

"No thanks are needed. I would do it a thousand times over, just for the chance to know you." Dean tipped my chin up with his forefinger and thumb, and his eyes drifted down to my lips.

The air became thick, my skin tingling in anticipation, and I was sure it was pure lightning that flowed through my veins at his proximity. He leaned in, pressing his mouth to my forehead, and I shut my eyes.

He pulled away. "Goodnight, Blair. Sleep well."

My body protested as his warmth left with him, nearly forcing me to trail after him. I inhaled deeply for the first time in what felt like hours, trying to keep the last of his lingering scent with me as I watched him walk down the hall and into his room.

I saw him pause just before shutting the door, and I secretly hoped he would come back. He didn't, though, and the click of the door echoed in the hallway.

I turned and shut my own door, leaning against the wood and staring at the ceiling. My traitorous heart was going to bring this pack trouble, and I couldn't let that happen. I didn't deserve someone as good as Dean. I brought my head down to see the cat lounging on the duvet, staring at me with knowing eyes.

"I know you need a name, but I don't have the energy to figure that out right now," I told her.

She blinked and nestled her head into her paws. I blew out a breath and began stripping down. I found a sleep tank top and threw that on before making my way to the bed. I slipped under the duvet and pulled it all the way up to my chin, cocooning myself in.

My nameless cat made her way up to me slowly, then curled into a little ball on top of my stomach. It was surprisingly comfortable to have her there.

I wasn't sure how long it was before I drifted off to sleep, but the last thing I heard before the darkness took me was purring.

Chapter Fourteen

The trees were unnaturally still as I walked the forest path behind my house. Unease trickled through me as I took in the familiar surroundings.

I didn't know how I had gotten here. To my right I could see the edge of my porch, as well as the steps leading up to it. I was vaguely aware that I was in the underwear and tank top I had gone to sleep in. Gooseflesh broke out along my bare legs, and I hugged my arms in close to my chest.

A twig snapped to my left, and I whirled to face the noise. I took a step back towards my house as I looked around for the source of the sound. Horrifically familiar red eyes were glowing from within the darkness of the trees.

Alistair.

He stepped out of the tree line with a sinister grin. He was dressed in an all-black suit that was tailored to his lean figure, and his pale skin stood out in the shadowy forest. On instinct, I called to the blade I had created, and with a silver glow it appeared in my hand.

"Well, well, well, Blair, learning a few new tricks, I see." His eyes drifted down to the short sword in my grip. "But I'm afraid it will all be in vain. I have friends in… well, maybe not high places, but let's just say very powerful friends." He continued, "So, why not just give in, Blair? I promise your pain will last but a mere moment, and then this will all be over."

I sneered, "And I'll be dead. Sorry if I don't jump at the opportunity to help your pasty ass." I shifted the blade in front of me and adjusted my feet into a fighting stance.

"I can make your death feel good, love," Alistair purred. My skin crawled from the way his eyes roamed over my body.

"Still not interested," I retorted.

"Aren't you even the least bit curious as to why we want you so badly? Other than the obvious." His eyes trailed up the length of my legs and then lingered on my nearly exposed chest. I wanted to vomit.

"Fuck off, fanger. No means no."

Chaos began churning inside me, begging to be released. I held it in but kept it close to the surface. He took a step closer to me, and I shifted back, keeping my legs ready to run.

"I'll give you a hint. It has to do with your blood. It's quite fascinating." His eyes shifted to somewhere slightly behind me, and his face grimaced in confusion. "What the hell…?"

I felt a strong, comforting presence at my back, wrapping around me like a cloak and offering protection. It felt like pure spiritual power, but it was familiar, and I couldn't place where I had felt this before. I couldn't spare a glance behind me, not wanting to give Alistair a chance to strike. But in my bones, I knew this shadowy presence was here to defend me.

"Come after me or any of my friends, and I will kill you. Delivering you to the gates of Hell is the only help you will get from me." A monstrous growl from the shadow behind me enhanced my point, and it gave me great satisfaction to see a flicker of unease cross Alistair's face.

"Your anger is misguided, and I am only trying to help my species. Surely, you can see the merit in that."

At his words I gave him a rude gesture, letting a small flicker of fire dance at my fingertip to enhance my point. His features hardened, no longer cool and relaxed. I saw the slight shift in his weight, and I knew he was preparing to rush me.

I let trickles of my chaos leak out of me, silver tendrils of light radiated from my body, and my sword lit up in an ethereal glow. I felt my magic caress the shadow behind me, as if it was greeting an old friend.

Alistair's eyes widened.

"Your eyes—" He shook his head. "Enough of this."

I barely registered that he had moved and suddenly he was in front of me, fangs bared in a snarl. Before I could blast him with chaos, the shadow exploded from behind me, and I finally saw the unknown protector.

Its inky form flew through my body, and a chill seeped all along my skin. The shape was distinctly feline but far too large to be any normal jungle cat, and shadows billowed off its skin the color of the midnight sky. Its fur was shiny and absorbed all light, with a long tail whipping through the air as it launched at Alistair, claws and teeth first. Its roar was deafening and shook the earth beneath me.

Alistair barely had time to turn before the feline brought him to the ground with its jaws clamped on his shoulder. The creature clung to him and began tearing through his flesh, its snarls vibrating my bones. His screams echoed throughout the forest, and I'd be lying if I said I didn't relish the sound.

The creature shifted its grip on Alistair's shoulder and tossed him like a ragdoll between the trees. I watched his body hit and wrap around a tree with a sickening thud, accompanied by his cries of pain. My shadowy savior whipped its head towards me, and I gasped at the sight.

Chartreuse eyes stared back at me.

I recognized those intelligent green eyes. This beautiful, terrifying shadow beast was the cat I had found in the forest. The beast prowled towards me, blood dripping from her maw, and I lowered my sword. She stood at my feet and gazed up at me with her large eyes.

Her fur was slightly longer in this form, and her ears had black tuffs of hair sticking off the point. Her fangs were much longer than any normal leopard, as they peeked out of her mouth slightly. Claws that were more like talons dug into the dirt, prepped and ready to strike again. A long, slightly fluffy tail whipped around behind her, along with beautiful inky shadows billowing out of her body, as if they were dancing with excitement.

I vaguely heard Alistair's muffled grunts as he tried to pick himself up off the forest floor. She tilted her head to the side, and I slowly reached out and touched her forehead. A silvery glow broke out where my hand came in contact with her head, and I tried to pull my hand away but found that it was stuck.

Panic set in, and I tried harder to yank my hand back, but it was no use. The beast began purring, and I looked up to see Alistair on his feet, his breathing ragged and his clothes and skin torn to pieces. His wounds were slowly healing, and the look on his face was nothing short of murderous as he stared at my feline friend.

The surrounding forest began slowly spinning, and as it sped up, I couldn't keep track of where Alistair was standing. Everything was blurred, and I could barely keep a hold on my sword.

I think I heard him screaming in anger, but soon that noise quieted, until there were no sounds except purring. I found myself leaning into my shadowy savior, clinging to her as the spinning continued. I shut my eyes at some point and clenched my jaw to keep myself from vomiting all over my new friend.

The horrible spinning sensation slowed, and I reluctantly opened one eye. The colors of the forest were replaced by bright blues and yellows. Within a few seconds, the world stopped whirling, and I lifted my head to take in my surroundings.

Starting with the oversized feline sitting in front of me. I eyed her, briefly wondering if she transported me to wherever this was just to eat me. She let out another chuffing sound, and her eyes twinkled with humor and mischief.

"You may remove your hand now," a throaty feminine voice murmured.

I yanked my hand away and staggered back, shuffling myself back into the tall yellow grass. More chuffing erupted from the big cat, and she stretched her legs out in front of her.

"I am not here to eat you, Blair. You can relax," the same voice echoed in my head.

Was this shadow cat speaking to me? And worse, was she reading my mind?

"Yes, to both questions. And I believe introductions are in order. My name is Ophelia, and I am your familiar." The cat—Ophelia—purred.

I felt my jaw drop. I could remember Vivian teaching me about powerful witches having familiars, but it was mostly legend. Very few witches across history had been blessed by Hecate to have one.

A familiar was a creature that was meant to guard and protect a powerful witch. Their duty was to serve and assist their assigned witch with their magic and protect them with their life. Familiars were an extension of the witch's power, enhancing their abilities, and they had a special bond, a soul bond, one that would last until death.

"You are my familiar? How the hell did that happen?" I blurted out.

She tilted her head but did not respond.

I hurried to clarify, "Not that I am not grateful for you helping me, Ophelia, I just don't understand how this happened. You—you were magnificent by the way, taking him down like that. Thank you for that. Asshole deserved that and more with all the sleep he's deprived me of," I rambled on while she just continued to stare at me.

She crossed her giant paws over one another and yawned before turning her attention back to me. "Your power summoned me. However, I have been watching over you for some time now."

I stiffened. Confusion and hurt filtered through me, even if I didn't completely understand the latter emotion. The thought of

Ophelia watching but not making herself known cut deeply, even though I had no knowledge of her existence.

"How long have you been watching me?"

"A few years, give or take. Though, I lost track of you for a while and have been searching for you since."

"And you didn't think to keep me company while I was holed up in St. Christopher's?" I exclaimed. My body vibrated with nervous energy, so I shot up and began pacing, the long stems of the grass falling over as I walked.

"As I said, I lost track of you for a while. I could not pinpoint your location until I felt you use your power. The more you used it within the past few days, the easier it was for me to find you. I had to approach you first, and you had to accept me. Familiars have rules they have to follow, a protocol. When you brought me into your home, you were accepting me into your service, and therefore I was able to protect you in your nightmare."

I stopped and changed course to walk towards her. Her green eyes glowed in the sunlight, and her fur stood out against the light colors of the grass and the blue hues of the sky.

"What about when I was attacked by vampires at the convent? What about the nightmare I had the other night? Did you know he was going to come for me tonight? Is that why you found me in the forest?" I demanded, the questions quickly flowing out like word vomit.

"I was searching for you, and when I felt your power for the first time in over a year, I rushed to you as fast as I could. Once I tracked you to New Haven, I had not had the chance yet to bond with you before your last nightmare, but as it happens, I felt another come to your aide. The Fates have taken a special interest in you. As for tonight, I did not know the vampire would be coming for you, but as our bonding had started, I was able to protect you." She gracefully adjusted herself into a seated position and wrapped her tail around her paws.

I shook my head at her information and pinched the bridge of my nose in frustration. "I'm going to put aside the sheer craziness of this situation to ask the more pressing question. Where the hell are we?"

Rolling golden hills surrounded us, the tall blades of the grass swaying in the slight breeze. The sky was a beautiful shade of blue, with not a cloud in sight. The air was warm, but the wind carried just the right amount of chill to keep it pleasant.

"I am not sure. I didn't bring us here. But it is a place of peace. Can't you feel its energy?" Ophelia closed her eyes and lifted her nose to the air, and the wind ruffled her whiskers.

I let my senses explore and felt the aura of the land surrounding us. A warm glow of peace and safety curled around me, and even though I knew we would not be harmed here, wariness sat hard in my gut. I had not brought us here either.

I felt his presence before he spoke. I whipped around with my sword and swiped it towards the other being to have saved me from Alistair.

Ponytail.

My sword cut through his white tunic, and my gaze wildly flickered between it and his face. In addition to the tunic, he was wearing a pair of black breeches and knee-length boots. His golden-brown hair was not in his famous updo but instead hanging loose at his shoulders, and his golden eyes were hooded by thick, furrowed eyebrows. There were no glowing wings in sight.

"Is this how you offer thanks to those who have helped you? You try to strike them down?" His voice was low but dripped with power.

"Well, that's what you get for trying to sneak up on a person!" I snapped.

I watched his brows lift in surprise as he seemed to contemplate my words. I took a step towards Ophelia, and she positioned herself in front of me, fangs bared, her ears flicked back.

"You did not feel my presence? I sent a connection to your familiar to follow my grace and bring you here away from danger," he replied, his tone serious.

It was my turn to lift my brows, and I looked down at the shadowy jungle cat next to me.

"I simply followed the pull to safety. I thought it was you, Blair." Ophelia looked thoughtfully at him, her shadows churning around her.

I turned back to him. "That still doesn't mean you shouldn't announce yourself. Especially when you are coming up on someone from behind and they're already freaking the fuck out because they were almost just killed by a vampire." Not to mention the fact that I was not wearing any pants. "Thank you for bringing us here," I mumbled.

Ophelia chuffed again, covering her laugh, and I ignored her.

"I apologize. I am rusty when it comes to human customs. Are you alright?" Ponytail asked as his gaze traveled down my body. "I don't sense any injuries from you that are in need of healing." His eyes on my body were not lustful but observant, and I stared at him. And then busted out laughing.

"Am I alright? Did you not hear what I just said? I was almost taken *again* by Alistair, who wants to use me for gods only know what. I just found out I have a familiar, who has been creepily watching me for a few years but only made her presence known tonight. I can hardly get one good night's sleep without being worried I'm going to have to battle a vampire.

"I recently was taken in by a pack of werewolves when I have hardly had any interaction with any other supernatural beings because all of my teenage to adult life, I was told to avoid them. And then there's you, who I know nothing about, but you have saved me once before, yet I know nothing about *who* you are or *what* you are."

"That is a lot to take in," he agreed. His composed response had me fuming. He didn't elaborate further.

Which only enraged me more.

"How about you give me some answers?" I seethed, gripping my sword tighter.

I had the sudden urge to practice using my new blade. Ophelia rubbed her head along my thigh and began purring. I ran my hand along her fur and scratched behind her ears. She had a soothing energy about her, and I found myself leaning into her for comfort.

"I will explain what I can to you. However, that will not be tonight. You need to return to your realm for now. Your wolf is growing restless." Ponytail took a tentative step towards me. "I will bring you back here tomorrow night when you sleep."

Knowing he must have meant Dean, I let out a sigh and nodded, even though I wanted to demand answers now, I felt like my head would explode tonight if I learned anymore new information. I was unsure if I could even trust him, but he had kept his distance, hadn't tried to attack me and apparently brought us to this place, away from Alistair. This was the second time he helped me, so I would hear him out.

There was also a sense of familiarity with him that I couldn't quite explain. His features were proud, sharp, and somehow, I recognized them—not just from the first nightmare he revealed himself; I had thought he looked familiar even then. A blurred memory I couldn't place, shrouded in shadows nipped at my mind, trying to reveal itself to me, but it was just out of reach.

"What is your name?" I asked him, needing one last piece of information for the night.

"Ezekiel. Connect with your familiar again, and she will guide you home." Ezekiel gestured to Ophelia.

"Alright, Zeke, but tomorrow night, I'm getting some answers." I pointed the tip of my sword at him.

His eyebrows raised in surprise, and whether it was from my nickname for him or the threat of my blade, I wasn't sure, but his golden eyes were churning with amusement. I went back to Ophelia, and she was waiting for me patiently.

Going off instinct, I knelt and placed my hand on the side of her furred face, her whiskers tickling the back of my hand. She nodded in encouragement, and I reached my chaos out to her. It was met by her inky magic. The two twined together like old friends, and suddenly the world was spinning again.

The bright colors faded away to black, and I no longer felt Ophelia's fur in the palm of my hand. I was falling into a depthless pit of darkness, until I wasn't.

I gasped and sat up in bed, and my head connected with a hard surface.

"What the fuck!" I bellowed, and one hand flew to my head to rub the pain away. The other held the sword defensively in front of me.

A voice echoed my own groans of pain. I opened my eyes to see Dean with a panicked look on his face, a slight bruise already healing on his forehead, and my blade inches away from his throat.

I quickly dropped my sword to the bed and felt Ophelia curled up in my lap in her house-cat form, staring up at the both of us with a bored look on her face. Dean's gaze flickered between her, the sword, and I, and it was then I noticed how heavy he was breathing.

"You... you were screaming, having another nightmare. And I came down here to wake you when I saw—I saw this black shadow covering your body. I couldn't reach you, and I couldn't touch you. I couldn't help you." Dean's words were broken up between breaths as he ran his hands through his hair. He glared at Ophelia and growled, "It was you, wasn't it?"

Ophelia met his angry stare with a deadpan look and sniffed at him.

Dean's alpha energy was filling the room, and his aura was angrily buzzing around the shape of his body. Ophelia let out a cross between a hiss and a growl as she puffed her fur out and shifted into a standing position on my lap.

I carefully shifted Ophelia onto the bed, and I adjusted so I was on my knees at the edge of the bed before him. He still stood taller than me as I looked up into his glacier-blue eyes. They were still locked onto Ophelia, who had moved beside my hip in a low crouched position, ready to pounce if he lost control.

Slowly, I reached out and wrapped my hands around his neck, pressing my body into his. His breathing was still fast, fighting the instinct to shift, so I tucked my head into the crook of his neck and took deep breaths, forcing him to match his breath to mine.

"She was just trying to protect me, Dean. You both were just trying to protect me." I murmured soothing words over and over until his breathing slowed and he gripped me tighter.

The warmth of his body curled around me, and I inhaled his scent. My own nerves calmed at his touch, and I felt my heartrate slowing and the harshness of the nightmare begin to fade away.

Dean pulled away slightly to look at my face. My body immediately protested at the sudden loss of contact. His eyes bore into mine, and I nodded at him, trying to let him know that I was unharmed.

Well, physically.

Mentally and emotionally, I was a hot mess.

"Are you okay?" Dean murmured. I couldn't help but raise a brow at him, trying to ease the tension. We both chuckled. "What I meant was that I hated how I couldn't be there for you. I couldn't break through whatever that was. I felt..." He broke off and dropped his eyes.

Helpless. He felt helpless that he couldn't do anything to protect me.

I moved my hands from his neck to cradle his face and force him to look at me. His eyes slowly roamed up my features, but they lingered on my lips before settling on my eyes. I felt the air electrify between us, and gooseflesh covered my skin.

Against my better judgement, I brought his face down to mine and pressed my lips against his. He raised his eyebrows briefly in surprise, but it quickly passed as he leaned into the kiss. His lips were soft and demanding as our kiss deepened. One of his muscular arms wrapped around my waist and pulled me flesh against his hard body, while the other went around the base of my head and fisted into my hair.

I vaguely heard Ophelia jump off the bed, and a soft click of the door soon followed.

Dean's tongue flicked against my lips, asking for entrance, and I opened my mouth to him. I matched every move he made, battling him for control, and he growled in approval. His hand by my waist started caressing the exposed skin, then slowly began running up the length of my body.

He paused at the swell of my breasts, leisurely stroking. My nipples pebbled in response and were on full display in the thin tank top I was wearing.

My hands began exploring his body, the hardness of his chest, the dips and grooves of his muscles, before I ran my hands through his hair, tugging him closer to me. He nipped my bottom lip, and I shivered at the sensation.

I needed more, wanted more. Lightning was flowing through my blood, and chaos was pushing at my skin. I felt lost in Dean, and I didn't want to be found.

He pulled away slightly and smiled against my mouth. We were both breathless, leaning against the other. He placed his hands on the sides of my face and brought my lips in for one more tender kiss. I shamelessly tried to pull him back him for more, still kiss drunk, and he chuckled.

"You are... extraordinary," he breathed.

His arms went from my face down to brush my arms, and then he pushed on me slightly, so I was sitting back on my heels, looking up at him. His... enthusiasm was hard to look away from, but I was trying to be a lady and not look directly at it.

"As much as it pains me to stop..." He licked his lips, and I clenched my thighs together. "I need to know what happened in your nightmare. And what the hell is your cat?" He came over and sat next to me on the bed, and I adjusted myself to face him.

Ophelia silently entered the room again and jumped up onto the bed while Dean's eyes warily tracked her every movement. She padded over to me and made herself comfortable, tucking her paws underneath her body and staring up at Dean with her intelligent green eyes.

I told him everything that happened, starting with how Ophelia was my bonded familiar, and she protected me and solidified our bond to one another. I relayed every detail of the nightmare, as well as when the nightmare changed to a dream, and I finally learned Ponytail's name.

Ezekiel.

Chapter Fifteen

Dean was nearly carving a path in the floor with his heavy pacing as I relayed everything to him. He started with a look of concern on his face, but it quickly morphed to one of rage the moment I mentioned Alistair. Once I was finished, he stopped to run a hand through his hair and let out an exasperated sigh.

"So, you now have a familiar, who can turn into a very large cat and is duty-bound to protect you. And Ponytail is some sort of supe who can direct your consciousness from a nightmare into an alternate dreamscape?" Dean quirked an eyebrow at me.

"That's about the gist of it." I nodded and let out a big sigh.

I wasn't sure how to stop Alistair from infiltrating my nightmares. It was still unclear whether he could hurt me when I was in the nightmare, and I didn't want to find out. We also didn't know if he was able to track me through my dreams. I needed answers, and soon.

Perhaps the mysterious Ezekiel would be able to shed some light on the situation. The thought had stones of terror sinking down in my gut, but there was also a slight weight lifted off my shoulders. There have been so many unknowns in my life, and the thought of having a few of those revealed felt like I could breathe for the first time in a long time.

"I think it's time we consult with a dragon. Or a dreamwalker. Either would work out." Dean's words had my eyes practically bugging out of my head.

"I'm sorry, a *what?*" I sat forward. "Like, a literal dragon?" I demanded.

He came again to sit with me on the bed. I figured more creatures existed than I could possibly imagine within the supernatural world, but dragons? I assumed at least that creature would be a myth.

"Yes, dragons are rare, but they do exist. Luckily, one of their many abilities allows them to conceal themselves from humans while they are flying, and many humans refuse to believe the unexplainable, even when they see it with their own eyes. Dragons can also break magical connections and offer protection and healing, as well as breathe their famous dragonfire. Though, it usually takes them some convincing to do so. Dreamwalkers can walk through dreams, obviously. They can walk themselves and project others into the mind of anyone they can manage to make a connection to. They are extremely powerful and can manipulate your entire subconscious to see what they want to you to see," Dean explained.

"Either one should be able to help block the magical influence from entering your dreams, and depending on the power of the supe, they can cut the link between you and the influencer of your dreams and possibly pinpoint their location." Ophelia's velvet voice filled the bedroom.

If it were possible, Dean's eyes would have fallen out of his head. Clearly, she was speaking to the both of us.

"Oh yeah, she can talk." I gave a small smile to Dean and then turned back to her. "Ophelia, are you saying we could not only find out who is letting Alistair into my dreams, but also find them and stop them? And stop the nightmares?" I asked her seriously. Maybe having her around would come in handy after all.

"Yes. We need to find a powerful one to help us accomplish this.

Perhaps the wolf knows of someone?" She turned her chartreuse eyes onto Dean.

He still looked slightly surprised, but he quickly shook away the expression.

"I think there is a dragon in New Haven, but I'm not sure. There's always whispers and rumors, just like any small city, but rarely is there a powerful supe like that roaming around without some talk of it. I'll see what I can find out. They may not grant us their help easily, Blair. It may take some convincing for them to offer their assistance." Dean's expression turned grim.

My brows furrowed. "Why would they not want to help?"

"Dreamwalkers and dragons both are very rare and highly coveted. And many other supes would kill to have something that powerful in their back pocket. Many dragons have been hunted and persecuted until near extinction, and dreamwalkers hardly reveal their powers for the same reason."

I contemplated his words.

"They are viewed as weapons and used as such. So, they usually keep to themselves."

Ophelia's voice murmured in my head, and I glanced over at her. Her eyes remained on Dean, as if she hadn't said anything at all. Maybe I had just imagined it, or she could choose when to speak to where only I could hear her.

"Yes, I can speak with you in your mind. All witches and their familiars have this ability. It is a part of our souls bonding together. As our bond grows stronger, less effort will be put into our communication, and it will be as easy as breathing."

I gave her a slight nod that I understood. I sent a thought to her about how she and I needed to have a little conversation about this new bond of ours.

"I will force their hand if I have to, Blair," Dean rumbled, and he gripped my hand tightly.

I smiled weakly up at him, rubbing my left temple, trying to somehow calm my brain down from the overload of information.

As if things weren't complicated enough with trying to figure out why a clan of vampires was after me, let's just add finding a *freaking dragon* or a dreamwalker and understanding this witch-familiar bond to the to-do list. I felt a headache coming on, and I groaned quietly, continuing to rub my temples.

"Do you want me to stay?" Dean murmured as he gently pulled my hands away from my head.

I peeked my eyes open to look at him. His were filled with concern as he gripped my hands into this much larger ones.

Warmth radiated from his skin, and I felt myself wanting to lean into him and snuggle into the sensation. Those baby blues were pulling me in in too, begging me to dive into their depths. That familiar tingling sensation was running along my skin, leaving goose-bumps in its wake.

"Blair?" His voice snapped me out of my haze, and I realized I was staring at him. A slow, cocky smile spread across his face, the one that revealed his dimple. That damn dimple.

I swallowed. "I think I'm okay for tonight. I doubt I'll be sleeping anyway, and I have Ophelia here with me. She'll come get you if anything else happens." I looked over to her, and she dipped her head.

"I will keep her safe, wolf," Ophelia promised him.

Dean nodded and squeezed my hand before standing and heading towards the door, taking his body heat with him. He stopped suddenly and prowled back to the bedside, his eyes smoldering as if they peered into my soul.

He brought his face down to mine and pulled me into another intense kiss. This one was intense in a gentle way, not as demanding and raw as our first. There were no wandering hands; they stayed up cradling my face and caressing my cheekbones. He pulled away, and I was dazed for a moment, staring back up at him. Before I could even recover from the intensity of the kiss, he leaned in and licked my lips up to the tip of my nose.

"Gross!" I squealed. I had barely begun rubbing his saliva off my face when he was walking out of my bedroom laughing. I let out a soft chuckle as the door shut behind him.

Ophelia and I sat in silence for a few moments. I stared at the door, feeling numb without Dean's presence. He was like both the sun and the moon, warm and effervescent, yet calming and strong. Despite his alpha aura, he had a charming nature about him that drew you in.

"I can go get him if you'd like," Ophelia purred.

I swung my head over to look at the feline, my mouth falling open.

She gave me a knowing look and placed her head on her delicate paws. "Try to get some sleep, Blair. We have much to discuss tomorrow, and you'll need some rest if you're going to be meeting with Ezekiel tomorrow night."

"I don't think I'll be able to go back to sleep. What if Alistair weaves himself into a nightmare again?" I murmured.

I hated feeling like I was afraid. I had felt afraid more times than I could count in my life. It wasn't that I couldn't handle the fear, it's what happened when I overcame it. I'd get angry, and I would lose control of my chaos. The silver bolts give way to the dark shadows, and then people get hurt.

"I will assist you with an incantation that will help you fall into a dreamless sleep. It isn't a permanent fix by any means, but it should do the trick for tonight. You'll awaken fully rested in the morning." She sat up and stretched before padding over to sit in front of me. With a flick of her tail, the bedside lamp clicked off, and all I could see was her glowing green eyes.

"Do all familiars know magic?" I asked her.

"We are brought into existence with a certain level of knowledge of magic. The longer we are alive, our knowledge base continues to grow. Partly with what the witch or warlock we are bonded with can teach us, and the rest is bestowed to us by Hecate."

I opened my mouth to ask so many more questions, but she stopped me with a little swat of her paw.

"We will have time for a history lesson later. You need rest. From the look of the bags under your eyes, your sleep has been nearly nonexistent for some time now. Now, concentrate and repeat after me." She closed her eyes, and I followed suit.

She began chanting ancient words through our connection and at first, I merely listened. The language was almost musical, and after listening to her incantation once, I was able to recite the words back to her perfectly. She instructed me to chant them six times, and by the sixth my body began feeling extremely heavy.

Keeping my eyes closed, I adjusted myself in bed to a comfortable position, cuddling one of the pillows. My body felt entirely relaxed, and as I drifted off, I felt Ophelia curl up in the small of my back, purring as she did so.

* * *

I was drooling. I could feel it pooling underneath my mouth and soaking the pillow, but I couldn't bring myself to move. The only thing ruining this beautiful sleep was the light streaming in through the windows.

Had no one ever heard of blackout curtains in this house?

Whiskers tickled my face, and a small wet nose began nudging my cheek. I groaned and gently pushed her away. Just a few more minutes. I couldn't even remember the last time I slept that hard without a nightmare interrupting it.

The nose nudging was replaced by a paw tapping my cheek. I shifted my face, so it was flat into the pillow, and in response, Ophelia sat on my back.

"Blame the wolf. He has been restlessly pacing outside your room since sunrise this morning. I told him that you were sleeping and that he should go piss on a tree or something. He didn't find it very amusing." She made a noise that was probably meant to be a chuckle but came out as a hissy laugh.

I laughed internally because my brain was not ready to make any complex noises yet. I slowly turned over and felt her jump off me to avoid being smushed before I stretched out my arms and legs, taking in a deep breath before opening my eyes. The light was jarring at first, but as I adjusted and sat up in bed, I noticed I felt... good. No lingering fatigue, no sore muscles. I wasn't sweaty, and there was no slight headache I always seemed to wake up with after I had a nightmare.

I shifted my legs off the bed and began walking over to the bathroom when I heard footsteps outside my door. I sighed and changed course, walking over to the door and swinging it open.

Miles stood in the doorway with his hand in the air as if he was about to knock. His eyebrows were lifted in surprise, and as his gaze traveled down the length of my body, they lifted even higher. I couldn't help the wave of disappointment that crashed into me at the sight of Miles instead of Dean.

"Well, good morning to you too, little witch." A slow smile crept across his face. "If I would have known this was the dress code, I would have dressed accordingly." He winked.

"I'm not sure you could pull the look off, wolf." I lifted my chin at him, crossing my arms. I glared at Miles, my mood slightly soured that it wasn't Dean crowding my doorway.

He chuckled. "Dean got called away to a council meeting. I believe he's meeting with a few of them afterwards to find out if any of them have information about Alistair and if they know of any dream-fixing-supes in the area. Do you want to train with Calian and I after breakfast?"

"Sure, I'll get dressed now. Thanks." At my words, he nodded and turned towards the stairs. I shut my door and immediately went to put some workout gear on.

This should be interesting.

Chapter Sixteen

Watching Ophelia train with the werewolves was a hilarious experience. At first, none would even approach her, so Miles took it upon himself to challenge her. And boy, did she answer.

Having a much more lithe and agile body of a jungle cat, she was able to wiggle out of his hold easily as well as use the surrounding trees to her advantage. Calian loved having the variety of training partners, between Ophelia and I, and we were invited to train with them whenever we liked.

Selene was in the garden with Hayley when we got back, so I made quick work of prepping wraps with various meats, cheeses, and vegetables I found in the fridge. Miles and Cal found some chips in the pantry, and we made ourselves comfortable sitting together at the island. I made extra for Hayley, Selene, and Dean and left them in the fridge.

I was mid-bite when Dean walked in, dressed in a leather jacket with a gray V-neck underneath, as well as dark jeans and motorcycle boots.

His hair was wild like he had continuously run his fingers

through it, and his stubble was more grown in today. The food nearly fell out of my mouth at the sight of him. I felt my chaos push up against my skin, desperate to wrap its energy around him.

He strolled over with his eyes zeroed in on me. I slowly chewed my food, not taking my eyes off him either. I swallowed roughly as he pulled up the last barstool close to mine, invading my space, his large figure looming over me and wrapping me in his scent.

"Can I help you?" I quirked a brow at him, continuing to take a bite of my wrap. His blue eyes twinkled with mischief. "What the hell are you smirking at?"

"I just like the way you eat," he chuckled, and I nearly growled at him.

Miles coughed, covering his laugh, and I turned my glare onto him briefly before turning back towards Dean.

"And how do I eat?" I popped the last bit of wrap into my mouth and leaned against the countertop.

"Like an animal." His smile was wicked, and I opened my mouth to comment on his perception of my eating habits, but he cut me off. "I heard it was a very successful training session this morning. Thank you both for working with the sentinels. It's always good for them to practice with new supes. Keeps them sharp." He reached out and twirled a piece of my hair around his fingers.

"I enjoyed it thoroughly." Ophelia purred and turned her eyes on Miles.

He scoffed and gave her the finger. Calian let out a bark of a laugh, nearly choking on his food.

"It just feels nice to use my body again." I turned towards Dean.

"I could think of another way you could use your body," he rumbled in my ear, and I nearly fell right off the barstool. Before I could utter a retort, he changed the subject, "I wanted to take you into town this evening and show you around the city. If you'd like."

His expression was hopeful, and when I nodded yes, he smiled so big that damn dimple made its appearance.

He leaned in and pressed a soft kiss against my cheek, murmuring, "Thank you for the food. I'll eat while you get ready."

I felt my cheeks flush, and I gave him a nod, muttering a see you later to Miles and Calian before rushing up the stairs. Ophelia's soft paws followed me into my room, pausing briefly to stretch before jumping on the bed and settling in for a little catnap.

Even though I wanted to be quick and get back downstairs as fast as I could, the hot water of the shower felt so good on my aching muscles. I felt the tension ease up the longer I stayed in, but finally I finished and began working towards getting ready.

I found myself nervously chewing on my lip as I started brushing through my hair. I was nervous because of how much I craved being around Dean and desperately excited to finally see the whole of New Haven, a city for supernaturals, a place where we did not have to hide.

Once I had wind-dried my hair and it sat in loose curls down my back, I made my way over to the closet.

I went for a pair of skinny jeans, an emerald form-fitting tank top, and paired everything with my new favorite leather jacket. My generous cleavage was a bit on display in this top, and I almost went to change into one of the vintage band t-shirts I spied in the back corner of my closet, but I decided to be bold.

I finished up the look with combat boots, giving the outfit a classically edgy look. I was just about to head downstairs when I saw an over-the-shoulder bag and I quickly grabbed it. Ophelia eyed it, reading my thoughts and hopping into the opening, settling herself inside. She poked her head out of the top, content with being carried. *Spoiled familiar.*

It should have frightened me, how instantly important she became to me. Our bond thrummed between our souls, and it was strange to think of a time without her tied to me. It was an indescribable feeling to be totally understood by someone, and despite my recent immersion into this world of supernatural beings, I felt like I was finally where I was meant to be.

I turned down the stairs, careful not to jostle Ophelia too much, and strolled into the kitchen. Miles and Cal were gone, leaving Dean sitting beside the counter, reading a book. Dean looked up, and his eyes slowly raked over my body, his irises a blue blaze of lust.

"You look... angelic, as always," he rumbled, dropping the book onto the counter as he swaggered over to me.

I snorted. "I doubt angels wear combat boots."

He hardly left any space between us before he brushed my cheek with his thumb, and I had to hold back a shiver. I licked my lips as I looked at his plush mouth, then up to his eyes. The lighter hues of blue looked like bolts of lightning brightening up a darkened sky.

"They would after one glimpse at how bewitching you look." He traced his thumb down my cheek and brought it to my bottom lip.

Feeling a little wicked, I quickly bit down, and his responding growl made my knees wobbly. I released it after a moment, and his gaze down at me was purely predatory.

He licked his lips. "Wild thing."

"If you two are going to continue that, will you please let the cat out of the bag?" Ophelia quipped. Dean chuckled, and I cleared my throat awkwardly.

He grabbed my hand, and we walked through the living room, then exited the house through a pair of ornate double-doors. There was a gravel circle driveway in front of the house, and directly in front of the porch steps was a motorcycle.

My jaw dropped. It was flat black, with chrome detailing, and adorned on the side of the fuel tank was an outline of a crescent moon. He strolled over to it—I stood back gawking—and he leaned up against it with a cocky smile.

"Wanna ride?" he asked.

Oh, what a loaded question that was. Ophelia's hissy laugh sounded from the bag, and I scowled at her before turning back to Dean and giving him a nod. Truth be told, I had always wanted to ride on a motorcycle.

He opened one of the leather bags on the side, and I slipped my bag in; he made sure to leave the flap open so Ophelia could stick her head out. He sat on the bike first. His powerful body looked massive, and the bike groaned slightly under his added weight. I threw my leg over the side and sat on the seat behind his, pressed up against his back.

The heat from his body radiated against my skin, and I found myself snuggling in closer to him. His responding rumble sent tingles into my chest and my center. The engine flared to life, and my whole body was vibrating from both the bike and anticipation.

Fifteen-year-old Blair would be swooning right now seeing me on the back of a motorcycle with a bad-boy-type.

Well, maybe big-bad-wolf was more accurate.

We peeled out of the circle driveway, gravel spraying out behind us, and I let out an excited squeal. I felt Dean chuckle as I pressed up against his back, my arms wrapped around his muscled torso. I glanced down to see Ophelia with her head slightly out of the leather saddlebag, her tipped ears flicking back with the wind.

The gravel was soon replaced by dirt as we traveled towards the edge of the pack territory, and once we were closer to the main road, the trees thinned slightly.

I felt us pass through the magical protections that lined the border of pack territory, dusting over us like static mist. Dean slowed slightly to make the turn onto the asphalt, and then he twisted the throttle, lurching us forward again. Trees lined the road in an endless sea of green, continuing into the horizon.

My dark hair whipped out behind me, and even though we were travelling at a high speed, my hold on Dean loosened slightly. Closing my eyes, I tilted my head back and relished the feeling of the wind caressing my face.

This must be what flying feels like.

Chapter Seventeen

I leaned forward onto him, relishing the heat his body produced as the wind whipped around us, gripping him tighter with both my arms and thighs, getting as close to him as I could. I angled myself to glance at his face, and I saw his mouth was pulled up into a sultry smile, exposing his dimple.

Soon, the trees started spreading out, giving way to scattered homes, all varying in style and color, and Dean slowed his speed. It was refreshing, as human homes had all begun looking the same in recent years. The further into town we rode, the more homes popped up, and with them came the supernaturals of the city.

Dean turned down a street that eventually led us into the downtown sector of New Haven. The single-family homes were replaced by gorgeous brownstone apartments adorned with iron gates and small gardens on their stoops.

More creatures appeared as we travelled along the streets, a few of them giving Dean a wave. Some appeared as near human, while others were obviously otherworldly in their appearance. With their varying features came their varying aura colors, but I was pleasantly surprised to see that they were all relatively peaceful.

Dean jumped the curb and parked the bike in front of a red brick building before he cut the engine and dismounted. He opened the saddlebag Ophelia was in first, which she promptly jumped out of before shaking out her fur. He then grabbed my bag, shouldered it, and reached out his hand to help me off the bike.

Even with both feet on the ground, he didn't let go of my hand as he slipped the bag over my shoulder and started up the steps of the building.

There was no sign in front, but as he turned the knob on the black door, the smell of bourbon hit my nose. The bar was dimly lit, with flickering candles inside the iron fixtures. The candles cast more light than normal, so they must have been spelled, but the orange glow across the worn-in bar gave the room a homey feel to it.

Bottles lined the wooden shelves across the back wall, and I found myself giddy with excitement. I *loved* bourbon.

"What do I have to do to get you to look at me like that?" Dean murmured. His gaze was heated, and little bolts of lightning raced underneath my skin.

I pressed my thighs together as I turned my eyes on him, letting my gaze travel the length of his hard body, and as I reached his eyes again, they were glowing a bright glacier blue.

"Dean! Been a long time since you visited the pub. And look! You've got a *dame* with you. A mighty pretty one, if I do say so myself." A tall male came around the bar and clapped Dean on the back. He had wild curly onyx hair that trailed down his back and striking moss-green eyes that nearly glowed against his dark complexion.

I wasn't sure what species of supe he was right off the bat, but his energy suggested he possessed some sort of magic.

Dean barely glanced at the man. "Brodie, it's been a long time. This is Blair. She's with *me.*" There was a distinct claim in his statement, and Brodie's smile only widened as he looked back at me, his aura pulsing a deep purple, slightly tinged with yellow at the edges.

His aura was giving off strong sexual energy, as well as amusement. Ignoring the oddness of it, I gave him a mock salute in greeting.

A harsh meow had us all glancing down to Ophelia on the floor, her ears pinned back in annoyance. "Sorry, this is my familiar, Ophelia." She sniffed and then stalked off towards the bar, hopping up on one of the stools.

"Pleasure to me you both. Come on, let's drink." He gestured to the bar, and we followed Ophelia's path. I took the seat directly next to her, and she head-bumped my elbow as I rested it on the bartop. "What'll it be?" Brodie threw a towel over his shoulder, a sultry grin curving his lips as he looked over my face.

"Bourbon, neat please."

Brodie's emerald eyes sparkled with mischief before he turned and grabbed a crystal decanter from one of the shelves. Dean signaled for the same, and Brodie quickly poured our drinks, including one for himself, and set the bottle in front of us.

"You're from Atlantis. A siren, if I'm not mistaken." I nearly choked at Ophelia's blunt words, but I didn't want to waste any bourbon.

I swallowed and coughed a bit before glaring at her. Her green eyes remained locked on Brodie, while her shadows wrapped around me protectively, their touch like a cool caress of darkness.

Atlantis was the realm of the God of the Sea and Waters, Lir. My eyes widened at Ophelia's words. I had never met a supe from that god-realm before, but they were rumored to be both extremely sensual and vengeful beings.

He took a swig form his glass and nodded. "Don't get your tail in a knot there, pussycat. I promise not to use my gifts on this beauty." Brodie leaned in close, his moss eyes filled with heat as his gaze snagged on my lips. "Unless she asks me to."

Dean growled a warning before he pulled my barstool closer to him.

Brodie threw back his head and laughed, the sound musical and alluring. "Easy, Dean, I'm only joking. Besides, I'm guessing you're trying to figure out what she is?" Brodie's face turned curious as he glanced over to Dean and then back at me.

I blinked in surprise, a nervous sweat sliding down my back.

"I'm a witch. Dean knows that." I sniffed before I took another sip, looking between the two males. I'd be damned if a siren tricked me into revealing my true nature.

Brodie studied me for a moment, and I kept my face blank as I held his stare. "A witch? I see, my mistake." He winked before leaning against the bar, inching towards my face.

I felt his siren magic reach out towards me tentatively, like a cool wave kissing the sandy shores, begging me to dive into the water. My magic defiantly rose within me, a dark beast full of storms and shadows, and slapped his sultry magic away without a thought. He chuckled.

Dean looked between the two of us, curiosity evident on his face. I gave nothing away, but Brodie's eyes twinkled with mischief.

"Quite the female you've brought into my pub, Dean. Reminds me of our dear friend Valerie." Brodie sipped his bourbon, never tearing his gaze away from mine. Ancient knowledge lurked in those emerald depths, and I feared he knew exactly what I was.

"Valerie?" I turned my head to Dean, attempting to steer the conversation away from me.

"Valerie is a friend of ours. She is an extremely rare kind of supe. Your power reminds me of hers, and I already asked her to come meet with you. She said she would, whenever she gets a break from that mysterious job of hers." Dean's gaze shifted to my own, and for a moment, I thought I saw concern flicker in his eyes.

"What kind of supe is she?" I asked.

Dean and Brodie exchanged a look, and Brodie put his hands up in front of him with a shake of his head.

"It's not our place to say. You'll just need to meet her. But she is an ancient, powerful supe. Very intense. I think you'll like her." Dean's lips tilted up into a small smile. I nodded.

"Enough of the heavy. Let's drink and be merry." Brodie waved his hands as if to banish the seriousness of our conversation.

He then picked up his glass and threw it back, slamming it back on the counter when he was finished. I chuckled and let Ophelia return to her barstool. I finished my own drink and nearly shivered at the familiar, beautiful burn in my chest.

We drank a few more glasses and exchanged stories of our youth, sticking to the happier memories and laughing together. Ophelia even shared a few stories of her previous charges, as she called them, and I was happy to know that she had other witches in her long life that cared about her as much as I was growing to.

Familiars were not demons, as much as human folklore made them out to be, but witches who had passed on and felt a debt was owed to Hecate and agreed to serve the next generation of witches. They were granted magical knowledge necessary to perform their duties and two forms to shift between, whichever would better assist the witch, as well as a soul bond to the witch they were assigned to.

This bond allowed them to communicate telepathically, sense the other's presence, and share energy when necessary. The whole thing was a lot to understand, but it explained this attachment I felt towards her already.

I found myself feeling a little buzzed, despite my usually high tolerance for alcohol. My limbs felt warm and tingly, and I couldn't stop smiling.

Dean leaned in and murmured, "All supes have a high alcohol tolerance. Brodie and the other barkeeps tend to spell the liquor to affect us the way it affects humans." My eyes widened as I took in the tingling sensation of the spelled bourbon.

I shrugged and finished my drink.

A few other supes trickled into the bar throughout our conversation, offering greetings to both Dean and Brodie. Eventually, the bar was in full swing, and I even recognized a few pack members sitting at tables. The energy from the crowd was almost overwhelming, so many kinds of supes that I had never been around, each aura vastly different.

Brodie became busy slinging drinks to his patrons, and Dean gestured to the doors. He murmured for Brodie to put the drinks on his tab, and we both stood to take our leave.

A hand snaked around my arm, pulling me back, "Where you going, sweetheart? The night is young. Stay a while."

Dean stiffened in front of me, and he let his power slip into the room, quieting the supes closest to us. Dean turned, letting out a growl of warning, blue fire blazing in his eyes as he stared down the male who still had his hand wrapped around my arm. A few of his pack members growled, slowly creeping in towards their alpha. Brodie cursed, and Ophelia silently shifted into her jungle cat form, ready to defend me if I needed.

Ignoring them all, I plastered on my sweetest smile, slowly turning towards the male.

The man was barely taller than I was, with windblown auburn hair and russet-colored eyes. His grin revealed crooked teeth, and it only widened as I took a step further into his space. Shifter, I decided, his aura a hazy swirl of lust and jealousy.

"Remove your hand from my arm, *now*, or you will lose it," I purred. I kept my magic under control, not letting an ounce of it flow through me.

His eyes darkened, and his hand squeezed tighter, to which Dean let out a warning snarl. Chaos cackled within me, begging me to punish him for his unwanted touch. I pushed the urge away and resorted to my favorite form of punishment.

Good, old-fashioned violence.

I let my smile grow a fraction before swinging quickly, my fist connecting with his nose with a joyful crunch. He shrieked in pain, his hand letting go and flying to clutch his now bleeding nose as he crumpled to the floor.

"Let that be a lesson to you about consent. Sorry about the mess,

Brodie." I straightened my jacket and turned, earning a grin from Brodie and a hungry smile from Dean.

I sauntered around the bar, leaning around Brodie to grab a towel before giving him a peck on the cheek. I tossed the towel over the bar onto the handsy shifter, but before I could trail after Ophelia, who was already making her way through the door, Brodie pulled me in for a quick hug. There was no hesitation in my embrace back to him, and I felt the heat of his magic embrace my own, but it demanded nothing, just danced around it teasingly.

He winked as I pulled away, before he turned back to his customers, yelling at the shifter to clean up his mess of blood off the floor.

Dean was suddenly at my side and stepped around me to lean down and whisper in the shifter's ear. Whatever he said, the male shifter turned a ghastly shade of white, and his mouth dropped open before he sputtered apologies to Dean and then to me.

I rolled my eyes, but my toes were curling in my boots as Dean pressed his hand against the small of my back. We made our way out of the bar to where Ophelia was waiting for us by Dean's motorcycle, her tail swishing against the pavement.

"Where to now?" I asked, turning to Dean, and even I was surprised at the huskiness in my voice.

He inclined his head, and we began walking down the streets of downtown, with Ophelia trotting behind us. We stopped in various shops he wanted to show me. Some were the same as they would be in the human world, while others were filled with items I had never seen or heard of. Dean and the shop owners explained everything I had questions about, and my head was swimming with all the new knowledge I had of the supernatural world.

We even made a stop at Hayley's shop, where one of her workers showed us various items Hayley had set aside for us.

I was shocked again to see how in-tuned she seemed to be with my taste, even though we were still getting to know one another.

When I questioned Dean about it, he merely shrugged and explained she had always had a sense about those things, just as his mother had. He asked for the items to be packaged up and said that he would be by to pick them up later.

Dean kept a hand on me the entire time, and my chaos was thrumming with delight. Eventually, he pulled me into a restaurant—after a particularly loud growl from my stomach—called the Wolves' Den, and we were immediately seated by the hostess in a booth in the back. The restaurant was cozy, colored with various hues of reds and oranges, like the flames of fire. The space was buzzing with such happy energy; the sounds of laughter and conversation swirled around, coaxing me to relax. I was in complete awe of this entire city.

It's amazing, isn't it? To be around others like yourself. Not having to hide what you are. I can hear your heart singing, Blair. But do close your mouth. You'll catch flies like that.

My eyes nearly bugged out of my head as I snapped my jaw shut and shot a look at Ophelia. But she was right; this city was amazing. I felt that pull of magic visiting Sage in Flagstaff, but I never imagined it was trying to pull me here, calling me home.

Dean's eyes danced as they studied me. "It has been such a pleasure to see you experience this city for the first time. Your reactions are so genuine and sweet. I couldn't imagine seeing the city like this for the first time." He angled his body to face me better, sprawling out, his knee bumping mine under the table.

Dean's compliment caught me off guard. I wasn't used to a man saying exactly what he was feeling, so naturally I had to ruin it with my sarcasm.

"I don't think anyone has ever described me as sweet." I snorted.

The waitress came by then, a petite young woman with chestnut hair and striking gold eyes.

Dean ordered us each another glass of bourbon, and as she quickly trotted off towards the bar, I noticed she had furry legs adorned with hooves. Dean must have noticed my expression, as he quickly explained she was a satyr.

I nodded and began looking over the plethora of choices on the menu the waitress had left behind and found myself nearly drooling after reading the descriptions of each item. Ophelia's little paw reached up and tapped what her choice was, murmuring that she would share. I giggled at that.

Our waitress came back then, and she began taking our orders. My eyes widened when Dean ordered not one but *several* dishes for himself.

As the waitress walked away, he laughed at my expression. "Werewolves and other shifter types tend to eat more than the average supe. It's believed it's because of our animal side, as having two forms requires more fuel for power apparently. Different supes require different forms of energy. While you and I and many other types of supes eat food, there are others that sustain themselves on different sources. For example, vampires obviously sustain themselves on—"

"Blood," I interrupted him, wrinkling my nose.

He nodded, his mouth set in a grim line.

"Right. Sirens, elves, and the fae get their sustenance from energy. Sirens and elves use human emotions like lust, sadness, anger, happiness—whatever emotion is strongest in their source during feedings. Fae use elemental energy to keep themselves strong, drawing from nature and ley lines. All of these supes can eat normal food as well, but it doesn't keep them strong like energy does."

I filed all this information away. Neither Sage nor Vivian had gone over any of this in our lessons of the supernatural. Maybe Vivian never thought I would need that knowledge considering how secluded our lives were. She focused on teaching me what I would need to know to protect myself and to control my magic.

She probably never imagined that I would end up in a place like this. Hell, I'd never imagined I would either.

And Sage liked to speak of the gods and their realms, the Fates, and even though she answered most questions I ever asked, it's hard to question things you know nothing about. Perhaps she thought I knew more, with all the lessons Vivian insisted on having with me.

Our friendship was so much more than our connections to the supernatural, so really it didn't surprise me too much that it never came up with her.

Still, my lack of knowledge of the supernatural was slightly alarming, especially for having a witch for an adoptive mother and a psychic for a best friend. And Dean and Ophelia seemed to be the only ones willing to share.

"What else?" I demanded, eager to learn as much as I could.

Both Dean and Ophelia chuckled. Dean finished his glass and set it back on the table, humor gleaming in his glacier eyes as he indulged every question I asked.

Our plates finally arrived, and we began digging into our food. I had ordered the ribeye plate with roasted potatoes, broccoli, and cauliflower. While Dean ordered the same thing, he also got a plate of pasta with meatballs, a whole roasted chicken, and another smaller steak dish.

The flavors were beyond anything I had ever tasted.

A slight noise of pleasure slipped out after the first bite of juicy steak and Dean rumbled, a devilish grin adorning his face as he watched me. After a few more bites, he finally started in on his plates.

My eyes wandered over to one of his dishes, and I bit my lip at the sight. I heard Dean chuckle as I quickly brought my gaze back to my own food. A fork with a meatball appeared in my peripheral vision, and I turned to see Dean offering me a bite. I quirked my brow at him, surprised at the gesture, and he jiggled the meatball in front of me expectantly.

Feeling a little wicked, I quickly snapped out and took over half the meatball into my mouth, chewing slowly.

He laughed. "And they call me an animal. That was completely vicious." He looked between me and the now bare fork he held. "I liked it," he nearly purred, and I swallowed with a loud gulp.

Wolves never share their food, you know.

I continued eating but spared a glance over to Ophelia. She was looking out into the restaurant, but a flick of her ears told me she knew I heard her. I vaguely remembered Sage telling me that werewolves were extremely territorial about nearly everything, including food.

So why had Dean offered mc some of his?

Chapter Eighteen

After we had finished and Dean paid, we walked along the now quiet streets again. There were hardly any lights on, so you could see the night sky very clearly. It reminded me of beautiful home, where every night, it looked as if you could reach out and touch the stars. A gentle breeze ruffled my hair as I stared up into the endless depths of stars overhead.

"Beautiful." I broke my gaze from the night sky to look at Dean, his eyes staring at me, glowing in the light of the moon. He grabbed my hand. "I want to show you something."

Before I could utter a reply, he tugged me along behind him, pulling me further into the city.

The buildings began spreading out and getting larger until we finally stopped in front of one with large pillars in front of wide cathedral doors with intricate golden handles. Dean pulled over the massive wooden doors and ushered me inside.

Luminous light like burnt sunsets cascaded from the lamps and onto the mountainous bookshelves. The building was at least three stories tall, and as I gazed up, I saw the beautiful vaulted ceiling adorned with a magical illusion of galaxies swirling in the dark sky. I walked towards the massive shelves and spied book nooks furnished with oversized chairs, blankets, and side tables for readers to relax and enjoy their chosen titles.

Dean remained silent at my side, watching as I moved through the shelves, touching the spines of the books as I delved deeper into the library. I couldn't believe the variety of books I was seeing on the shelves from history, romance, grimoires, classic fiction novels, and even research texts. There were also many titles I did not recognize, some even in languages or runes I couldn't make out.

I stopped suddenly and turned to Dean. "I don't even know what to say," I breathed.

He was smiling, dimple and all, and it made my skin warm like I was sitting near a fire. The glow of the lanterns highlighted his sparkling eyes, the various tones of blue shining brightly.

"I thought you might like it here, considering I've seen you go through about half of my personal library at home since you joined us," he chuckled, and I smiled at him.

"Reading has always been a comfort to me, one of the only constants I've ever had," I admitted, wringing my hands together nervously. Dean's eyes softened slightly, knowing bits and pieces of my dark past.

"There is always a librarian here, one during the day and the other at night, so you can come here whenever you'd like. Should you ever need help finding something, all you need to do is ask, and she will appear before you to assist."

I nodded and looked up at the starry ceiling again, breathing in the smell of aged paper and leather binding.

He couldn't possibly know how much this meant to me. He offered me sanctuary, not only within this city, or within his home, but a space where I could get lost in the pages of books and have a sense of normalcy.

I don't know how long I stood there like that, filled with peace and comfort. But when I opened my eyes and turned to thank him, I found Dean had stepped closer, our bodies nearly flesh against each other. The heat radiating from his body caressed my skin, and my magic nearly vibrated within me from the closeness.

I had to look up at him as he towered over me. His eyes were trained on my mouth, until they slowly made their way back to meet my stare.

"Thank you." Those two words were all I could manage under his soulful stare.

He reached up and placed his hand on my cheek, his thumb caressing the skin there. Despite my usual disdain for physical contact, I leaned into him. I could never seem to help drawing closer to him.

A hearty rumble escaped him, and it took all my willpower not to bury my face in his muscled chest to feel the sound vibrate upon my face. His eyes searched mine, and I felt like he was peering into my very soul. Yet as he did so, he didn't pull away from whatever darkness he found there, and I didn't pull away from his.

He brought his other hand to cup my cheek and slowly brought his lips down to my own.

Dean's kiss was captivating, and my arms reached up to pull him closer. His kiss electrified my body, and I felt bolts of chaos flooding through my veins, singing at the feel of his plush mouth on mine.

The kiss soon deepened, and his tongue flicked my lip, asking for entrance. I opened to him, our tongues stroking one another, and my hands wandered along the planes of his hard muscles. His hands caressed my skin from my face down to my back and then rested briefly on my hips, grinding me against him, before one hand came back up to rest behind my head, pulling me closer, deepening the kiss.

I bit his lip playfully, earning a growl from him, and I smiled against his lips. He quickly picked me up, and I wrapped my legs around him just before he pushed my body up against the nearest wall, narrowly missing one of the bookshelves.

Dean kissed all along my jaw and down the column of my throat, and I let out a breathy moan. Each kiss felt like an electric shock pulsing through my body that left me tingling with pleasure. His hardness was pressed up against my core, and he captured my next moan with his mouth. I shoved my hands underneath his shirt, needing to feel his skin and tracing my fingers along the curves of his muscled chest and stomach. Dean let out another groan at my touch, and I relished the feeling of it reverberating through my body.

A throat clearing behind us put a stop to our feverish movements. We both were breathing heavily, and Dean continued to hold my body up against the wall. Dean growled and scented the air as I peered around him to see who was standing behind him.

A short female with large purple eyes and pointed ears was tapping her foot, giving us both a stern look. Her wispy silver hair sat in a bun on the top of her head, revealing delicately pointed ears peeking out, and she wore wide leg slacks with a white shirt tucked in. Her skin was a cool brown, and bright white freckles dusted her face, like the stars decorating the ceiling.

"Lumen, nice to see you again," Dean's voice echoed in the library, and my cheeks burned with embarrassment. I squirmed and tried to push him away from me so I could reclaim some sort of dignity.

"Dean, as an alpha *and* a council member, you of all supes should know that there is no *canoodling* allowed in the library." She crossed her arms and shook her head in disapproval.

Dean finally let my legs go, and I swiftly got to work righting my clothes.

He gave me a wink and slowly turned around. "There was no canoodling here, Lu, just showing Blair here around the city. I knew she would find the library very stimulating, as she is an avid reader and is currently researching everything there is to know about our world. She's new around here."

Her eyes swiveled towards me, and I gave her a small wave.

"Yes, clearly it was the library that held her attention." She rolled her eyes and shrugged her shoulders. "Just no frisky business in the library, okay? No one else is here during the night, and it echoes in here." She shuddered, and I felt a blush creep down my neck in embarrassment.

"Is the library only filled with non-fiction texts?" I blurted out just as she was about to walk away.

She stopped and turned back to look over me again. She then strode up to me, and I felt her starry magic gently pressing at my aura.

A black shadow flew down from the second story railing and landed right next to me with an ethereal grace. Lumen let out a little squeak in alarm, taking a step back as Ophelia held her large head high as she came to sit at my side, shadows whipping around curiously.

Lumen cleared her throat nervously. "No, we have an array of fiction titles as well, written by both supes and humans. This library runs similarly to any human library, we just have a bigger selection. Is there anything in particular you're looking for?"

My smile widened as Lumen studied me with interest.

"As silly as it is, I'm a sucker for fantasy and paranormal romance. I'm loving learning everything I can about supes, but I do miss the smut I normally read." I gave her a wink, which earned me a shy smile.

"I can leave some recommendations that I personally enjoyed in that genre. I can also make some recs about familiars and the gods. I think that'd be an excellent start to learn where each species came from with Soliel, the day librarian, so you can come back at a more suitable hour." She wrung her tiny hands together, and I couldn't help but notice a hint of bitterness in her tone.

"I'd rather just work with you, if that's alright. I'm kind of a night owl myself." I gave her a genuine smile, hoping she wouldn't refuse.

Lumen's face lit up, her freckles nearly glowing, as she nodded her head excitedly. "Oh, yes! I'd like that very much, Blair! Give me a couple of nights and then come back around this time, and we shall go over what I'm able to dig up!" She clapped her hands, and I smiled even bigger at her excitement.

We said our goodbyes and made our way out of the library and back to where the motorcycle was parked outside of Brodie's bar. Ophelia walked straight up to the saddle bag and gingerly lifted the flap to nestle inside. The street was serene and silent, the scattered lights of the city providing a soft glow that didn't interfere with the white light of the moon and stars.

"How did you know Lumen would take to me?" The question flew out of me before I made any moves towards the bike.

Dean ruffled his dark locks and gave me a one-shouldered shrug.

"She doesn't get many visitors, and I thought she could use a friend. She's been through a tough time, and though I do think she enjoys the quiet, she does get lonely. I thought you could use a friend too." Dean gave me a small, encouraging smile, and my heart squeezed.

Curiosity bubbled up within me, and I couldn't help but ask, "She's been through a tough time?"

Dean sighed, and the smile faded from his lips, turning down into a frown. "Yes. Family drama. There are four courts within the Fae species on Alfheim, all created by Gaia, the Goddess of the Fae. They are solar-based, so there is the Day Court, the Night Court, the Dawn Court, and the Dusk Court, and each have their own special magics. Lu's family is considered royalty at the Day Court, and Lumen... well, she was born different. Her magic hails from the Night Court, while her twin sister, Soliel, has magic from their home-court. There hasn't been a Night Court fae born in their royal line in centuries, until Lumen."

He paused, his eyes flicking to me, waiting to see if I had a question. When I didn't, he continued.

"Her parents used her birth to make plans to create permanent ties between the Day Court and the Night Court and arranged a marriage between Lumen and the Prince of the Night Court. When she came of age, she refused to marry, and her parents were outraged. She fled from her own home and wound up here. Her parents spun it as a postponement to allow Lumen to finish her studies and 'get some real-world experience' and sent her sister here to keep an eye on her, and trust me when I say that is not a good thing."

My mouth hung open, the story far beyond what I had imagined. The sheer idea of courts and court politics was way outside my realm of knowledge. But I admired her courage to stand up for herself, and it only made me want to get to know her more.

"Wow," I breathed. "Her parents sound like dicks."

Dean chuckled, "You're not wrong there. She is also a brilliant researcher, and I thought she could help. Besides, who could resist such a charming face?" He gave me a dazzling smile as he gestured to himself, and I laughed.

"Pretty sure I was the one who asked her for help," I pointed out as I took steps towards the motorcycle.

Dean shrugged as he kicked up the stand and took a seat, the metal groaning under his weight. I made quick work of settling in behind him, snuggling a bit closer than I needed to. His body rumbled again at my touch, which sent a shiver through my body.

"And again, I ask, who could resist such a charming face?" He winked before he started the bike, and I let out a breathy laugh.

The roar of the engine drowned out any other noise as we raced off into the night. The chill of the air paired with the warmth of the werewolf in front of me gave me a semblance of peace, and for a moment, I ignored the looming presence of the scheduled meeting with Ezekiel.

Chapter Nineteen

The ride back to pack territory was far too quick, and nerves were starting to set in. Any lingering effects of the magic-infused alcohol had left my system. The house was quiet when we walked in, and neither of us spoke as we made our way upstairs. The creek of the old steps and Ophelia's padded feet were the only noises that broke that silence.

We both paused at my bedroom door, an unspoken question lingering between us.

Dean casually leaned against the doorframe, but I could see the tension lining his body. I couldn't help but want to have him there with me while I met with Ezekiel. His presence soothed me, provided me a sense of safety and belonging, no matter how much I wanted to deny it.

I opened my mouth and shut it, unsure of how to go about asking him to come inside. I usually didn't mind being forward and saying exactly what I wanted. But with Dean, I was more wary. Not out of nervousness, but of the fear that I would ruin it all.

"Just go ahead and invite him in for Hecate's sake. I thought this evening proved you two were done dancing around each other,"

Ophelia's voice broke the silence as she flicked open the door with her magic and strolled inside.

My jaw dropped at her words as I looked back at Dean, who was clearly holding back a laugh.

He swaggered in behind her, and I gave myself a mental shake before following them inside. Dean kicked off his boots and shrugged off his jacket before hopping onto my bed, throwing his arms behind his head as if he didn't have a care in the world. The sight of him in my bed stirred something inside me, and I had to quickly file those dirty thoughts away before my lustful scent filled the room.

I rushed through my nighttime routine, eager to get some answers from Ezekiel. I stepped over to the dresser and found a pair of loose pajama shorts before making my way to change in the closet. I pushed to shut the door, stopping short and leaving it cracked just enough so the view was unobstructed from the bed.

From where Dean was laying in my bed, watching.

I don't know what caused such boldness, but I found myself slowly taking off my clothes with my back turned to him. I felt his eyes on me as I replaced my skinny jeans with the shorts and removed my top. I unclasped my bra, vaguely hearing a rumble coming from the bedroom, and a small smile played on my lips. I let the lacey bra fall to the floor before I slowly reached for the oversized band t-shirt and pulled it on.

I walked back into the bedroom and plopped down onto the bed without even looking at Dean. He made no move to get under the covers with me, only adjusting himself once, but I continued to make myself comfortable, fluffing my pillow before laying down.

"I'm not going to be able to fall asleep with you sitting there staring like that, so lay down, wolf," I chided.

He chuckled before sliding underneath the covers, keeping his clothes on and staying on his side of the bed. Ophelia moved from the accent chair and hopped onto the bed, nestling herself behind my back as I laid on my side.

I reached to pull a pillow to cuddle up with as I usually did to fall asleep when Dean suddenly stopped my hand and scooted closer. He pulled me into his body and rested my hand upon his hard stomach. I wordlessly moved my head onto his chest and listened to the beat of his heart, focusing on the sound of his breath.

"Thank you for tonight," I murmured, already finding my eyes drooping closed. The warmth of his body wrapped around me like a cocoon, and his scent was like aromatherapy, lulling me to sleep.

"You're welcome, Raven," he rumbled, his fingers tracing little circles on my back.

I smiled at his nickname for me before falling into the darkness.

* * *

I opened my eyes to familiar golden rolling hills, a warm, gentle breeze swaying the tall grass. In the distance, waves crashed lazily against the cliffside. I felt Ophelia brush her head against my thigh, having shifted into her larger form.

To my surprise, I wasn't wearing the pajamas I had gone to sleep in. Instead, I was wearing black leather armor. The pants clung to my form and were lined with some sort of fur, but it had a cooling effect rather than making them too warm. The top was sleeveless, cutting off right around my shoulders. The leather was thicker, like a vest, protecting the vital organs underneath, and was lined with the same fur. The intricate detailing on the leather looked like feathers from wings, and the boots laced up all the way to my knees.

"Battle leathers from our armory. I thought these would be more appropriate than your sleepwear," Ezekiel's voice rang out from behind me. I turned to find him in a similar outfit, only his leathers were a deep brown instead of black. "Good evening, Blair. Ophelia." He looked between the two of us, his honey-colored eyes serious, and his jaw ticked despite having a small smile.

"I want answers, Zeke." I didn't bother with pleasantries. He had information I needed, and I refused to wait any longer to get them.

He nodded once and motioned for us to follow him. We walked a short distance over one of the golden hills, the grass swishing around our legs. A small cabin soon came into view, with a large wooden porch adorned with two rocking chairs. I raised a brow as we went up the steps and into the small home.

He gestured for me to sit in one of the leather armchairs that faced each other in the living room. Ophelia sat next to me, her body pressing up against my leg in comfort. I stroked her head absentmindedly, staring at Ezekiel. That nagging feeling prodded me again, trying to tell me something.

As he sat, he pulled his hair back into a ponytail, securing it with a leather band, the action shining light on a memory cast in shadow.

I had just come in from walking within the border of our property. Sage had called, and we had been discussing the latest book we read together, so it was far later than the time Vivian usually wanted me home by. I was hoping to sneak in quietly and face her wrath in the morning.

But when I crept into the front door, I heard a stranger's voice. Ezekiel's voice.

"Do you realize what you ask of me?" he boomed, and curiosity got the better of me. Vivian never had guests over. I leaned around the wall just enough to catch a glimpse of who she was talking to.

Fire danced in the fireplace, although she had spelled it not to put off heat, as it was the middle of summer in Arizona.

The stranger glared down at Vivian, towering over her, and she glared right back, her emerald eyes fierce as she stepped up to him. He was handsome, his nose straight and proud. Each feature seemed perfectly etched, almost too perfect. Golden brown hair hung loose down to his shoulders, and he wore a smart black suit. The male gathered his unbound hair into a ponytail, securing it with a leather band, as if he was bracing himself for battle.

"I don't have much time left. Please." She placed a hand on his broad chest, and after a few seconds, the stranger deflated, pressing his hand on top of hers.

"Alright. You have my word. Consequences be damned."

Vivian visibly relaxed at his words and opened her mouth to say more. My damn phone started buzzing, and I rushed to silence it, but it was too late.

"Blair? Is that you?" Vivian called out. I inwardly cursed.

"Yes! Sorry I'm late, Sage and I got a little carried away." I stepped out into the living room, eyeing the stranger and my adoptive mother, who were now standing several feet apart from one another. "Who's this?" I asked, genuinely curious.

Vivian flicked her eyes to the male, whose attention remained wholly on me, the gold in his eyes seeming to glow in the firelight. "One of my clients. He needed to reschedule some sessions, and he happened to be in the neighborhood. He was just leaving." She gave the male a pointed look, and when he did not move, she walked over to him and grabbed his elbow.

But his focus remained on me, even as Vivian practically dragged him out the door, nearly slamming it in his face.

She never mentioned him again.

I sputtered, "You knew Vivian! I saw you at our house just a few months before my nightmares started!" At this, Zeke's eyebrows lifted in surprise.

"Yes. I am surprised you remember that. Our encounter was very brief." He didn't say anything else at first, which damn near made my eye twitch. He studied me for a moment before he continued, "Vivian and I were friends of sorts. And she asked me to look after you."

Shock struck me at his words. Vivian never would have trusted anyone else to look after me. And no matter how badly she wanted me to be safe, she would have never entrusted what I was to another supernatural.

"Why would she do that?" I eyed him warily, feeling very exposed at the possibility that he knew what I truly was.

He ignored the question. "How much do you know about your mother?" He leaned back in his chair, and the leather squeaked.

His question caught me off guard, but I kept my expression cool as I answered.

"Not much, other than that she was a very powerful witch. She died shortly after I was born. Why?" I leaned forward, eager to see how much he knew. Necromancy was not a power many witches held, and witches who possessed this ability were usually outcast from covens for their power over the dead.

"Your mother was a powerful witch, yes, but she was known as the most powerful necromancer in the world. But you already knew that." I stiffened at his words. He continued, "I will answer all your questions, Blair, but before we continue, I need you to know that you can trust me. The information I am about to reveal to you is dangerous even for me to know, but I have not told another soul, nor do I plan to."

I stared at Ezekiel, wondering if his words were truthful. His golden eyes bore into my own, and his large body was tense, even though he was in a relaxed position within his chair.

I narrowed my eyes. "Trust is earned, not freely given. So, I'm going to need to know something about you, since you so clearly know enough about me. What are you?"

He gave me a small smile. "Funnily enough, what I am directly has to do with what *you* are."

He stood from his chair, strolling behind it before turning back to me. I heard a brief ringing in my ears before light burst from his back, the same way it had the first night he appeared in my nightmare. An iridescent glow filled the room, burning so brightly I nearly had to shut my eyes. They adjusted quickly, and when they did, the light faded to white feathers splayed out behind him.

I nearly felt my jaw hit the floor.

"I'm an angel. Warrior of the legion in Elysia. And you, Blair, are a Nephilim. A being that is half angel and, in your case, half witch." Zeke's voice was deeper than it was a moment ago. His skin was brighter, and his eyes shined a fearsome gold. His enormous wings filled the entire space of the living room, the feathers so white I could hardly comprehend how perfect they looked.

I couldn't form thoughts, let alone words as I continued to stare at him. He tucked his wings back behind his body, waiting patiently for a response from me.

I almost laughed right in his face and walked out, but instead I was frozen in my seat, the sincerity in his voice and the feeling of truth ringing in my head as I continued to stare at him. Then a laugh mixed with a scoff bubbled out of my mouth, which earned a confused look from the angel across from me.

"Oh, if only Mr. Yates found out that he had chained up a half-angel in his cellar instead of a demon like he thought. He would shit himself." My laughter died off as I let myself come to grips with what Zeke was telling me. I was half angel. The girl with darkness swirling inside of her was the spawn of an actual angel. While there were about a million burning questions I wanted to ask him, the first one I rattled off was, "Who is my father?" Quickly followed by, "Is that why Alistair wants me so bad? Because I'm half angel?"

Zeke's wings disappeared in the blink of an eye, and he joined me again in the chairs.

"Although angelic blood itself is extremely powerful given that we are all made by Odenus himself, Nephilim blood is even more so, and many would kill for even a drop of it. Unfortunately for you, being that your mother was a witch and a powerful necromancer, your blood is even more rare, mixed with both the light magic of angels and the dark magic of witches *and* demons. As for your father, that is one question I unfortunately can't answer. I don't know who your father is. But based on the immense power of your magic and energy surrounding your soul, I've narrowed it down to one specific kind of angel. I believe your father is an archangel."

I rapidly stood up and began pacing in front of my chair. My mind was racing, and I felt the need to move my body to catch up with my brain. I rubbed my temples as I paced, with Zeke and Ophelia quietly waiting for me to be ready for conversation again.

I whirled and looked to my familiar.

"Did you know?" I exclaimed at her. What other reason could there be for her being so calm? One of her ears flicked back, but she kept her chartreuse eyes on me.

"I suspected, but I could not be sure. Right now, your magic is not evenly balanced, so it has been difficult to get a read on you. But I will admit that I have known more about you than I have let on. Withholding the truth from you was not right, so I will apologize for it now." She paused.

I don't think I was even breathing; there was so much I didn't know about myself, and to think she had been keeping something from me cut deep, the bond between us aching painfully.

Her next words sliced through me like a blade to the chest.

"Vivian knew what you were when she adopted you, and she was working for a demon."

Chapter Twenty

"**B**ullshit!" I spat at her. She at least had the sense to look ashamed of her words, her ears flat against her head.

"I know it to be true because the charge I was assigned to before you was investigating Vivian for demonic involvement. They were in the same coven at the time, and there were very strict rules against summoning and working with demons." Ophelia's words were grave, and much to my horror, I sensed the truth through our bond.

Zeke remained quiet, listening intently as Ophelia explained, her words cleaving my heart in two. It couldn't be true; they must have been mistaken. Vivian loved me like her own daughter. She would never hand me over to demons.

"We didn't know why a demon would want a child. Sure, we had heard whispers and rumors, but nothing we could prove, nor could we prove Vivian's involvement. The first night I saw you was the night she pulled you out of the cellar. The moment I saw you, Blair, I knew what you were, and I knew we were connected. I almost left my post with my current witch to protect you myself, but Hecate whispered to me that it was not our time yet, and even though you were there right in front of me, I was still dutybound to Imogen."

I saw pain flash in her eyes at the mention of the witch.

She continued, "I watched over you during your years with her. She had only treated you with kindness, and you were growing to be such a strong female. We began to think maybe we had made a mistake... We didn't. The night you disappeared was the night we were ordered to bring Vivian in for questioning. It had been a lengthy investigation, because fraternization with a demon is hard to prove, but the coven issued a warrant for her arrest. As we were closing in on her location, a Hellhound showed up looking for something. Looking for you. It saw us as a threat, and Imogen... Imogen was killed. Vivian fled the scene."

Every lesson I'd had with Vivian had been geared towards defending myself, how to fight off attackers, how to escape and honing each ability within my magic to use as a weapon. There was always a darkness she tried to hide from me, but there were times when she couldn't.

The ferocity of her training, her paranoia with me meeting anyone new... I just thought they were results of her own past, and I grew used to her strange overprotectiveness with me.

I couldn't even look at Ophelia. Vivian's betrayal hurt me, gutted me from the inside, and I barely registered that I was storming out of the house. Black magic rolled within me, hot and angry, pushing against the boundaries of my body, desperate to seek retribution for the betrayal.

It started coming out in small whisps of smoke, just from my hands as I stormed to the top of a nearby hill. I struggled to rein it in, to control the magic and not let the darkness take me over completely. Tears streamed down my face as my mind tried to comprehend that the only maternal figure I'd ever had in my life had only rescued me to turn me over to demons.

Darkness spilled out of me as I screamed at the heavens. Black smoke billowed out of my palms, slowly spreading across the hillside, whitling the golden stalks of grass until they turned to ash.

I felt the power coursing through my veins. With each scrap of life it took, it flowed back into me, feeding my death magic. She was a hungry beast, and I had been starving her.

The dark magic obscured my vision, all I could see were the inky vapors whirling around me, with streaks of lightning flaring on the inside like a storm. Sorrow and rage and pain all swirled within me. The love and trust I had placed in her now seemed like a cruel joke. I filtered through every memory I had with her, questioning whether any of it was real.

Images of her teaching me how to drive, movie nights in with us cuddled up on the couch with far too many fuzzy blankets and way too much popcorn, the trip we took to California just so I could see the beach, only to find out I couldn't stand to be around so much sand.

I closed my eyes, fighting back the tears. More memories resurfaced.

Those early nights after the adoption was finalized, and I still had nightmares of what Mr. Yates had tried to do to me, she had held me while I cried, stroking through my hair, rubbing soothing circles on my back until all the tears dried up. Each time I failed at a spell or task with my magic and I felt discouraged, she would lift my chin up and encourage me to keep trying, telling me that I could do anything I set my mind to.

Was it all just an act? A lie to make sure I stayed with her?

All I could think about was how Vivian intended to hand me over to a demon. Vivian, who I had come to think of as a mother, was raising me to deliver me to one of the vilest species in this realm so they could do gods knows what with me. The knowledge was too much to bear.

I didn't even care that half of my magic was considered dark. I always accepted the darkness inside myself and learned to control it. But being half angel was something I could not come to grips with.

I was not inherently good; I never have been. The capacity to walk the path of light died out of me a long time ago, and I chose to walk within the gray.

The earth quaked beneath my feet as death pulsed into the ground. The sky darkened above me, rumbling with the intensity of my rage. I could tear it all apart, I realized. I felt the power to do so, the endless well of my power banging against the locks that held it trapped.

In my mind's eye, I tentatively reached out towards the door, prepared to unlock the cage.

Nothing exists without both light and darkness, Blair. True power lies within accepting all parts of yourself. You will be a fearsome sight to behold when you do.

Ophelia's voice was like a beacon of light in the raging storm of my mind, a tendril of that soul bond between us, strong and true, offering a lifeline. I reached out to the darkness, reining it back in with every ounce of strength that I had. Sweat broke out along my brow as I ground my teeth at the process.

As the swirling smoke came back to me, my vision cleared, showing Ophelia sitting calmly just outside my circle of destruction on the golden hill, with Zeke at her side.

I fell to my knees, trembling as the last drops of my power came back to me, settling in my chest. Ophelia tentatively made her way over to me, stopping just in front of my bowed head. She rested her head on top of my own, and our mental bond thrummed with sympathy and a much stronger emotion. A deep connection between a witch and her familiar. It wasn't quite love, but a connection between souls, and it felt like unyielding devotion—an extension of my very self.

Ophelia rubbed her cheek against my own, lifting my head up, and as she pulled away, I was able to look into her chartreuse eyes. Many emotions lay within them, probably as many that spiraled within my own. But she grounded me, and I was able to breathe easier knowing she had my back.

With a long exhale, I pushed a small amount of my power out to the dead grass around me, then pulled the death back into myself, restoring the golden stocks to their former liveliness.

Once more they swayed in the slight breeze, the light of the returned sun reflecting off their bright color. The death I had taken floated in my blood, and I directed it to my magic, adding it back to the well of power that lurked within me.

"Only an angel with archangel blood could wield that much power," Zeke broke the silence of the hillside and strolled up to us, as if I hadn't almost just destroyed the area surrounding his home. "Vivian knew what you were and knew the dangers she faced for the deal she made. So, she sought to make another deal. I vowed to her that I would look after you, to keep you safe."

His words threatened to break me further, so I cast them away and ignored them fully.

"Do you have any better idea of who her father is based on what you saw?" Ophelia's voice was soft, as if she was trying not to spook me with talk of my father. I shakily rose to my feet and gave her an affectionate scratch behind the ears, silently thanking her.

Zeke looked thoughtful for a moment, looking me over again, as if the answer of who my father was would be written across my forehead. "I have theories, but the necromancer blood makes it difficult. Your powers have blended in a way that have never been seen before. Necromancers reanimate the dead, but you can deal out death as well as give life. It's very curious."

"Ha. Curious? Try horrifying." I gave him a dark look, trying to push the memories of my past away. Being a thirteen-year-old girl was hard enough, but being one with emerging abilities to control death was a much more difficult feat.

His eyes softened, as if he knew the details of my haunted upbringing. He probably did. But I decided to just take it as a good sign that he hadn't killed me yet. Instead, he was helping me.

"I'm sure it made for a tough childhood, but it has no doubt shaped you into the female I see before me. Strong. Unrelenting.

Fierce. All traits that angels admire." I nearly snorted at his strange compliment. He continued, "I would like to train you as we angels are trained. Teach you our ways. Your existence, if the other angels found out... it would be a bloodbath. You need to be able to protect yourself."

I studied him as I considered his offer. I did enjoy combat training, and though the wolves provided that now, I worried that I would lose control and hurt them.

"If I agree to train with you, I have one condition. I want you to not only train me in combat, but I also want you to help me figure out who my father is." I stood a little straighter, finding strength in the desire to know more about my heritage, and maybe find out who my estranged father was, and why he left my mother for dead.

"Deal. Are you ready for your first lesson?" Zeke gestured back towards his little cabin, his face serious, his cold warrior nature showing through in his golden eyes. My brows shot up.

"Right now?" I spluttered. Ophelia chuckled next to me but kept her gaze firmly on Zeke.

"Come. We'll focus on something small today." He turned on his heel and began making his way down the hillside, giving me no choice but to follow.

I glanced down at Ophelia, who gave me an encouraging nod.

I followed him, stopping as he turned to face me in front of the steps leading into his home. With a snap of his fingers, a table appeared next to him with an array of weapons covering the surface. There were varying sizes of swords, curved blades, bows with matching arrows, daggers, and even crossbows. I did notice there were no shields among the pile of weapons.

"I already have a blade, remember?" I asked him. At the mention of it, my hand tingled and burned, bringing the blade to me.

His eyes widened slightly at the sight, but he quickly composed himself. "Yes, and while it is good you have your own, every angel is trained with various kinds of weapons in every realm's arsenal. These are just a few that I thought we could get you familiar with in addition to your blade." He paused before snapping his fingers again and bringing forth a sheath fit my sword. The blade would rest on my spine with two loops for my arms to go through. "You'll need this."

I pulled the sheath on and with a very careful attempt not to stab myself, I managed to get my sword into the scabbard. I adjusted the loops to my liking with a few pointers from Zeke until it felt comfortable, yet tight and sturdy. The black leather matched the battle leathers I was wearing, and a small feeling of belonging spread through me.

We ran through various drills with my sword first, making sure I was the most comfortable with my own blade. While I trained and he instructed, I asked him several questions about angels, and he answered every one of them. Despite the training pushing my body to new limits, I couldn't help the smile creeping over my face. Ophelia watched with her chartreuse eyes glowing with pride.

I learned that angels guarded the realms, with each god or goddess commanding the legions, minus Purgatory, the Realm of Gray. Odenus created angels as warriors with help from Hecate.

Zeke was in the legion that protected Elysia, what humans most commonly referred to as Heaven. He was under the command of the archangel Michael, the first angel ever created by Odenus. Purgatory was not governed by any god or goddess, much to my surprise, but an archangel. Zeke did not say his name, only that he was grumpy and usually kept to himself.

We moved through the weapons on the table, and I quickly discovered which ones I favored over the others. My own short sword being obvious, but I found myself being very drawn to a pair of curved blades. They were mainly used for close quarters fighting, and you held them curled in a fist, jabbing out as you would throw a punch.

My kind of weapon.

"Are all chaos witches actually Nephilims?" I asked just after I let out a shot with the crossbow, hitting just a little to the left of the target.

I watched Zeke's facial expression carefully as he contemplated his answer.

"Yes. Angels were forbidden from reproducing with anyone other than their own kind, a law passed by the gods because of their potential to hold great power. To sire a Nephilim is a death sentence."

The thought made my stomach roll, but I kept my face impassive. The spell Vivian performed to learn more about my parentage proved that he was alive, but that didn't mean he wasn't rotting in some sort of angelic angel jail, or worse. Or perhaps he didn't even know she existed? Or perhaps he did, and he chose to stay away to keep his act a secret? I didn't know which option I found to be worse.

"Vivian always taught me to be careful about how much magic I used. She warned me that others would come after me if they knew what I was," I murmured, setting the crossbow down.

Ezekiel studied me for a moment, mulling over my words. "She was protecting you. When you use a large amount of magic, it could be felt by other angels across realms, and if the angels found out about you, they would have killed you on sight. If that happened, her deal with the demons would be broken, and they would kill her for it. Vivian likely knew this and trained you to fear expending too much to avoid discovery. It was in her best interest to keep your existence a secret."

My heart squeezed painfully at his words.

"I think that is enough for today. These trainings will help you learn to control your grace expenditure in a safe environment, as well as learn how to fight like an angel." He smirked, and I let out a breathy laugh. I felt good, despite the emotional turmoil rolling around in my gut. More in control.

"Thanks, Zeke. I look forward to our next lesson. Don't forget to hold up your end of the bargain." I gave him a mock salute before taking a step towards Ophelia.

Zeke grabbed my arm. "Here. These belong with you. Not a common weapon for an angel to carry, but you are exceptionally good at handling them." He handed over two thigh straps with holsters for the curved blades I had been admiring. As I was strapping them on, he continued, "Guard your secret carefully, Blair. If more find out what you are, not only you will be in danger."

I nodded solemnly and clapped him on the shoulder in thanks.

Ophelia appeared at my side, holding her head high as I reached out to her to pull me back into our realm. A vortex of wind blew around us, fading the golden hills and wooden cabin of Zeke's home.

Warmth surrounded me, and a rumble vibrated against my head. I reluctantly opened my eyes. Tan skin dusted with dark hair and linen sheets were the first things that came into focus in the early morning light.

Dean's large arm pulled me closer, and I let out a sigh of contentment before glancing up to meet his gaze. Sunlight shone in through the massive window, casting beautiful morning light across his face, illuminating his sky-blue eyes.

"How'd it go?" His deep voice was sleepy and sent shivers down my body that had nothing to do with being cold. I tried to pull away on instinct, still not entirely used to so much physical affection, but his arm tightened around me, holding me in place.

I sighed, settling back in before looking back up at him. "I'm not sure you're going to believe what I'm about to tell you."

Chapter Twenty-One

Dean listened patiently while I relayed to him everything that happened in the dreamscape with Ezekiel, minus the part about my own heritage. Although Dean had shown himself trustworthy so far, I still was not ready to share my secret with him. His face remained attentive throughout my story, his eyes searching mine, as if he sensed I was leaving things out.

"So, you've got an angel watching over your shoulder, huh? Seems like you'd have to be important to the gods to have one of their soldiers looking after you." He stretched, his corded arms flexing. "I make a great listener, you know, so whenever you decide to let me in on all that is going on up there, just know I'm here." Dean tapped my temple.

My face gave away nothing, but I offered him a nod. Dean's eyes looked weary, and guilt twisted around my heart at the realization that he had stayed through the night just to watch over me.

As if he could sense the direction my thoughts were going, he leaned over and planted a kiss atop my nose. "Don't worry about it, Blair. I'd stay up all night for you any time." He winked, ever the flirt.

I gave him a small smile, but after everything I had learned, I was even more terrified that I was putting him and his family in danger.

It was a grim history for the Nephilim, and though I had known the dangers of my powers before I knew exactly *what* I was, that fact increased my unease tenfold.

"This doesn't change anything, you know. You can stay here as long as you need, and my pack protection still stands," Dean assured me as he slipped off the bed, and I gave him a grateful smile.

Ophelia, sitting atop the dresser, let out a tired meow, bringing my attention to the neatly folded pile of leathers next to her. Next to them lay the matching sheaths and the daggers.

I leapt out of bed to examine them. The leather felt smooth yet heavy-duty in my hand, and I looked over each piece, noting that they looked and felt exactly how they had in the dreamscape. A sense of rightness settled in my chest as I handled them, feeling remarkably attached.

The mirth of my inner thoughts faded as they strayed back to the more morbid implications of my newfound lineage. I was a blend of the lightest and darkest powers across the realms. The perfect weapon, untethered to the gods, a child of many realms, primed for the taking.

Though I couldn't prove it, I had sneaking suspicions that Sage knew the truth of what I was. She had to. She was psychic after all, and she always alluded to the fact that there was more to my dark history.

Zeke's warning played over in my mind, *"Guard your secret carefully, Blair. If more find out what you are, not only you will be in danger."* Panic gripped my gut. Regardless of whether Sage knew the truth about me, others would assume she did because of her gift and her close relationship to me.

I quickly turned to Dean, who immediately straightened at my rigid posture.

"What is it, Blair?" he asked, taking a step closer and brushing a stray hair from my face. His touch was soothing, but it was not enough to calm my pounding heart.

Even though I had no right to ask this of him, I knew he would not deny me.

"I think I need to bring Sage and Vivian to New Haven." I looked up at his handsome face, hoping he would agree to help, despite the risk it posed his pack.

No matter what, I would bring my family to the safety of New Haven. Despite the information that had come to light about my adoption, I still cared for Vivian and could not stand the idea of any harm coming to her. That realization sat like a heavy weight in my stomach, nearly making me sick, knowing what she had done and what she intended on doing with me.

But Vivian was one of the only people who I had ever cared for in this world, who had saved me when I could not save myself.

"Blair, the demons may have already captured Vivian for not following through on her deal. Demons aren't very forgiving creatures, and their contracts are binding, straight down to the level of the soul." Ophelia's voice was gentle, but there was a hardness to it, and I felt guilty over the situation.

Ophelia's previous witch had died trying to apprehend Vivian for demon involvement, and yet here I was, trying to save her. But she was going to have to come to grips with the situation, because Vivian was the only family I truly had, and I would do anything in my power to keep her safe. She owed me answers, ones I was determined to get.

I stepped around Dean to come face to face with her sitting on the dresser. Her chartreuse eyes stared up at me, and there I saw flickers of pain and concern. I stroked her fur, and she accepted the gesture stiffly.

"I know," I murmured, "but we can't take the chance that she hasn't been. If they have already taken her, then they will torture her for more information. She could put Sage in danger. And... despite everything she has done, she's like a mother to me. I can't just leave her unprotected," I nearly begged her to understand.

And with a huff and a twitch of her ears, she nodded.

I turned back to Dean. "I'll need to borrow a car. Just something large enough to bring them into the city. I can work to pay for their lodgings." I wrung my hands out nervously under his gaze.

"They're your family, Blair. They can stay here on pack grounds, as there are available cabins they can stay in. As for a vehicle, we'll discuss with the group on who will go on this mission." I spluttered out a protest before he held up a hand, silencing me. "This isn't up for discussion, Blair. What would have been the point in rescuing you for you to go back out into the human world, unprotected and getting captured?"

I snorted, "Who's saying I would get captured? Have some faith in my skills, wolf." I flashed a cocky look as he ran a hand over his face.

"I have no doubt you can take care of yourself. Any idiot could feel the power you possess. But I can't take the chance that something would happen to you. Everyone should be back at the pack house by tomorrow morning. We'll talk about it then."

The finality in his tone had me bristling, but I had enough respect for him and his family that I backed down... just this once.

The rest of the day went by painstakingly slow, but somehow, I managed to keep myself entertained. I decided to continue working on the moves Zeke had taught me in the training clearings, which were thankfully empty for most of the day.

Dean left me to my thoughts, though I felt eyes in the surrounding forest watching me, probably relaying information back to him.

Ophelia offered her critiques based on what she saw during the training with Zeke and her hundreds of years being involved with various witches, though only a few of them bothered to train in hand-to-hand combat. At some point, Dean had purchased training dummies to use, so I was putting my new blade skills to the test and letting my brain process the past twenty-four hours.

Each time I swung my blade, I slowly came to grips with a small piece of information I had learned. With each slice of the dagger, I let go of some of the anger I felt welled up inside of me. Every kick, punch, and movement of my body was aimed to bring me towards the acceptance that I was half-witch and half-angel.

A Nephilim.

I had already made up my mind that I wanted to visit the library again to see Lumen. Now that I officially knew what I was, I could do my own research in the library on angels and Nephilims. I would have to convince her I didn't need help finding what I was looking for, which could pose difficult, but I was good at figuring things out on the fly, so I didn't let it worry me too much.

The sky darkened, and I made my way back to the main house. Sweat drenched my clothes, my muscles aching and my body wholly exhausted. I felt a sense of calm I hadn't felt in a very long time. After a delightfully hot shower, I dressed in the softest sweatshirt I could find with a pair of leggings and made my way back downstairs with Ophelia in tow.

My growling stomach announced my arrival in the kitchen, and I was greeted with smiles from Dean, Hayley, Selene, and Miles. Cal was still off speaking to some contacts within New Haven and wouldn't return until the following morning. The kitchen smelled of some sort of pasta, and I practically groaned. Even though my body was screaming at me to sit down, I rolled up my sleeves, found an apron, and got to work helping Selene.

Laughter and teasing filled the air, mixing with the decedent scent of garlic and other spices. Selene caught Dean trying to sneak a taste of the vodka sauce we were making, and she gave him a slight swat to the hand before shooing him back towards the bar.

I found myself smiling at the scene in front of me, and the feeling of home settled in my soul.

Dean caught my eye as he poured four glasses of bourbon, and my smile widened. He saluted me with his drink and set mine in front of me with a wink. It was getting harder and harder to keep him at arm's length.

Somehow, he was making himself a home within my heart, and the feeling scared the hell out of me.

Dean's hand rested on my knee under the table as we ate, occasionally sliding up my thigh until I would give him a warning look. With a chuckle, he would back off and idly stroke his thumb on my knee. The sensation of his touch sent sparks along my skin, and I found myself scooting my chair closer to him to chase that feeling.

Chapter Twenty-Two

Surprisingly, I slept through the night without any vampiric or angelic visitors. I had even slept in, the late morning sun flowing freely into the room where Ophelia was staring out into the forest.

Calian is back, and Dean has called the wolves to the house for a meeting.

I yawned a thank you to her before stumbling into the bathroom to get ready for the day. I emerged from the room wearing my usual ripped jeans, motorcycle boots, and a denim jacket over a black tank top, with my hair pulled up in a messy bun on the top of my head.

The energy was tense as I entered the kitchen, as if the impending conversation was sitting over the house like a dark cloud, threatening to storm.

Dean was tense, his body was rigid as he moved with the intensity of the wolf that lurked beneath his skin. Miles and Hayley kept casting worried glances over at him, but they quickly averted their eyes when Dean caught them. This trip of mine clearly had this wolf's tail all tied up in a knot.

After breakfast, Miles, Hayley, Selene, and Cal followed Dean and I into the family room spreading out throughout the space, while Dean pulled me into the leather loveseat next to him.

"We need to conduct an extraction of Blair's family. Her best friend Sage, who lives just outside Flagstaff, and her adoptive mother, who lives north of Phoenix, near Cottonwood. I will go with Miles tomorrow afternoon and take the SUV. Everyone else will stay here."

Dean's voice held so much power and dominance, the wolves exposed their necks to him, submitting and nodding in agreement to his plan.

But I was no wolf.

I jumped up and snarled, "Like hell I'm staying here!"

The tension between us was so thick it became hard to breathe. The room vibrated with warring dominance, but I would not back down. Ophelia came to stand beside me, still in her housecat form, her ears firmly pressed back against her head, the threat in her posture clear.

The alpha-asshole calmly stood up, the motion gracefully deadly, and gave me a stern look. "You need to stay here, where it's *safe* and the pack can protect you."

I stepped in close to his face and bared my teeth at him.

"There is not a force on earth that will keep me from coming with you to pick up my family. Try and stop me Dean, I *dare* you," I seethed.

He growled at me, baring his teeth right back, a peek of canine showing beneath his lip. The sheer volume of it shook the entire room. No one dared to intervene, not even Ophelia.

I dropped my voice, as if that could give us an ounce of privacy in a room full of werewolves. "They're my family, Dean, and they're only in danger because of me. I need to do everything I can to ensure their safety. Surely, you can understand *that*."

It was a low blow, but one I knew would hit home with him. I knew Dean respected my choices, even if they angered the hell out of him, but I was unsure if this moment would push him too far. His wolf instincts demanded he dominated everyone weaker than him, but that was the problem.

I wasn't weaker.

And I wasn't a werewolf that would cower in his wake.

"Everyone *out*." His voice was sharp and commanding, and the wolves quickly made their way out of the room. The only one who lingered was Miles, and he threw a worried look between the two of us before he too exited.

We stood in silence for a few minutes, pinning each other with our fierce gazes, eyes never wavering, neither one of us backing down. Our power bases were pushing against each other, resulting in a slight shake of the furniture around us. The tension was palpable, like the earth waiting in anticipation before a bomb dropped and reaped its destruction across the land. I broke that tension first.

Not out of submission, but out of total irritation.

"You have no right to keep me here. You may be their alpha, Dean, but you can't push me around like one of your wolves." I poked him in the chest, putting a little bit of chaos behind it so he stumbled back a step. He quickly gained back the space he lost, bringing his face mere inches away from my nose, our chests nearly flesh against each other.

"I'm doing it to protect you!" he roared back at me, his power filling the room, trying to dominate me into submission.

I felt the power that I kept locked away tapping on the door, begging me to release it and show Dean my full potential. To show him what I truly was.

But I pushed those thoughts away and wrapped myself in my familiar darkness. Ophelia immediately shifted into her larger form at my side, her lips curled back in a warning as she let out a low growl. Her shadows whipped out around her, furling around my legs.

"I don't need your protection! I'm not some damsel in distress! I've been taking care of myself my whole life, and I don't need some arrogant alpha male coming into my life and ordering me to stay behind! Now give me one good reason why I shouldn't be there with you and Miles to rescue my family!" I screamed back in his face. A little bit of ethereal magic slipped through its barrier, and lightning flickered around my fingers.

"Because I can't lose you!" he roared so loud the walls shook, and I faltered back a step. He was breathing heavily, his glacier eyes filled with emotion as he stared down at me. "I'm... afraid. I'm afraid I won't be able to protect you, and something will happen to you. I can't lose anyone else I care about." His voice softened, and he reached out to grab my hands.

I stood there frozen, trying to find words.

He gently pulled my hands to rest on the sides of his temples. "Can you look into my memories, the same way you let me into yours?" he breathed. I raised my brows and nodded. "Look at the night I was given the vision of you, a few days before you were almost taken by the vampires."

I swallowed, nodding again as I concentrated on bringing my chaos to my hands. Silver light bloomed in my palms, casting light on his face, making his eyes glow before he closed them. I closed mine as well and crossed that threshold into his mind.

The sitting room fell away to darkness as I let Dean's memory wash over me.

The air was cool, a slight breeze filtering through the forest as he ran a familiar trail through his territory. The trees were a blur as he pushed himself faster, trying to force the stress of leading a pack out of his body. Sweat trickled down his shirtless chest, but he didn't stop.

"Dean." A trio of whispers stopped him dead in his tracks.

His eyes darted around in the trees, trying to figure out who had called his name.

The voices sounded again, this time coming from his left side. He rumbled a growl as he stalked deeper into the forest. There were strangers on his territory, and he would do whatever it took to eradicate the threat.

The whispers grew louder as he tore through the bushes. He inhaled sharply, trying to get a scent from the trespassers but finding nothing aside from the stench of death and ether.

Clouds began rolling in, covering the dark sky above. The sound of thunder filled the air, and he hoped it covered the sound of his movements. The voices became louder, and Dean slowed his steps. Lighting crackled in the sky above. The energy in the forest shifted, even the trees seeming to be waiting in anticipation. Dean looked around warily, his wolf raising its hackles beneath his skin.

A lightning bolt curved out of the sky and struck the ground right in front of him. He swore and jumped back in surprise. The ground glowed, smoke wafting up from where the bolt connected with the forest floor.

Dean slowly crept towards the charred earth, and without warning, lightning struck again.

The electric current surged through his body as he flew back. The world moved in slow motion, his body almost floating as the bolts wrapped around him. Images filled his eyes of the most beautiful female he had ever seen.

It was me, reading in an oversized chair, smiling to myself and my dark hair tumbling around my face. The image changed to me sipping a glass of bourbon alone at a bar. It shifted to me training in the makeshift gym shed I built in my yard, sweat pouring down my body as I threw combination after combination. Another image of me laughing at something Sage said.

The sound of my laugh wrapped around his mind like a warm breeze as each image blew away like whisps of smoke.

"Bound by lightning and called to by the moon. Forged in the darkness of a swelling storm, she is the destruction and salvation of the realms. Save her, Guardian, or the realms will descend into a soulless darkness," the same trio of voices whispered as he hit the ground before the vision changed to the vampires hauling me out of the convent.

I was fighting hard, but they managed to get cuffs on me, press the damp cloth over my mouth, and throw me into the trunk as I went limp. *The moon was full in the sky, providing ample light as they sped away from the convent, with my screams fading to silence in the trunk.*

Dean's heart was racing as the black car sped away and faded into smoke. The dark swirls gave way to another string of images that caused his soul to ache. Images of Dean and I together, smiling, laughing, kissing, training, snuggled up with one another. And in each image, he was staring at me with an emotion so intense I dared not label it.

"This is what you stand to lose if you let him have her. Protect her."

The images faded away along with the voices, and he reached his hand out as if to bring them back. His mind whirled from the aftershock of seeing those images, of seeing me, and one word came to his mind as he sat up off the forest floor.

Mine.

I pulled out of Dean's memories and gasped for air. His rough hands against mine were warm and didn't let me go as he stared down into my eyes. Energy buzzed between us as our breath mingled. His eyes flicked once towards my lips, and I didn't dare move.

He whispered, "I cannot lose any more people I care about, even if we haven't become that to one another yet. That... happiness I saw. I won't lose you." He shook his head, and my heart swelled at his words.

I rubbed my thumbs along his stubbled face. He closed his eyes, and a rumble escaped his chest.

"Please do not ask me to stay behind while my family is in danger. I'll stick with you the entire time, silly wolf. I will be fine." It was a dangerous promise to make, but the words came out before I could stop them, an overwhelming need overcoming me to reassure him.

I couldn't acknowledge those images of him and I together, but I secretly held onto those images and let them wrap around my untrusting heart.

"You aren't going to stop arguing with me on this, are you?" he sighed, and I smiled coyly while shaking my head. His lips turned up in a small grin before he rolled his eyes. "Fine, but stay close to me, and *try* to listen to orders. I command people for a living, you know."

I snorted. "You know I can't promise that. Don't go all alpha douche on me, and we should be fine. And don't worry, I'll protect you from the big, bad bloodsuckers," I teased him, pinching his cheek.

He playfully nipped at my fingers. I laughed and shoved him away, stepping out of his space. My body instantly missed the warmth Dean's body provided.

Something had shifted between us now. The knowledge of the premonition he had been given shed some light on this undeniable attraction between the two of us, and even though the possibility had my soul yearning for it, I feared it being ripped away from me, like everything else good in my life.

"Have you kissed and made up yet?" Miles shouted from the hallway, and we both jolted out of our own little bubble.

Dean sighed as Miles, Selene, and Hayley rushed back into the room, taking their seats again. Cal was slower to return, his amber eyes wide as they took in my unscathed appearance. Ophelia shifted back, still slightly glaring at Dean before stalking over to the couch.

"Blair and Ophelia will be joining us on the mission. Cal, you're in charge while we're gone. Shift around the schedule to bring more sentinels to pack territory instead of the city watch." Dean paused when he got to Hayley. "And Hayley, try not to be a nuisance."

She uttered a curse and threw a pillow at her brother, which he caught with ease.

"We'll leave tomorrow afternoon right after the council meeting. We should be able to get both Sage and Vivian by tomorrow night, but we'll be back here late. The sooner we get everyone into New Haven territory, the better." At this, I nodded in agreement.

Sage lived in Flagstaff, which was fairly close to New Haven. Sage may not have known about the city, but she must have felt the mystical energy coming from the protected sanctuary. Some humans could be in-tune with the energy of supernaturals, even if they didn't know what exactly they were feeling.

Vivian lived in Cottonwood, which was further south and more of a desert terrain. She lived in a house in the middle of nowhere, preferring privacy. I realized now that was probably because she was in hiding from demons hunting her.

"Should you let them know that you're coming?" Hayley asked me.

I shook my head. Zeke's warning had me wondering whether vampires were watching Sage and Vivian, and any change in behavior could tip them off that we were on our way. I didn't want to put them in any more danger than they were already in.

Chapter Twenty-Three

The sun had set by the time we made it into the city of Flagstaff. The city was busier than I remembered it, and despite it not being filled with the immense magic that New Haven held, I could still feel whispers of it in the air as we made our way through town.

We parked the SUV a few miles down the road behind an old, abandoned barn. It was on the edge of Sage's property line, giving us the perfect vantage point.

Sage had moved to Flagstaff a few years ago to help run a yoga studio there. It was only an hour away from where I lived with Vivian in Cottonwood, and she still managed to make time to come back and visit all the time.

I had begged Vivian to move in with Sage, but she had refused and blamed it on there being too many supernaturals in the area. It was our biggest fight, but one I eventually let go, knowing Vivian was only trying to keep me safe. Now I just wondered if it was only to keep me close for whenever she was to deliver me to the demons.

Dean and Miles stayed in their human forms as we made our way through the forest. I whispered a spell to make sure we were silent and unable to be heard by vampiric ears.

Ophelia trotted at my side, already shifted into her jungle cat form, her shadows wrapping around me protectively. I kept my breathing steady, despite my rising heartrate. The angelic leathers Ezekiel gifted me were surprisingly cool despite the nervous sweat dripping down my back, and they helped keep me hidden in the shadows with their dark color.

We came to a stop when her white cottage-style house came into view. It looked undisturbed and just how I remembered it. There were beautiful vines crawling up the sides of the windows and planters filled with various greenery adorning the front porch, some dangling down the side of the railing. Her car was parked in its usual spot on the gravel, but there were no lights on in the home.

Unease prickled in my gut. Something in the air felt off. As we slowly crept closer, my jaw dropped in horror as I noticed her front door was ajar. A low growl rumbled out of Ophelia, and I removed both of my curved blades out of their thigh sheaths. My chaos swirled at the connection, the blades a conduit of my power.

Dean took the lead as we reached the edge of the house. Ophelia crept along with us at my side, blending into the shadows, only her sharp eyes and gleaming teeth visible, with Miles bringing up the rear. Dean turned and nodded, signaling for us to start on the porch steps.

We slid along the wall to the door, only pausing when a loud *thump* sounded from upstairs. I shoved past Dean, earning me a low growl as I tore up the stairs in search of my friend.

I reached the landing, only to pause as my boots crunched along broken glass.

A picture had fallen off the wall and shattered. I slowly bent and picked up the frame to see a picture of Sage and I at the top of Mount Humphreys. She was all smiles, her silver-blonde hair blowing in the wind and an arm draped around me. I was rolling my eyes at her but embracing her back.

It was one of the only times Vivian let me visit Sage in Flagstaff, only agreeing if she was able to accompany me, which she did, and she was the one taking the picture. What you don't see in the picture are the various protection spells and charms Vivian had insisted on. All of which now made much more sense.

I smiled at the memory, focusing on the happiness of it as I tucked the picture into my leathers and crept up the remaining steps.

Miles had caught up to me now, and he quickly signaled that Dean was sweeping the ground floor. I peered into the hallway, satisfied I didn't see any vampires lurking, and nodded towards the room at the end of the hall to the left, which was Sage's room.

Ophelia stalked ahead of me, keeping her body low to the ground. Miles went in the opposite direction, heading towards the two guest bedrooms at the other end of the hallway. I halted just outside her door, pressing my ear up to the wood and listening for any movement. Ophelia gave me a nod as I slowly turned the knob.

She burst into the room, teeth bared and shadows ahead of her, checking every corner for intruders. I quickly followed and scanned the space. Her bed had been left unmade, but everything else in the room seemed to be in its rightful place. Ophelia furiously sniffed the air, trying to catch any lingering scents.

Fear struck my heart with the worry that Alistair already had her in his grasp, but Ophelia shook her head, letting me know there was no scent of a vampire in this room.

The sound of metal clanging against a hard surface sounded from the end of the hall, followed by Miles yelling in pain. Ophelia and I tore off to the spare bedrooms just as Dean raced up the stairs, the wood groaning under his weight.

"Are you *fucking* crazy?!" Miles bellowed.

We burst into the room to find Miles on his knees rubbing the back of his head, grimacing in pain, and Sage up on top of a dresser next to the door with a stainless-steel water bottle in her grasp raised over her head as if she was going to strike again.

Her breath was ragged as she glared at the werewolf, but her eyes widened as she turned her gaze to me standing in the doorway.

"Blair?" She hopped down from the dresser, nimble as a dancer, and warily glanced at the hulking presence of Dean standing behind me and Ophelia sitting at my feet.

She paused, her face wary of all the strangers in her home. Her eyes landed back on me, the gold ring around her pupils nearly glowing as she took in the leathers and the blades strapped to my body, as if she had seen the new garments before.

"Hey, Sage." I flashed an impish grin. "If I would have known you liked knocking around werewolves, I would have picked you up a lot sooner."

Dean chuckled as his hand made its way to rest upon the small of my back.

Miles glared at us all, still rubbing the back of his head. He stood up with a huff but remained near Sage, eyeing her curiously.

"I had a vision that someone was coming for me, so I raced home to pack my things to get out of town and go try and find you. When I got here, the air felt off, and I *saw* someone in my kitchen, so I ran in here to hide." She turned to Miles. "I'm so sorry for whacking you over the head. Blair is usually the one prone to violence, not me." She blushed at Miles and offered him a smile, her voice light and airy, calming in a way that mine would never be.

A small grin turned up Miles's lips, and he gave her a slight dip of his head.

That was Sage for you; she could win over almost anyone with her sunshine personality. Everyone she met fell in love with her, and Sage may be psychic, but she was blind to see the affect she had on people. Her calming aura brought peace to your heart, and she was truly the kindest soul I had ever known. It was why her yoga classes were so popular in the Flagstaff community.

She nearly glided over to me, her movements always graceful, and I inhaled deeply as she embraced me. She smelt of eucalyptus, and I instantly felt at ease knowing she was safe. I peeked my eyes open to see Miles looking at Sage with interest, and I winked at him in response. He rolled his eyes with a smirk and leaned against the bed frame.

Sage pinched my back hard, and I yelped in response when she pulled away. She looked sternly at me and scolded, "Don't you do that to me again, Blair. I was worried sick about you."

"You were the one who told me to hide!" I exclaimed, throwing my arms out in frustration.

She crossed her arms and continued to glare at me, wrinkling her nose.

"I know that! But I didn't hear from you this entire year! I thought you were dead! I tried to *see* if you were safe, but the Fates wouldn't give me any information. You know I can't control what they allow me to see! You should have called, Blair," she shouted back at me, and I fell back a step. Sage never raised her voice. I saw the worry and hurt in her eyes, and guilt pooled in my gut.

"I-I'm sorry Sage. I thought that if I called, someone would use you to figure out where I was, and I couldn't bear the thought of you being hurt because of me. Your life matters to me, Sage, more than my own, and I would be lost to the darkness if something happened to you," I murmured, a little embarrassed to be having this conversation in front of Dean and Miles.

Her face softened slightly as she blew out a breath. "When are you going to realize your life matters to me just as much as mine matters to you? We are family. You don't have to be alone in all of this."

My eyes began to well with tears, and I worked to suck them back in. I shook my head and sighed. Sage pulled me in for another hug, this time without the pinching. Before being surrounded by touchy shifters, Sage was the only person I ever allowed physical affection from. There was something about her touch that was healing, and I let that energy wrap around me once more.

"As sweet as this is, we should really get going. We need to get you back to New Haven as soon as possible." Miles swaggered over to us and clapped me on the back. "In case you wanted to know the name of the person you throttled with that water bottle, I'm Miles." He gave her an award-winning smile that deepened the blush on her cheeks.

"Again, I am so sorry about that. I don't keep weapons in the house, so I had to improvise. Worked out fairly well, though." She glanced at her makeshift weapon and tested its weight by thrashing it through the air once more, earning a wince from Miles.

Dean cleared his throat, and I gestured to him. "Sage, this is Dean. I've been staying with him and his pack for the past few weeks. He saved my life." I gave her a meaningful look to convey that he was the one she saw in her visions. "And this is Ophelia, my familiar." I waved towards her.

Sage just smiled and nodded, not at all fazed by the weirdness of this situation.

We descended the stairs together, with Dean taking the lead and Miles trailing behind us. Just as we reached the threshold of the door, Dean froze, and I peered around him to see what had caused him to stop.

He inhaled deeply and let out a low growl when I saw the lone figure dressed in all black sniffing around Sage's car.

No one spoke, though the vampire likely was aware of our presence by our scents alone. I still had the spell in place to keep our movements silent, and Dean slowly brought his arm back to push us towards the kitchen and back exit. His eyes never left the door as we lightly stepped back into the hallway. Sage let out a slight squeak when she bumped into Miles, who had stopped just as suddenly as Dean had and was peering into the kitchen. I saw movement by the back entrance to her house and cursed.

I looked to Ophelia, silently pleading with her to protect Sage at all costs. Her shadows rippled out of her body in anger, but she gave me a slight nod before adjusting herself closer to Sage.

Sage's sea-colored eyes were wide with fear as she glanced between the three of us, clutching her water bottle closer to her.

Miles slowly lengthened his claws as the back doorknob jiggled slightly. The vampire in the front was closing in on the front porch, a menacing smile spreading across his face, his fangs gleaming in the moonlight.

Cut the veil and drop us all by the SUV, Ophelia silently commanded.

My eyes darted over to meet hers as I contemplated it. I had never taken another person across the veil, only myself and various objects. She gave me a look that said *you got this.*

The vampire at the front was on the porch now, each step echoing loudly, as if each thump against the floor signaled our impending death. I heard the doorknob in the kitchen get broken off, splintering wood raining down on the floor. My heart thundered in my chest, and I prayed to the gods that this would work.

Ophelia lightly grabbed Miles's pant leg with her teeth and tugged him closer, wrapping her tail around me as I gripped Dean's arm, preventing him from taking another step, before pulling Sage close to me. I gathered my chaos and sliced my hand through the air, opening up the veil directly beneath our feet.

The five of us fell through the floor just as vampires burst into Sage's home, screeching wildly.

Chapter Twenty-Four

I never stopped and looked at the surroundings whenever I traveled using the veil. But as we fell through the dark, smokey emptiness, I could have sworn I saw silver eyes staring directly at me from the void, watching curiously as we fell.

We landed a few feet from the SUV, with only Sage stumbling a bit upon re-entry into this plane. I reached out a hand to steady her before I started ushering her into the car. The two wolves stared at me with wide eyes before I snapped at them to get moving. They were jumping into their seats in a matter of seconds.

Gravel flew behind our wheels as we took off into the night, away from Sage's first home. She held my hand as she looked back with sadness, as if she would never see it again. I feared the same.

I let the others talk while I sat back silently, contemplating the next part of this rescue mission. Sage asked Miles about a million questions, which he happily answered, ever the gentleman. Dean's eyes flicked back to me every so often through the rearview mirror; whatever emotion lay there, I could not place.

Ophelia had shrunken back down into her house cat form, much to the surprise of Sage, and curled in close next to me, purring softly.

Pride flickered down our bond as I murmured a thank you to her, not only for giving me the idea, but also for having the confidence that I could do it. I made a mental note to practice more, because the strain of pulling four addition beings through the veil had me slightly drained. I closed my eyes for a bit, drifting off as the SUV rolled on.

* * *

We were closing in on Vivian's secluded desert home. Pine trees had given way to cactus and dirt, and dust flew out behind our car as we made our way down the lonely road. The moon was high in the sky now, casting shadows along the rocky terrain.

I signaled for Dean to stop about a half mile away from her house.

I could see the twinkling lights of her patio from here, and the glow of a fire coming from the back of her house through the large windows that made up the walls of her living room, giving you a clear view straight through her house. Vivian loved the sun and refused to have a house with small windows. Being so far out in the desert, she really didn't have to worry about privacy.

Sage tried to follow us out of the car before I shut her back in. She argued, trying to pull the door open, but her human strength was nothing compared to my own. I used magic to lock the car doors, and they would only unlock for Dean or myself.

"Ophelia, I need you to stay here and guard Sage." I looked to my familiar, who was clearly ready for this argument. Sage pounded on the glass window, screaming at me to let her out, and I winced. I would get an earful for this later.

We are stronger when we are together, Blair. I am duty-bound to protect you, she snarled at me, and I sighed.

"Ophelia, I am trusting you with the life of my dearest friend. We'll be in and out. Please. I'll call if I need you." Whatever she beheld in my eyes was enough, and she growled before sitting in front of Sage's door, glaring at me as we walked on.

I spelled our movements silent once more, and we lightly jogged up to the gate of Vivian's property. I couldn't see her through the windows, but with the firepit roaring on her back patio, I knew she was home. I disabled the wards she had protecting our home to allow us inside.

We entered the house and searched it quickly, but she was nowhere to be found, and just as a slight panic began to set in, I saw her walking back from her shed with more firewood in her arms.

She appeared the same as the last time I had seen her over a year ago. Her long caramel-brown hair was pulled back into a braid with many strands falling out of it, and she was wearing a long burgundy skirt and an off-shoulder white top. She was barefoot as usual; she enjoyed being grounded to the earth as much as possible.

As if she sensed me, her green eyes snapped up and spied me through the window. She dropped the wood and watched as I slowly made my way out onto her patio. Tension filled the air as we stood mere feet away from one another, with only the fire between us. The wolves offered us privacy, fading back into her home.

She took in my leathered outfit, the weapons strapped to my body, and gave me a sad smile. "Your outfit suits you. How much do you know?"

She made no move to come closer, and neither did I.

"Most of it. I just need to know why. What could make you so desperate that you would make a deal with a demon? You made me trust you, and the whole time you were conspiring to hand me over to them so they could do gods knows what with me. What did they promise you, Vivian?"

Tears welled in her eyes at my words, but I held my ground, keeping my face hard as I waited for an answer.

Her eyes were solemn as she took in my harsh features. "I was married once, to a man within my coven. We had been trying to conceive for so long, and we weren't having any luck. We tried all the herbs and remedies that various coven members suggested to us. We prayed for the gods to bless us with a child, but we were met with silence."

A single tear slid down her cheek, and she hastily wiped it away.

"I knew he was pulling away from me. The stress of it all and the possibility that I could never give him children was too much for him. So... he left. I tried the one thing I could think of that would give us a child. The one thing we were warned never to do throughout all our lives in the coven: I summoned a crossroads demon."

She nervously rubbed her hands together as she continued.

"The demon was powerful, way too powerful for a normal cross-roads demon. He knew exactly what I wanted and promised he could give it to me. I was so *alone*, Blair. I just wanted a baby and my husband back.

"So, we made a deal. I would bring him the child he wanted, and he would give me a child of my own. He gave me your location and instructed me to move there and watch you, get to know your patterns and report to him of anything strange. Even from afar, I could sense the power in you, Blair. I knew you were different from any witch I had ever met.

"I got to know you a little bit, and I saw what those awful people were doing to you. I had to believe that whatever the demon wanted with you, it couldn't be as bad as that. He was surprisingly charming and never gave any indication he wanted to hurt you. That's what I told myself, at least. Then came the night with the priest. You were going to kill them, Blair. I felt the death leaking out of you when I arrived, and I knew I had to get you away from them. I found that I... well, I cared for you. When I got custody of you, he told me to raise you, to foster your magic and allow it to grow, to keep you safe and away from other supernaturals, and he would be back when you turned twenty-five, when all witches come into the full extent of their power.

"So, I raised you, and gods, Blair, you were the daughter I had always dreamed of having. I did everything I could to train you up and make sure you were strong, because I knew he would eventually come for you. I thought that somehow, I could keep you safe from him. All I knew was that I couldn't turn you over to him. I even made a deal with Ezekiel to protect you from the mistakes I made. I was such a fool. The night you disappeared, a Hellhound arrived at my door to collect what its master was owed."

She was sobbing now, and I felt tears of my own rolling down my cheek, but I made no move to wipe them away.

"Imogen was killed because of me, because of the deal that I made. I don't know what happened to her familiar. They were both in my coven with me before I left; they were my friends. I managed to convince them that I had hidden you away, knowing that the coven was coming for me, and when I went looking for you, I couldn't find you. I feared that they had gotten you. Despite Ezekiel's assurance that you were alive, I was so terrified for you, Blair."

Her story left me unable to breathe. Tears still stung in my eyes, and I fought to keep my emotions in check so I didn't lose control of my magic.

Grief consumed me, grief over the lies she spun and the truth that was hidden from me, but there, an ember in the dark, was the love I still held for her. For everything she had taught me. For the love she had given me when no one else had.

"Blair, please, you must know that I truly love you. You were the daughter I was meant to have. It's why I taught you everything that I did. I couldn't go through with it. You mean more to me than anyone else in this life. And I am truly sorry for my lies." She fell to her knees and sobbed into her hands.

I struggled for a moment with her words, with my feelings of the situation. No matter what the story was, I loved Vivian. She saved me when I couldn't save myself. She brought me out of a dark place that I didn't think I could escape, away from abusers I couldn't escape.

Vivian taught me to be strong, taught me to fight, to defend myself, taught me to control my magic and not let it control me. She was still my family.

Wordlessly, I walked over to her and sank down to my own knees, pulling her in for a hug. "I forgive you," I breathed. She sagged in my arms and clung to me. I held her close and inhaled her scent of lemons and lavender.

Dean burst out of the back door with Miles in tow and growled, "We have company."

I pulled Vivian up with me and hauled her towards the wolves. Just before reaching Dean's outstretched hands, Vivian was ripped away from me, and I was thrown clear across the patio, crashing through the far wall.

Chapter Twenty-Five

I stumbled out of the debris, coughing slightly at the dust from the stucco before rushing out to take in the chaos before me. Dean and Miles were grappling with six vampires, a mass of snarling, flying fists, and claws. Vivian was being dragged away into the desert by Alistair, who turned just enough to flash me a malice-filled smile, his fangs dripping with her blood.

I took off without a thought, and I distantly heard Dean roaring for me to come back. Ophelia pushed against our bond, pleading with me to call her to help, but I blocked them both out. She needed to stay with Sage and keep her safe, and I needed to deal with Alistair once and for all.

A female vampire emerged from the shadows, blocking my path, hissing and eyeing my neck with an intense hunger.

I flicked out my curved blades, the hilts warming in my palms as I launched myself at the vampire. She was quick and skilled in dodging the onslaught of attacks. She slashed out with her bare hands, screeching as I evaded her grasp.

A howl sang through the air, and her eyes flickered to the carnage I was sure Dean and Miles had wrought. I used that distraction to take her to the ground, and as she snarled, I plunged my blade into her heart. Her scream cut off quickly, and as dark blood pooled beneath her, I sheathed my blades. I set her body alite before I tore across the desert, willing my feet to take me faster.

Just as I was gaining on Alistair, he suddenly whirled around and hauled Vivian flesh to his chest. Her face was contorted with fear as she looked around wildly for a way to escape. I skidded to a halt as another figure stepped out from behind a saguaro cactus, a dark red aura pulsing around him, making my skin crawl.

"Hello, Blair." His voice was lovely, just as the rest of his appearance was, with his defined lips, curly dark hair, and aristocratic nose. He was dressed in a black suit perfectly tailored to his tall yet lean build. Everything about him was alluring, designed to draw you in, except his eyes. There was no ring of color around his pupil, only darkness that seemed to absorb all light and hope laid there.

I whipped out my sword from behind my back and braced my body for a fight. "Let. Her. Go," I growled, the ground quaking beneath me. Vivian's face paled as she took in the dark stranger, and when she looked back at me, I knew exactly who was standing before me.

The demon she made a deal with.

"Come now, Blair, where are your manners? I thought Vivian had taught you well after all these years." He strolled over to her and stroked a finger down her cheek.

She screamed in pain as the smell of burnt flesh filled the air. Her skin seared where his fingers had touched, his demon power pulsing with delight at her pain. Lightning cracked on the edges of my vision as rage coiled within me.

"Do that again and you'll become all too familiar with what she taught me." I took a step closer.

He laughed and held up a finger at me, a warning not to come any closer. I stopped short, but I pooled my chaos at my fingertips, ready to strike.

"My name is Gadreel. And I have been looking forward to

meeting you for some time, Blair. Though, I had to wait a bit longer than I anticipated." He gave a pointed look at Vivian. "But I am impressed, nonetheless. You are so much more powerful than I thought you would be." He cocked his head to the side, as if he could indeed feel the well of power within me.

"Flattered. Now let her go, and I won't have to kill either of you," I replied flatly.

Alistair snarled at my words. His bloodred eyes were hungry for me, trailing down my neck. Vivian whimpered when his hold tightened on her, and the sound only fueled the rage mounting within me.

"You are quite a female, Blair. I think I will enjoy breaking you." Gadreel's smile was menacing as he took a step towards me. Twin howls broke out into the night, and the demon paused. "I see you have made some interesting friends. Perhaps we should let them join the party." His grin only grew bigger, and my stomach churned.

I launched myself into action, flicking one of my blades out towards Alistair and praying it didn't hit Vivian, while swinging my sword towards Gadreel. He was the puppet master here, pulling the strings, and I needed to cut them before it was too late.

His movements were swift as he avoided every swipe of my blade, smiling as he did so. He was playing with me, I realized.

So, I stopped mid-swing, curling my magic within me and sending out a stream of chaos from my fingertips. His eyes widened in surprise as the streaks of lightning singed his jacket, narrowly missing him.

I had never done that before.

The thundering of Dean's paws grew louder, and I knew I was running out of time. I turned, launching myself towards Vivian and Alistair, only to be stopped short by Gadreel, his hand curling around my throat as he yanked me into his chest. His touch singed my skin, and I bit my lip to hold in the scream threatening to escape.

Vivian struggled harder when she saw him wrapped around me, and she shrieked every curse in the book, begging him to let me go.

I fought in his hold, but he was so strong, and every move I made only burned more flesh. He brought my neck back farther, nearly resting my head against his shoulder, and I gagged on his sulfuric stench.

"Stop struggling or she dies." He held his hand in front of him, ready to snap his fingers, and I stilled.

Alistair tightened his grip on her once more. Vivian raged at me to keep fighting, and she managed to throw her head back, crunching it into Alistair's nose.

She stumbled forward and ran towards us, falling on her knees before Gadreel. "Take me instead. I'm the one who made the deal. Take my life and let her *go*." I shook my head against him, and his fingers tightened around my neck. Smoke billowed up from the burns.

"No! Take me and let them live," I whispered, barely getting the words out. The pain of the burns was excruciating, every movement pure agony.

Alistair slowly crept up behind Vivian, waiting for Gadreel to give an order. "You'll come with me without a fight, and I will let them live? That's the deal?" Gadreel murmured in my ear, slightly licking the flesh there.

I nodded, nearly vomiting at his touch.

"No, Blair! Let her go, you bastard!" Vivian screamed, and I could see her gathering her magic. The ground began to shake from her earth elemental abilities.

Gadreel merely chuckled as he petted my hair.

He turned my cheek towards him and said, "Deal." And he pressed his lips against my own. I heard Vivian rage, and the ground continued to shake. I kept my lips firmly shut as he tried to coax them open with his tongue. He pulled away and turned my face back towards Vivian before hissing, "Here's the thing, Blair, when making a deal with demons, you need to be *painfully* specific. You see, I agreed to let *them* live, but you did not specify who or for how long. Besides, Vivian forfeited her life the moment she decided to keep you from me."

He snapped his fingers, and Alistair struck.

Alistair was a blur as he tore out Vivian's throat. The earth ceased its trembling as the light went out in her eyes. I stopped breathing as Alistair drank her blood greedily, crimson staining his clothes and the sand beneath him before he dropped her lifeless body to the ground.

My eyes were locked on her crumpled form, blood splattered all over her clothes, her empty eyes staring up at the star-filled sky.

Time seemed to move slowly. Her spectral form rose up from the ground, and she stared at me, her eyes full of sadness and peace.

She gazed off in the distance, towards Dean and Miles racing towards us, and then to a new shadowy figure appearing out of a tear in the veil. A beautiful woman dressed in black armor, her ruby-red hair braided intricately along the sides of her head, walked out of the tear and murmured words I could not hear to Vivian.

She nodded, and with one more look at me, her smile small, she grabbed the mystery woman's outstretched hand and walked into the veil with her, disappearing. The tear in the veil closed slowly behind her, the finality of it nearly bringing me to my knees.

Vivian was dead, she was gone, and it was my fault. I choked on my sob.

Pure grief suffocated me, stealing the very breath from my lungs as I stared at the spot where Vivian had disappeared into. Tears were flowing freely as I fought for breath, clawing at my chest, at my throat, for the pain of her loss was too much to bear.

Alistair licked his lips and swaggered over to me until we were nose to nose, unaware of the entire exchange that only I could see behind him. "Delicious," he purred as he wiped his bloodied hand across my face before ridding me of my weapons, tossing them to the ground with a hiss as the blades seared his skin.

I snarled at him, fighting to get out of Gadreel's iron grip to rip Alistair to shreds for what he had done.

The stench of Gadreel's magic filled the air as he tightened his hold. "Now, now, Blair, be still or I will kill the mutts, too. And that would be a shame. I have big plans for *him*."

My blood chilled at his words, and I immediately stopped struggling.

Alistair moved to stand next to Gadreel and I, and my heart broke when I saw Dean and Miles in their wolf forms barreling towards us. Ophelia shouted at me through the bond, demanding to come to me. Tears streamed down my face, but I remained still as Gadreel's magic wrapped around us and sucked us into the void.

The last thing I heard before falling through space and time was the mournful cry of a wolf.

Chapter Twenty-Six

I was dropped hard onto a stone floor as I fought for breath. The stench of sulfur was everywhere, and I emptied the contents of my stomach on the floor.

Vivian was *gone*, and it was my fault. I retreated into my own mind, pulling my power deep within me, enveloping myself in it, even though my rage and despair demanded vengeance. The image of Vivian's soul leaving her body replayed over and over in my mind as I laid there, waiting for whatever was next to come. Whatever it was, I deserved it.

My only comfort was that my friends were safe. Sage would return with Dean and Miles to New Haven, and I knew he would protect her. As long as she was safe, I didn't care what happened to me.

I didn't care when winged demon creatures with long, spindly arms and arched claws dragged me into an adjoining room and chained me to a metal table. I didn't care when another demon cut away pieces of my leather to expose my skin, leaving me almost bare on the table, with only a sliver covering my breasts and nether regions.

I made a deal that I would not fight, even if Vivian still paid the price.

Dean and Miles were still alive. Sage and Ophelia were still alive. And maybe if I didn't fight, maybe that would spare them long enough to get back within the protective wards of New Haven.

Ezekiel... please keep them safe. I sent out the silent prayer, hoping that he could hear me.

They left me strapped to that cold table all night, alone and shaking with fear. The stone walls were covered in strange runes made of blood.

Whatever they were, the marks pushed away the connection to my magic. I couldn't touch the roaring winds or the burning fire, nor the chaos that ran through my veins. I couldn't even feel the darkness I kept locked away. I couldn't feel anything.

I knew that was about to change as Gadreel strolled into the room.

I could barely see any of my surroundings, as my head was strapped down, but I managed to catch glimpses of him as he set up a rolling table and pulled it next to me. He had taken his jacket off, his sleeves rolled up to his elbows, and covering his chest was a leather apron. His smile was purely feral as he took in my bare skin under the harsh overhead light, his black eyes gleaming with whatever plans he had in store for me.

Under his elbow, he carried a leather sleeve that he laid out onto the table. As it unrolled, I heard the telltale sound of metal scraping against metal.

I allowed myself to be scared for a moment, and then I locked it down and stared at the stone ceiling, letting myself fall further into my mind, away from this place. My face remained impassive, even as he brushed his fingers down my arm, burning the flesh there.

I bit my cheek to contain my scream but could do nothing against the single tear that escaped.

"I don't understand why we can't do the ritual *now*, Gadreel," Alistair grumbled from the doorway, his eyes tracing over every inch of my exposed skin. Pure rage flared within me as I glowered at the vampire. Alistair gave me a cruel, knowing smile as he licked his lips, as if he could still taste Vivian's blood on them.

I lurched once against the bonds binding me and cursed whatever magic was keeping my own at bay. Gadreel turned and slammed his hand against my chest, pressing me hard down into the table. I gasped for breath that was robbed from my lungs, the smell of my burning flesh filling the air. I squeezed my hands into fists so hard my own nails drew blood, fighting the urge to scream out in pain.

"We need a very specific moon for the spell to work, Alistair, as I have already explained to you. The blood moon will link her blood to yours, which will ensure the ritual will be successful. Besides, we need to make sure she's the one we're looking for. So, until the timing is right, I will have my fun with her, *and you will not question me again.*"

His voice echoed with power, shaking the room with it. Alistair grumbled, clearly displeased, but he remained where he was for a moment, staring down at me with hunger, before he turned to leave.

Despite the agony I felt, charred flesh ripping more with each breath, I rasped, "I'll kill you for what you did to her." Alistair stopped, while Gadreel's eyes flicked between the two of us, his devilish smile widening at my pain. "I'll drag you to Hell myself," I vowed, letting my words flow into the universe. A death promise, one I would fight to keep.

"I'm going to enjoy drinking you dry, Blair. And once I'm done with you, I'll drop your body on the wolf's doorstep and watch him shatter at the sight of you before I kill him too."

I lurched against the chains, ignoring my sizzling flesh as I imagined ripping Alistair to pieces, but I only managed to give him the finger before he laughed and finally left the room.

Gadreel peeled his hand from my chest, some of my skin departing with it before he gingerly wiped it off on a nearby towel. He then grabbed a blade at random and began to sharpen it, the zing of metal against metal causing my heartrate to spike, but I fought the urge to flinch.

He leaned against the table and looked down at me, his soulless eyes boring into mine. He smiled. "Let's get started, shall we?"

"You will not break me. There are no whole pieces of me left," I hissed at Gadreel. His smile only widened.

"Oh, my dear. I am not trying to break you. I am trying to *unleash* you."

With a flash of movement, his dagger sliced into my stomach, and pure fire razed into my blood as the blade slashed through my flesh.

My vision went white. There was only burning.

I screamed.

* * *

I don't know how much time passed. I was constantly in and out of consciousness, passing out when the pain became too much, only to wake up to more pain. I don't know how many times he cut me with his various knives and other torture devices he brought into the stone room, now stained with my blood. Some of them hurt worse than others, burning me from the inside out, my body only able to heal the wounds from the knives that merely cut, not the ones that burned.

Perhaps it was because there were similar runes etched into those blades that adorned the walls. Whatever the reason, I didn't care.

I didn't scream anymore. I couldn't.

My voice was gone, just one more thing Gadreel had taken from me.

He artfully carved into my skin, sometimes using the fire blades, but lately he had been favoring ones covered in some sort of poison. He allowed me just enough give in my bonds so I could throw up over the side of the table, until there was nothing left in my system.

My body slowly healed the poisoned cuts, but the burning blades left angry scars all along my skin. I didn't care. This was to be my fate until the ritual, and I accepted that. My eyes had now dried of all tears, and I merely laid there as Gadreel or some other demon repeatedly flayed me open, the sounds of my flesh being ripped apart replaying over and over in my mind.

His special blades were tortuous to endure, but I found there was no comparison to the feel of his demonic claws shredding into me.

It was a curiosity he indulged, whether I would be able to heal wounds given directly from his own hands. His claws had sliced me open from rib to hip, the pain so great I immediately passed out, which I considered a blessing. To his surprise, they did heal over, leaving jagged gray scars across my skin. The thought alone made me want to vomit.

Any time I was rendered unconscious, Alistair's dreamwalker controlled what I saw in my mind's eye, and without my connections to Ezekiel and Ophelia, I was completely powerless to change or escape whatever false realities the dreamwalker spun.

Vivian's death replayed over and over, the blood pooling at my feet as I tried to go to her, trying to stop Alistair from ripping her throat out.

But I was always too late. Other times, I saw my friends, bloodied and beaten on the ground, dead eyes staring up at the black sky above. I couldn't reach them. I could only watch as their blood soaked the earth.

The dreamwalker used other tactics to mess with my mind. Visions of everyone moving on after my disappearance, not caring whether I was alive or dead. Sage had found a new best friend and moved her into my home across from hers. Ophelia had a new charge, a young witch with immense gifts and no darkness residing in her soul. Dean moved on, took Rose on as his mate, and the pack hardly even noticed my absence.

Though those nightmares were meant to wound me further, they were a reprieve. I was forgotten, and they were safe. They were better off without me.

The only break from the cutting and the nightmares were when demons would drag me by my hair into a different room to beat me until I was utterly broken and limp on the floor. Gadreel's only rule was no blows to the face. He claimed it was too pretty to be marked.

No matter what they did, I didn't fight.

As time passed, however long, Alistair had become increasingly frustrated. I heard him arguing repeatedly with the demon posted outside my room, demanding to see me or Gadreel. Impatient to get his prize. He was either answered with silence or guttural snarls. More time must be passing than I realized. Gadreel often materialized out of a cloud of black smoke straight into the room, clearly to avoid Alistair's incessant nagging.

I almost started to be relieved when he came to torture me instead of the other lower-level demons that worked for him. That thought alone made me hate myself—more than I already did.

At least the strokes of his blade were neat, clean, and skillful. When his demons tore into me, they were brutal and messy. They slashed wildly, sometimes losing control completely, going feral with bloodlust until my flesh was nothing but bloody ribbons. Whenever the bloodlust faded, they usually shoved a healing tonic down my throat, only to begin again as soon as the wounds had healed.

Sounds of screaming and sizzling flesh echoed throughout the stone room, nearly bursting my eardrums from the intensity.

The walls shook from the pain that emanated from this place. I didn't have to see them to know the halls outside this torture chamber were riddled with broken souls, spirits cursed to endure an afterlife of misery. I could *feel* them.

Hell.

I was in Hell.

And maybe, just maybe, I deserved to burn.

Chapter Twenty-Seven

I was flipped onto my stomach, the pressure on the still tender claw marks nearly making me sick. The demon in charge of torturing me today was striking my back with a multi-tailed whip. The flesh on my back had been reduced to a bloody pulp, and I could hear the blood dripping onto the floor and being splattered across the wall with every raise of his arm.

My energy was dwindling, and I felt utterly empty without the connection to my magic. Every now and then, I would feel my dark power pressed against the locked door inside myself, desperate to get out and reap violence on them all, but I didn't possess enough strength to even let it free.

Gadreel wanted to break me. But he didn't know I was already broken.

I heard the heavy iron door open followed by calculated footsteps I knew belonged to Gadreel strolling up to the bedside. The demon stopped whipping and without a word set the weapon down and scurried out of the room.

Drip, drip, drip.

Gadreel walked around the table to the side where my head was positioned, staring at the wall where drops of my blood slid to the floor. He knelt and flicked his eyes to the marred flesh on my back with hungry gaze before bringing them to mine. I looked at him, unflinching as his black eyes looked at me with a calculating gaze.

What new kinds of torture did he have planned for me tonight?

"Well Blair, this is going to be harder than I thought. Every demon in my circle doesn't know whether they should be impressed with you or furious with themselves. They pride themselves on being master torturers, you see."

I met him with more silence.

"I'm starting to wonder if I have been going about this all wrong. After all, there are so many ways to achieve our goals. This method of torture usually works. Perhaps you take more after your father than I realized." My mind perked up at this, but I willed my features to remain the same, empty of all emotion.

Demons lie, I had to remind myself. He wanted me to react. Gadreel probably had no idea who my father was. And it didn't matter if he did; I wouldn't ever be leaving here to meet him.

Despite my empty expression, his lips curved into a smile. "Ah, yes, I know who your sire is. That's what makes you special, more valuable than anyone could realize. The blood that courses through your veins, that now coats my floor and walls, many would kill to have even a drop of it," Gadreel purred as he swiped his finger through a trail of blood leaking from my back and onto the steel table.

"For something you claim is so valuable, you seem to be wasting a lot of it," I croaked, unable to keep in the retort.

He smirked at my words, as if he had won something by eliciting a response from me.

He propped his elbow on the table next to my head and stared down at me, bringing his bottom lip between his teeth before responding, "It is not a waste for my purposes. Every cut chips away at your control; I can sense the shift within you. It won't be long now. Though, I must say it is a bonus that red is an *exquisite* color on you."

I bared my teeth at him, which only made his eyes dance with delight.

I laughed, the sound dry and scratching my throat as it escaped before I rasped, "Keep slicing away. Bleed me dry, Gadreel. I don't care. Nothing you can do to me will cause me to shatter. That I can promise you." I flashed him a cocky smirk and stared down my nose at him, even though I was strapped down to a table.

At my words, his frown deepened, his power radiating through the room, causing a few stones to fall from the ceiling. My grin only widened at his frustration, and I let out another harsh laugh.

But from one breath to another, his face returned to his usual cunning smile, as if something had just occurred to him. He cleared his throat before he leaned in closer to me, looking over every detail of my face. I could see my reflection in his black eyes, and I hardly recognized the empty girl staring back at me.

There was no fire in my eyes, my soul, just an empty husk of darkness and pain.

"Fear not, Blair, I have other ideas. Though, I'm sure my associate will not be too happy about it. He will be disappointed either way, I'm afraid, but that is another issue entirely." Gadreel stroked my cheek, pushing a sweat-soaked piece of hair out of my face. This time, there was no burning, just the touch of his surprisingly cool fingertips.

I felt his magic swirling in the air. The foul stench of sulfur quickly filled the room; I was so used to the scent now, I didn't even gag. The bonds around my body loosened until they fell away completely.

Run, my magic whispered.

That kernel of grace flickered inside me, urging me to get away. But I remained on the table. I couldn't move, could hardly even take a breath without an extreme amount of effort. And he knew.

"I will see you again *soon*, Blair." Gadreel stroked my hair once more before leaning back casually on his heels.

Confusion swept through me, and I eyed him, waiting for him to flick out a blade to slice into me when I wasn't expecting it.

His black eyes remained on my face, while his hands remained neatly folded in his lap. The current of magic continued, and the surrounding room began to fade away. The sounds of screaming went silent, and I felt the air in my lungs being sucked out, until everything went dark.

And then I was falling.

My body tumbled through the air, the coolness of it stinging my open wounds as I fell. The crisp night brought me peace, and the smell of pine filled my nose instead of sulfur.

I prayed this wasn't a trick, another illusion from the dreamwalker, and I was truly out of that dungeon.

I could let go now.

I embraced the fall, letting myself smile slightly at the irony.

I hurtled through the air like a falling star, streaking across the night sky. Only to be slowed down when I hit several trees, bringing them down with the sheer force of my descent. The pain didn't even register, not with the wounds I already carried. The earth shook from my impact, creating a boom that echoed through the forest.

I grunted as dirt flew up around me, coating my skin and wounds, the vibrations spreading around me like an earthquake.

I made no move to get up as the earth settled.

I felt myself fading in and out of consciousness again. I barely managed to curl my knees towards my chest, shivering now at the cool air pressing in around me. I looked at the moonless sky above, the stars being the only comfort as I laid on the forest floor, waiting for my death.

A flash of silver light lit up the sky and was streaming towards me. I could only watch as it landed right at the edge of the crater I had created with my crash. Spots danced in my vision as the light faded to a figure of a large male, black wings splayed out behind him, with energy identical to my own.

Death had come for me.

Silver eyes gleamed in the night as he walked towards me. They were the last thing I saw before fading into a depthless pool of black.

Chapter Twenty-Eight

A blissful darkness wrapped around me in a soft embrace, and I wondered if this was what Elysia was like. Just an eternity of this.

I sighed and leaned into the sensation, waiting to fade away.

I vaguely heard a male voice murmuring something, hands pressing against wounds that I had forgotten, a slight stinging sensation making me groan in pain. The memories of the dungeon, the cutting, the falling, Vivian, and death came rushing back, and my eyes snapped open.

I was on my stomach again, laid on a soft bed of cotton sheets, my entire body stripped of whatever scraps of leather had remained during my time with the demons. My backside was covered, and there were no bonds holding me down.

I didn't have the strength to move, though.

Fear coiled around me, tightening its grip on me until I was breathing quickly, panicking about where I was, who held me captive. My muscles tightened in anticipation of another blade slicing into my skin as I desperately tried to get up, the echoes of it causing me to flinch.

A cool salve pressed into the open flesh of my back, and I hissed at the sensation, my eyes wildly trying to orient myself. Barely mustering the strength, I began thrashing, desperate to get away from the hands on my body.

"*Hold still.* I am almost done," a deep voice sounded from behind me, and I stilled.

I let my senses reach out towards him, only to be met with that same energy I felt in the woods before I passed out. It was grace that I was feeling, but it was not the energy of Ezekiel that was greeting my own.

No, this felt more... familiar.

Eventually, the entirety of my open wounds was covered, and the stranger closed the tin of whatever healing agent he'd been using and set it down on a surface I couldn't see. He laid linens over me, the cloth sticking to salve, and my shivering stopped.

Black leather pants like the ones Zeke had given me were the first thing I saw.

I strained to look upward, glimpsing a white tunic speckled with my blood, along with silver eyes set under thick brows paired with raven-black hair like my own pulled into a bun, and a similar set of high cheekbones.

"The salve will help close the wounds, but I'm afraid some of them may scar. The demon blades Gadreel used are infused with demonic magic that is toxic to angels. Your grace was depleted, so some of the wounds could not begin the healing process... I'm unsure of whether your back will scar or not." His voice was deep, commanding, and cold.

I knew the answer before I even asked it, and though my throat was still raw and aching, I whispered, "Are you my father?"

My heart thumped wildly in the silence that followed, each second that passed only quickened the beats. Finally, I heard him stand, and I held my breath. Curiosity and fear rolled around alongside my racing heart, warring with each other to stay and meet the man whom I'd wanted to meet my whole life, or run away, afraid of what he thought of me and why he abandoned me.

He pulled a stool to sit directly in front of me, his face holding no emotion as he said, "Yes. I am Azrael, the Angel of Death." My eyes widened at his words. I was Death's daughter. "You need to sleep now. We must wait for the wounds to close and your grace to replenish to travel, and then I can take you back to New Haven."

My father was the Angel of Death. My mind reeled at the revelation of his identity, but I was struck speechless.

It felt as if a missing piece in my being had finally snapped into place, even if anger for his absence from my life still swelled within me. Despite this, I was grateful he had come for me when he did, even if during my fall I had wished to fade away.

His command was clear, but my eyes stayed wide open as I took him in.

There were no wings behind him now, but I saw so much of myself in his features. His skin was the same olive complexion as my own, and his black locks were wavy as a few pieces hung outside his bun. My lips were fuller than his, a trait I must have gotten from my mother.

My mother. The necromancer.

"H-how did you find me?" I rasped, unable to articulate all the questions rolling around in my head.

His eyes flashed, and I saw sadness there, along with a twinge of regret as he stood up abruptly to grab a glass of water. He brought it to my lips and supported my head as I drank greedily.

"One of my reapers informed me that you were taken. I began searching for you the moment Gadreel stole you away, but he must have kept you in a fortress with heavy warding, making it impossible to track you. I was only able to find you when I felt your grace again, as you fell into the woods just inside the Canadian border." He gave me more water. "I was searching for you for months."

His words turned the water to lead in my stomach. I had been tortured by Gadreel for *months*. I thought of Dean and the pack, Ophelia and Sage, and hoped that they were safe.

Before I could ask, Azrael murmured, "Your friends are safe inside New Haven. Ezekiel has been monitoring them, as has one of my reapers who is close with the alpha." I gave him a slight nod and a quiet thank you, my heart calming slightly knowing my friends were safe. "Sleep now, Blair."

I couldn't fight it as my eyes drooped closed, and I fell into a dreamless slumber.

* * *

I don't know how long I slept for, but when I woke up, there was no sting of open wounds. I was alone in a bedroom, adorned with homey wooden furniture and charcoal linens. A marble fireplace was crackling with a fire, and I basked in the warmth as I slowly got up.

A bowl of soup and bread with a goblet of water was waiting for me on the nightstand. I pulled the sheet around me, covering my body before slowly devouring everything in sight. I let out a soft groan at the taste.

In between bouts of torture, to keep me sustained, I had been force-fed stale or moldy bread and murky water. But those meals were few and far in between, and I slowed my eating as my stomach began to feel too full too quickly.

I shakily climbed to my feet, my muscles quivering to find a black velvet robe hanging on the armoire, and I delicately put it on, wincing slightly as the fabric slid over my tender flesh.

I soon located the adjoining bathroom, finding all the necessary human toiletries. Seeing my body surprisingly clean, I skipped the shower for now, did my business, splashed cool water against my face, and brushed my teeth for what felt like ten minutes. Before heading to the door to find Azrael, I paused, looking at the mirror leaning against the wall. I kept my gaze on my eyes at first, noticing how silver had bleed into the brown, right around my pupil.

Sucking in a harsh breath, I mentally prepared myself for what I would see, as I shifted the robe down to look at my skin.

I choked back a cry. Though I knew my skin did not reflect all the cuts and marks Gadreel and his demons had left on me, my skin was still littered with scars from where he'd used the demon blades on me.

My back seemed to be the worst, the skin there riddled with angry red slashes and raised, but it was no longer open and bleeding. It would scar, the marks of the whip forever living on my skin, evidence of what had been inflicted on me.

There was a long-clawed scar that went from the ribs on my right side all the way to my left hip bone where Gadreel had grown sharp black claws and slashed me open to look at my insides. Scars from his claws were tinged gray, and I ran to the bathroom to vomit at the sight of them.

I tightly closed my robe after rinsing out my mouth and shakily made my way out of the room. The bright light filtering through the windows nearly blinded me after having been locked underground with hardly any light for weeks. I kept close to the dove-gray walls and found Azrael in an office two doors down.

His silver eyes flicked up at me and then to a plush leather chair in front of his desk, his request clear. I sat gingerly, my body still aching despite the healing.

"Where am I?" I croaked.

"Purgatory. This is my home, and I run the realm for Odenus and Morana, ushering the souls of the dead to the appropriate afterlife." I nodded at the information, my mind still reeling that I was sitting here with my father. The Angel of Death.

"Your resiliency is admirable. Very few have withstood what you went through and lived," he continued. Even at his praise, I felt empty. Like Gadreel cut out everything I held within myself and left me a husk. "It reminds me of your mother."

My mind perked up at this. "What was she like?" I asked quietly, slowly bringing my eyes to him.

His brow furrowed. "Your mother was a powerful witch, but she faced her own hardships. She was born into a coven who wanted to use her unique gifts for nefarious purposes, but she escaped, wanting to make the world better, not worse. She was strong—stronger than any other being I have come to meet. She was also stubborn, quick-witted, and a force to be reckoned with. I see a lot of her in you."

I mourned her loss all over again and cursed the Fates for being so cruel as to not allow me time to know her. What would she have thought of me?

"Was she kind?' I murmured, my voice breaking as I clenched my fists.

Too much. This was all too much. But I had to know.

Those quicksilver eyes softened slightly. "She was. Even to those who did not deserve it."

I nodded but kept my head down, trying to hold back my sobs.

"She would be proud of your strength. Just as I am," Azrael said quietly.

I bit down hard on my cheek, trying to distract myself from the well of emotions threatening to cleave me in two.

I never knew my birth mother, and the very idea of her seemed so distant and intangible. Vivian was dead now, because of me, and she had been the only mother I had ever truly known. Even with her dark past, I mourned her loss as deeply as I mourned my birth mother's. And now I was sitting before my father, the father who I had always assumed abandoned me, who I always wished to know more about, and he was telling me he was proud of me.

Red skin, raw and irritated, caught my eye, and nausea churned my gut. I was nothing to be proud of.

"Blair, look at me," my father ordered.

I realized I had been staring at the scars on my wrist, where the endless rubbing of the rune-covered chains had worn through my skin.

"Glad I was able to impress," I mumbled in reply. My voice was flat, devoid of any emotion. I pulled the sleeves of the robe down and looked up at him. His face was hard as he looked over me, seeing straight through my emotionless words.

"I will return you to New Haven after you have eaten at least two more meals. Your wounds have healed significantly as you slept over the past few days, but you will need to continue to rest when you get back there. I have instructed my Commanding Reaper, Valerie, to keep watch on you and ensure you do. She has a home in New Haven."

I recognized her name. She was a friend of Dean and Brodie. I merely nodded, not having the energy or care to form words.

My father continued, "Once you have regained your strength, you will train with her, get to know the ways of our reapers. I will meet with you periodically to monitor your progress."

"Reapers?" I asked, furrowing my brows in confusion.

Azrael clasped his hands together, his posture straight as he cleared his throat. "The reapers are in the realm's employment and consist of angels, Valkyries, and other supes connected to death. They reap the souls of the dead and bring them here for judgement. From there, the souls are either taken to Elysia or Hell, for peace or punishment."

"And you want me to train to what? Be one of them? To work for you and reap the souls of the dead?" My tone was clipped. I couldn't believe that it hadn't even been five minutes into having my first real conversation with my father and he was focused on my career choices.

"Given your abilities, it seems like it would be more than appropriate for your skillset. Unless you prefer slinging drinks at the local pub for mediocre tips like so many humans," he scoffed.

I bristled at his words. "You don't know a damn thing about me, and I'd be perfectly happy slinging drinks if it keeps me away from supes like *you*," I growled, pulling at the sleeves of my robe, wishing it would swallow me whole, if only to cover the evidence of what I had endured.

Azrael caught the movement, his silver eyes zeroing in on my wrists before he murmured, "I have instructed my reapers to be on the lookout for Gadreel and Alistair,"—I winced at their names—"and we will deal with them accordingly."

"I want to kill them," I muttered.

He solemnly nodded, as if he could feel the intense rage I felt, the need for vengeance nearly overwhelming. I focused on it. Held onto it so tightly it filled my entire being.

I felt my magic swelling inside me, building and building until it filled every crevasse of my body as my breath quickened. The room began to shake, and black smoke billowed around me. I clenched my jaw, not even bothering to bring it back in. The lights flickered, and the room was filled with the scent of ether and thunder. Lightning flickered at my fingertips, and I relished in the feeling of power.

The door that held that immeasurable magic at bay cracked beneath the wave of magic that was slamming against it. I tried to ignore it, to rein it back in, but it continued to fill me, to fuel me, to protect me.

Azrael immediately rose to his feet, his eyes zeroing in on my hands. His own power filled the room, and I found it to be powerful like my own, both wild and dark like an impending storm. His eyes flicked back to mine, the silver in them looking hard as a steel blade. As if he could sense the shift inside me, he commanded, "You *will not* go after them without my consent."

I let out a growl. I was not some petulant child he could order around.

"You do not own me. Father or not, I do not answer to you." I felt that darkness filling me up, ready to strike, coiling like a cobra and rearing back to deal a blow.

His eyes narrowed. The furniture in the room shook as our twin energies pressed against each other.

"He caught you without sparing an ounce of his demonic power. Kept you bound and unable to escape or fight back for *months*. You think you can take him on by yourself, with your full potential locked down within yourself so deep? Without training?"

"Fuck you," I spat.

"You will not go after him by yourself. You will not endanger yourself like that again. Revenge is a fool's errand, Blair. It can only end in bloodshed." His power flickered throughout the room, but I did not cower. I let my own power seep out of me and reveled in the slight widening of his eyes as he felt a sliver of what was inside me. "I'm trying to protect you, Blair. Despite what you may think of me, I have always fought to protect you."

I laughed, the sound harsh. "Protect me? You have let me suffer my entire life, and *now* you wish to protect me? Save it for someone who needs it. I can take care of myself. I have been for the past twenty-five years." I shoved out of the chair, snapping my power back into me and stalking out of the room without looking back.

It was childish, but I slammed the door to the room. I sank down in front of the bed and let out a few shaky sobs, before wiping my tears and tearing through the armoire to find soft black pajamas, the pants long and cuffed at the ankles, and the shirt long-sleeved and loose. It covered my entire body below the neck.

I sat on the edge of the bed, waiting to be taken back... where I would have to face my friends.

Later, a meal appeared on the nightstand, and I begrudgingly ate the warm soup before falling into another deep sleep. When I awoke, the smell of eggs and potatoes had me turning towards the table again, and this time I ate without a second thought, knowing it was the only way I would be able to return home.

After I finished, a light knock came at the door. I put on a pair of slippers that were also in the armoire and opened it. Without looking at him, I cinched my robe tightly, somehow still feeling like too much skin was showing, and turned back to him.

His silver eyes assessed me, and I balled my hands into fists, ready to strike out at him if I found an ounce of pity in their steel depths. All I saw was hardness, and maybe pride.

I found I wanted to hit him for that, too.

He reached out a hand, and I flinched at the sudden movement, then thoroughly cursed at myself for the reaction. Still, his hand was an invitation, and he did not move until I pressed my own into his, albeit reluctantly. He pretended not to notice the grinding of my teeth as I got used to the feeling of someone else touching me.

I swallowed my embarrassment, and the world around me whirled at the familiar sensation of traveling through the veil.

Chapter Twenty-Nine

The smell of the forest hit me first, and I inhaled deeply, bringing the fresh air into my lungs. I recognized the tingle of the barrier that surrounded the city of New Haven, keeping out humans and unwanted supes.

I jerked my hand from my father's and stepped away. He cleared his throat, and out of the tree line, just inside the barrier, stepped a female.

I recognized her immediately, barely hearing my father introducing her to me.

The very reaper who had reaped Vivian's soul.

Valerie.

She wasn't dressed in armor as she had been that night. Instead, she was wearing a pair of leather leggings with a cream sweater, her crimson hair pulled up into a delicate bun. Her eyes were not silver, I noted, but a brilliant hazel that nearly glowed against her golden skin. Freckles were smattered across her button nose, and her full lips were colored a deep red that matched her hair.

She inclined her head to Azrael and brought her eyes to me, taking in my disheveled appearance. I stood taller.

I did not want her pity, and she didn't offer it.

With a flick of her hand, a door-sized break in the magical barrier opened, and she nodded her head towards the forest.

I glanced back at my father, who was staring down at me, his cold mask effectively in place. "Let yourself heal, Blair," he murmured. I snorted before stalking over to Valerie. Just as I was inside the barrier, I let out a long breath and turned back towards my father.

"Thank you. For coming for me," I grumbled, not meeting his gaze.

Without another word, he unfurled his wings and launched himself into the sky. I watched his powerful wings beat in the current of the wind before I turned back and walked next to Valerie.

"Don't be ashamed of the scars. Wear them with pride. They are a testament to your strength and sacrifice." She didn't look at me as she spoke, instead keeping her eyes trained forward.

There was no way she could see any of the scars, as I was covered almost head to toe, but the ones she could see in my eyes, the scars hidden beneath the skin, the ones that still burned, and were festering with anger and guilt.

"If I wanted your opinion, I would ask for it," I snapped at her.

She merely nodded and kept walking. The rest of the walk was silent.

She led me to a sleek vehicle parked on a hidden dirt road within the forest, and we wordlessly slid inside. Within a few minutes, we were off the dirt road and on the main street that led outside of the downtown square, heading towards Dean's pack territory.

My grace was fully awake now, and I curled it tightly within myself, holding it close, as if that alone could quell the rage burning within me. I didn't bother using it to try and heal the scars, even though I knew it was impossible.

Let them be a reminder.

"There is something you should know," Valerie said quietly.

I turned away from the window to look over at her, urging her to continue.

"Dean has... not been himself since you were taken. He has barely shifted back to his human form since that night. Miles managed to capture one of the vamps that was there, and they brought him back here, where Cal tried to get information out of him. Dean lost himself to his wolf and killed every vampire that was involved with Alistair they could find. The trail led nowhere, and anyone else involved has gone into hiding... They only just got him to come back to New Haven two days ago."

I sucked in a deep breath. He hadn't stopped looking for me.

A flicker of gratitude and devotion swept through my chest, and it became painful to breathe. Tears stung in my eyes as I thought of how I had wished he'd moved on, had never looked for me, but knowing he never stopped made my heart squeeze.

I gingerly wiped the tears away and nodded.

"We think you're the only one who can bring him back. He won't let anyone near him," she stated, and I nodded again.

The thought of Dean raging and trapped in his wolf form was such a harsh contrast to the sweet touches and wicked smiles I thought of when I had been taken. From the first moment I saw him, I was entranced. Those blue eyes and cocky grin pulled me in, even when I didn't want to like him. He showed me a whole new world, accepted me for everything that I am, and never once faltered when I kept him at arm's length. He broke down my walls with those smiles, his laugh, and his caresses and kisses that I never knew how much I needed.

I held those memories so close, and at times, I felt like they were the only things that kept me from breaking. I even thought at times that I heard the mournful cry of his wolf, a sad serenade to our story that I didn't think I would be able to continue.

I wondered if that had meant something, that perhaps Selene had been right, and the Fates had deemed me worthy of being his mate. Regardless of whether that was true or not, and I didn't believe the Fates would be so kind to me, I would bring him back to himself. I owed it to him, for all he had done for me.

As we closed in on the territory, I felt the tether of my bond to Ophelia tighten, as well as her relief trickling through it. Her emotions seemed muted, like she was holding back as if to not over-whelm me. I sent her silent words of thanks and a *see you soon* before I turned my attention back to the scenery.

I didn't know how I was going to face them. I could hardly stand to be touched, hardly stand to look anyone in the eye, because I knew what I would find there. Pain. Emptiness. Broken shards of my sanity and soul.

Flashes of blood and knives appeared in my mind's eye, and I started sucking in quick, shallow breaths.

Terror took over as I struggled to inhale. I began clawing at the doors, needing to get out, needing to get away from *him*. I heard his laugh, felt his hands all over my skin. I heard the knives sharpening, claws ripping, the laughter of the other demons as they waited their turn to mark up my flesh. The smell of sulfur invading my lungs and sticking to the inside of my nostrils.

The burning, horrible burning—it was in my veins, and I couldn't get it out, couldn't get away.

My body lurched against the restraints holding me tightly against the table, my magic no longer within my grasp. I was strapped down again, waiting for endless pain and torment. I hadn't gotten out.

A velvet voice pierced through the flashes of torture I was reliv-ing, "Look at me, Blair. You are free. You are not back in that place with him. I will not hurt you. I will not touch you. Deep breaths, Blair." Valerie began inhaling and exhaling loudly, trying to get me to mimic her. Her magic reached out to me, a cool blanket of gray, soothing my own which had risen to come to my aid.

I struggled for a while, tears streaming down my face, until finally my breathing slowed, the visions of blood and pain fading away, and my grace settled again.

Her hazel eyes came back into view and flicked to my hand. I nodded, meeting her halfway to grasp hands. She anchored me, and as I squeezed her hand, she squeezed mine lightly back. A lifeline in the pool of pain I was drowning in. Bringing me back to the present.

I continued breathing deeply, and she rolled my window down, letting the cool breeze brush my face. Her magic, like an old friend, continued to caress mine, reminding me that I was safe.

"I am what most of the world calls a Valkyrie, and I have seen many battles, suffered many losses, and possess my fair share of scars, as well. I have been where you are. I know many warriors that have been where you are. You will get through this because you are strong enough. You are unbreakable. Say the word, and I will turn this car around and take you to my townhome within the city, and we will face this another day. You have my word."

A sense of kinship was forming between us, another bond, glimmering into fruition before my eyes as they locked with hers.

I couldn't get any words out, not now. But I gave her a nod and continued to slow my breathing. We sat there for another few minutes before she slowly peeled out onto the road. The intense memories began to fade with each deep breath I took, until finally, I only saw the road ahead. I kept her hand firmly in mine, and she did not pull away.

We turned down the familiar path and passed through the glittering barrier that encompassed Dean's territory. The forest seemed eerily silent as we continued down the gravel drive. Feral and lost within himself, Dean was a beast to be reckoned with, and the creatures lurking within the woods knew.

My stomach churned as we drove up to the mansion, and I saw Ophelia and Miles sitting calmly on the front steps. Even as we parked, they made no move towards us, though I could see in Ophelia's tense form that she wanted to run to me.

"Whenever you're ready," Valerie murmured, giving my hand another gentle squeeze.

I took a few more moments to myself, locking down the horrific memories and overwhelming feelings before letting go of Valerie's hand and stepping out of the car. She met me around the front, and I grabbed her hand again before we walked together up to the steps where my familiar and Dean's second-in-command were waiting.

Miles shifted forward, as if he was going to pull me into a hug, and I quickly blurted out, "I do not wish to be touched. *Please.*" His green eyes showed a slight hurt, but they quickly shadowed in understanding, and I looked away from him before his emotions became too much to bear.

I glanced at Ophelia, and her chartreuse eyes glittered with nothing but understanding.

She dipped her head in acknowledgement and came to sit next to me at a respectful distance. Her shadows danced at the sight of me but did not touch. The bond between us thrummed, the closeness strengthening it once again.

I am glad you are back, Blair. I missed you. Sage is inside and will see you when you're ready.

Ophelia's calming energy centered me, and I sent a thanks down our bond before turning back to Miles. "Where is he?"

His face was grim as he motioned for me to follow him.

We walked around the house and into the forest, past the large barn where the pack gathered for dinners and past the pack members' cabins. The territory was silent, and I didn't see any of the other wolves as we made our way further into the forest. He led us to a familiar area on the other side of the lake, where the mountains met the trees.

Ophelia tensed beside me as the snarls of Dean's wolf reached us. I saw flickers of a black form pacing back and forth within the trees. The ground was rumbling from the pounding of his massive paws. I knew in his current state that it could only be me to approach him.

Without another word, I left the group and walked into the tree line towards Dean. The growls were getting louder, nearly vibrating my skin as I approached him. Just as I was nearly at the break in the trees, the breeze changed. He lifted his snout to the air and whirled around. His responding snarl shook the trees.

My heart nearly broke as I looked into those icy eyes, wilder than

I had ever seen them. I had done this to him. Sadness and guilt threatened to consume me as I took him in, but they were overpowered by the determination to bring him back.

"Dean. It's me. I'm-I'm home," I choked out.

His growling stopped, and he stalked forward. His blue eyes were wild and feral-looking as he looked over me, the lightest blue I had ever seen them, and his lips were still pulled back, revealing his incredibly sharp teeth.

I took a step forward, "Dean. Come back to me. *Please.*" And despite every instinct telling me not to, I held out my hand to him.

A sense of calm overtook his eyes. He crept forward and gently reached his paw towards my outstretched hand. A bright light flashed over his form, and in the wolf's place now stood Dean, his hair wild and body covered with dirt and smeared blood, evidence of his wrath in my absence.

He took my hand, and I found I didn't want to pull away. The warmth of his skin was calming, the touch seeming to settle us both.

"Blair..." he murmured, and I saw the sadness and relief pooling in his eyes as he looked over me. I couldn't bear it. I couldn't face the reality of what had happened to me. I needed to feel anything else but the overwhelming rage and emptiness that sat heavy in my chest.

So, I abruptly pulled him close and pressed my lips to his, hoping to drown in him instead of my pain. Dean would never harm me; I trusted him, and I knew he would give me what I needed. At first, he stood there shocked and stiff, but with a few flicks of my tongue, he melted against me and kissed me with the ferocity that I was hoping for.

That I *needed.*

I let my hands roam all over him despite his filth, exploring every muscle, tangling my fingers in his hair. He was being gentle. One hand cradled the back of my head to give him better access to my mouth, while the other lightly rested against my hip, just above where Gadreel's claw marks ended.

His tongue danced with mine, sending tiny bolts of lightning towards my core. I needed to be closer, needed this distraction to keep me from falling apart. My hands roamed lower, and I grabbed his hard length in my hand.

I gasped. Dean groaned at my touch but stopped kissing me. He pulled away to caress my cheek. I stroked him again, marveling at the size. He made to grab my wrist, but I used my other hand to stop him.

His eyes were wide as they took in the scar peeking out from the sleeve of the robe. They darted back up to mine, and just as he was about to say something, I interrupted, "Please don't. I need this, I need *you*." He looked bewildered, as if he was about to pull away. "Please," I whispered once more.

I waited for what seemed like an eternity for him to step away, unable to push his questions aside. His eyes never wavered from mine, and I got lost in the deep pools of varying blues.

Instead, those same eyes turned molten, and he pulled me in for another devastating kiss. He gently lifted me up and wrapped my legs around his torso, his hands cupping my ass as he held me close. He kissed my jawline, my neck, gently nipping at the sensitive skin there, and I melted into his touch.

Using the last bit of strength I had regained from the past few days, I cut the veil beneath us, and we landed softly in my bedroom in the pack house.

Chapter Thirty

Dean did not stop kissing me as he walked us into the bathroom and turned the shower on. Steam began to fill the space, and he gently set me down on my feet. He took a step back, his eyes filled with hunger and lust.

He was already naked, and my eyes raked over every glorious inch of him. I hesitated for just a moment before I began slowly removing my robe. Valerie's words came back to me, offering me strength and confidence that I never thought I would have.

Don't be ashamed of the scars. Wear them with pride. They show what you endured and came back from.

Dean monitored every movement like the predator that lurked beneath his human form, calculating and unwavering. I stepped out of my slippers next, then slowly removed my top, followed by the long pajama pants. A low growl erupted out of Dean as he took in my scars, but he did not move. He did not utter a word.

And as I brought my gaze up to meet his, dreading the look of pity I would find there, I only found rage—and a feral thundering of lust.

His heated gaze took in every inch of my skin, and my face

flushed. I had been naked with men before, but this felt different. This felt like I was baring my soul to him, every dark secret, every insecurity, every desire and dream laid before him. And he was not turning away from me.

Wordlessly, we collided, like a lightning strike to the earth.

Still intertwined, we managed to make it into the shower underneath the hot water, only adding to the heat between us. I barely broke our kiss to lather his body with soap to wash the grime off his skin. The sensual touches earned me low rumbles that vibrated all the way to my core.

Dean took his time washing me, making sure he was gentle with the angrier skin. His calloused hands provided the perfect amount of sensation that had my head leaning back against the shower wall, a sigh escaping me. He gave extra attention to my breasts, rubbing and flicking the peaked buds that had me moaning at his touch. When the bubbles were all washed away, Dean lowered himself to his knees before me, his hands tracing small circles down my hips and thighs. My breath hitched as he lifted my leg up to rest on top of his shoulder.

He pressed gentle kisses along my inner thigh, stopping just before he reached the apex of my thighs. I bit my lip as I gazed down at him, staring at my pussy with animalistic hunger.

He looked up, giving me a lustful smile as he purred, "I think I rather like being on my knees before you, Blair."

I squirmed with need, making my want increasingly clear.

He chuckled darkly before bringing his mouth to me. I barely kept in my moans of pleasure as his tongue started out with slow strokes, building me up touch by touch.

One of his hands reached up to palm my breast, teasing my nipple into an aching peak, while the other traced up my thigh until he reached my entrance. I gripped his hair as he ravished me, a silent command, and as he slipped two fingers inside, my knees nearly buckled.

Dean licked, sucked, and nibbled all while fucking me with his fingers until I screamed with pleasure, barely able to stand on my own. He growled as I came, only adding to the already overwhelming sensations coursing through my body. He licked me clean as I shook from the aftershocks of my orgasm.

My legs were a shaking mess, and Dean stood up slowly, supporting me. He picked me up, wrapped my legs around his body, my core pressed against his hard length, and carried me out of the shower.

I was a puddle of mush in his arms as he brought me to the bed, laying me down on my back. He towered over me, his blue eyes glowing with desire.

I suddenly felt vulnerable underneath him, in a position so similar to being strapped to Gadreel's table, and I pushed him away, gasping for breath. Visions of the demon flashed before me, leaning over the table, black eyes mocking me as he cut into me. No, no, no. But Dean was before me, not Gadreel. Dean would never hurt me. Still, my heart thundered, fear coiling within me, my power rising with it. I was gasping for air, scrambling backwards.

Even if I knew he wouldn't hurt me, that he wasn't Gadreel, I couldn't lie beneath him. I wouldn't be put in that position again. He leapt off the bed to give me space, his eyes laced with concern now.

"Blair, we can stop," he rushed out.

I clenched my shaking hands into tight fists and closed my eyes. I focused on my breathing, inhaling slowly, holding that breath, then exhaling slowly. I pushed away images of the torture I'd endured at Gadreel's hands, replacing them with Dean's kisses, the way blood rushed to my cheeks with each heated glance he gave me, his gentle touches that were so at odds with his animalistic nature.

With each set of breaths and each memory of him, my heartrate slowed, and the shaking stopped.

I regained that space, reaching out a finger to his lips. I needed this, to take my body back. To feel something other than pain when someone touched me.

He truly looked at me, searching my eyes, peering into my soul in the way that only he could, seeing every fractured piece inside me. We stood there a few moments as he continued to look, the realization dawning on his face, a mixture of understanding and devotion, before he began slowly kissing me again.

Dean only pulled back once to murmur, "Take what you need, my Raven. I'm yours."

I guided him to the bed, laying him on his back and straddling him. I knew it was hard for him to be like this, in a submissive position beneath me. But he didn't flinch even as I placed my hand on his chest, pinning him there.

Because he knew what I needed in this moment.

He let out a rumble of pleasure as I stroked him a few times before bringing him to my entrance. I paused, wondering if the size of him would even fit before I began lowering myself onto the hard length of him. He groaned with each inch I slowly sank down, and I moaned at the delicious ache he was creating within me.

Once I was fully seated, I leaned down to kiss him again. One of his hands tangled in my hair, the other caressing my neck before traveling down to my back.

Dean suddenly stopped. His fingers felt the marred skin from the whip. But instead of pulling his hands away, he traced patterns along the scars that sent tingles down my spine, chasing away pain with pleasure. A slight burning sensation prickled between my shoulder blades and down my spine, and I leaned into the deliciousness of him.

I rode him slowly at first, getting used to his size, but I increased my tempo with the buildup of my impending climax. His hands gripped my hips, urging me on but allowing me total control. He adjusted his own hips, so he was hitting a spot inside me that caused sparks to dance in my vision. My entire being quaked with pleasure as my body erupted. I screamed out his name just before he roared along with me, finding his own release.

I collapsed on top of him, breathing hard. He gently slid me off him and pulled me in close to his side. I laid my head on his chest, breathing in his beautiful scent of leather and amber. Sleep found me quickly, and I curled up into the darkness.

* * *

I don't know how long I slept, but when I awoke, I was still naked, and Dean was still lying next to me, now staring at me with concern. He brushed my tangled mess of dark hair out of my face.

"Your eyes are different. There's a ring of silver just around your pupil, leaking into the brown," he murmured, stroking my cheek with his thumb.

I continued to stare at his handsome face. The varying blues in his eyes and how the dark lashes made the color pop. His hair was longer than the last time I'd seen him, and my eyes traveled lower to his sensual mouth, his sharp jawline.

He was devastating.

Something felt different between us. Like we crossed some unknown barrier, and our souls were dancing with one another. His energy held flickers of my own, and I felt his twirling with mine. I reached up to hold his cheek as he was holding mine and caught sight of the brutal scar on my wrist, along with the other scars trailing up my arms. I pulled back.

The flashes began again, and I recoiled, squeezing my eyes shut as if that would make them disappear. I heard him saying my name, but I couldn't distinguish between Gadreel and Dean. I was shoving him back, desperate to get away.

I heard the rip of Vivian's throat as Alistair tore into it. Saw the light fade from her eyes. The sound my skin made as the demons tore into it echoed in the room. The burning, I felt my skin burning, the smell of it filling my nose until I was choking on it.

I felt myself fall off the surface, my feet caught in sheets or bindings, I didn't know which, and I scooted back into the corner, pulling my knees into my chest and curling my head inward, desperately begging for it to stop.

"You're safe with me, Blair. You're home. You're free. You're *free*. No one will hurt you like that again." I sobbed at his words, because in my heart I knew I couldn't allow them to be true.

My breathing was labored and uneven as I fought to push away the terror. Dean was my salvation and my undoing, and I didn't deserve the liberation he offered me.

Ophelia and Valerie barreled into the room, and I finally calmed my breathing enough to look up at Dean. His eyes revealed the warring of his emotions, a mixture of concern, rage, and helplessness. He was kneeling before me, his arms outstretched but not touching me, his face twisted with grief as he looked at me.

"I'm sorry. I'm-I'm so sorry," I gasped, looking wildly from Dean to my familiar and Valerie.

The first two were sad, but Valerie was looking at me with grim understanding. Movement caught my eye, and I saw Sage's head peeking around the corner, but she did not enter. I felt more of my soul shatter as she looked at me.

She had made it out. We got her here safely.

But Vivian didn't make it out.

My heart thundered at the images that replayed before me. Vivian begging to take my place for Gadreel. How I refused to let her die for me, and I made that deal with Gadreel to spare them, not realizing how vague my words were, and how he used that to his advantage.

I had been so stupid. I should have chosen my words more carefully, should have realized how he would have twisted my words.

Alistair's snarl filled my ears, followed by the tearing of his fangs into Vivian's throat. Her screams of agony had turned into gurgles as her blood spilled out of her, Alistair drinking from her deeply until her skin faded to a pale, sickly color, and the light burned out of her emerald eyes.

I couldn't escape the images, couldn't escape the guilt and sorrow and rage that welled up inside me, threatening to rip me apart. I had failed her. Failed the only mother I had ever truly known. Vivian was dead because of me.

Anger quickly overtook my fear and grief as I glared at Sage.

I shot up to my feet and pointed at Sage, though she tried to remain in the shadows. "Did you know what would happen to her? Did you *see it?*" I snarled at her.

Her eyes widened with shock and hurt as she came forward into the doorway.

"What? No, Blair, I would have warned you all if I had seen that. You know I can't see everything, only what I am allowed to see." Her shoulder-length blonde hair was pulled in two low buns, and she was in her usual yoga outfit of a skintight bra top and leggings. Totally whole and unharmed. "I would never keep something like that from you!"

"*LIAR!*" The room shook as my rage leaked out of my body. I felt the darkness inside myself filling me. She was lying. And if she wasn't lying, then there was no excuse as to why I couldn't save Vivian.

It was my fault.

And I *deserved* what happened to me.

"Don't think like that, Blair," Ophelia's voice rumbled to everyone as she took a step towards me, her body rigid with concern.

I snapped my eyes to her, looking for the next victim to take out my rage on.

"Stay out of my head," I hissed. She squared up with me, despite the hurt that flashed in her eyes. Her tail swished behind her with anticipation.

Valerie stepped forward, pushing both Sage and Ophelia behind her. "You want to pick a fight with someone? Pick a fight with me." She was in a warrior's stance, her hard honey eyes shining with that infuriating understanding. Her red hair was now pulled back into intricate braids that decorated her head, and I couldn't help but think she looked like a Viking princess.

"Let's go then," I growled, as she nodded.

She turned to the dresser behind her, pulling out a new pair of leathers, along with my sheaths and blades. The room continued to quake, but she had no trouble storming out, tugging Sage with her. I heard another door slam shut down the hall, then Sage's protests muffled by the now shut door.

I ripped through the sheets that were wrapped around my feet before shoving around Dean to put on the training leathers. They were still soft and strong like I had remembered them, and I felt empowered again to have them protecting my body.

"Blair, I—" I whirled and held my curved blade in a defensive position in front of me.

I bared my teeth at him, feeling every bit the animal that lurked beneath his skin. He took a step forward, letting the blade press into his neck. A drop of blood rolled down his skin as he looked over me. "If this is what you need, then I will not stop you. I will be whatever you need me to be. Anything you throw at me, I will not yield. I see you, Blair, and I am not afraid."

I withdrew my blade from his neck and walked out.

Chapter Thirty-One

Valerie had changed into leathers like my own, though the color was a rich brown instead of black. The Valkyrie seemed to be the only one to understand that all I needed was to burn off this fury I felt scorching inside me, and she was the only one who wasn't looking at me with such sickening sorrow.

I wasted no time and no words as I launched myself at her, striking out with my fists, leaving my weapons sheathed. She dodged me easily enough and met me blow for blow.

Her red braids whirled in the sun, making them look like blood spattering through the air. The sight of it threatened my mind with flashbacks, but I pushed through them, continuing my assault, focusing on the feel of our traded blows.

I was vaguely aware of Dean's presence lurking within the forest, though he didn't approach and didn't say a word as he watched me.

Valerie landed a few punches that stung, as she hit a few of the angry scars beneath the armor. I hissed and hit back with enough force to rattle the trees around us. She took each blow, barely grunting as she did and letting me make contact again and again as we sparred, until I was completely numb. She was a graceful savage with her movements, so different from the precision and poise that Ezekiel held when we trained.

I reveled in the violence of it, letting the monster inside me take control.

The sun was beginning to set by the time I finally slowed, dripping with sweat and breathing heavily. I backed away from her and collapsed in a heap.

She silently padded over and sat next to me, her breathing just as labored as mine was. Dean was standing next to Ophelia, his expression unreadable as he murmured something to her; I could not hear what it was over the roaring of my blood.

"Same time. Tomorrow," was all Valerie said as we sat there, watching the sun fade away through the trees.

There was a cool breeze that sent a sweeping chill across the exposed, sweat-soaked skin on my face. I closed my eyes at the sensation, breathing deeply before nodding. The memories and flashes of blood and screaming had gone quiet, leaving me with only my thoughts.

"I think I need to stay at your place for a while," I whispered quietly.

I felt Dean stiffen at my words, and the rejection I knew he felt sliced through my heart. But I couldn't stay here. I couldn't let him get any closer to the sharp edges that were left of my soul. He was safer if I stayed away. They all were.

Valerie merely nodded, as if she had been waiting for me to utter those very words since I entered New Haven. She softly told me she would gather my things and meet me at the car. She motioned for Ophelia to follow, and she reluctantly went after a glance between Dean and myself.

I slowly peeled myself off the ground, and Dean was on me in an instant.

I shielded the jagged pieces of my heart with fire and black stone, impenetrable and deadly to any who tried to reach it, because this male would try to piece me back together, but I didn't deserve to be fixed, and he didn't deserve to bloody up his hands trying.

"Please don't do this." He reached out to graze my arm, and I flinched away from his touch. He pretended not to notice, but I saw the pain flash in his ocean-filled eyes as he lowered his hands. "Don't go. Don't push me away."

My heart twisted, and a single tear slid down my cheek.

"I can't stay here anymore. You're all safer here without me. I can't—I can't do this," I barely managed to get out. He took another step towards me, and I let him, silently inhaling his scent and committing it to memory.

"You don't have to do this alone, Blair." He palmed my cheek, and I cursed myself for slightly leaning into the touch. "Please just let me help you. Let me in."

My heart broke as I took a step back out of his arms.

"You can't help me, Dean. I made that deal to save all your lives, and Vivian was *murdered* all the same! I would let them repeat everything they did to me for eternity if that kept them away from you! Vivian is still dead because of me, and I won't let the abomination I am be the death of you too!" I screamed, tears streaming freely.

Dean's face crumpled with sadness, silver lining his eyes as he watched me back away.

"I-I break and ruin everything around me. I will not allow myself to be the ruin of you. I will not tarnish you with my stained soul," I whispered in between sobbing breaths, feeling my chest cleave in two, my soul descending into that endless pit of nothingness as I looked at the devastation on his face.

He didn't follow me, stuck in stunned silence as I ran back up the path leading to his house. I rounded the corner and went straight to Valerie's car, flinging the door open. I let out an angry cry, my body shaking from the pain I felt deep in my soul. Within moments, Valerie opened the back seat, placing a few bags there and allowing Ophelia to hop in, before she came around to the driver's side.

I peeled my face away from my hands as she backed out of the drive, seeing Dean there, looking like he wanted to follow as we drove away. His star-flecked cerulean eyes stayed with me, and just as we made our way to the border of their territory, a mournful howl filled the air, and I sobbed even harder.

* * *

Valerie's brownstone apartment was filled with cream and rust colors, clean lines, and a breathtaking view of the mountains surrounding the town. It was elegant yet warm, just as she was.

Over the following weeks, I moved like a shell of a person through the apartment, eating when I was told, sparring with Valerie in her home gym to quell the anger when it became too much. She had even started bringing in other reapers to challenge me with their various fighting styles, an order from my father no doubt, to ready me for the role he wanted me to accept.

They didn't ask questions, didn't do much talking either. Whether it was an order from Valerie or whatever they beheld when they looked at me, I wasn't sure.

My body became leaner and hard with muscle, though my curves remained intact.

I was dangerous before with hand-to-hand combat, but I had now become completely lethal, a death dealer. I now fought with the same graceful savagery Valerie did, along with the cold calculation of a soldier of Elyisa that Ezekiel had drilled into me. I was precise with my weapons, both the curved blades as well as my sword, and I always kept them within arm's reach.

Valerie had been heavily encouraging me to leave the apartment over the past few weeks, not pressing too hard, as the mere thought of rejoining society had me running to the toilet to vomit, but still she insisted. And I knew she was right. So, we compromised, and I agreed to visit the library in the dead of night to visit Lumen. Not quite back in society, but still requiring to be slightly social.

But I was still unwilling to just walk all the way to the library, so

Valerie mercifully allowed us to cut the veil from within her apartment and exited just outside the doors of the library. The night air was brisk and made my new scars prickle uncomfortably, so I pushed my way through the large double doors, with Valerie and Ophelia in tow.

Lumen was sitting at the front desk, her nose buried in a book. She startled slightly at our entrance, her half-moon glasses sliding down her small nose.

Her stark white hair was styled into a beautiful, braided coronet atop her head, and she was dressed in a navy sweater that hung off her shoulder, exposing her rich brown skin and silver freckles.

"Blair! Oh my goddess, I am so happy to see that you're alright! Miles told me what happened..." Lumen stood, rushing around the front desk but stopping short when her amethyst eyes took in Valerie.

Tears welled in my eyes at her words, a painful reminder of why it had been so long since I had been here. What I had endured.

That first night exploring New Haven with Dean was so long ago, it felt like a hazy dream.

"I-I'm sorry, Lumen." I couldn't get any other words out, as flashes of Vivian bleeding out before me, each cut into my skin at the hands of demons, and of Dean's devastated face as I left played over and over in my mind.

I shut my eyes and began shaking, fear squeezing my heart as I tried to form words. Sweat trickled down my face and I bared my teeth at the memories, wincing at the sound of each cut into my skin.

"I told you it was too soon!" I barely heard Ophelia growl at Valerie over the roaring in my ears.

I had to get out. I needed to get out.

Cool, delicate hands wrapped around my own, and I opened my eyes to see Lumen before me, her large round eyes twinkling up at me with such gentleness I nearly fell to my knees. Star-kissed magic flowed from her fingers, wrapping around my scarred hands, and tiny glittering lights misted out from her slight figure.

The rest of the library lights dimmed at the use of her magic, only illuminated by the stars of Lumen.

"You are amongst friends dear, Blair. I swear that no harm will befall you while you are in my presence. I will shield your back, protect your secrets, and provide you comfort. That is my vow to you." Lumen stood before me like a beacon of light in a sea of darkness, and a single tear slid down my cheek at the spectacle of beautiful magic.

I gave her the barest of nods and squeezed her hands tightly in mine.

The stars faded away, and the ones tickling my hands traveled back into Lumen but left an iridescent sheen of glitter along my skin. The nightlights of the library glowed once more, but Lumen made no move to step away, her hands still holding my own.

"Thank you," I whispered. Ophelia wound herself around my legs, purring loudly, and Lumen gave me a small, understanding smile.

"I would like to show you something. Would that be alright, Blair?" Lumen's voice was like the chiming of delicate bells. I nodded, and she waited a beat for me to let her hands go before she began leading us deeper into the library.

She brought us into a small alcove in between shelves, a beautiful nook with a large plush chair, a side table, and lamp. Many pillows and blankets were scattered throughout the space, along with a rich mahogany coffee table piled with books and a kettle with teacups.

"I set aside this space for you to visit after we first met all those months ago and began collecting books I thought you might like to leave for you here. Even after Miles told me, I left them here for you, for whenever you returned." Her cheeks blushed a slight purple color, only illuminating her silver freckles even more.

I was speechless. The space was so warm and inviting, much like the reading room I had created in Vivian and I's home. Before I could utter a word of my gratitude, she continued.

"I, uh, I have a confession to make." I raised a brow, and she gave me a sheepish grin. "I have been setting aside ancient texts I think would be most beneficial for *you* to read." She gestured to the books on the table, all thick and worn with age.

I glanced at Valerie, who was regarding Lumen warily now before I went and picked up the book on the top of the pile. At first glance, the text appeared foreign, and I could not make out the language, but as I studied the cover, silver magic flashed over the book, lighting up the faded words on the cover and morphing them into words I could recognize. The title read: The History of Angels.

My eyes nearly bugged out of my head as I whipped around to look at Lumen, whose blush had deepened, spreading from her cheeks down to her neck. Valerie blocked the exit to the nook and leaned casually against the wooden bookcase. "Explain." That velvet voice hardened to steel as she studied the fae female.

Lumen shrugged. "I'm a researcher, and when I felt your magic the first night we met, I knew right away what you were." She wrung her hands together nervously as her amethyst gaze flicked between Valerie, Ophelia, and me. "I've met angels, been around them a lot in Gaia's realm, and your magic is similar, but also so much more complex, containing traces from more than one realm. Naturally, I started looking into why you were so much more powerful, and I just made an educated guess. You needn't worry about me telling anyone. I don't exactly have a lot of friends; my sister has made sure of that. I only want to help you, Blair. I swear it."

I looked to Valerie, finding her golden gaze was assessing Lumen with those warrior eyes. Then they flicked to me, and she gave me a shrug as if to say, 'Your call'.

"She speaks the truth, Blair. I can smell it on her. We can trust her," Ophelia piped up from the plush chair, already curled into a little ball, her chartreuse eyes glowing in the dim light.

"Well, Lumen, teach me what you know about the Nephilim." I gathered a few pillows and a blanket, making myself a little nest near the table as I looked at her expectantly. Lumen smiled brightly as she sat across from me, crossing her legs and grabbing a book to pull into her lap. Valerie smiled and joined us, and we all nestled in for a long night.

Chapter Thirty-Two

Other than late-night library visits with Lumen and my rigorous training, I indulged myself with bourbon, which Brodie begrudgingly dropped off a crate of for me once a week. I didn't know why he indulged me the way he did. Maybe he understood the pain I felt. I didn't care either way.

But even the bourbon wouldn't keep the nightmares away.

Zeke was having to swoop in and save me from the raging Alistair as he invaded my dreamscape more and more frequently, furious that I had escaped his clutches. I didn't bother to correct him, that Gadreel had willingly let me go.

It was a fact that kept my mind busy during the nights where I was too terrified to go to sleep, but the only conclusion I could draw from it was far more terrifying than the nightmares Alistair's dreamwalker conjured. Gadreel wasn't done with me yet. And that thought alone made my blood run cold and my insides twist up in fear. Memories of a mention of a ritual of some sort resurfaced, but no matter how much I tried to remember the details, if any were ever disclosed to me, I couldn't. Whether my brain was trying to protect me from the horror of those memories, or if they simply didn't exist, I wasn't sure.

While in the dreamscape, I trained with Zeke. I was now proficient in all angelic weaponry, even though it took some encouragement to even touch a blade after having so many cut through me over and over again.

He was a good and patient teacher, and he never pried too much as to what I had gone through, although the scars probably said enough.

On what few nights Alistair stayed away, the memories of torture at the hands of Gadreel tormented my dreams. The light blinking out of Vivian's eyes, and blood, so much blood. Skin and muscle being torn apart, bones being broken over and over again. My screams rattled the house, my magic a constant unstable beast, threatening to decimate the entire block.

Valerie and Ophelia had to work together to rouse me awake, and when they did, I usually ran to the bathroom to vomit, whispering broken apologies between sobs.

Dean checked in and asked to see me a few times each week. Miles, Sage, Hayley, and even Cal had come by as well. And every week I had denied them, while ignoring Ophelia's pleas for me to just let them see me.

The weather was turning cool in the city, and I liked to watch from the window all the preparations for Samhain next week, which the city threw massive celebrations for. Lights and decorations were being hung throughout the city's streets, and laughter and excitement floated up through the windows. I lifted my current bottle of bourbon to my mouth and drank heavily.

Samhain was my birthday.

The last birthday I celebrated, the year before I checked myself into St. Christopher's, I had spent it with Vivian and Sage, drinking until they passed out under the stars.

It was the perfect birthday. We had gathered out on Vivian's patio with blankets and pillows next to the firepit and stared at the night sky laughing, dancing, and singing along to whatever song came on Sage's playlist blaring over the speakers.

The doorbell sounded, and I sunk lower against the windowsill. The smell of leather and amber wafted up in the breeze, and I breathed it in, torturing myself with his scent. I heard Dean's low voice at the door. Ophelia joined me, peering over the ledge and giving me a pointed look. I shook my head and swigged again. She let out a sigh and snuggled into my lap, her warmth curbing the bite of the autumn breeze.

I heard the door shut and watched as Dean stalked down the steps. Just as he was about to turn the corner he stopped, his head tilting up slightly, as if he could hear the way my heart was pounding at the sight of him. He turned and looked right at me, despite my efforts to remain hidden behind the rust-colored curtains. Even in the distance, I could see his glacier-blue eyes staring directly into my soul, pinning me to the spot.

That faint tether between us tugged at the sight of him, and if I had less self-restraint, I would have leapt out the window to go to him.

But I was not ready to face him. The wounds on my body may have been long healed, but the ones inside me had not, and I couldn't bear to let him see the still broken pieces. My heart longed to embrace him, embrace the light he brought to my shadow of a soul, the lone spark in the endless darkness. But he deserved more than my broken self.

He gave me a sad smile, and I felt what remained of my heart fracture, because I saw in his eyes undying devotion for me, and that he would keep coming back. With a slight dip of his head, he turned and continued down the street, avoiding the decorators, and faded into the night.

Valerie walked into the room and plopped down on the armchair in the corner with an envelope in her hands. Wordlessly, she handed it to me. The silver wax seal had a crescent moon with the head of a wolf howling adorning the center.

My hands were shaking as I opened it.

It was an invitation to the council of New Haven's Samhain celebration at the mansion of one of the council members. The attire was formal, and it would take place on the holiday itself. Behind the invitation was another piece of paper that read:

Blair,
For your nightmares.
Hamish Thornblood.
Ever yours,
Dean

"We're going. Only a dragon or another dreamwalker can break the connection of your subconscious away from Alistair's control. That'll take care of that problem at least," Valerie murmured, giving me a hard look as I glowered at her.

"And what of the other nightmares?" I snapped.

Her face softened only slightly as her honey eyes assessed the state of me. Dark circles sat beneath my brown and silver eyes, my hair was in a tangled heap on the top of my head, and I only ever wore pajamas and the battle leathers I used to train.

I know what she saw when she looked at me. No light. No hope.

"I think an evening out would do wonders for your aching heart. Especially with a certain male who has visited *every night*, even if he doesn't always approach the house. Your heart needs to heal, Blair. You can't keep everyone at arm's length away for the rest of your life."

I snorted at her. Like hell I couldn't.

Her brows furrowed. "And what of my life? You live with me. I am in as much *danger* as Dean's pack for harboring you," she reminded me.

"You have the Angel of Death's protection, oh powerful reaper. You command legions. I think it would be rather difficult for anyone to harm you," I drawled, flourishing my arms.

"Excuses. Death and danger are at the mercy of the Fates, and they favor no one. I would know. Valkyries used to reap the souls of unsuspecting warriors in battle, many of them thinking themselves invincible," she retorted, voice flat. "You're afraid, and it is not a weakness, Blair. To care for others. To love. To let others share the burden of your pain." Her eyes turned sad, and she stood, heading for the door but pausing right before the threshold. She turned and murmured, "If it weren't for the darkness, light would never shine."

Chapter Thirty-Three

"I am not wearing that." I grimaced at the satin fabric lying on the bed, then looked back at Ophelia and Valerie. I eyed the dress and then flicked my gaze to the mirror hanging on the wall, wincing slightly at my disheveled appearance. It was the night of the Samhain celebration, and despite promising I would attend, I was having second thoughts.

I wasn't sure I was ready to be around so many supes, nor to attend such a formal event, something I had never experienced before.

In addition to that, it was my birthday, and even though I knew attending the gala was in my best interest to find this Hamish Thornblood guy and convince him to sever the connection between myself and the dreamwalker, I didn't feel like celebrating, and I wished I could just curl up in bed alone.

The day just felt meaningless. I didn't think I was worth celebrating, and the memories of previous birthdays spent with Vivian and Sage only threatened to bring me to tears. Which was also why I didn't tell Valerie or Ophelia what today was. Even if I suspected

Ophelia already knew, she didn't mention it, respecting my feelings on the matter.

Over this last week, I cut back on the bourbon, showered every day, got up at a semi-reasonable hour, and busied myself with more than just fighting, drinking, and reading.

Valerie and I walked throughout the city, visiting merchants and shops, stopping in restaurants, a new one each day. Though, by the end of the week I was slightly worn out from the daily outings, so I skipped shopping the day prior, wanting to bury myself in a pile of books at the library with Ophelia at my side.

Valerie did most of the talking during our outings, while I focused on breathing and trying not to flinch every time someone's arm brushed against mine on the street. As the week went on, I became more comfortable with wearing clothing that showed the scars on my arms and legs, ignoring any strange looks directed my way, although there were far fewer than I would have expected.

"Yes, you are. This is your punishment for not going shopping with me yesterday, so you have to wear what I bought you. And don't act so disgusted, I have excellent taste." Valerie sniffed, plucking some invisible lint off her black velvet dress that hugged her every curve.

It had thin straps that crossed at the back, the neckline a deep V-cut that nearly went to her navel, showing her generous cleavage. Her lips were colored a deep wine to match her hair, and gold simmered on her eyelids, making her eyes glow.

I looked back at the dress she had picked for me, so simple yet stunning. I sighed, resigned to the evening ahead of me.

I shucked off the robe I was wearing and slipped into the dress. The satin was cool against my skin, and the tight bodice was surprisingly comfortable. Before I could look in the mirror, Valerie ushered me into a chair so she could begin on my makeup and hair. My eyes were wide as I watched all the various tools and brushes she used, having never gone to a salon before. Whether Valerie realized this or not, she explained what she was doing and why she used each product, and I was grateful for the distraction. Nerves had been building up within me the entire day; the event was yet another thing that was new and foreign.

She worked with the precision and seriousness she held with all things, and despite my constant griping when her brush snagged on a tangle, or when a makeup brush got far too close to my eye, she continued briskly. She finally stepped away with a satisfied smirk, gesturing for me to look in the mirror.

I hardly recognized who was staring back at me. The dark circles, by some miracle, were gone. My face had its natural olive tone instead of the pale mess it had been since returning to New Haven. My eyes were lined with black eyeliner and winged out giving me the perfect siren-eyed look, bringing out the upward angle of my eyes. My lips were full and plump with a dusty-rose color, nothing too bright to take away from the dress.

The bodice of the dress was like a second skin, and the cowl neckline showed off the swell of my generous breasts. At the waist, the dress flowed out and pooled at my feet, with a slit running up the side, almost all the way to my hip.

It was by far the fanciest article of clothing I had ever put on, and I was struck speechless.

The satin was the brightest silver, nearly matching the ring of color in my eyes. The shade of the dress gave my skin a luminous glow, even with the scars, now healed completely and no longer angry and red. I found I wasn't bothered anymore at the sight of them. They told a story of strength.

I turned to find my raven-colored hair hanging in loose curls down my back, slightly wild looking, as if the wind had styled it. Even as my hair moved and I caught sight of the scars from the whip peeking out from the top of the dress, I didn't falter.

I found myself smiling, and Valerie placed simple silver heels at my feet, which I donned quickly. Without thinking, I whirled and pulled Valerie into a hug.

She had managed to breathe a little bit of light back into me, and though I was still broken, I was healing. She was slow to embrace me back, caught off guard by my sudden affection, but eventually she gave me a slight squeeze.

"Thank you, my friend, for everything," I choked out, trying to suck the tears back into my eyes to avoid ruining my makeup.

She held me tighter, and we lingered there for a moment.

Even though this started out as a job given to her by my father, our connection was deeper now, a fierce friendship that was felt deep within our spirits. The pain of losing Vivian still cut through me, making me nearly break all over again, but with Valerie around, the ache was slightly dulled, manageable.

We exited her apartment together, clad in our finery, including Ophelia, who was in her larger form, sporting a stunning jeweled collar around her neck. Her shadows whipped happily around her. I ruffled her ears, and she looked shocked at first but began batting my hand away playfully. My heart squeezed; I had shut everyone out, including my familiar, whom my soul was bonded to so closely.

Her chartreuse eyes turned to me, twinkling with understanding as she nudged my hand with her head in reassurance.

I slashed a hand gently through the air, opening the portal, and we stepped through, emerging next to a large fountain facing an immaculate sandstone mansion with ornately carved columns lining the front entrance.

"Lucky we didn't land in the fountain," I joked, and my companions chuckled.

Together we walked along the gravel path leading up to the monstrosity of a house. Valerie dipped her head in greeting for a few of the supes she knew, and I clenched my jaw tightly at how many supes I was already surrounded by.

I had worked hard to be comfortable in public again, but I still found myself counting my breaths and focusing on the cool caress Ophelia's shadows provided as they wound around my legs. I didn't deserve her.

Hecate deemed us worthy of each other.

I smiled at her, giving her a slight nod as we finally made our way up the many steps leading into the house.

The foyer was breathtaking. A spiral staircase led to the upper levels of the house and was decorated with lights and various wildflowers and viny plants, giving a forbidden forest vibe. There were candles everywhere, illuminating the space with a warm glow that softened the stark white walls.

Valerie grabbed my hand to pull me along into what I could only describe as the ballroom off to the right. We were greeted by a waiter that handed us flutes of champagne before he continued to mill about the room.

I felt him before I saw him, like a tingling spark deep within my chest. Dean was standing at the far end of the room at the bar, ordering a drink.

Gods, he looked *good*. He was dressed in a black suit with a crisp white shirt and a smart tie that was loosened from his neck in the sexiest way. I saw his nostrils flare slightly, and he turned his head towards me, his eyes raking over my entire body hungrily, making my toes curl.

The bartender handed him a glass filled with amber liquid, and Dean grabbed it quickly and began making his way through the crowd straight to me.

I couldn't deal with him just yet. Liquid courage, that's what I needed right now. I quickly downed my flute of champagne and mumbled about getting a drink to Ophelia and Valerie before I hurried to the bar on the opposite side of the room, where the bartender gladly filled my order and watched me slam it just as quick with wide eyes.

"You look like a vicious little thing."

I glanced to my left, where a tall male was leaning against the bar with an intrigued look on his face. His hair was a remarkable silver blond, and it hung to his chin with a slight wild wave. His eyes were a blueish gray, like a storm cloud, and he was dressed in a suit of similar colors.

"Vicious doesn't even begin to cover it," I snapped at him before signaling for another drink. I was in no mood to entertain a drunken flirt. Not with an alpha wolf no doubt stalking me through the crowd and the nervous ball of energy buzzing in my gut.

"I like that," the stranger purred, and I rolled my eyes.

He stepped closer, and I felt his energy swirling around me like vapor and pulsing with strong, wild magic that matched his scent of smoke and embers.

"What are you?" I faced him, and he flashed me a lazy grin, his drink sloshing slightly as he bowed.

"A damn good time, that's all that matters. Hamish Thornblood, at your service." I stiffened, remembering the note Dean gave me. "Though, if you'd like to use my *services*, you'd need to speak with that gentleman over there, who owns my contract currently. Big bastard."

My eyes followed where he motioned, landing on the largest ogre I had ever seen, scowling at me from a high-top table a few feet away. His blue skin was marred with scars, and one of his tusks that protruded from his bottom lip was broken at the tip.

Great.

"Well, he looks like a peach. What do you mean by contract?" I swirled my drink around, attempting to be casual.

He shrugged. "Just a pretty word for slave essentially. I've been sold to various supe leaders for my gifts for two centuries now." He pulled up the sleeve of his shirt, exposing a tattoo around his wrist. The ink was blue, and it was intricately designed to look like chains buried beneath the skin.

He downed his drink as I wrinkled my nose in disgust.

Contracts such as his have been banned for centuries now, a decree made by the gods themselves. Though, if they were bound by old magic, it is possible that he is still bound into slavery.

Ophelia's voice flowed through my mind, and I felt her physical presence close by, but not close enough to alert Hamish.

"If your gifts are the kind of gifts I'm looking for, could I buy you out of it?"

"*All* of my gifts are the ones people look for. Doubt you could afford it, though, wicked temptress. Ogres are extremely barbaric creatures. He'd sooner have you challenge him for it than just sell it. He's not so eager to line his pockets with coin; his desires are more egotistical."

As if he heard Hamish's words, the hulking ogre came stomping over, his hands curled into tight fists that looked more like bowling balls. He and his clansmen all wore varying colored two-piece suits that were nearly busting at the seams at the sheer size of them.

"Back off, bitch, that's my property. I suggest you find someone else to warm your bed tonight. *This one* has other obligations." His voice sounded like he had rocks rolling around in his large jowls, and I felt a drop of spit fly out of his mouth and hit my cheek. A few of his clansmen came up behind him, all just as huge as him, glowering at me.

I simply wiped the spit away and finished my drink before turning back to him.

I pulled on that lingering swagger I had before being taken, letting it fill me up before I purred, "Since I'm feeling generous, I'll ignore what you just called me. If you're going to insult me, at least get creative with it. And as a courtesy, I won't break all the bones in your body for not keeping your spit to yourself." I paused, glancing at Hamish out of the corner of my eye, a wicked grin spreading across my face. "I challenge you for his contract."

The ogres all roared in outrage, causing the chandeliers overhead to shake.

"That's enough, Bane. This is a celebration, and I will not have you ruining this night for everyone." A tall female appeared at our sides, glaring at the ogre. She was slender, with pale skin and onyx hair, wearing a sparkling black off-shoulder dress that pooled like liquid night at her feet.

Her beauty was fearsome, but what held my attention most were her upwardly slanted glowing yellow eyes, with black slits down the middle.

He ignored her. "Tomorrow night, our woods at sunset. I'll enjoy crushing your skull between my hands, *bitch*," he boomed, spit flying, but I gave him a bored wave. He and his clansmen lumbered off with Hamish trailing behind, but not before he turned to give me a wink and a drink salute.

The woman in black shifted towards me, her brows pinched with displeasure. "I know you are new here, so I will give you one pass. Any fights or brawls that are a direct result of your actions, I will personally put an end to and then to you. Do I make myself clear?" Her aura was dark, and she radiated an ancient sort of power that nearly had me trembling. I gave her a small nod of understanding. "Valerie, keep her in check."

"Apologies, Nathara, won't happen again." I didn't know Valerie had been behind me, but she was a reassuring presence at my back.

Recognition flared inside me at the name. She was the council member Dean had wanted me to meet all those months ago, one of the first supes created by Hecate.

She titled her head as she looked over me, cataloguing every visible scar as she did. I lifted my chin, which only caused her to curl her purple painted lips into a smile. "Despite the unpleasantness of our first meeting, I am glad to finally be making your acquaintance, Blair."

I dipped my head in respect. "As am I. Your home is lovely."

Her smile widened at the compliment. "Thank you. I was pleased when I heard you would be in attendance. I wish to speak with you in private, so I will find you later in the evening." Her tone offered no room for argument, and I merely nodded again.

Nathara looked over me again with those snake-like eyes before she spun on her heel and disappeared into a throng of onlookers. I nearly shuddered as that ancient power slithered away with her.

"A little advice? Don't piss her off." Valerie paused, eyeing the ogres at the far end of the room. "Think you can take him? You haven't faced an ogre yet."

I scoffed. "Piece of cake. I'm stronger now, and besides, size isn't everything." I gave her a mischievous grin. She nearly spit her drink out, choking on her laugh, which only brought laughter to my own lips.

Gods, how long had it been since I'd done that?

"Her skin looks like she's been a chew toy for the past few months. You'd think she'd have chosen a dress that would have covered up those horrendous scars." Rose's voice snapped me out of my laughter, and I glared towards her.

She was wearing a short white corseted cocktail dress that left little to the imagination. She was snickering with another werewolf I didn't recognize, and they were both looking at the scars that littered my body.

Ophelia let out a warning growl, her elongated fangs gleaming in the candlelight, but I cut her off with a wave of my hand.

"Have something to say, Rose?" I asked her sweetly, turning towards her with my head held high. I brushed my hair off my shoulders, revealing more scars, wearing them like armor. Valerie remained at my side, looking down at the she-wolf with visible disdain.

Rose stepped up to me and popped out a hip as she smirked. "Just that it's a good thing a piece of trash like you moved out of pack territory. That those scars make you look like the miserable weakling that you are. You don't deserve Dean." She nearly spat the last words at me, and I saw the wolf flash in her eyes.

The room was nearly silent, everyone waiting and listening.

I stepped into Rose's space, so close she had to look up at me as I purred, "You think you could have survived what I went through, Rose? I'd have you begging for death within minutes of doing to your body what was done to mine. If you'd like a demonstration, I'd be happy to give it to you." The lights flickered above me as grace leaked out of me.

She tried to fight submitting as she continued to glare at me. I focused my power on her, pushing, making her squirm, and reluctantly she tore her eyes away to look at the floor.

I pulled my power back in with an easy breath, and low murmuring broke out among the guests. I knew it was risky, using my power like that, but I didn't think about the consequences. I only thought about how I wanted rip Rose's face off for how her words had stung.

I turned away from her, and she snarled, offended that I turned my back on her despite her submission. I already had my grace built up in an invisible shield behind me when I felt the familiar press of alpha energy slam into the space.

Dean's voice was a promise of death as he growled, "If you lay one claw on her, Rose, you will lose that hand. Don't. Fucking. Touch. Her." I turned back to see her claws phasing back into a human hand, her lip curled as she glared at me. "Get out of my sight," Dean snarled at her, and she turned tail with a whimper and left the room, taking her friend with her.

He growled again at the party guests who were staring, and they quickly found something else to be occupied with as the music started up again.

Dean sighed as he adjusted his jacket and turned to me. "Been here five minutes and you're already causing fights, huh, Raven?" Dean chuckled, moving in front of me with that animalistic grace that would have lesser creatures cowering in fear.

I snorted. "First of all, I didn't start anything. But I would have gladly finished it," I said sweetly, letting my gaze slowly take him in.

His hair was longer, dark curls nearly hanging at his shoulders now. His face was clean shaven, but his smile was still as cocky as it had always been. His chuckle was a deep, wonderful sound that I could listen to again and again.

"I have no doubts about that." He paused, looking me over again. "Happy birthday, Blair."

My eyes widened as he flicked his fingers at the bartender to order another bourbon before sliding the drink over to me. I felt Ophelia and Valerie fading into the crowd, giving us privacy. I took it, letting our fingers graze slightly, which sent shocks skittering up my arm and towards my heart.

"Thanks. How did you know?" I quirked a brow at him as he stepped closer, his scent overwhelming my senses. Everyone else in the room faded away as I looked into those cerulean eyes that twinkled with mischief.

"Sage. She filled me in on all things Blair." He gave me a wink, and I rolled by eyes before giving him a small smirk.

I surveyed the room, trying to look anywhere but at the devastatingly handsome werewolf before me. Nearby I saw Cal, Hayley, and Brodie grouped at a high-top table, acting like they weren't watching us. I rolled my eyes and gave them a tentative wave.

"Nosey mother hens. Sage and Miles stayed behind tonight," Dean explained, and I nodded, slightly sad. I had so much I wanted to say to my friends. To apologize.

"Dean, I—"

"You don't need to explain yourself, Blair. You lost your parent, and then you went through something so... I don't think most supes could have gone through what you did and still be standing here. Looking like fucking goddess, I might add."

I blushed, and when he reached up and caressed my cheek, I did not flinch.

He added, "Whenever you are ready to come back—*if* you want to come back, you'll always have a place with me and with my pack. I'm all yours."

Before I could say anything back, he was reaching into his jacket pocket, and I eyed him warily as he pulled out a square velvet box with a silver bow tied around it and set it on the bar-top between us. I inhaled sharply as I looked at the box, slowly bringing my eyes back to his, suddenly feeling shy.

"Aren't you going to open it?" he challenged me, and though his tone was joking, his cerulean gaze was filled with such raw emotion and uncertainty as he watched my reaction.

My fingers were shaking as they reached for the box and gently pulled the silver ribbon, setting the delicate fabric down before I pried open the box. Gleaming brightly inside was a necklace with a crescent moon pendent made from moonstone, identical to the one I had found and returned to Hayley he morning after I arrived in New Haven. Tears welled in my eyes, and I delicately reached out to stroke the cool stone.

Words were stuck in my throat, and my heart squeezed painfully as I looked back up to Dean, who peered nervously back at me.

"My mother had a second one made, identical to the one my father had made for her and gave it to me. She wanted me to give it to my... she wanted me to give it to someone special to me. I would like for you to wear it, if you'll accept it?"

I still couldn't speak, could hardly breathe as I looked back at the gorgeous necklace. I bit my lip, unable to stop the blush from staining my cheeks as I nodded shyly. Dean beamed, and I turned, moving my hair away from my neck as I did so. The metal was cool as he slid the chain around my neck, making sure to keep it loose, and quickly clasped it, only pausing to brush his fingers across my skin, which pebbled in response.

I turned back, letting my hair fall back into place. My hand reached up to stroke the pendant once more as I whispered, "Thank you."

His eyes sparkled with the intensity of the stars, but I couldn't muster the courage to say all I wanted to. So, I knocked my drink back and placed it on the bar top, choosing a more familiar emotion instead.

He was so understanding, so committed, *so handsome* it nearly made my blood boil. Surely, this was worse than pity. Shouldn't he be angry with me? Furious that I never answered the door when he came to check on me? Hurt that I used him for his body and left? Worried that I was nothing more than damaged goods now?

It was as if—it was as if he could see right through me.

"Dance with me," he commanded, holding out his calloused hand to me.

But it wasn't just a dance, was it? It was a step back into the life I fell into all those months ago. "No." My voice was shaky, and not convincing, and Dean quirked a dark brow at my rushed response.

"Afraid you'd enjoy yourself?" he challenged me.

The truth was, I was afraid. Not of the dancing, but of the emotions that stirred within me when I was around this male. I hesitated, only for a moment, before letting out a sigh and taking his hand. He smiled, killing his own drink before pulling me to his side as we made our way to the dancefloor.

The song was a beautiful melody as he twirled me around, his hand staying right on my hip, and I found I didn't mind the touch. Not from him. I trusted him, and whatever walls I had erected after being held captive seemed to fall away at his presence.

I didn't know if I had worked through enough anger, enough of the pain in my weeks of drinking and fighting, but I felt lighter. Like I could breathe again.

It was why I had avoided him all this time. Dean had the unique ability of breaking down any barrier I built up to keep others away. He made me near murderous with his alpha-hole nature, his overprotectiveness, his arrogance. But he also understood me on the most primal level that no one had ever even gotten close to seeing before.

That damn tether between us was constantly pulling me towards him, despite all the fear of letting anyone in, that he could get hurt because of me. That his family could get hurt because of me.

But being in his orbit calmed the well of power within me, centered my magic, soothed the twin beasts within our souls. It terrified me how much I wanted him, needed him. How I craved merely a whiff of his scent, and that I lingered by the window every night just hoping to catch the breeze of it when he left the stoop.

How I wanted to rip apart Rose for saying I didn't deserve him.

Because she was right, I didn't deserve him. He was the light to my darkness, and I was afraid that I would swallow up the light he emitted. Strike him down as sure as lightning lit up the sky.

Despite all of that, I kept dancing.

Chapter Thirty-Four

I found myself smiling and enjoying myself as the hours passed by, filled with dancing, drinking, and laughing at the cheesy pickup lines Dean kept whispering to me as he held me close on the dancefloor. I was so at ease with him that all the other supes in the crowd faded away into the background. There was only him.

But even he couldn't keep the guilt I felt at bay for having experienced one moment of happiness when Vivian died because of me.

I excused myself as the song ended, needing to get out of this room and out amongst the trees and the open sky.

But before I could find the exit, Nathara stepped into my path. "Leaving so soon, Blair?" A thin black brow lifted expectantly, and I cursed myself for not remembering, having been caught up in my time with Dean.

"Apologies, Nathara, I only needed some air." I avoided making direct eye contact, remembering Dean's advice from so long ago.

Her aura pulsed a bright yellow, amusement, and orange, which I guessed was curiosity.

She tilted her head, beckoning me to follow her from the room. I obliged but kept my magic close to the surface. Ophelia was nearby, I could feel it, but I reassured her that I would be alright alone with Nathara, even if I was unsure whether that was actually true.

Our heels clicked against the marble floor, echoing in the high ceilings, the sounds of the party fading away as we walked deeper into her mansion.

She paused in front of a painting that depicted the Goddess of Magic herself, each of her three forms visible, wearing her triple-moon phase crown gleaming starkly against the hues of purple and black background. The Maiden to the left of the artwork held a dagger up to the sky, the mischief and defiance in her eyes evident even in a painting. In the middle was the Mother, her features slightly older than the Maiden, her dress more modest, holding a large key in her hands. And to the right was the Crone, her hair entirely gray, her skin wrinkled and withered. She held up a torch, illuminating the space around them.

My skin prickled, as I felt Nathara's gaze no longer on the painting but on me as I stared up at it. "Your presence in New Haven has interested me for some time, Blair. I would have met you earlier, but circumstances were not kind to you."

I couldn't tear my gaze away from the ethereal artwork and only met her with silence, unsure of how to respond.

She continued, "I am glad our goddess was able to guide you back."

Finally, I looked to Nathara, curiosity getting the better of me. "Why does my presence interest you so?" I dared a glance into her yellow eyes and found the slits expanding with that same curiosity I felt within me. The corner of her lips tilted up slightly.

"Perhaps it was our connection to the same goddess? Or perhaps it was far simpler than that. Power calls to power, as you well know. There aren't many in this city whose power demands respect such as ours."

I stiffened at that, but she merely turned her round face back toward the painting, staring almost lovingly up at the goddess.

"I do not think what dwells within me deserves anything," I

murmured quietly, looking in my mind's eye at that locked cage where that darkness dwelled, flinching away from the purr it gave me.

"You're wrong, but deep down, I think you know that, even if you are too scared to admit it." I bristled at her accusation but said nothing. "But that is not why I wished to speak with you tonight. I merely wished to meet you and offer my assistance should you ever need it. I have been around a long time, and my vast knowledge could be of use to you, as would my close relationship to our goddess."

I raised my eyebrows, surprise filling me as I looked at the ancient being before me. "Why would you offer such a thing? You don't know me."

She turned back to me, and this time I held no fear as I looked into her eyes. Nathara studied my face, and in turn I studied her, trying to figure out what sort of creature lurked beneath that pale skin.

Nathara stepped in close, that ancient power pressing against my own, beckoning it to come out and play, and I had to work hard to keep it in check. "As I said, power calls to power, and you, Blair, are about to be drowning in it." Without another word, she walked away, heels clicking as she went, leaving me alone in the hallway, with only the painting of the Goddess of Magic to keep me company.

When I finally exited the mansion, the moon was shining brightly overhead, casting a luminous glow throughout the pines. The forest was quiet, singing a mournful song that called to the inner witch in me, to heal and to breathe.

I made my way to a flat, grassy knoll and sat down, letting the cool night breeze leave a chill on my skin. I soon felt Dean's presence behind me, his scent riding the breeze like a gentle caress. Ophelia lingered nearby, always my shadow, but she remained out of sight.

"I know you looked for me," I breathed as Dean joined me on the grass, overlooking a beautiful pond that reflected the stars. We sat so close our arms brushed against each other, and his blissful heat wrapped around me, shielding me from the crisp autumn air.

"I would have torn worlds apart to find you, Blair. I never would have stopped." His deep voice was so strong, filled with truth and conviction, and I felt his eyes on my face.

I gingerly took my heels off, letting my feet sink into the blades of grass. They were cool, slightly wet with dew, and I felt the gentle magic of the earth reach out to greet my own like an old friend.

I would endure it all again, I realized.

For him.

"I didn't think I'd ever see you again. Any of you. I thought I would die down there," I whispered.

Dean made a move like he wanted to put his arm around me but stopped and placed his hand back in his lap. I sighed and grabbed it, draping it over my shoulder and snuggling closer to him. His chest rumbled.

"I want to tell you what happened to me. And what happened after. I'm sorry I couldn't—I couldn't talk about it when I got back. I was so broken from Vivian's death and what they did to me, and I just needed you, needed to feel something that wasn't... I don't want you to think..." My voice faded, tears already falling down my cheeks.

"You wanted to feel something other than pain," Dean murmured.

I merely nodded, not being able to look at him, for he saw me so clearly, perhaps more clearly than I saw myself.

He gently grasped my chin between his thumb and forefinger, turning my face to look up at his. He quietly wiped the tears away before saying, "Whatever you need me to be, I'm yours. And whenever you're ready to tell me about what happened, I'm here to listen. And if you never want to speak of it again, I will not push you or ask." Dean studied my face, his breath mingling with my own, and I leaned in and gently kissed him.

His lips were soft and tender, letting me take the lead. He cradled my face like it was the most precious thing he held in his hands. He pulled away first, to press another kiss to my forehead, then drew me in closer to his body, resting his head atop my own, breathing in my scent.

And under the light of the moon, in the early hours of the morning after my birthday, I told him what had happened to me. Every detail of what I had endured in Gadreel's dungeon.

I told him the reason Gadreel and Alistair were after me. That I was a Nephilim, a secret I had not told anyone else since finding out. A secret that could be used to his own advantage if he wished it. But I knew I could trust him; I could feel it deep within the dark pockets of my soul.

Dean listened quietly, his eyes the only thing giving away his emotions, either widening with surprise or blazing a blue hellfire. And with each word, a shard of my broken self managed to piece back together. There were still cracks, like open wounds, but as I sat there, basking in the moonlight with Dean, I knew that they would heal in time. I cried and lost my words during some of my story, but Dean waited patiently for me to start up again, wiping away the tears and stroking soothing circles along my arm.

I finished, feeling like an immense weight had been lifted from my shoulders.

"Gadreel doesn't know that he did complete his task, not fully, but he did break me into pieces. I'm still broken. And knowing what I am only makes the guilt worse, like I'm constantly putting everyone in danger. I've been hiding—hiding from the pain, hiding from the anger, from happiness. Because in the end, after what happened to Vivian..." My voice broke, and I couldn't finish the sentence.

"You did not deserve what happened to you. Don't ever think that," Dean said fiercely, and I gave him a sad smile, but he continued, "After my parents died, I felt fractured, like there were these massive holes within myself that would never close. I blamed myself because I couldn't save them, that I wasn't there when it happened. I tortured myself, wondering if it would have been different if I had pushed harder to go with them.

"I lived with those holes in my heart for so long, until one day, they slowly started filling back up, piece by piece. At first, it was so small I hardly knew it was happening, but over time, I felt like I could finally let myself be happy again. But it wasn't until the first glimpse of you in that Fates granted vision that I felt truly alive, that every choice I have made in this life was leading me to you. And when I lost you, I could not go down that road again, so I refused to give up, refused to stop looking for you. Because you, Blair, you are where I feel at peace, where my soul can rest. You feel like home."

His dark-ringed glacier eyes shined with such truth, I didn't think I was breathing. And though I wanted to tell him the truth that was sitting right on my tongue, that he was my salvation too, I just nestled in closer to him as we watched the sunrise.

* * *

I slept the entirety of the next day, only to be woken up by Valerie barging into my room and throwing my leathers at me. I had missed our training session, and blessedly, Zeke hadn't summoned me in my sleep, nor had Alistair come to torture me.

I felt well-rested, which was good, as I was heading into ogre territory to challenge Bane for Hamish's contract.

Valerie helped me braid my hair up and away from my face, leaving half of it down in loose curls at my back. I strapped my blades to me, and Ophelia shifted into her larger form, her shadows swirling around her in excitement. Valerie briefly explained the challenge rules to me, and though they were not complex, they were considered law among supes.

The most important one being that if anyone interfered with the challengers, they forfeited not only their life, but the challenger's as well.

As we stepped out of her apartment, I was surprised to see Dean and Cal waiting for us at the bottom of the steps. Dean's eyes lit up when he saw me, and Cal gave me a slight smile and a dip of his head in greeting.

I walked up and gave Cal a hug, pushing through my unease at the touch, which he gently returned, always far more reserved than the other wolves. As I turned to Dean, his hands wrapped around my waist before he planted a kiss on my forehead. I closed my eyes as I breathed him in, immediately calmed by his touch and woodsy scent.

Something had been repaired between us after last night, and my draw towards him was stronger than ever.

We gathered together in front of the brownstone before Valerie cut the veil in front of us, and we stepped through, emerging at the base of one of the many surrounding mountains.

Twin boulders marked the entrance into their community, lined with torches and two green-skinned ogres, who waved us through with a sneer. As we made our way through the stones, I saw a large bonfire burning high, flicking embers into the sky. Many ogres were already waiting for us there. Massive stone homes were scattered throughout the thinned trees leading up into the rocky terrain of the surrounding mountains, some built into the base of them.

Dean growled, taking in the scene in front of us. "If I had known this was how to gain the dragon's help, I would have challenged Bane for his contract myself." He shifted his body closer, nearly blocking me from the view of the sneering ogres.

I rolled my eyes, even if a small smile graced my lips at his over-protectiveness.

He had told me that his contacts had only given him a name and that the dragon would be in attendance at the Samhain celebration. I patted his shoulder and moved around him. While I appreciated his protective nature and the small thrill it gave me, I didn't mind the challenge. In fact, I was looking forward to it.

Bane emerged from the gathering crowd, naked from the waste up, wearing a leather skirt decorated with teeth and small bones intricately woven into the waistline.

A few other ogres were wearing similar outfits, armed with shields and giant wooden clubs or swords, but the rest of the onlookers donned normal clothes, just ogre-sized. I never thought I'd see an ogre wearing khaki shorts and a polo, but there's a first time for everything apparently.

Hamish stood off to the side, looking bored at the entire exchange, but his body language was rigid and watchful. His storm-gray eyes swiveled to me, and I gave him a quick wink as I swaggered my way up to the bonfire. I let my shoulders roll and my strides appear lazy, exuding the confidence that I knew would throw Bane into a rage.

Dean was already strutting in a similar manner, and when Bane looked between the two of us, his face twisted into an ugly snarl.

"Don't look so happy to see me, Bane," I drawled as we came to a stop on the other side of the burning pile. His face turned a deep shade of purple, and he ground his teeth so hard, it sounded like rocks scraping together. "Do you answer my challenge for the contract of Hamish Thornblood?" I let my voice carry throughout the clearing, and the surrounding ogres stiffened, hanging on every word.

"I accept your challenge," he growled before giving a curt nod to one of the other ogres in uniform. The crowd parted, and the first female ogre I had seen gracefully strolled through the now empty path.

She was as tall as the males, but her body was leaner, although still stacked with muscles, and her skin was a perfect blush pink. She wore a warrior's dress adorned with freshly polished breastplates and spiked shoulder cuffs. Her lavender hair was braided into a single plait that draped over her shoulder, her features much softer than the males, and no tusks were sticking out of her bottom lip.

She was beautiful, and many of the male ogres seemed to agree as they all gazed longingly at her back.

Her voice boomed across the clearing, strong yet feminine, "The challenge for Hamish Thornblood has been accepted. There will be no weapons, and they must stay within the perimeter of this clearing. No assistance shall be offered by either side. You will fight until submission, or death."

At her words, I handed my weapons off to Valerie and cracked my neck, allowing my muscles around my shoulders and back to loosen slightly.

"The judge will hail from the defender's homeland and shall remain unbiased, under penalty of death." Magic swirled in the clearing at her words, binding the withered-looking ogre judge who hobbled out of one of the nearby stone houses. He wore loose linen black pants and a cut-off shirt, his teal skin slightly wrinkled, like he had spent many years in the sun.

His gaze was hard as he surveyed the crowd and gave a brief nod to Bane and me.

We both stepped forward as the crowd was shuffled back by Bane's clansmen. Dean gave me a wicked grin and wink, his stance still lazy, as if he didn't have a care in the world. Cal and Valerie were alert and tense, sizing the ogres up in case anything went awry. Ophelia sat next to Dean, and she gave me a dip of her large head in confidence, the little tufts of her ears flicking with the movement.

"Begin," the old ogre's voice rang out across the clearing, and I barely had a chance to ready myself before I was narrowly avoiding Bane's fist flying towards my head. I dodged the blow and spun around his back, landing a few punches there, causing him to grunt in pain.

The month of training and continuous fighting gave me an advantage. My body was swift, and I landed more blows than Bane did. He fought savagely, his fists flying with brutal precision, but he relied too much on his brute strength. It made him slow, and I was able to dance circles around him.

But even with my supernatural strength and quick feet, when Bane's fist finally met its mark, I flew across the clearing. Dean's growl sounded from where he stood, but he held his stance, not daring to interfere. Alpha or not, if he got involved, we would both die.

I had already regained my composure before I even hit the ground, letting my body sail limply through the air and grunting out in pain when I landed.

I grappled to my feet clumsily before dusting myself off slowly, acting like the blow had me dazed. Sure, it had hurt, my jaw now throbbing in pain, and I tasted blood, but I still had a firm grip on my consciousness. His face was smug as he lumbered towards me, only pausing when I looked up at him.

I flicked my tongue out, licking up the blood that was leaking from the outer corner of my mouth. Bane's steps faltered. I gave him a smile so crazed, so feral, that it would send even the gods running for the safety of their own realm.

"I'll let you have that one."

I flew back at him with the combined moves I had learned from Zeke and Valerie, each strike precise and calculated.

I unleashed myself on him, letting only half of the strength I possessed filter in through my blows. After all, I wanted to beat him, not kill him. Dust flew as we fought across the clearing, his clansmen roaring with support for their leader, save for the judge who merely watched.

Bane's steps started to slow, his breathing ragged and his punches becoming sloppier. I knew this was my chance. He made a grab for my body to throw me into the ground, and I slipped between his legs—avoiding eye contact with whatever was underneath the skirt—and jumped onto his back.

He whirled and tried desperately to dislodge me, flailing his arms about, grasping for a hold on my leathers. But I had already scrambled up to his shoulders, and I wrapped my legs around his throat in a chokehold that Valerie had taught me for larger opponents. I pulled with restrained strength, not wanting to pop his head off, but just enough to cut off his airway.

His breathing became labored, wheezing as he continued thrashing and swinging, pulling at my arms and desperate for breath. He soon dropped to his knees and threw himself onto his back, trying to squish me beneath him, but I didn't let go.

I applied a little more pressure, using his weight to my advantage, and Bane's body seized with panic.

He was gasping now, and his clansmen were casting worried looks at each other. One even took a step forward, as if to break us up, but one warning growl from Dean had him stepping back in line. Hamish looked positively delighted at the scene.

Bane's arms were weakening; he could hardly hold them up to pull at my own. I turned my gaze to the judge, his face unreadable and assessing. I squeezed a bit harder and bared my teeth at him. Slowly, Bane reached up with a shaky hand and tapped my elbow twice, such a human gesture that I nearly laughed, but I held firm, waiting for the judge to call it. The old ogre narrowed his eyes at me, and I stared right back, unyielding.

Bane's face was turning a concerning shade of purple, his breaths barely a wheeze. His now bloodshot eyes flicked wildly towards the judge, and his fingers tapped my elbow again before his arm slumped to the ground.

"The challenger wins. Hamish Thornblood's contract now belongs to *her*. Release him," the old ogre croaked, and I let go of my hold on Bane's neck.

I shoved him off me, while he was still coughing, trying to breathe. His clansmen and the female ogre rushed to him, pushing him into a seated position as I strolled towards Hamish, who was now standing between Valerie and Ophelia.

"Vicious might be too nice of a word for you. Death incarnate might be more appropriate." Hamish looked over me with a bit of wonder in his eyes.

I laughed; he had no idea how true that was.

Dean was looking at me with an uncontrolled desire, and that cocky grin widened just enough to show his beloved dimple. His eyes glowed with hunger and pride as they traveled the length of my body, only flashing briefly with anger at the smeared blood on my lip.

"Here," Bane rasped as he appeared behind me, a scroll rolled tightly and secured by a leather band in his hand.

I snatched it quickly and unrolled it to check over the document. The entire thing was written in what I assumed to be blood, and at the very bottom was a release of ownership that Bane had signed, the red liquid fresh and yet it did not smudge.

He handed me a bone quill with no ink, but as I began to trace my name with a quirked brow, I felt a small prink in the palm of my left hand. Blood welled slightly as I continued signing my name, the makeshift ink appearing under the quill. Once finished, the bleeding stopped, the quill vanished, and my wound healed.

"Pleasure doing business with you, Bane." I saluted him, rolling the scroll back up and motioning for my friends to follow me.

"She fights well for such a tiny thing," the female ogre muttered to Bane as she checked over him.

The ogres watched in silence as we left with Hamish. Once we had exited the twin boulders at the front of their territory, I cut open the veil, smiling wickedly as I heard Bane scream to Elysia with pure fury that rattled the trees.

Chapter Thirty-Five

We settled into Valerie's living room, which seemed far too cramped with three hulking males taking up most of the space. One of which decided to take the seat right next to me on the luxurious cream sofa. Dean plopped down with the arrogance only an alpha male would possess, dipping the cushion just enough that I nearly fell into his lap, which he made no objections to.

Cal remained close to the door, watchful as always, his dark eyes observing every move Hamish made, assessing for threats and weaknesses. Valerie lounged on the chaise with Ophelia curled up in her lap. Hamish sat in his own armchair, eyeing the group warily, until his gaze landed on me, his expression turning inquisitive.

"You must have a dire need of one of my gifts if you were willing to risk challenging Bane. I've seen several supes go up against him and not survive. He's had my contract for over a century." He leaned back, still surveying each of us with his storm-gray eyes.

My eyes nearly bugged out of my head, Hamish had been a slave for over a century. Disgust coiled within my gut, and I wished I had hit that ogre a bit harder.

Dean answered before I could, "A risk would imply that there was a chance she would have been unsuccessful. I think you observed that there was *never* a chance of that." His words were laced with pride—and a warning.

Hamish's eyes flicked between the two of us, curious.

"Indeed. What'll it be then? After all, I do *serve* you now." His words were clipped, and I laid the contract out on the table before us, its ends still curving inward.

"I'm in need of a dragon. Someone has control over my dreams, and I want them out."

Hamish's eyes widened slightly, but he quickly regained his composure. He adjusted his ashy hair from his face, tying it out of the way as he contemplated his answer.

"And how do you know I am what you are looking for?" Hamish replied calmly.

"Does it matter?"

"Not to me. I'm at your service. But I do believe the constant favors people will ask of you regarding my abilities will become taxing." He was pressing. I had made it very clear what I thought about his contract at Samhain, and he was testing me. "You're young to have such powerful enemies. What's so special about you?"

Ophelia growled at my side, the room seeming to darken with her irritation. Her shadows billowed out from her angrily as she bared her teeth at Hamish. She only uttered one word: "Careful."

Hamish's eyes missed nothing as he looked over my familiar, cool and calculated as he brought his gaze back to me. Ophelia leaned against my leg affectionately, purring slightly as I stroked her fur in thanks. Such a protective familiar.

I picked up the contract in one hand and brought fire to my fingertips in the other. The blue flames cast a glow throughout the room, and Hamish stiffened. My friends remained unfazed as the flames danced across the planes of my fingers.

"I'm not special, Hamish. I just need these assholes out of my head for good." The gray in Hamish's eyes seemed to swirl like storm clouds as they flicked between the flames and his contract. "I have no need of a slave. You help me with this, and I swear I will free you of this contract and you will walk away a free male."

I half expected him to agree immediately, but he narrowed his eyes, distrust lining his features. "Why? I have been a slave for centuries, and many have promised just what you are claiming to me now, but as you can see, that didn't exactly pan out. Why should I trust you will hold up your end of the deal?"

"Because I know what it's like to suffer at the hands of others," I said quietly, trying to block out the images of Gadreel cutting into me from my mind's eye.

The whole room quieted, and Hamish studied whatever he saw in my eyes. I bore to him the shards of my soul that were barely put together, let him see the pain and rage, my suffering. But I also displayed my desire for vengeance too, and whatever he saw there must have satisfied him, as he nodded.

I did not move. "This is a contract for work, not one of slavery. You have your freedom, and you may come and go as you please. I'll make sure you are compensated for your efforts to rid me of the dreamwalker. And once it is done, you are free to go. Or stay, if that is what you so choose." I flicked my eyes to Valerie, and she dipped her chin slightly, confirming that my father would pay Hamish for what he was doing for me.

The scent of magic filled the room, and the contract changed its wording at my command, now reflecting a work contract and releasing him from his previous slave title, making him a free male. His eyes widened as he read the new terms of our agreement and dipped his head again, waiting for me.

I extinguished the flames before I leaned forward and gripped his hand, shaking it only once, sealing our deal. As we shook, I felt ancient magic fill the air as a band of flame appeared on my wrist, right over my scars. His chain tattoo faded away, only to be replaced by the same flames, glowing a soft orange from his wrist. I felt the magic settle, and the bond between Hamish and I flowed around our joined hands, glittering for a moment and then absorbing into our skin.

Hamish leaned back, heaving out a breath. It was then I noticed how haggard he looked. There were slight purple bags under his eyes, his clothes were wrinkled, and there was no light in those stormy eyes as he relaxed into the chair.

"Get some sleep, and we will begin once you have rested." I leaned back into Dean before looking to Valerie. "I can go back to the pack house, so you will not have to house him too." At this, she shrugged.

"It's no consequence to have him here. I have the space. Even if you went back, I would go as well. Where you go, I go. Boss's orders."

I rolled my eyes at her reminder. I hadn't heard from my father since he dropped me off here with Valerie after he found me, but I knew he was checking in with her regularly.

She motioned to the stairs, and Hamish began to follow her as she disappeared up them. As he reached the stairs, he turned, his eyebrows were furrowed as he looked at me, disbelief clear in his gaze as he studied me. He opened his mouth and shut it once, twice, before his lips lifted up into a small smile as he said, "Thank you."

I nodded and he continued up the stairs after Valerie.

* * *

The autumn breeze ruffled my hair as I made my way down the quiet streets of New Haven, heading towards the library to see Lumen. I had swapped out my leathers for a warm pair of leggings and a sweatshirt paired with sneakers, but even the warm clothes could not keep the chill of the air away from my bones.

The werewolf walking beside me took care of that.

Dean insisted he accompany me to the library, giving me no other reason than he wanted to. Ophelia trotted along my other side, still in her large form, with her shadows dancing out in the night air. Valerie begrudgingly agreed to stay behind with Hamish, as none of us fully trusted him quite yet.

Once we reached the doors and stepped inside, the lingering chill dissipated, and I was greeted by one of my favorite smells in the world: books.

Lumen immerged from behind one of the shelves, her moon-white hair braided and hanging over her shoulder. She smiled widely when she saw us. "Blair, I recently found an ancient text that I think you will find most helpful." She suddenly noticed Dean was standing there. "Oh! Dean. What a surprise. Will you be joining us?"

Her purple eyes flicked between the two of us. I nodded, looking over to see Dean lifting a brow at the question.

I strolled over to Lumen, my companions right on my heels, pausing to embrace her quickly before following her back to one of the private research rooms, which housed a coffee table and four plush lounge chairs surrounding it. A pile of books sat upon the table, most in ancient languages that I was desperately trying to learn but was failing miserably at.

The History of Angels sat open on the table, a book I had read cover to cover during my many nights researching here with Lumen about my angelic heritage. I sat down and looked over the pages Lumen had left open, and the Enochian runes becoming legible as it recognized my angelic blood.

"According to this text,"—she pointed to a line on the page—"it says that the siring a Nephilim is strictly forbidden, a law passed by the gods after a prophecy foretold by the Fates. A prophecy that stated a Nephilim's power will far surpass the power of their sire, and if the Nephilim ever reached maturity, the Nephilim would bring on a new age of power. The penalty for an angel breaking that order is the fall from grace, but for an archangel, the penalty is death."

I remembered the particular passage she was referencing, having read over it nearly a thousand times myself. Ezekiel had told me the same thing all those months ago when he revealed to me what my true nature was. If it was true, and it appeared that it was, how did my father escape this fate?

"And there has never been a Nephilim sired from an archangel before?" I looked at Lumen to confirm.

"The seven archangels are far more powerful than the other angels. Each one serves one of the gods in their corresponding realms, all except for one. Your father is the only archangel that is essentially the master of his own realm, but he reports to gods of the after-realms, Odenus and Morana. Even though there is no god that directly rules Purgatory, Odenus and Morana reserve the right to kill him for the crime of procreation.

"It has been rumored for some time now that Azrael is the most powerful of the archangels because of this, despite the angels revering Michael as the strongest, and being the first created angel." She sat down across from me, running a hand through the free strands of her braid.

I worried my lip as I mulled over the information again.

Why would the gods allow their first creation the ability to sire a child that could rival them in power?

Remember who history is written by. I would not be surprised if certain details were erased for their own gain. Ophelia looked thoughtful as she stretched out next to me.

I gave my familiar a slight nod, agreeing with her assessment. The gods were selfish, and they would do anything to protect their own power.

"If Nephilim are outlawed, why did Ezekiel agree to help Blair and not kill her on sight?" I winced at Dean's words.

"Ezekiel and Vivian were friends, and somehow she convinced him to watch over me, to protect me, in case she could no longer do so." My words were quiet, and I rubbed a hand over my heart, trying to quell the ache of her loss.

Dean rested a hand across my thigh and squeezed lightly, a silent comfort to my still mourning heart.

"Be that as it may, it is possible that Blair has thrown out her power in such a way that other angels could be aware of her presence. Perhaps they are biding their time to figure out who her sire is." She flipped the page. "Here it states that as the Nephilim awakens to their power, they are unable to control the power surges in a time of high emotional response. The surge is pure grace leaking out and sending a pulse across worlds. The awakening begins when the Nephilim is around twenty-five years old, but there's no information as to what happens when the Nephilim fully awakens, because none have ever reached maturity."

She swallowed as she looked at me again, her amethyst eyes calculating.

"The peculiar thing about this text is that in all my other research, I can't find any other mention of the Nephilim in history. No mention of their mighty power or this supposed prophecy from the Fates. This book alone is the only one that mentions they ever existed." Lumen rubbed her temples, confusion wrinkling across her forehead as she stared at the books, as if the answer would jump out at her.

Why would only one text in this entire library mention the Nephilim and how dangerous they were? And what would the gods do when they found out about me? The daughter of Death.

Ophelia's voice rolled through my head. *There must be a reason why your father would risk the god's wrath to sire you. To the most powerful necromancer of the millennia, no less. Regardless, I am here with you. Until Hecate calls us home.*

Chapter Thirty-Six

If Valerie knew anything about the reasonings behind my birth, she kept it silent as we relayed everything we learned from Lumen.

Her face was serious and contemplative, not betraying any emotion within her stern gaze. At the end, she simply hopped off her island counter and said, "Azrael must have had his reasons. It is not for us to assume anything. Whether it was a play for power, love, or an act of defiance, you are here now, and we can only move forward."

She pulled her satin gold robe tighter across her chest, and my gaze narrowed on her.

She began to walk out of the kitchen, heading for her bedroom before she paused and looked back. "Your father plans on checking in with you soon. Ask your questions then." I widened my eyes at her words. And although my skin began itching with nerves at this upcoming sit down with Azrael, I gave her a nod, and she left the room.

The heat of Dean's arm curled around me, and I found myself leaning into him. He pressed a gentle kiss to my forehead and murmured, "Whatever you need, I am here for you."

I looked up into his eyes, the two pools of blue churning with devotion as they roamed over my face, pausing briefly on my lips. His look became heated as I slightly bit my bottom lip. "Whatever I need?" I purred, curling my hand around his arm, pulling him closer.

A low growl rumbled out of him as he leaned in, his breath mingling with my own.

"Wicked little Raven," he breathed before capturing my lips with his.

I vaguely heard Ophelia pad out of the room as Dean's hands traveled up my body to cradle my head as he kissed me deeper. Each touch was like bolts of lightning all over my skin, need coiling in my core, desperate to be released.

Somehow, I gathered enough willpower to break the kiss. Our breathing was ragged, but he didn't push for more. I wasn't ready to take that step with him again, despite my body protesting, that tether pulling us closer. There were still so many things I needed to make right. Steps I needed to take to make sure those I cared about would be safe.

"Tomorrow, Hamish is going to try and break the connection between me and Alistair's dreamwalker, and I'd like you to be here. For me." I pressed a light kiss to Dean's lips, and he smiled.

He paused, pretending to think it over. "Only if you come to the pack run for the full moon in a couple of days." He gave me a cocky smile that exposed his dimple, and I nearly pulled him in for another heated kiss. "I've missed having you there, and I know Hayley has too, even if Sage has been keeping her company in your place." I straightened at that.

Guilt coiled in my gut as I remembered the way I had screamed at Sage after I came back to New Haven. The grief and trauma of Gadreel's torture had made me say those words to her, even if deep down I knew they weren't true. She could not control her visions, and she couldn't predict everything.

"She misses you." He cupped my cheek. "And so does the rest of the pack." I nodded, leaning into his hand.

"Okay, I'll come for the full moon," I agreed, and his responding smile nearly made me melt right on that barstool. But as we made our way up to my room, an unspoken agreement that he was staying with me, that guilt came rolling back, keeping me from falling asleep.

* * *

At some point during the far too early hours of the morning, I couldn't stand to just lie awake, staring at the ceiling, so I padded downstairs to sit in the reading room. I busied myself with a book, cozied up underneath the warm glow of the lamplight. I contemplated going back to the library to see Lumen, but Ophelia was dozing on the plush chair next to me, and I couldn't bring myself to wake her. Even if I left without her, the bond would tug her awake, urging her to follow me.

The sun started to rise, and as the golden rays beamed through the windows, I got up to make coffee. I waited perched on the counter, leaning against the cabinet with a blanket pulled around me. I let out a sigh as I shut my eyes, listening to the sounds of the coffee being brewed.

I woke up with a jolt, strapped to *the table*, the cold biting against my exposed skin. The stone walls were covered in familiar bloodred symbols, designed to ward against my magic, and to keep anyone from finding me. I pulled against the thick chains, but those too were covered in the same symbols, further weakening me. I looked around wildly, trying to orient myself as to what was happening.

It was all a dream. I had never gotten out.

A choked sob tore out of me as the sound of a knife sharpening broke the eerie silence of the torture chamber. A menacing laugh followed, and out of the shadows appeared Alistair. His bloodred eyes were glowing with dark delight as they took in my body strapped down, completely powerless.

"Miss me, love?" He smiled, revealing his fangs. The same fangs that had ripped out Vivian's throat.

I snarled at him, despite the tears streaming down my face, despite the fear and anguish threatening to cleave me in half.

"You know, I never understood the obsession with knives," he quipped, tossing the knife onto the nearby table, where countless other torture devices waited. "I much prefer doing the work with my own hands. And my fangs, of course." He chuckled. "There's just something so... *riveting* about ripping someone open with your bare hands."

He was at my side in a blink, his smile promising pain as he looked down at me with wicked delight. I barely had a chance to utter a response before he struck and plunged his hand into my side, ripping through skin and muscle.

I screamed so loud the walls shook, the blinding pain leaving me breathless as I tried to refocus my vision from the blaring white. I felt him moving his fingers, poking and prodding my organs, each movement pure agony. I cried out, fighting for breath as his finger scraped the edge of my heart, his smile widening, his fangs now on full display.

He tore his hand out suddenly, and I gasped for air, gulping it down greedily. His hand was dripping with my blood, and he stared at me as he licked it clean.

I was sobbing now. This was my fate. The price I had to pay to keep my friends safe. Gadreel freeing me had all been a dream. A pain-induced last scrap of hope, my mind trying to protect me one final time.

Alistair paused, his smile falling away as he looked towards the massive stone door. A quake rattled the walls, causing small pieces of stone to crash to the ground. The pressure in the room seemed to change, the edges of the surfaces becoming blurred. Even Alistair was hazy in my vision.

"If you let that connection sever, you are dead. I will rip you apart!" Alistair roared to the ceiling.

I didn't know who he was talking to, but I didn't care, I started struggling against the bonds holding me to the table. The scent of magic was heavy in the air, thick as I fought to free myself.

He whirled toward me, eyes swirling with fury. "You belong to me, Blair. You were promised to me, to give me and my nest the gift of walking in the sun, and I will kill everyone in my path who gets in my way. Just like I killed Vivian." More stones fell from the ceiling, and even the table underneath me shook from the force of magic. "Only, your blood will be so much sweeter than hers."

"I will kill you for what you did to her, you filthy bloodsucker!" I raged against the metal cuffs, surprised to find they had a little give. His eyes widened slightly before he bared his fangs in a hiss. He lunged for me but smashed into an invisible wall of magic.

"No!" he screamed, pounding against the barrier, speeding around the room and checking all sides around me but finding no way to get in.

A horrible burning seared through my head, and for a moment I thought it was going to rip me in two. I screamed again, the barrier causing the sound to echo back to me. The chains and straps fell away from me, and long silk pajamas appeared on my body as Alistair continued to pound into the shield. The gaping wound in my side closed as if it had never been there at all, the blood disappearing from the table, taking the pain with it.

The walls began to burn away, the entire scene set ablaze, magic fire banishing it completely, closing in on the vampire. He snarled and hissed, recoiling from the powerful fiery wave of magic. I pulled my knees into my chest and watched as the magic swallowed him whole, leaving me alone and surrounded by the flames.

Then the magic parted, allowing in a doorway of light, and out stepped Hamish, his ashy hair messy and his jaw set hard with determination. Smoke billowed from his nostrils. He wasn't wearing a shirt, allowing me a view of various scars on his body.

Scars like mine.

He held out his hands, showing me his palms as he slowly approached me. "I know that seemed very real, Blair. Alistair has access to an extremely powerful dreamwalker. Lucky for you, dragons are much more powerful," he tried to joke. I eyed him warily. "Let me show you a place of peace, and then I will wake you up."

He reached for my hand, pausing halfway, waiting for me to take it.

I reluctantly did, my hand shaking. The magic surrounding the shield swirled and began sparkling like the galaxies before shooting up towards the heavens, creating a beautiful night sky. I was no longer sitting on a stone table but on a sandy beach, facing the ocean.

Hamish was at my side, his hand still wrapped around my own. The waves crashed along the shore, the water illuminated by the stars above and beautiful glowing jellyfish beneath the surface.

I released a breath before inhaling the salty air. I squished the sand between my toes, saying nothing as we stared out towards the sea. Without looking at me, Hamish murmured, "Dragons are immune to most magics and can break connections of a magical nature. I can use this ability to help others if I choose to." He paused, inhaling deeply before continuing, "This is a place I used to go to escape. Before my enslavement. I feel such peace here, even in the dreamscape."

I nodded, as my heartrate slowed, and my tense muscles relaxed. The waves continued to crash, washing away any lingering fear. I was free. I was in New Haven, away from that place. The pain was not real, the dungeon was not real. Even this was not real.

I was free.

"Thank you," I whispered, giving his hand a slight squeeze.

"I was able to sever the connection between you and the dreamwalker and have placed some temporary warding in your mind to continue to keep her out. Once you're awake, I can place a permanent one."

I turned to him, unable to hold in my tears, and pulled him in for a hug.

He was stiff at first, surprised, but he soon relaxed and embraced me back. "Are you ready?" he murmured against my shoulder. Without letting him go, I nodded.

Magic slid over my skin, and the sand disappeared beneath me. I could no longer taste the salt in the air or feel the ocean breeze caressing my skin. The glow of the jellyfish faded, and flames of his magic burned the rest of the serene beach with it, until all that was left was the stars.

I woke up to strong hands sliding underneath me and lifting me up off cool tile flooring. I opened my eyes to peer at my surroundings, as the warm hands held me close, but I groaned as the light nearly burned my eyes out.

"She'll need to rest. Breaking a dreamwalker connection takes a toll, especially one of that strength. I need to stay with her in case she tries to reform the connection to Blair," Hamish spoke seriously to someone.

Leather and amber scents filled my nose and I sighed, leaning closer to the smell. "I can take care of her," Dean snarled softly as he carried me up the stairs, reaching my bedroom in a matter of seconds. He laid me down gently, and I groaned as my head swum at the sudden movement.

"Right, and what will you do if the connection is somehow made again? Growl at her as she has her mind invaded and is shown her deepest fears?" Hamish demanded, and Dean's responding growl shook my entire body as he nearly laid over me protectively.

Thump! Dean grunted, and Ophelia snarled, "Enough of this male pissing contest. This is about what is best for Blair! We both failed her tonight, yet Hamish was the one who managed to pull her out. Put aside your moronic alpha-possessiveness for the night and let him help her!"

Dean muttered something about her giant murder mittens as he stretched out next to me, gently pulling the covers over me.

"I only wish to help her. What I saw... what that dreamwalker was making her see, I will not let her relive that again." Hamish's voice became soft, haunted even, and I felt Dean stiffen at his words. "I, too, know what it is like to be unmade at the hands of others."

A contemplative silence followed, the two males exchanging a loaded look before Dean grumbled, "You can sleep on the ground." He then pulled me against him, underneath the soft sheets. I sighed, snuggling in closer, with Ophelia pressing against my back.

"Are you sure you don't want my company? I'm a great snuggler," Hamish purred from the edge of the bed. Dean's snarl shook the entire room, and Hamish merely chuckled.

I vaguely heard Hamish pulling a blanket out of the closet before settling in on the ground next to the bed before I drifted away into a blissful darkness.

Chapter Thirty-Seven

A slight tickling under my nose roused me from sleep. I peeked open an eye to find Ophelia's tail brushing my nostrils as she sprawled out next to me, the black fur on her chest rising and falling with her breath. Dean's arm tightened around me slightly, and I turned my head to find the alpha still sleeping as well, his face peaceful. Hamish groaned from the floor as he sat up and stretched, his face twisted into a grimace.

He peered over at me and gave me an assessing look as I felt his strange magic reach out to my own. Whatever he found, he merely nodded as he stood, beckoning me to follow him. I gently untangled myself from Dean's embrace as he murmured sleepily and slid Ophelia into his arms. They were an adorable sight.

Hamish and I didn't speak as we made our way down the stairs and into the kitchen. I plopped down onto a barstool, my body protesting at the movement, and Hamish busied himself with making the coffee, despite what I assumed to be the late afternoon hour.

As soon as it started to brew, he turned to me.

"How are you feeling?" he asked, his stormy eyes looking over me again.

"Tired, and like my brain is a bowl of jelly. Thank you, for what you did," I murmured, unable to say much more.

I felt as if my soul had been bared open to him, as he saw me at my weakest, sobbing and terrified, unable to escape what Alistair's torture. But as I looked back at him, I saw no pity like I expected, only understanding.

"Breaking a mind connection like that takes a toll on the body. That dreamwalker is powerful, and the connection must have been in place for a very long time; it had its hooks deep. But if you are ready, I can place the permanent warding on your mind to prevent any future mind manipulation." I merely nodded. "Were they all like that? The nightmares," he asked, and I shut my eyes, willing the flashes of torture away.

I took a deep breath before answering, "More or less. They were different before I was... taken, but still just as horrible. It's been going on for over a year now."

He swore at my words as the coffee maker beeped, and he angrily poured me a cup.

He stalked around the counter, and as he placed the drink in front of me, he brought his hands up and asked me to face him. I swiveled the barstool and took a centering breath before nodding at him to get it over with.

His hands were warm as they pressed into the sides of my face, and a slight burning sensation tingled along my skin before burrowing itself into my mind. I grimaced slightly; it felt like a brand on the inner corners of my mind. It was over as quickly as he started, and he stepped back, giving me an approving smile.

Valerie came down the stairs then, clad in her champagne-colored robe, with a lace nightgown peeking out of the top, unworried at the late hour of the day. Hamish's eyes widened with heat at the sight of her before he swaggered back around the counter to pour her a cup as well.

We all drank our coffee in comfortable silence before Valerie began working on preparing breakfast. I made a move to get up and help, but I was pushed back into my seat by the two of them, acting like a couple of mother hens. I rolled my eyes as I sat there, watching them work surprisingly in sync.

Soon, the scent of bacon and sausage filled the kitchen, which brought down both Dean and Ophelia, the former shirtless with a sleepy grin adorning his face. He pulled a barstool closer to my own, leaning in and placing a kiss on my neck before rubbing his face on mine. His stubble rubbed against my cheek in a way that sent heat pooling between my thighs.

Valerie groaned, "Keep your scents to yourself, please."

I blushed as Dean chuckled and leaned away, although not far, and moved his hand to rest on my knee, his thumb tracing small circles.

"Thank you for what you did for her, dragon. It appears I am in your debt." Dean turned his gaze to Hamish, who arched a blond brow at the werewolf. "You'll have the protection of my pack should you choose to stay in New Haven." Even I raised my brows at that.

Hamish dipped his head in acknowledgement before replying, his face serious as his gaze flicked between the two of us, "I didn't do it for you, I did it for her. Even when she breaks the contract, I am in her debt."

"Speaking of," I muttered as I summoned the contract from the magical tattoo on my wrist. His eyes widened as I incinerated the large scroll, and golden ashes fell in a small pile on the countertop. A warm buzzing tingled across my wrist as the binding magic disappeared, and I lifted my head to see that his vanished as well.

He turned to me, his jaw dropping as he marveled over the now smooth skin along his wrist. Hamish swiftly moved away from the barstool and knelt before me, gazing up at me.

Before I could reprimand him to stand up, he looked at me seriously as he vowed, "You freed me from an eternity of slavery and misery, keeping your word, lifting a curse cast upon me by a resentful god. I have beheld your wild flaming heart, a twin to my own, burning with the desire for *peace* in a world of war. So, where you go, I will follow."

I opened and shut my mouth several times, at a loss for words. Whispers of destiny tickled my ears as we stared at one another, an understanding clicking into place between us, a sense of kinship, a sense of likeness.

I pulled him to his feet and smiled. "Welcome to the pack."

* * *

The air was crisp as the five of us made our way down the main drag of New Haven towards Brodie's bar. Winter was nearly upon us, and if the weather here was anything like the other northern regions of Arizona, we should be expecting snow here before long.

We soon made it to the bar and found Lumen waiting for us at one of the larger tables, chatting with Brodie animatedly about a fae territory they both loved in Alfheim, Gaia's realm. Greetings and introductions were kept short as we all quickly sat around the table. Hamish was eyeing Brodie curiously, and I watched with interest as Brodie gave Hamish a sensual smile and a wink.

Lumen cleared her throat before pulling various books from her bag on the ground. "According to the texts, vampires never had the ability to walk in the sunlight, as they were created with insatiable bloodlust, and magic demands balance, the balance being they could only hunt at night. However, I have heard whisperings of forgotten legends that this was a curse, and there was a spell to remove it, which would allow all vampires to walk in the sunlight."

"That only leaves one question then. What do they think they can accomplish by kidnapping *you*? Only a power that was born of the gods could achieve such a thing," Brodie asked, arching a dark brow in my direction.

A sense of dread pooled in my stomach as I glanced at Lumen, her silver brows pinched together as she worried her lip. She gave me a slight dip of her head, confirming what I knew to be true in that very moment. Brodie's moss eyes flashed a brilliant shade of green when I brought my gaze back to his.

"I'm a powerful witch, Brodie, you know that. The demon has probably tricked Alistair into some sort of deal, one that will no doubt benefit Gadreel over Alistair. He has Alistair convinced that I'm the perfect ingredient for the spell, even though it's a fool's errand." My voice was confident, final, as I stared down the siren.

"And what of the torture you endured for those months? What purpose did that serve?" Brodie challenged me, trying to force my hand to admit what was none of his godsdamned business.

Before I could even muster up a retort, Dean's growl shook the glasses on the table, his alpha power filling the room, demanding blood for what Gadreel had done to me. I pushed my grace out, letting it tangle with his magic, coaxing it to calm down.

Everyone around the table remained perfectly still at Dean's outburst. Hamish tried to control his smirk but at least had the sense to stare at the table, not daring to even glance in Dean's direction. Lumen's eyes were cast down too, but her head was tilted slightly, listening to the magics filling the air.

I felt Dean's eyes snap to me as I slowly stood, his lip quivering as he fought against the need to shift, to kill, to protect. I kept my movements graceful and calculated as I walked over to his chair, pausing to look down at him.

His eyes were more animal than human, though they were still their usual brilliant blue. I gently sat in his lap, exposing the side of my neck to him, letting my legs dangle off the side of the chair. His arms immediately snapped around to pull me closer to his chest, a possessive growl leaving his throat as he glared at everyone else at the table.

His nose traveled up the curve of my neck, inhaling deeply, which sent goosebumps all along my flesh.

"Mine," he growled, and Valerie had to stifle her chuckle.

I rolled my eyes but allowed him to keep snarling like a brute for a moment. It was in his nature to be possessive, and if I was being honest, this primal side of him made my toes curl. His hands continued to pull me closer, his muscles tensing as if he was going to leap to my defense at any moment.

Feeling the need to break the tension, I slapped him on his hard chest and chastised, "Down, boy, we all know you're a big bad wolf." I kissed him gently on the nose, and slowly his alpha energy reined back in towards his body, making it easier to breathe, and everyone relaxed slightly. Dean nipped at my earlobe before nestling closer to my neck, breathing me in.

"Call me boy again, and I'll show you how *bad* this wolf can be," he murmured against my neck, his hot breath sending chills down my skin.

I let out a throaty laugh before turning back to everyone at the table.

Lumen cleared her throat. "Blair's right. That would be the only explanation as to why Alistair and Gadreel have been hunting her all this time."

"I have some fellow reapers looking into him. All we know is he was one of the original angels that fell and transformed into a demon, making him extremely powerful. He's considered one of the Princes of Hell." Valerie's words sent a chill through my bones.

I had read a bit on the hierarchy of hell when I was staying at the pack house, but the possibility of Gadreel being a Prince of Hell had never crossed my mind while I was being held captive.

"And you didn't think to mention that to me until now?" I snapped at Valerie.

She smirked and shrugged her shoulders, taking a sip of mead as I stared at her.

"Don't get your panties in a twist, Blair. I just got the report this morning. I only waited until now so I didn't have to repeat myself." She sniffed.

I rolled my eyes at my friend, my anger subsiding, and she gave me a wink in return.

Dean pulled me closer, pressing a reassuring kiss on my neck before growling, "I will not let them take you again." I mutely nodded, focusing on the heat from his body and not the cold dread pooling in my gut.

Chapter Thirty-Eight

"Your father has requested your presence." Valerie breezed into the living room, clad in her black armor, red hair pulled back into intricate braids and an impassive look on her face.

Ophelia immediately shifted into her larger form, her shadows flicking about around her. I sighed, making a move to get off the couch, but Dean pulled me back into his hard chest.

I raised a brow at Dean, who was sporting an impish grin that revealed his dimple. But when I looked into his cerulean eyes, I saw the worry there, and I leaned in to press a kiss to his forehead. "I'll be back soon. Try not to cause too much trouble while I'm gone."

He finally released me with a chuckle, and I smoothed out my band t-shirt and began pulling on my combat boots.

"Raven, you're the *only* kind of trouble I want to be in," he rumbled as he pulled me in for another kiss. His stubble scraped against my skin in the most sinful way as he nipped at my lip. I gasped, which gave him full access to my mouth, his tongue stroking my own, his hands gripping my hips.

Valerie cleared her throat, and I begrudgingly detangled myself from Dean, my cheeks hot with lust as he gave me a hooded look. I found it harder and harder to stay away from him, and I knew he felt the same. He'd stayed here at Valerie's nearly every night over the past few days, only leaving to deal with pack business and council meetings.

He grabbed my oversized black coat for me, placing it around my shoulders before walking us out to the stoop. Before he could walk off, I pulled him in for one more quick yet passionate kiss before he sauntered off towards his motorcycle, smirking with pure male satisfaction as the bike roared to life beneath him.

Valerie made a mocking vomit noise next to me, and I elbowed her, the both of us letting out a laugh. She extended her hand, which I grabbed, keeping the other placed on Ophelia's head. With a flick of her wrist, she cut open the veil beneath our feet, and we dropped together into darkness.

The three of us landed softly in a large hallway with vaulted glass ceilings that allowed a view of the night sky. The stars looked incredibly close, and the sky itself was glowing with inky blues and purples between the millions of stars.

The hallway itself had smooth stone walls and marble floors, and at the end of the hallway I saw massive wooden doors with some sort of intricate carvings adorning them. Still hand in hand, we walked down the silent hallway. As we neared, I heard the buzz of voices, and I pet Ophelia nervously, trying to keep busy to hide my trembling.

I hadn't seen my father since he rescued me and healed me after being imprisoned and tortured by Gadreel. He had seen me in such a vulnerable state, broken, bleeding, and grieving, and I had this stupid notion to want to prove that I wasn't weak. That I had overcome what had happened to me.

Valerie gave me a moment to steady myself as we stood before the massive wooden doors. I studied them as I took some deep breaths, admiring the intricate carvings of the three afterworlds. The top depicted Elysia, with Odenus looking over the clouds filled with gardens and the rays from the sun streaming down on the souls who dwelled there and the angels overseeing it. The middle showed the reapers bringing in the souls of the deceased across a river to the gates leading to Purgatory, where an angel with black wings stood with the scales of judgement in his hands. The bottom of the door was jagged with its carvings of fire burning and demons torturing the souls of the damned, all of it being overseen by the Goddess of Hell, Morana, sitting atop her throne in her castle of brimstone.

I gave Valerie a nod, and she flicked her fingers, opening the doors with her magic. I raised my brows at the sight before me. There were reapers everywhere, each clad in the same black armor Valerie wore, with the addition of a dark hood shrouding their features and gray-feathered wings. The reapers were ushering in souls and checking on them as they stood waiting to be judged.

Souls of the dead looked just as they did at the time before their death, the only change being all color faded from their forms, and they became incorporeal.

My necromancer gift flared to life inside me, called by the overwhelming number of souls in the room, sending out a pulse of power. The reapers and spirits stilled, all turning their attention towards me. The reapers' faces were no longer hidden within the shadow of their hoods, all stark with curiosity.

"Shit. I didn't mean to do that." I gripped Valerie's hand tighter as the spirits began to drift towards me, despite the reapers trying to herd them back in line.

The spirits were crowding us, their spectral forms casting the rest of the hall into a blur, and I could *feel* them, feel their sorrow, their confusion.

Pure instinct took over as I let my gift fill my very being before calling out in an ethereal voice, "Your fates await. Please step back in line for your judgement."

They all stopped about a foot away from me, pausing briefly before turning and taking their places back in line in front of the Scales of Judgement. I locked that part of me down, slightly afraid of how my gift had reacted to being in this realm around the souls of the in-between.

The reapers regarded me curiously but returned to their duties. A few of them waved at Valerie as we made our way through the crowd towards another hallway.

This place called to my soul like no other, and my grace felt endless as we walked further into the realm of Purgatory. I let out a breath as we stepped out of the room and loosened my grip on Valerie's hand.

"You sure know how to make an impression," Valerie quipped, a smirk playing on her ruby lips. I snorted and shook my head; the last thing I needed was the attention of all the reapers under my father's command.

"The souls of the dead were very taken with you, and you even held the reapers in a trance for a moment." Ophelia looked up to me with both pride and worry in her eyes.

As each day passed, and my abilities grew, so too did my fear of the consequences of the power I held.

We soon arrived at an all-black arched door at the end of the hall which opened as we approached it. Valerie gestured for me to go inside. She gave me a reassuring nod, and Ophelia and I stepped through the threshold. The door abruptly shut behind us, and I looked up to see my father sitting behind his desk, his wings nowhere in sight.

"Blair, you look well." His face remained impassive as he looked over me appraisingly.

Despite the anger still simmering for my father, I felt the urge to shy away from his gaze. Ophelia pressed against my leg, and I lifted my chin, refusing to let him see any weakness. He gestured for me to take a seat, and I swaggered over and lounged in the chair.

Ophelia shrank to her house cat form and jumped into my lap, facing him with her chartreuse eyes narrowed. Azrael's gaze flickered between the two of us as I casually stroked her back.

"So, what is this about? I'm sure you could have gotten all the information on my well-being from Valerie." My words were pure venom as I stared down my father.

"There are some things we need to discuss. First, I want you to know that we have not been able to locate the demon Gadreel or the vampire Alistair. Wherever they are hiding, it appears that they are—"

I cut him off, "There are runes all over the walls that I believe repel angels from being able to enter or find the location. I read about the symbols at the library in New Haven."

One of his dark brows lifted slightly, the only sign that he was surprised. "It seems you've been doing your research. What else have you learned?" He sat back in his seat, bringing his hands to rest in his lap.

His expression was serious, but his eyes shined with an eagerness I did not understand. This was a male who had allowed his daughter to be raised by strangers, alone in the world with no idea who her family was. I wasn't a fool; I understood the risk of any involvement he could have had with me, if the knowledge of my existence had been discovered by others. The circumstances of our situation didn't make me feel any better, didn't make accepting it any easier.

I steeled myself against that olive branch I could so clearly see him offering, embracing the one emotion that would not allow the risk for the hurt of abandonment again, of that loss.

"Let's just skip the bullshit, shall we? I know you have been keeping tabs on me, so tell me what you wanted to speak with me about so I can go home," I tossed back, tired of this game.

His jaw ticked, his irritation showing, but he kept his face a cool mask.

"I have only asked about your well-being, not your personal life. I am not interested in violating your privacy; I only wanted to know that you were healing and safe." His words were clipped, as if he was working to keep his voice under control.

I ignored the truth I heard in his words and the colors of pain and regret swirling in his aura as he looked at me. I was aware my anger was irrational, knowing what would have happened if he had made his presence known to me, if he had allowed himself to be involved in my life. But I couldn't stop the hurt that he didn't even deem me worth the risk. That the only reason I had come to meet him was because I was tortured by the very demons he sought to keep me away from.

I couldn't stop my next words from flowing out, the anger at what had been taken away from me too much for me to contain.

I let out a harsh laugh. "That's rich, coming from the male who had no regard for my safety and well-being all my life. Spare me from the fake caring father act. You never gave a damn about me, and now you're only worried your little secret accidental act of rebellion against the gods will get out! You only care about yourself."

He stood up, knocking over the chair behind him as he snarled, "Do not speak of things you know nothing about!"

I jumped up as well, Ophelia leaping off my lap and shifting instantly into a defensive position in front of me, letting out a growl as she bared her teeth at Azrael.

"It must have been important for you to defy the laws of the angels, to risk the fall and even death itself all to conceive me," I seethed, my grace leaking out of me, making the room vibrate.

His brows creased together at the show of power, and I could practically hear his teeth grind at my words, his quicksilver eyes burning as they stared down at me.

But still, he said nothing.

I raged on, "Is immortality that boring? Needed some entertainment? Got a random wild hair to defy the gods? To put not only my life but everyone I hold dear's in danger. Tell me why!"

In an instant, he was in front of me, his black wings bursting out behind him.

"It was love!" Azrael roared, his magic rising up to meet my own.

I faltered a step back, regret filling me instantly. It was a possibility I had never considered. That my father, an archangel, could have loved my mother, a witch. Perhaps it was because I had never even known of his existence, the concept of a father seeming so far out of reach that when presented with the idea that he had truly loved my mother, it was too unbelievable.

The hard lines of his face softened in anguish as he pinched the bridge of his nose and let out a harsh breath. "You were conceived out of love, Blair. I loved Yvaine, your mother, and she loved me." He sat down on the edge of his desk and buried his face in his hands before looking back up at me, his eyes glistening with tears.

"You... you loved each other?" I whispered.

"Still do. Even death cannot stop a love like we shared. It... it nearly killed me when she died." He paused. "I'm sorry to disappoint your already low opinions of me, but there was no ulterior motive of your birth. Even still, I suffered all the same. I may not have fallen, but a piece of me fell away as your mother's soul was ripped from her body. And even more when I had to let you slip away from my grasp, the last piece of her in this world, to protect you from the dangers that came with your heritage. But it appears I failed at that as well."

Tears sprung to my eyes as I took in my father. His dark wings draped at his sides, as he looked up at me with eyes desperate for forgiveness and a sadness I felt deep within my soul. He appeared like a fallen dark king, broken from a love lost. Even Death himself could not defy the will of the Fates.

"I'm sorry you lost her," I murmured, the burning rage I came here with fizzling out at his words. I wished I could take back the angry words I'd hurled at him, the guilt making me shrink back in shame.

He nodded and replied, "I only wish she could have seen you grow into the fierce warrior you are today. She would be proud."

My father's lips turned up into a small smile, and I relaxed slightly. I righted the chair and sat down in front of him, letting out a shaky breath.

"Please know that there was not a day that I didn't think about you or wish things could have been different. I searched for you, but the cloaking spell your mother placed on you before she was killed was too powerful even for me to overcome. It only broke when the awakening started, and even then, I had to be careful about not drawing too much attention to you."

I blew out a breath as his words echoed in my mind. He *had* been looking for me.

We sat in silence, staring at one another, unspoken words flowing between us over the lost time we would never get back.

"True mates are a rare and treasured phenomenon, and losing one's true mate is a tragedy that most cannot bear. Most will turn to madness or seek death to join them in the afterworld. The only reason I remain here is you, the last piece of her I have. I hope you never have to feel that never-ending pit of loss with your true mate." Azrael placed his hand over his heart, his silver eyes burning into me with such emotion, I nearly reached out to comfort him.

Instead, I offered him a snort, "I'd have to find my true mate first, which is a doubtful feat in itself." Even if a certain male werewolf came to mind at the words 'true mate', I couldn't let myself even consider the possibility. I didn't deserve someone like Dean, and he certainly didn't deserve to be shackled to me.

"Power calls to power, Blair. Your power will call for its equal, and when united it will be a fearsome thing to behold." Azrael studied me quietly, as if he were searching for something, a question needing an answer.

"I have enough trouble with my own power. No need to add more to the pot." I waved him off, wishing we could move on from this subject.

Azrael shifted his gaze from me to Ophelia.

"Your bond to her is not the only one residing within her soul. The wolf?" he asked her, and my eyes shot to my familiar.

Ophelia's round eyes shifted between Azrael and I before she answered, "Yes, though it is not clear what kind of bond they share. They are drawn to each other, but the nature of what is between them is still concealed by the Fates."

"Are either of you going to clue me in to what the fuck you are talking about?" I shouted, my irritation flaring.

"The bond is solidifying between the two of them and yet none of you told her what was happening? He did not tell her? Explain it to her?" Azrael demanded of Ophelia, who bared her teeth in response.

Lightning shot out of my fingertips, skittering across the stone floor, my power blasting from within as I stood up and snarled, "Tell me what you know!"

Ophelia squared up with me, her tail swishing around nervously as she looked up at me. "You and Dean share a bond. That tether you feel, tugging you towards him, urging you to be near him, it is some sort of bond forming between you two. A link between your souls, like the one you and I share."

I didn't think I was breathing, hurt and confusion swirling within me. I took a deep breath, pulling my wild magic back to me before I deigned to speak.

"And you don't know what kind of bond it is?

Ophelia cast a wary look between Azrael and me again. "As I said, it is unclear. It initially formed the night you two met, Fate twining your destinies together, and has only grown stronger with the time you have spent together. The nature of your bond will probably not reveal itself until it is complete."

I readied myself to ask one more question, and judging by the unease in her gaze, she knew what I was about to ask, and the answer was likely going to make me angry.

"Does Dean know?"

I was met with silence.

Chapter Thirty-Nine

I didn't think I was breathing as her silence roared throughout the room.

So many emotions were rolling through my gut, but the most powerful was hurt, and I was unable to control the grace that was seeping out of me. Lightning coated my fingertips, coiling up my arms and casting a fearsome glow that contrasted with the orange flames that burned in the sconces adorning the walls.

"Does he know?" I growled, my gaze flickering between Ophelia and my father, both looking uneasy. I tried to rein in my magic, but the raging storm inside me would not quiet as I stood there, feeling absolutely betrayed. How many more truths could possibly be withheld from me?

"He likely knows of a bond forming, as wolves are keenly aware of bonds, being pack creatures. Like you, he probably has no idea what kind of bond is growing, just that he wants to be near you, to protect you," Azrael answered.

I struggled to rein in the storm of emotions rolling through me, desperately grasping at the grace leaking out and pulling back into my chest. Ignoring the hurt of being lied to by the people I cared most about in this world, I shut my eyes and took a deep breath.

Later. I would deal with this later.

I set my face to appear impassive, though I was pretty sure I wasn't fooling anyone, and adjusted myself in my seat. The lightning receded back into my skin, and my magic quieted.

"You didn't bring me here to talk about those bound to me. Why am I here, Azrael?" I drawled, picking at my nails in a bored fashion.

His brow quirked up, and he looked at Ophelia briefly before squaring his shoulders and moving on. "Your powers are growing stronger, and you are nearing your awakening. There is talk across the realms about a Nephilim roaming the Earth. We're here to discuss your options. The gods will not intervene until the rumors are deemed true, and many angels from all realms are out searching for you, eager to gain favor with any of the seven gods.

"Ezekiel is feeding me information he hears within Michael's legion in Elysia, and I have trusted a few within my own legion that are working to distract from your power surges."

I raised my brows at his words, surprised at how closely he worked with Ezekiel.

He continued, "The only way to completely take away the threat of the gods smiting you for what you are is to ensure that you are not a threat to their reign."

"And how would I ensure that?"

"By becoming a servant of the afterworlds and taking on the mark of the reapers and working for me." I paused, staring at the serious-ness on his face, then laughing at the ridiculousness of his words. My father's expression darkened. "I don't see what is humorous about this situation, Blair. I'm trying to protect you against the wrath of the gods."

I snorted. I would not cower and beg for forgiveness to live out my days serving gods who never gave a damn about me until the awakening started. I didn't ask for this power. I didn't ask for any of this.

"If you think me working for you in Purgatory will spare me from the wrath of the gods, you are a fool. If they find me, they'll kill me. It's that simple." I pushed back from my chair and began walking towards the door.

His power pulsed in anger as he called out, "You'd put everyone else at risk for your own selfishness? Working for the realm of Purgatory could save your life, save thousands of lives! You think Morana or Odenus cares about casualties when it comes to destroying threats to their power? She oversees the entire realm of the damned, Blair, and he the realm of eternal peace. They have the most to lose at your awakening. An untethered Nephilim will upset the power of the realms as we know it."

I stopped just before the door. "How could *I* upset the balance of the god's power?" The question escaped my mouth before I could stop it, curious to see if he would tell me what I already suspected to be true.

He answered, "You are the child of the Angel of Death, a celestial being sired by the gods, and master of death, Yvaine, a resurrector, a holder of the Phoenix Flame bestowed on you by the Primordial that created this very universe. You hold both life and death at your disposal, the two most powerful power bases the gods possess."

A shiver ran down my spine at his words. He was Odenus and Morana's son, and my mother was a resurrector. More truths withheld. "I have always been told my mother was a powerful necromancer," I whispered.

His silver eyes flashed with anguish as his mouth set into a hard line.

"Come with me." He stood up abruptly, flicking his fingers as he turned, and the bookcase to the right of his desk swung outward to reveal a dark passageway. When we passed through the threshold, silvery lights lit up the narrow space as we made our way down the passage.

Ophelia stalked behind me, ears flat against her head as she protected my back, despite being in my father's presence.

We walked for a few minutes, the sounds of our footsteps on the stones echoing off the walls. As we made our way around a rounded corner, an arched doorway loomed before us. Two sconces with grace-light cast a silvery glow along the black door with etchings of a hooded figure standing before the gates of Purgatory.

The door opened at my father's approach, and the whole room lit up with the ethereal glow, revealing shelves lined with small opaline floating whisps, each one unique with varying hues of colors. My eyes widened as I took in the thousands of rows that filled the seemingly endless room, as whispers too soft to understand reached my ears. The hairs on my arm stood up, the gift that connected me with the dead vibrating deep within my chest, calling me to touch the whisps and hear their stories, see the memories of those that had passed on.

In the middle of the room sat a round altar made of obsidian stone. As we walked closer, the grace-light grew brighter, and the stones began glittering as if they mirrored the night sky. The top of the altar had a round inlay surrounded by Enochian carvings along the edges that read: *A glimpse into the soul before Judgement.*

Azrael motioned for me to stay next to the altar while he walked over to a nearby shelf and waved his hand. The shelves around started moving, and new ones rose from the floor, shifting and twirling until one stopped directly in front of him. He held out his hand to a whisp on the top shelf that was nearly opaline, with brilliant hues of blue and flecks of purples and greens, and it floated into his palm.

He sighed, a sound filled with sorrow, as he watched it dance along his calloused hands and brought it over to me, placing it gently down into the round inlay on the top of the altar.

"This room is called the Archive of Souls. It's how we judge the souls brought in by the reapers to determine where they go, Heaven or Hell, as many humans call it. This,"—he gestured to the dancing whisp floating just above the stone altar—"is a small gathering of memories that belonged to your mother. My Yvaine, my star."

At the sound of his voice, the whisp seemed to burn brighter, and I struggled to swallow over the lump forming in my throat.

That dancing, glowing wisp, was the only piece of my mother left in this world. Neither one of us spoke as we stared at the gathering of memories flickering and sparkling before us. Ophelia felt my pain and longing through our bond, and she leaned heavily against the side of my leg, offering what she could to quell the sorrow.

After what felt like an eternity of stillness, my father gestured for me to place my hands on the glittering surface of stone. I watched warily, and as his hands met the stone, his eyes clouded with a milky white, and the whisp burned brighter than before. I followed suit, placing my hands down to find the stone cool to the touch, and before I could even take a breath, a whirling sensation overtook my mind as my consciousness was sucked into the wisp.

Chapter Forty

I was dropped next to my father in an unfamiliar hospital hallway. The smells of disinfectant and sickness made me wrinkle my nose and look to Azrael, but his eyes were locked on a window that offered us a view into a patient's room. A child lay lifeless in the hospital bed as a team of nurses and doctors tried to revive her.

The child was pale and had a bright pink beanie on her head. Her eyes were closed as if she was sleeping, but the stream of beeping machines and frantic hospital workers gave away the reality of the scene.

The child had passed on.

Her mother was howling in the corner, and the raw pain in her voice cut me to my core, making tears spring to my eyes.

The doctors slowed and stopped working, glancing at the clock to call a time of death. The mother's sobs filled the room as the nurses silently filed out to give her a moment alone with her child. I wanted to look away, the scene seeming too private as the mother shakily stood and leaned over the bed to hug her child one last time.

She brushed her fingers along her daughter's cheek, tears streaming down her own, and just when I was about to look away, *she* appeared.

My mother.

She slipped into the room, her wavy, wild golden hair falling gracefully down her back as she approached the bed. She was wearing scrubs, but they were loose and baggy, like they weren't hers. The mother snapped her eyes up, still sobbing, and rasped, "She's so young. She had her whole life ahead of her." My mother nodded silently.

I walked into the room, needing to get closer to her. She was beautiful, with golden skin, a round face, and lips with the same plushness as my own. The similarities were staggering; even though I got my coloring from my father, there were so many pieces of her within my own features.

My mother, Yvaine, gently reached out and grasped the child's hand, and the grieving mother stared, tears streaming down her face, finally realizing how odd this situation was. As she opened her mouth to likely dismiss my mother from the room, light began to glow out of my Yvaine's hand, radiating through the child's arm, creeping up until the light shone all over the child's body.

"Come back, sweet child, it is not yet your time."

I watched as the light shined brighter beneath the child's skin, until it was nearly impossible to see the features of their face. I squinted against the intensity of it, but just as I almost closed my eyes to block out the burning rays, I saw it.

The spirit of the child appeared from behind the mother with an excited grin on her face as she floated towards her body and scrambled onto the bed, settling back into her skin. The woman gasped as the light faded, and revealed the child's chest rising and falling, the color blooming along her cheeks, replacing the pale hue of death.

I was utterly still as I watched the child's eyes flutter open and the corners of her mouth tilt up in a small, tired smile. Her mother released a sound between a wail and sigh of relief as she pulled her daughter into a hug. The machines began beeping with her vitals once more.

Yvaine slipped out of the room quietly, quickly dodging the nurses running back into the room with disbelieving looks. It was then I noticed a reaper watching my mother silently behind the nurse's station, invisible to the humans milling about. The reaper cut the veil without a word and slipped back to Purgatory.

I followed my mother as she briskly walked out of the hallway and into a stairwell, where she tossed off the scrubs, revealing an oversized t-shirt and leggings.

She pushed out of the doors into the dark alley, only to stop when she saw a silhouette of a large male figure leaning against the building, as if he was waiting for her.

He stepped into the light, and my eyes widened at the sight. It was my father, without his wings, dressed in his black armor, his scythe attached to his back with a harsh look on his face, quicksilver eyes glowing in the darkness. I glanced back at my father, the real-time version, and his face was filled with more emotion than I had ever seen before. Gone were the hard lines of his face, the general furrow of his brow, the coldness in his eyes. There was warmth and longing as he stared at my mother.

I pulled my gaze away from him and back to my mother, squaring up to the Angel of Death with a wicked grin on her face as she brushed golden hair off her shoulder. She was fearless as she swaggered up to him, looking up as he towered over her.

"Wings, are you familiar with the term, 'stalker'?" She popped a hip out with familiar sass. Azrael's dark brow lifted as he crossed his arms. "Oh, I've done it now. There's the brow, making its appearance. I'd love to stick around and chat, Wings, but I'm a busy girl. I've got places to be." She sniffed as she moved to walk around him.

He stopped her, grabbing her arm as she tried to pass. "You did it again. I *warned* you to stop," my father growled at her, dipping his head down towards her. It was probably meant to frighten her, but her smile only widened.

"I don't know what you're talking about," she purred, tipping her head up to him. Leaning in, she continued, "And I'm warning you right now that if you don't let go of my arm, I'll gut you right here in this alley and not think twice about it."

I didn't know where she had been keeping the knife, but before my father could take a breath, she had a curved blade pressed against his throat.

Now I was smiling, as I saw the shock register on my father's face as Yvaine pressed in slightly to further convey her warning.

"The lives you are saving, it has been enough for me to take notice. And if I have taken notice, then I am sure the gods have taken notice as well. You're in danger, *resurrector*." Azrael let go of her arm, but she waited for a moment before pulling the knife away and shoving it in the waistband of her leggings.

She snorted. "I can take care of myself. Besides, if the gods weren't so cruel as to request souls *before* their time, I wouldn't be so busy." She turned away from him, swishing her hips as she went. Azrael followed her.

"It is the natural course of life. Death is not cruel nor unnatural," he argued.

She whirled around to face him, her golden hair flying around her, eyes fiery like molten coals as they burned into him.

"My gift calls to me, to protect the souls that are not meant to die yet, and I answer that call." She looked down her nose at him, despite the height difference. "And the look on that mother's face when I brought her child back to her would make any wrath of the gods worth it," she snapped before whirling again, leaving my father with his jaw dropped staring after her.

The vision swirled, and I strained my eyes, trying to get one last look at my mother as her image drifted away like smoke, and I was dropped back into the glittering room in front of the stone altar.

I inhaled a deep breath and mumbled, "Why did you show me that?"

I kept my eyes cast down towards the altar, not wanting my father to see the many emotions swirling within them. She was so beautiful, so firm in her beliefs and powerful, and I would never get to know her.

"To show you why you are unique. Why it is vital that you do not bring unnecessary attention to yourself. Why you need to pledge yourself to my legion, to Purgatory. So I will not lose you, like..." he drifted off, closing his eyes, as if he couldn't bear to say the words.

Like he lost my mother.

I didn't know how to respond. The loss we both felt, while both losses were vastly different, it connected us. I grew up with the sorrow of not ever getting to know my mother. He knew her, loved her, then lost her. And shortly after, he lost me.

The only piece of her he had left.

"Your mother was blessed with Phoenix Fire, a gift given by a Primordial being, one who helped create the realms and even the gods. Phoenixes were natural healers and life bringers, sentient beings burning brightly throughout the universe, creating worlds in the wake of their flames. A millennium or so after Odenus's creation and his rise to power, he began hunting down the Phoenixes, wanting to be the only creature that could control life and creation. Odenus succeeded in part, having killed several of the Phoenixes who remained in this universe. But what he did not know is that many of the Phoenixes began mating with supes from other species.

"Thus, carrying on their bloodline and mixing with the many beings that were born of their godchildren. No child from those matings resulted in a full-blooded Phoenix, however, most of those children can heal themselves, but rarely could they stop death completely. That power remains with the Fates and the gods. Which is why it is imperative that you align yourself with Purgatory. Come work for me as a reaper so I may protect you."

Each word from his mouth had my mind spinning. There was so much more to the history of gods and angels than I could have ever imagined, and a messy one at that. Still, even with the knowledge of my heritage, my real heritage, I could not bring myself to take him up on his proposition.

"I don't know if I can agree to that. You say it will protect me, but I don't think the gods will forgive my existence so easily. You work too closely with Odenus and Morana. And after what—after what Gadreel did, I don't know if I can." I barely managed to get the words out. I looked up to see his features soften.

He walked around the altar to stand in front of me as he reached out and gently grabbed my hand. "I am trying to ensure that will never happen to you again. You would have the realm's protection."

I looked down at his calloused hand holding mine and sighed. As I contemplated his offer, I caught sight of the scars from Gadreel holding me captive. Torturing me.

I would be aligning myself with someone who worked with and submitted to both gods of the afterlife. The thought of that made me sick, and every bone in my body was screaming at me to deny him. That I was made for something more than submission, and that he was too. I would not be at the mercy of anyone ever again.

My mother's words keep repeating in my head. She said she was protecting the souls of those who were not meant to die. Her cause resonated with me, called to me. As I considered those words, a sense of destiny washed over me.

Despite the revulsion rolling around in my gut and the words I was about to say, if only to buy myself more time to understand, I murmured, "I'll think about it."

My father arched a brow at me, his eyes skeptical, but he nodded and released my hand.

The walk back to his office was silent, and I kept one hand firmly on Ophelia's neck, needing her support.

"Valerie will escort you back to New Haven. I'll call you back soon." He looked me over, as if he wanted to reach out and embrace me before sighing and adding, "Stay well." He flicked his hand, and the door opened. Valerie was waiting outside, her golden eyes glancing between the two of us.

I dipped my head at my father and strode from his office. I didn't speak as we made our way through the halls, back towards the large double doors. My mind was racing with all that I had learned. My mother was not just a necromancer, she was a rare anomaly, blessed with Phoenix Fire that could bring a soul back from beyond the veil.

And Dean... I couldn't even finish the thought.

I snapped my head over to look at Valerie and stopped just as we were under the gorgeous vaulted ceilings in the stone hallway we arrived in. She stopped, not uttering a word as she turned towards me.

"You knew. About the bond Dean and I share." It was a statement, not a question. Her golden eyes searched my face as she lifted her chin before nodding. "Why didn't you tell me? I thought we were friends." My words were laced with venom and hurt.

"You were in no state to learn that kind of information. Do you remember what it was like, those months after your father brought you back? You were a ghost, Blair, barely surviving. When I first saw you the night Vivian was killed, I saw your heart break. I saw it shatter into a million pieces before my very eyes and yet you still sacrificed yourself to save *him*. I saw how traumatized you were the day Azrael brought you to New Haven.

"But at the mere mention of Dean, you woke up, the spark in your eyes returned, and you went to him without a thought as to what you had just gone through. You needed him, your soul needed that tether, and it kept you from breaking completely. Your bond with him saved you. In more ways than one."

I shook my head at her words, tears springing to my eyes.

She had not ever mentioned Vivian; I didn't even think she had remembered it.

My hands trembled, and she reached out to grasp them in hers. "I still deserved to know," I whispered. "I feel like you were all lying to me."

Valerie gave me a small smile. "And for that, I am sorry. But without knowing the nature of the bond, it would be difficult to explain. I know you have felt the pull towards Dean, and I think you have suspected there is more between you two than merely raw attraction."

I had done it all for him. Made the deal with Gadreel. To keep him safe.

Valerie slashed her free hand through the air, opening the veil and gently pulling me through with Ophelia trailing behind. A cool wind ruffled my hair as we landed just outside Valerie's townhouse in New Haven, and I sucked in a deep breath to clear away the tears that threatened to escape.

I soon felt Dean behind me, and a quiet rage coiled in my gut. Did he truly know about the bond forming between us? Why was it that everyone around me felt the need to keep these massive, life-altering secrets from me?

I whirled, letting go of Valerie's hand, and faced him. His bright eyes and smile for our return quickly faded as he took in my expression, which was twisted into a snarl. Lightning snaked down my arms, and even Cal looked at me warily, taking a small step closer to Dean, ready to protect his alpha if necessary.

Dean waved him back, not breaking eye contact with me. "What happened?"

I let out a harsh laugh as I looked at him. Valerie cursed behind me, as a few onlookers on the street began to stop and stare. I didn't care; let them see what I was. All of Hell and Elysia seemed to know I existed anyway.

But as soon as I looked at him, and that bond between us seemed to pulse with acknowledgement, I knew my rage was irrational, an overreaction. That anger swiftly faded to hurt, and I had to bite the inside of my cheek to keep the tears at bay.

Concern flickered across Dean's face as he took a step closer.

Lightning struck from my palm and cracked the stone beneath me, a warning to stay back. "Did you ever plan on telling me, Dean?" His dark brow lifted, and as he opened his mouth to respond, I cut him off, "When were you going to tell me about the soul bond between us?"

Chapter Forty-One

He stared at me in disbelief, and even Cal's stoic face had wide eyes as he looked between Dean and me. I vaguely heard Hamish chuckle from the steps of the townhome. I tried to rein in the swirling grace inside me, not wanting to lose control any more than I already was.

"Well?" I demanded, my lip trembling slightly.

He took a step towards me, earning a warning growl from both Ophelia and Hamish. The latter shocked me, but I didn't have the time to dissect what that was all about. Valerie just took a step away, a giggle slipping from her lips. Thunder clapped above us, causing the onlookers to rush away to escape the impending storm.

"Blair, I didn't know how to tell you." My lightning cracked the stone again, a warning. He cleared his throat. "I wanted to tell you, planned on telling you after we brought Sage and Vivian here."

Pain sliced through my chest, my heart squeezing at the sound of her name.

He continued, "Then you... you were taken. And I nearly tore the world apart looking for you. I feared I'd never get the chance to tell you. I felt your pain, Blair. Through the tether that binds our souls, I felt how much pain you were in, and I was in *agony* that you were suffering."

His words struck a chord within me, and I thought of the long nights of never-ending pain. I had thought I was losing my sanity at the time, but I swore that a howl accompanied my screams.

"The pain and guilt and rage I felt kept me in my wolf form, tearing through any vampire who possibly had any connection with Alistair. When you came back, I could hardly bear to see the look of emptiness, pain, and fear that was in your eyes, and all I wanted was to rip those bastards apart. But you needed me, needed me in the most primal way—and I did try to tell you then, tried to explain, but the look in your eyes... I would have torn my own heart out of my chest and given it to you, if you had asked. I would have done *anything*."

Tears sprung to my eyes at the memories. The pain nearly brought me to my knees.

Dean was in front of me then, a few pieces of his dark locks brushing his brow, looking down at me with his ocean eyes. I knew what he would say next, continuing to rip open all the wounds I had tucked away and ignored.

"Then you left. And even though it nearly killed me to let you go, every instinct in my body screamed at me to bring you back and never let you go again. I knew you needed to heal, needed to work through the horrors that you went through on your own, because you felt like you needed to protect everyone."

Hazy bourbon memories surfaced, of him asking Valerie if he could come see me, his delicious scent drifting up to my open bedroom window as I laid there in bed. It hadn't made sense to me before, why I had moved the bed near the window. Part of it had been because without a window, I felt trapped again, felt the walls closing in and the pain ripping through my body once more. But I also knew he would be there, outside the window, our bond pushing me to grasp onto any part of him I could.

I looked up into his beautiful azure eyes pleading with me as they looked down upon my face. His scent wrapped around me again, and I hated that I inhaled deeply, letting it fill me, center me.

"I will always come back to you. I see you, for all that you are, and I am not afraid. Never have been," he murmured, reaching up gently to brush a stray hair out of my face.

I sighed and tilted my head higher, closer to his. His eyes widened in shock, then gave way to a blazing heat as he leaned down, his gaze falling to my lips. His dark lashes hooded, and just as our breaths mingled together, I stopped.

"Pretty words don't change the fact that you should have told me sooner," I whispered.

My bottom lip quivered slightly as I looked up at him, the rage fading to the real emotion I was desperate to keep hidden away. The hurt and betrayal I felt, for being kept in the dark. The same feeling I'd felt when Vivian's involvement with demons came to light rose to the surface; yet another person whom I cared for had hidden things from me, lied to me. It was a heartache I didn't want to bear again.

Dean's brows pinched together, understanding flashing across his handsome features. He didn't fight me as I placed my hands on his chest and pushed him away slightly, taking my own steps back, needing to put space between us, to allow my emotions to settle. I inhaled deeply, allowing my magic to calm as well before I lifted my chin.

"I don't have the capacity to deal with this right now. I already have my father trying to dictate my life, and angels and demons out to kill me." I flicked my dark hair over my shoulder and adjusted my jacket. "Don't ever keep something like this from me again."

Dean's mouth kicked up into a small smile as he promised, "Never again, my Raven, I swear it."

* * *

"Fuck the gods and fuck your father's offer," Dean snarled as we sat in Valerie's living room once more.

After our little spectacle in the street, we all made our way inside and I told them all what had transpired during my trip to Purgatory. Dean dismissed Cal, and Hamish made himself scarce, doing whatever he wished with his newfound freedom.

Dean respectfully gave me my space, but he paced the room like a caged animal, as if it was the only thing keeping his wolf in check.

"Have you ever pulled back a soul from death?" Valerie asked, her golden eyes contemplative as she lounged on a nearby chaise.

"I have only brought back a soul from beyond the veil once. It was an animal though, a cat that had been hit by a car when I was a teenager. I didn't know what I was doing." When I had told Vivian about it, she brushed it off as necromancy, and that after my power faded the cat had probably given in to death again after a short while. It was obvious now that she had been trying to hide from me what she already knew. That my mother was a resurrector, and both Elysia and Hell would tear apart the world to kill me. "But I haven't done it since, because honestly it scared the shit out of me."

Valerie snorted. "Rightfully so, apparently. Clearly, your mother caught the attention of Morana and Odenus and paid the price. Your father revealed this to you to protect you, and to keep you from meeting the same fate." I inwardly flinched.

"Where do the demons and vampires fit into all of this? If this is god business, wouldn't it only involve the angels?" Dean asked.

"Demons are agents of Morana. She had tried to create something similar to angels by herself, but without the assistance of Hecate, something different was born of her death magic. Odenus and the other gods were furious and used their power to banish demons to reside in Hell. That amount of power created rifts in the world, small tears where the demons could crawl back up and wreak havoc on Earth. Thus, it became angels' main duty to hunt demons and dispatch them back to Hell, as well as protect their god and their realms of course," Ophelia's velvety voice projected to the three of us.

Sometimes I forget how old Ophelia was, being a familiar. She had lived countless lives aiding powerful witches until their time in this world came to an end.

I stood up abruptly. "I think I need to head to—"

"The library," the three of them chorused, and I stuck my tongue out.

"Well, yes. Lumen might be able to point me to some relevant texts about resurrectors. I left Purgatory with more questions than answers."

"I'll go with you." I stiffened as Dean began following me out. I turned, looking into Dean's pleading azure eyes and giving him a brief nod.

I didn't wait for him as I made my way down the steps of the brownstone and started down the quiet street towards the library. Ophelia trailed close behind. The three of us walked in silence, the sounds of our steps echoing against the buildings that lined the street.

"Are we going to talk about this?"

He was so close I could feel the heat coming off his body. His rich scent curling around me, begging me to forgive him.

I shrugged. "No."

"Why? I freely admit that I should have handled it better. Hell, I should have brought it up to you sooner, but you were taken before I had the chance to." He stepped in front of me, blocking my path, and I glared up at him. I tried to sidestep him, but he matched me. "Is it so bad to be bonded to me?"

Hurt gleamed in his gaze, even if his tone was joking, and I stopped.

He thought I didn't want to be bonded to him?

"Gods, Dean, is that what you think this is about? That I don't want to be bonded to you?" He just stared at me, the hurt and uncertainty still there, and it gutted me to see it. "You are exactly the kind of male that I would like to be—no, that I would be *honored* to be bonded to, to be mated to, if the Fates deemed me so lucky."

His eyes softened, a spark of hope returning to those cerulean depths.

Dean stepped closer, and I allowed it, inhaling his scent of leather and amber deeply. He raised a hand and caressed my cheek, and I leaned into it. "Then what is it?"

A single tear slid down my cheek, the truth almost being too much to reveal, too much to allow him to see. "I can't stand these secrets anymore. I was—I am hurt that you didn't talk to me about it. You, Ophelia, Valerie, shit even Hamish, you all knew, but I was left in the dark, wondering what this was between us. I was left wondering if I was the only one feeling this unexplainable pull. My entire existence has been one secret revealed after the next, when all I have ever wanted was peace."

"You have consumed my every waking thought from the moment the Fates granted me the vision of you, and I am *haunted* when I am not with you. You have shifted my whole world, bewitched my wolf, and have held my heart captive from the moment we met. I want to protect your peace, and I swear, I will never disrupt that peace again," Dean murmured, his eyes unwavering as he looked at me.

From what I had learned at the library, soul bonds were all extremely rare and varied between supe to supe on what they could mean.

The most well-known was a true mate bond, a bonding of two souls perfectly made for one another, and it was the rarest of the three. The second, the kind Ophelia and I shared, was a spirit bond. It was a bond between witch and familiar and was only given to those deemed worthy by Hecate. There have been cases of intense bonding between friends, making them more like family, or enemies so fierce wars were fought to end the feud.

The specifics of the bond were only revealed by the Fates, whenever they deemed you worthy of the knowledge.

Dean continued, "I never expected your estranged father to bring it up before I had the chance to. Knowing you were—*are* still learning about our world, I wanted to explain it, even if we aren't sure what kind of bond it is." His glowing eyes nearly burned through me as he stared down at me, a determined tick to his jaw only visible in the light of the streetlamps. "And what I feel for you, Raven, not even the gods themselves could rip you from the depths of my heart, of my soul, that you have made a home in."

I shuddered, the whisperings of the Fates surrounding me as my eyes roamed over his beautiful face. Searching, searching for anything that would contradict those words, any sign that he didn't truly mean them, even if in my heart, I knew he did. My brows pinched together in an effort to continue holding back the tears and the emotions I had kept at bay for so long.

Perhaps he thought my expression was one of apprehension or uncertainty, but Dean stepped in closer, and my breasts brushed up against his chest with each intake of breath. The air around us grew thick, and it took every ounce of my willpower not to lose myself in his delicious scent wrapping around me.

"You can be mad at me all you want, Raven. In fact, I welcome it. You can scream at me, fight me, stab me with one of your pretty curved blades, and I will take it all. I will meet you word for word, blow for blow, and keep fighting for you." He bent his head down until his lips were nearly touching mine, and I was too stunned at his words to move, too entranced by his devastatingly handsome face. "Because you are the storm I never want to end."

I let his words wrap around my heart, holding it close, thickening the tether I felt between us. This male before me saw me at my lowest points, where I felt the darkness that haunted me would consume me, but he did not balk, he did not waver; he kept coming back to me, offering up his light even when I pushed him away.

He saw me for everything that I was, and he was not afraid.

That wall around my heart crumbled, and I basked in the glow that was Dean, my light in an endless abyss of darkness. My grace thrummed within me, singing with pleasure, and I closed my eyes at the sensation, letting my lips curl into a small smile.

When I opened my eyes, Dean's eyes widened as tiny sparks began coating my skin, casting him in a silver glow. Before he could utter a word, I pressed my lips to his. He was shocked at first, completely still, until I flicked my tongue across his lips. A growl escaped him as he pulled me close with one hand grasping my hip, the other against my jaw, deepening the kiss.

We explored each other, our tongues tangling as his hand curled around my backside. A sigh of pleasure escaped me, and he devoured the sound with his own rumble.

When we broke apart, we were gasping for air, caught in a lustful haze. In that moment, nothing else mattered. He was the light side to my dark moon, the piece of myself I felt that I was missing my entire life—even when I felt like I was enough. He broke down every wall I erected, chose me even when he knew nothing about me, and still when I laid myself bare and broken before him, he still did not waver.

"This doesn't mean you're off the hook for not telling me sooner," I breathed.

He chuckled against my mouth, the sound sending shivers down my spine. "I will do *anything* to make it up to you." The way he purred those words sent a throbbing need to my core. "Are you sure we have to go to the library to study some dusty old books? I have a few other things in mind I'd like to look over in *great detail*." He leaned in and captured my bottom lip in between his teeth before pressing another brief kiss to my mouth.

I shivered at his wicked words. "As tempting as that is, we need to arm ourselves with knowledge. But as far as your other offer, maybe later... if you're lucky."

I playfully pushed him away and walked towards Ophelia, who was waiting patiently for us at the streetlamp up ahead. I heard Dean groan before jogging to catch up with us. We made it to the library a few moments later and pushed open the great doors. Ophelia sniffed the air and led the way around various shelves, leading us towards Lumen.

I had never seen the night fae in such a disarray before. Her silvery white hair was thrown up in a messy bun, with various pieces hanging down against her face and neck, and her clothes were wrin-kled as if she had fallen asleep wearing them. A heaping pile of books covered the table in front of her, with a few open as she looked between them and scribbled down notes.

"Lu?" I cleared my throat, startling her as she looked up, dark circles under her eyes. Ophelia shifted into her smaller form and hopped up onto the table, pressing her face into Lumen's cheek.

She exclaimed, "Oh! I'm sorry, I didn't hear you come in. But you are just the supes I wanted to see!" She waved us over to the table, pushing her hair out of her face before organizing her notes in front of her.

I exchanged a look with Dean as we made our way to the table and stood on opposite sides of her chair, peering over her shoulder.

Her eloquent handwriting was scribbled over several pages, some with drawings and sketches of large wolves, the symbol of the seven realms and angel wings. "Since our last visit, I had become curious about Dean's ancestry, after feeling the strength in his magic."

"You mean when he went all alpha-hole in the bar room?" I quipped, earning a playful growl from Dean.

She nodded. "Yes, exactly. It was not the same as any other alpha shifter I have ever encountered. And it reminded me of something I read about the gods and their protectors of the realms."

She shifted her papers and pulled an open book from her pile, placing it on top. The yellowing page held a picture of two massive beasts, one standing in front of a gate of light and clouds, the other in front of a gate of fire and bone. The former was a massive wolf with silver-colored fur and bright green eyes; the similarities between the wolf on the page and Dean were unnerving, despite the color differences.

The second wolf was a dark color from what you could tell, as most of the fur seemed to have been singed off, and its eyes were a glowing red that matched the fire behind it.

"Odenus and Morana desired to create beings that would serve as guardians of the realms of the afterlife: Hell and Elysia. In an act of self-preservation and selfishness, they looked to the other gods' children and creations to use for the task. Blessed with the power of the moon, incredible strength and agility, and the ability to shift between humanoid and beast form, two of Lunae's children were chosen for the spell, Fenrir and Grem.

"But before they could complete the spell together, Morana stole the spell from Hecate herself and created something far worse than just a Guardian of the After-Realms. She took away Grem's free will and his soul; thus, his only duty was to serve Morana, her realm, and her disciples. As a result, Grem became the first Hellhound."

Her delicate finger rested right underneath the picture of Grem, and my stomach clenched.

"Odenus, furious with Morana's deceit, demanded Hecate to give him the same spell to bind Fenrir to him in the same way Grem was bound to Morana. Hecate refused at first, until Morana unleashed Grem upon Earth, eager to see how many souls she could drag into her realm with the use of her Hellhound. Hecate, desperate to restore the balance of magic to the universe, granted Odenus his wish, and in turn, Fenrir was bound to Odenus. A great battle was fought, until both Guardians were called back to their own realms, as war nearly broke out among the gods because of the Guardian's destruction.

"Descendants of Fenrir and Grem were lost and remained hidden throughout the centuries, but if a line was ever discovered, they would mysteriously disappear, never to be seen again." She paused, looking over her shoulder at Dean. "You come from a long line of alphas that have been larger than any other wolf shifter in history. You have power that I have never felt another shifter possess. I believe you and Hayley are descendants of Lunae's children."

Chapter Forty-Two

I looked over the symbols on the page, each of them vastly different. The first, underneath the Elysian Guardian, had seven golden circles, two at the top and two on the bottom, with three intertwining in the middle, and overlapping the circles was a golden spear. The Hellhound symbol was a crimson five-pointed star, with a thick black circle encasing each of the points, and small red glyphs were etched between the lines of the star points.

"Do you have a copy of the spell that was used?" I asked Lumen. I felt Dean look at me with a questioning expression, but I ignored him, focusing on the symbols on the page.

"No, it is said that Hecate felt such remorse for aiding in the enslavement of Lunae's children that she destroyed the spell in order to keep the peace amongst the gods." Lumen rubbed her temples before adjusting her notes again on the table.

There is someone here in New Haven that might have knowledge of the spell. Or at the very least has contact with Hecate.

I smiled at my familiar before looking at Dean. With a wicked smile, I said, "Call Nathara and ask her to meet us here." His eyes widened in shock, and Lumen paled further. But without question, he pulled out his phone and made the call.

* * *

We waited in silence, other than Lumen shuffling her notes and books every couple of minutes while she worried her lip. I could understand her nerves, as my last encounter with Nathara had started out less than pleasant, but in the end, she offered her assistance should I have questions. And I had a feeling she would possess the knowledge I sought.

The energy shifted, and we all looked towards the hallway that led into the private study room. Ophelia shifted into her larger form and sat in front of me, her ears pulled back against her head, and her inky shadows wrapped around my body protectively.

Nathara entered the room, her long onyx hair pulled back into a sleek ponytail that trailed down her spine. She wore wide legged black trousers and a skintight black lace corset that had a pattern like snake scales. She was hauntingly beautiful. Her upward-angled yellow eyes narrowed as they flicked over the four of us, a slight hiss escaping her chest as they lingered on me.

Dean spoke first, "Thank you for coming, Nathara. I wouldn't have called if it wasn't important."

Nathara's gaze never left mine, and I did not grant her the satisfaction of looking away. Two predators, analyzing their opponent. Her ancient magic slithered throughout the room, the echo of a hiss following in its wake. Lumen whimpered slightly, but Dean and Ophelia let out growls of warning.

I let my own power meet hers, and the room quaked from the amount of energy that filled it. Nathara's lips curled into a lethal smile before she purred, "You are getting stronger, Nephilim." She pulled her power back into herself, and after a moment, I pulled mine back in as well. "How may I be of service?"

I motioned for her to approach the table and pulled the book of

Guardians to the top of the pile. "What do you know of the spell that created the Guardians and Hellhounds?"

"I have to admit, when you called me here, this is not what I was expecting." Her soft voice sent chills down my spine. "A very complex spell. One that started such conflict among the gods. Why do you want to know?" She trailed a finger over the image of Grem as her yellow eyes flicked to Dean, an action I did not miss.

I shrugged, feigning bored curiosity. "Just reading up on some lore. Thought the oldest supe in New Haven might be able to shed some light on the ancient tale."

She chuckled, as if she saw right through me.

But she played along, "Hecate was furious when the spell was stolen from her, and though the original was stolen and corrupted, all evidence of it was destroyed. These symbols here represent the gods, binding the beast to their will, their powers, until their death. Though the creation of the spell held good intentions, it was used for a moronic power play between Odenus and Morana and resulted in destruction and death across the Earth."

I nodded, mulling over that information. "So, the symbol is inter-changeable to the being the beast is bound to. Can the symbol be changed or removed?"

"Perhaps. If the being held enough power of the gods." Nathara smiled at me, the slits in her eyes expanding and contracting as she studied my face.

"What being would have the power of the gods?" Dean asked.

She said nothing, her eyes never leaving mine. The hairs along my arm raised up, and the air felt thinner as the ancient being before me stared. Her only response hinting that she even heard the question was the subtle lift of one thin eyebrow.

I changed the subject, "Has Hecate ever created a spell that would reverse the curse that banished vampires from walking in the sun?"

Her brows furrowed at my sudden change of subject, but I kept my face calm and impassive.

"Vampires have always been creatures of darkness. Walking in the sun is not an ability that was taken away. They simply never possessed it."

"Are you certain?" Dean demanded, taking a step closer to me.

"I was several hundred years old when vampires were first created by Morana; I would know if their nature had been changed. Regarding the Guardians, I can see if Hecate will grant you any more information, since you seem to have a vested interest." Nathara's eyes flicked to Dean so quickly, I was sure I was the only one who caught the movement. Hearing that she was able to contact a god sent a chill through me. "I will let you know soon."

And with that, she flicked her ponytail over her shoulder and started towards the entrance to the room.

"Why are you helping us?" I asked, just as she reached the threshold of the door.

She looked back at me over her shoulder, a venomous smile playing on her lips. "I know where this path leads." Her yellow eyes flashed with knowing as she stared at me before she strode from the room.

We stood in silence for a few moments before Lumen whispered, "Holy shit. Nathara was here, in the library. You earned favor with one of the first supes, a favorite of Hecate, a BASILISK!"

I chuckled at her whisper-scream and plopped myself down in the chair across from her.

Basilisks were an extremely rare supernatural creature, one of the first that were created, and there were rumored to only be a few in existence. They were feared due to their extremely poisonous venom that could either enslave you to their will or kill you slowly and painfully.

Legend also said that if you dared to hold a basilisk's gaze, they could send visions that were so real, you didn't even know they had ensnared you and keep you captive until you died.

"I can't help that I'm extremely charming." I put both arms behind my head. "Now, we wait for information." Lumen's mouth opened and closed several times before she sat back in her seat, processing everything. I sighed, "Go shower and rest, Lu. Dean and I can hold down the fort until the sun comes up."

"But I—" she began to protest, but I silenced her with a look. "Right, extremely charming. Thank you." She stood up wearily before patting Ophelia on her head and walking out of the study room, yawning as she went.

"Why did you ask her about the Guardian spell?" Dean took the seat to my right, hooking his foot under my chair and pulling it close to his. He picked up my legs and draped them across his lap, and I let myself relax into him.

I studied my nails before replying, "I just wanted to know a bit more about your ancestry. I am a witch after all, and I found the spell interesting." He stared at me, and I knew he didn't believe me, but my shrug of dismissal silenced him before I spoke again. "Knowledge is power, and so is having ancient beings on your side."

His satisfied smirk faltered a bit as he said, "Are you not concerned that Hecate will know you exist? That she will alert Odenus and he will unleash legions to kill you?" Worry laced his voice as he studied my face. I shook my head.

"If Nathara already knew what I was, then chances are Hecate already does too. Besides, I have witch blood within me, and I am hoping she will keep my secret from the other gods to protect me." I only prayed I was right, but it seemed like a logical conclusion.

"I think Blair is correct. I was sent specifically by Hecate to protect her, to become her familiar. I do not think she would have done so if she wished Blair dead." Ophelia shifted smaller and hopped up on the table.

I pushed away from the table and stood up, twirling my fingers, and the books began closing and shutting, putting themselves in neatly stacked piles, with Lumen's notes in the middle of them. I didn't dare attempt to put the books away. After many nights with Lumen studying, I learned better than to try and put them back myself. The night fae was very particular about their placement.

I wandered out of the study room and began lazily looking over the shelves. The library always brought me a sense of calm and quickly became a sanctuary during the months after I was brought back from *there*. The seemingly endless shelves and ceiling that perfectly displayed the star-filled sky brought me comfort, that I was not locked away, that I was free.

I took a turn into the small nook that I used frequently during my recovery. I smiled at the sight of the number of cushions lining the floor, as well as the plush oversized chair with plenty of room for me to spread out and read.

A sigh escaped me, as my thoughts instantly calmed upon entering the space. Books that I had been reading were laid out on the side table, left for me by Lumen, still deeming this space as mine.

Ophelia trotted ahead of me and made herself comfortable on her favorite cushion, curling into a tight ball and tucking her paws underneath her body. I followed suit and plopped myself down on the large chair, pulling the knit blanket hanging off the arm around my body as I leaned back. Dean paused between the stacks that served as an entryway of sorts into my little reading nook, taking in every detail of the space.

His azure eyes flicked to mine, as if asking permission to enter the space, which was something I appreciated. I gave him a nod, and he slowly walked over, carefully avoiding the cushions.

He took a seat on a cushion that was near the arm of my chair, leaning against the wall after he plucked one of the books I had set aside on the table and opened it without a word. I stared at him for a few moments, looking over the details of his face, the way his hair was much longer now, nearly to his shoulders, his strong jawline, and the way his glacier-blue eyes sparked with mirth as he read the fantasy romance novel I was entertaining myself with in between research texts.

Of course, he would have picked up that book.

I grabbed another book from the stack, one that detailed the history of how each archangel was assigned to each realm and god they served. The silence between us was comfortable, and I found myself enjoying his warm presence.

My mind wandered to the bond that seemed to be thrumming between us, the words on the page not registering as I kept stealing glances at him.

The hurt I felt that he had not told me what we were to one another was still aching within my chest, but I acknowledged the truth behind his words. If he had told me that as soon as we'd met, I would have probably laughed in his face and possibly made a very vulgar gesture.

My mind wandered to what he had said earlier about how he dealt with me being taken, how he said he could feel my pain. I remembered the sound of those mournful howls I often heard while Gadreel and his demons were slicing into my skin. In my soul, I knew the sound was real, even though there was no rational way it could have been him. The sound reminded me that he was safe, and it made every cut, every blow, every slice of my skin on my soul, worth it.

The wolf spoke the truth. Though your bond was barely formed, it was strong enough for him to feel an echo of the pain and anguish you were feeling. It was similar to the way I could feel it, as our spirits are bound as one.

I looked over to Ophelia to find her eyes still closed, but she continued.

He nearly went feral, Blair. Just at the echo of pain he was sensing from you, he was ready to tear worlds apart to get you back. The stupid wolf even attempted to summon a demon to make a deal to get you back.

It took great effort not to react to that statement, and Ophelia's tail flicked with amusement.

Don't worry, I stopped him, though I think he may still be quite bitter about me dragging him away from the summoning circle by the leg. We fought for a good while before he calmed down enough. She let out a soft chuffing sound, almost like a giggle. *The guilt of what was happening to you was destroying him on the inside, Blair. Though you were in pain, you were alive, and I told him to focus on that, and that we would find you, but that you would kill him yourself if he made a deal with a demon. The point is, Blair, he spoke the truth, and what you two have is so strong, he could feel everything you felt.*

I focused on the tether between us, the bond that bound our souls together. It gave off a faint hum within me, like the charge of my lightning, and I followed it, followed it to the end where it resided within his chest.

Warmth bloomed within me, like sitting next to fire, and it spread through my body as I felt him. It felt like happiness, contentment, peace. Sitting here, next to me in my little corner of the library, a place where I found sanctuary, he felt content, just being here.

The realization nearly made tears spring to the surface, but I inhaled, trying to suck them back in.

"Dean," I murmured.

His head lolled to the side lazily as he looked up at me with a crooked grin. "Hmm?" Whatever he saw on my face caused him to sit up straighter and angle his body towards mine. "What is it, Blair?" he asked seriously, his hand reaching out to hold mine.

"I'd do it all again. For you. I'd withstand Gadreel's wrath and burn for all eternity if it meant keeping you safe."

"Blair…" Dean reached up and cupped my cheek, and I leaned into the warmth of his palm, the callouses rubbing my skin.

"You once told me that I was your peace, but you are mine. You've saved me more than you realize, given me something to hold onto after I was utterly shattered inside, and you did not falter. I can't even begin to explain how much that means to me." A single tear rolled down my cheek, but I felt like I was drowning in emotion for this male before me.

He leaned in and kissed the tear away before plucking the book I held in my grasp and setting it on the table.

He made quick work of sliding in behind me, his arms wrapping around me as he hauled me against his chest, cradling me in his arms as he took over my seat, keeping me snuggled up to him. I inhaled deeply as we settled into a comfortable position, the warmth of his skin seeping into my own, warming me to my core.

"Just no more secrets, okay? Not with me. I don't think my brain or my heart could take any more in this life," I mumbled as he pressed a kiss into my hair.

A rumble escaped his chest, which vibrated against me. He picked up the book I was reading and propped it open for me, before settling his chin on the top of my head. "No more secrets, I swear it."

Chapter Forty-Three

Over the next few days, we all spent our time with our heads buried in various dusty books, learning anything and everything about my heritage. Dean had also commanded Cal to use their various contacts throughout New Haven to try and track down Alistair or Gadreel, despite my father's wishes to let him handle it.

We searched the library for any texts on resurrectors and the extent of their powers, and why the two gods of the afterworlds would be fearful of anyone with that power. To which we found nothing, nor had we heard back from Nathara since our meeting in the library.

In a desperate attempt to try and release some of the tension I was feeling over the situation—and to take a much-needed break from these old books that weren't providing any help—I decided that it was time to go back to the pack house and see Sage. I had been avoiding it long enough, and the guilt I was feeling was getting to be too much with all the information that had recently come to light. I just needed to see my best friend.

I nervously tucked my hair behind my ear and chewed my lip.

Ophelia was a steady presence at my side, the bond between us humming with shared magic, offering me support. I checked the bags that were lined along Valerie's counter, all filled with enough food to feed Dean's entire pack.

Valerie came down the stairs then, wearing her usual sweater and legging combination with a pair of sherpa-lined slippers. Her ruby hair was half up in her Viking braids with large golden hoop earrings hanging from her ears. My own outfit was similar, though I spiced mine up with my usual combat boots and leather jacket, as the temperature this week had dropped significantly over the past couple of days.

"Are you ready to go?" Valerie smiled brightly at me.

I gave her a nod. I had to be ready; this was my stupid idea after all. I hadn't been back to pack territory since I had initially been returned by Azrael from my imprisonment with Gadreel. I hadn't seen Sage since I had screamed at her in the wake of my grief and trauma, and that was months ago.

Hamish joined us as we started taking the bags into Valerie's car, piling everything into the trunk. He was surprisingly easy to be around, just another lost soul like the rest of us, trying to make it in this world. Hamish had taken up residence in Valerie's place unofficially, and he seemed to be making no moves to leave, his vow to me still holding true—another powerful ally on our side.

After a few trips, we settled into the car and started making our way to Dean's territory. Valerie assured me that she warned him we were coming this morning, but that did nothing to quell my nerves. Sage might not even want to see me after the way I'd yelled at her.

The memories of that day were a grief-ridden blur, but I remembered the way I had accused her of not warning me of Vivian's death, and I remembered the hurt in her seafoam eyes.

We passed through the magic barrier into Dean's territory and followed the gravel path to his circle drive. My breath hitched when I saw Dean, clad in his dark jeans and black shirt that clung to his muscular form, waiting for us on the stone steps of his massive house.

The bond between us sung a sweet song, happy to be close to him once again.

Valerie smirked knowingly as she threw the car into park. Sage was nowhere in sight, but as soon as we exited the car, Hayley and Selene rushed out of the house. I froze, not knowing how they would react to seeing me again after I had put their alpha, their family, in danger and left without saying goodbye.

They both brushed past Dean despite his protests and growls of warning and came running towards me. Ophelia and Valerie both paused, tensing and ready to intercept them if I needed them to. Hayley's dark hair flew behind her as she threw her arms out, and I flinched before they pulled me in for a hug. I was rigid in her arms, until a small whine escaped her, and I wrapped my arms around her too.

She held me close, and I soon found myself gripping her just as tight. No words were said, but her touch spoke louder than any words could have. Hayley and I had been close before everything happened, and I had shunned her just as much as I had shunned her brother.

She rubbed her face against mine, her wolf instincts coming through as she marked me as one of her own, a member of the pack. More guilt threatened to choke me, but she pulled back, her cerulean eyes lined with silver, and she shook her head, as if she sensed the direction of my thoughts. I nodded, offering her a small smile as she let me go to help Hamish and Valerie with the food.

Selene was gentler, but she embraced me all the same, murmuring, "Welcome home, Blair." She patted me lightly on the cheek, wiping away the rogue tear that slid down, before turning away too.

I sucked in a breath as the lot of them disappeared into the house, leaving me alone with Dean.

"Hey, angel-face." He strolled towards me with that cocky smirk that made my toes curl.

I groaned. "Please don't start calling me that. Raven is bad enough."

His grin only widened at my words, knowing it was utter bullshit.

His woodsy scent wrapped itself around me as he stopped in front of me, and I tried not to audibly inhale it.

"What's with the brunch brigade?" he asked, a curious glint in his eye.

"An apology? For nearly getting their alpha and beta killed. And I need to see Sage. To apologize to her. She's a sucker for brunch." I nervously picked at the sleeves of my sweater. His calloused hands came to rest over mine, stilling my movements. I looked up at him, his glacier eyes soft.

"There is nothing to apologize for. But I'm sure those savages will all appreciate the food." As if to punctuate his point, howls and yips of joy rang out from behind the house, and we both smiled. "Come on, I think Sage and Miles are out by the garden."

I quirked a brow, not pegging Miles for the gardening type.

Dean kept my hand in his as we made our way through the house and out the back door, the gravel crunching beneath our feet as we stopped in front of the iron gates that encircled the garden.

I saw Sage's silvery-blonde hair piled high into a bun as she bent over one of the many aboveground planters, with Miles peering over her shoulder curiously. She had a little bit of dirt smeared across her face, and as she turned to look at Miles with a sweet smile, he gently wiped it off her cheek.

I stole a look at Dean, who waggled his eyebrows at me as he glanced back towards the pair, who were still entranced in each other's eyes. Without taking his eyes from hers, he held a basket out as she deposited the herbs she had been harvesting in it.

I almost didn't want to disturb the scene and nearly pulled Dean away just as the wind changed, and Miles inhaled sharply, his eyes locking onto us.

Many emotions flashed across his face as we looked at each other. Finally, after what seemed like a lifetime, he gave me his famous lopsided smile. I released a breath I didn't know I had been holding as he murmured something to Sage that made her head snap up immediately.

Dean placed his hand on the small of my back, grounding me, and I suddenly had the urge to bolt back into the house.

Sage's eyes found mine, tears threatening to fall. She dropped all of her gardening tools, and like barriers had been lifted, we both sprinted towards each other. Tears fell freely down my face as I threw my magic to open the iron gate and turned down the path to meet her outstretched arms.

I buried my face in her hair, the smell of eucalyptus and lemons filling my nose. We both whispered apologies and soothing words as we held each other and cried, uncaring of how much time was passing. All that mattered was that all was forgiven.

We pulled away, both wiping the other's faces, even though her hands were covered in dirt—and now so was my face—and smiled broadly at the two werewolves and a familiar waiting patiently behind us. Miles was still holding Sage's basket of herbs in his hands, looking between the two of us with a grateful gleam in his eye.

I gave Sage a gentle squeeze before I trotted over to Miles, just as he set the basket down to wrap his arms around me and gently lifted me off the ground. Only a few seconds had gone by before Dean let out a warning growl, although it held no real threat. Miles obliged and put me down, rolling his eyes at his alpha before giving me a wink. I turned back to Sage to find Ophelia curled up in her arms, purring loudly as my friend scratched her chin.

"I brought brunch!" I blurted out to the group, unsure of what to say after such an emotional greeting.

Miles's stomach growled, but he made no move to race off towards the banquet barn. Instead, he picked up the basket and made his way to stand next to Sage.

"Oh, did you bring mimosas as well?" Sage asked excitedly, as she let Ophelia down and wiped her dirty hands on her overalls.

I nodded, and she linked her arm with mine before taking the basket away from Miles as she pulled me along with her to walk out of the garden with the males falling behind us.

"I've missed you, my friend." She leaned her head on my shoulder as we walked, and I rested mine on hers.

"I've missed you too. More than you could ever know. And I want you to know how sorry I am for what I said to you. I wasn't... I wasn't in my right mind, Sage. I will never forgive myself for how I treated you," I murmured to her, shame threatening to steal my breath away.

Her cooling aura tightened around me, reminding me of the chilling effect of eucalyptus as she shook her head. "You were in so much pain, Blair. I only wish I could have *seen* it so I could have possibly prevented it. The sight can be such an incredible gift... but also a curse." She paused. "I miss her too, Blair."

Those words threatened to let more tears break through, but I just squeezed her arm in acknowledgment.

We made our way to the old barn where the pack gathered for large meals and full moons, one of which would be taking place in a few days. Which was also another reason we came here. I made a promise to Dean that I would be here for the next full moon, and I meant it.

At our approach, many of the wolves turned and ran forward to run their hands across Dean in greeting. But before they turned back towards the food and tables, they paused and sniffed the air around me and dipped their heads. They did not attempt to touch me as they had Dean, but their eyes gleamed with that same respect as they looked at me.

Many of the wolf pups were creeping up towards Hamish with curious glints in their eyes, who was taking in the scene as he leaned up against a tree, his near silver hair hanging loose around his face.

Hamish's lips lifted in a smirk as he formed his lips into a ring, and a small fireball escaped his mouth. The pup's eyes widened as the fire took shape into a small dragon and began flying over their heads. They broke out into excited yips as they chased the fire dragon around the clearing, nearly knocking over a few adult wolves in their pursuit.

"You hungry?" Miles asked Sage hopefully, and she nodded,

smiling brightly up at him. Before she slid her arm from mine, I pulled her close to me, bending slightly so my mouth was close to her ear.

"I will be needing some details about *that* situation later," I whispered, even though I knew werewolves had excellent hearing and Miles likely heard me.

She giggled. "Not before I hear details about yours," she shot back before grabbing Miles's hand and walking off towards the tables of food.

I whirled on Dean as the last of his pack members dipped their heads and left us. "How long has that been going on?"

He laughed. "Ever since she wacked him over the head with her water bottle. He's been smitten ever since."

We both glanced over to find Miles piling food on both of their plates, the wicker basket still on his arm as he smiled warmly at Sage, refusing to let her hold anything as they made their way towards one of the tables. The scene made my heart squeeze, and I smiled brightly.

One of the sentinel wolves I recognized from training approached us, holding two plates in hand, both already piled with various breakfast meats, eggs, and toasts. He extended them towards us. "We made up some plates for you." His eyes were a bright amber as they flicked between the two of us, and I glanced towards Dean, unsure of what to say.

Dean accepted both plates and offered the wolf a thank you, which made his smile brighten widely as he took off back towards the group.

"What was that all about?" I asked.

Dean took a step closer to me, keeping his voice low as he murmured, "It's a wolf thing. I'm their alpha and you... you are important to me, and they respect that."

"But I'm not an alpha or a werewolf." I snorted.

His eyes were like a blue fire as they looked down at me. "You are *mine*, Blair, and they can scent my feelings for you, as well as your insane attraction to me," I glared at him as he chuckled. "It's just werewolf customs, sweet Raven. Don't get those lovely panties of yours in a twist about it."

He leaned down and pressed a kiss to my forehead, effectively banishing my glare as I breathed his scent in and felt our bond hum between us. In that brief moment, nothing else mattered. The noise of the chattering pack faded away, and all that remained was him.

I was his, and he was mine.

Chapter Forty-Four

Being back in Dean's territory felt like an immense weight had been lifted off my shoulders. Even though some wolves held more adoration in their gazes when they looked at me, it felt easy, natural to be back here. With him.

Valerie already knew several of the wolves within Dean's pack, so she easily slid into the pack dynamic, though she always kept me within eyesight. Hamish kept close to her, still slightly uncomfortable with all the attention he seemed to be getting, but I doubted it was merely because he knew her. There was something forming between the two of them, and I shot her a wink from where I lazed with Dean against a large tree as Hamish smiled at Valerie, the gesture lighting up his whole face.

Sage and Miles were only a short distance away from Dean and I, and she was currently positioning Miles into a yoga pose. The sight was quite funny, as Sage was so small and slender next to Miles's hulking form, and seeing him trying to stretch out into a downward dog pose was something I never thought I'd see. His brows were scrunched at the unfamiliar stretch, and then Sage placed a hand on his back. At her touch, his face relaxed.

Ophelia was playing hide and seek with a group of young wolves in the surrounding trees, and I giggled to see her perched on top of a branch, her smaller house cat form pressed down into the bark in a shadow, making her nearly invisible. The only pop of color you could see was her glowing chartreuse eyes as they darted to each of the children below, scrambling to find hiding spots with squeals of excitement.

"Why can't it always be like this?" I sighed as I turned my head to look up at Dean.

His eyes were closed, his face wholly relaxed. If it weren't for the small smile that played on his lips at the sound of my voice, I would have thought he was sleeping.

He turned, pressing a kiss into my hair before he murmured, "These are the days we fight for. These are the days that make all the fighting, all of the grief and pain, worth it. We fight for that spark in the seemingly endless sea of darkness, Blair." Dean shifted and ran a thumb along my chin, and I closed my eyes at his touch. "I would like to show you something."

I nodded, and he pressed a light kiss to my lips.

Dean stood first and offered a hand to help me up. As I stood, I caught a glimpse of Rose across the clearing with a snarl etched onto her face. She was nearly vibrating with anger as she glared at me, the threat clear in her dark eyes.

A spark of jealousy ignited within me as I looked at her, knowing what she felt for Dean, what she wanted from him. Possessiveness washed over me as I grasped Dean by the shirt with one hand and pulled him tightly to my chest before using my other hand to bring his face down to my level. I crashed my lips to his in a savage kiss, a claiming kiss not just for Rose, but for everyone to see.

He met each stroke of my tongue with the veracity of a starved beast, hungry for more as his hands roamed along my spine and down onto my backside, where he squeezed slightly, making me let out a soft moan.

He bit my lower lip before licking away the pain. We pulled

away from each other reluctantly, and I gazed up into his wintry blue eyes, which looked like blazing hellfire filled with uncontrollable heat. A growl rumbled out of him, and my toes curled at the sound.

"Never pegged you as the jealous type," Dean murmured, his voice husky and deep, and his lip curled into a smirk.

I shrugged, like I wasn't sure what he was talking about, and he let out a throaty chuckle before grabbing my hand and pulling me towards the dirt path that led to the base of the mountain.

The sounds of the pack faded away as we made our way through along the winding path that led deeper into the forest. My grace thrummed within me as we neared the mountain, and I almost couldn't keep the invisible door shut that blocked the dark power behind it. It was pounding against its cage, desperate to be let out, wanting to answer the call of whatever lay within the mountain peaks.

"What is this place?" I broke the silence as the terrain turned rockier and we breached the threshold of the tree line.

"This is Lupes Mountain. It's the mountain that New Haven was founded around because it is said to be one of the thinnest places between worlds, a well of great magic connecting this realm to the next," he explained as we paused before the rocky path leading up along the mountain.

A chill spread along my skin at his words and hummed in my chest. A nagging feeling poked the edges of my thoughts, and in my bones, I knew this was a natural tear in the veil between this realm and Purgatory, the natural next step between this realm of life and the realm of death.

"And how did your pack come to live on the lands where the mountain is?"

He smiled. "Lunae favors her wolf children, as we were the first beings she chose to create. The land called to us, and she gave her blessing for us to reside here." He paused, turning to face me before continuing, "It's a pretty long hike, but I can shift and carry you up there, if you'd like."

Looking down at my not hiking appropriate shoes, I nodded with a smile. He immediately shucked off his shirt before pulling a small, folded pack from the back pocket of his jeans and placing the shirt inside.

I raised a brow. "That's nifty."

He continued to undress, and I found it hard to pay attention to anything other than the hard planes of his body. But I managed to listen as he agreed, "It's actually something Cal had come up with. We were shifting so much while we were tracking down the vamps, trying to find you, that we were going through a lot of clothes. He worked with Brodie and Hayley on the idea, and this is what they came up with. The straps can adjust to the shape of our bodies after the shift."

All he had on now was his underwear, which did little to hide anything, and I had to force myself to shift my gaze upward.

His dimples were showing as he smirked, pure male pride on display in his azure eyes. He slowly pulled down his underwear, keeping eye contact with me as he did so, until I pulled my gaze away to look at his perfect body. As he stood up and placed the last of his clothes into the pack, I stepped in close to him, heat thrumming through my veins, and I inhaled his rich scent. His eyes hooded as I came in close enough to feel the heat of his own body without touching.

I shifted up onto my toes so our lips could nearly brush against each other and murmured in a husky voice, "Let me help you with that."

The evidence of his arousal was pressing into me, and a low growl escaped him from my words. I playfully flicked my tongue out to lick his bottom lip before I snatched the pack from him and danced away before he could trap me with his arms. I laughed as he nearly pouted at the distance I put between us.

"I'll chase you for however long it takes, Blair." Dean's voice was a deep growl, but the tone was somehow softer, filled with an emotion I couldn't focus on before he let the shift take over. Iridescent light glided over his body as his bones lengthened and changed at a rapid pace, and within a few moments a large black wolf stood in front of me.

He was magnificent, and I couldn't help but walk forward and reach out, stopping just before I touched his fur. I paused, asking permission, and he responded with a soft chuffing sound before pressing his massive head into my palm.

His midnight fur was softer than I expected, and up close, the coloring held an almost blue hue to it that made it that much more striking.

We stood like that for a few moments, with me softly running my hands along his elongated face, and then up behind his ears. I moved along to his side, and when I came to his muscled shoulders, he knelt so I could straddle him more easily. I couldn't help but let out a giddy giggle as I seated myself on his back and grabbed some tufts of fur between his shoulders to hang on to.

Once I was fully adjusted, Dean turned his head to look at me, his glowing eyes churning with mischief as he suddenly took off fast down the path.

I squealed in excitement as I held on for dear life, even though I knew he wouldn't let me fall. His feet pounded the hard ground as he raced along the mountainside, his wolf form faster than I would have ever thought possible.

The world around us was a blur, and if I couldn't hear his powerful paws pounding against the earth beneath, I would have wondered if they were even touching the ground. I let out an excited whoop as he turned, spraying rocks out behind him and over the edge of the mountain that overlooked the entire city of New Haven. Dean howled, the sound sending goosebumps across my skin, and our bond tingled within my chest. I joined him, howling at the sky, pure joy releasing out of me that I had been too afraid to have for so long.

It was like a blockage had been released inside me, letting the joy and the pure devotion I felt for Dean fill up my entire body. It felt like I was burning from the inside out, at risk of exploding with the emotions at any moment and letting them tear across the sky. I felt our bond strengthen, that tether becoming thick and impenetrable between us, and I swore for a moment I thought I heard his voice whispering along with my own thoughts.

Our howls were answered by his pack, the haunting harmony filling the entire valley like a symphony of love. The packs howls continued even after Dean and I let up, and Dean's steps slowed as we came to a landing of sorts near the peak of the mountain.

The area could have easily been missed, as there were luscious pine trees crowding the entrance. Dean managed to wind around the branches so none of them touched my body until we stood in the middle of the strange clearing.

There were beautiful white rounded moonstones placed in rows on the mossy floor, and all around were purple lupine flowers swaying in the slight breeze. As he walked closer to the first row of moonstones, I noticed etchings carved into the tops of them. I felt it then, the staggered presence of spirits, like an invisible force pressing all along my skin, and the whisperings of them curling around me. It was then I realized what the markings were.

Names of the dead.

He stopped near the edge of the clearing where there was one moonstone placed slightly away from the others, closer to the tree line. Blue lupines grew around it, and I felt my heart stop as I read the name carved upon the stone.

Vivian.

A choked sob came out of me before I could stop it, and Dean whined in response as he gently lowered himself all the way to the ground.

I dismounted on shaky legs, dropping the small bag holding Dean's clothes, and fell to my knees as I looked at her name upon the stone. I hadn't asked what had been done with her body; I was too afraid and too broken to even acknowledge that she was truly gone, her death caused by me.

Tears flowed freely down my cheeks, and I clawed the mossy

ground beneath me, as if it would help the pain I felt at her loss. I heard Dean shift behind me and shove on his pants before he came to kneel next to me, gently placing a hand over my own.

We sat like that for a few moments, until my breathing slowed and the tears stopped streaming.

He spoke first, his voice soft and gentle, "I thought you would like a place to visit her, a place of peace that has been used by my pack to remember the fallen for generations. Each moonstone is found in one of the caves with an opening at the top where you can see the moon. It's tradition for their next of kin to choose the stone for their loved one, but... I wasn't sure when we would get you back. Ophelia and I went down there together and found this one."

I turned my head to look at him, his eyes solemn as he peered at the moonstone in front of us.

He continued, "Ophelia informed me that it was tradition for witches to be burned after their death, so we burned her body and placed the ashes here. She rests near my parents." He turned to the two stones nearest to Vivian's, and my heart both swelled and broke for him.

"Thank you," I murmured, unable to say anything else without risking falling apart all over again. He squeezed my hand, and I turned my own over to grasp it tightly, as if I could pull his strength into me.

"I'm so sorry you lost her, Blair. What she did for you, risked for you, it will not be in vain. I will not let anything happen to you." Dean turned his head so our eyes met, electricity passing between us, charging the air, stirring the power within me until I could hardly contain it.

I turned and pulled him into my chest, burying my head into his shoulder as I felt my magic wind around the two of us as the tears began to fall. He gripped me tightly, inhaling my scent into his lungs, as if I was the oxygen he needed to survive.

Lightning burst from within me, wrapping around the both of us, swirling with the essence of our bond as it strengthened it.

Dean providing me a place to visit the only mother I had in this world, in a space reserved for his pack members and family no less, was an act of pure love and devotion, and my fractured soul could hardly take it.

I'm sure he knew it already, but I was finally able to utter the words that would change everything and nothing, despite the fear in my heart of losing someone once again, knowing that I would set the world on fire for this male, and he would do the same for me.

We were thunder and lightning, shadow and light, the moon and night sky, and I loved him with everything that I was.

I lifted my head up to gaze into those beautiful eyes of burning azure, to look upon the male who never feared me, never stopped coming for me, despite the jagged edges that surrounded my heart and soul. It didn't matter what kind of soul bond we shared, what the Fates deemed us worthy of. He was mine, and I was his.

"I love you, Dean," I whispered, my voice a quivering mess as I repeated the words again, letting the truth of them ring out into the heavens. "I love you."

His answering smile rivaled even the beauty of the moon before he kissed away the stray tears tracking down my cheeks. Dean pressed a kiss to the tip of my nose and murmured, "I know." He held me then, until the tears stopped, and my lightning faded, whispering the words my heart had longed to hear for so long, that he loved me too.

Chapter Forty-Five

When we returned to the pack clearing, a party was in full swing. The music was blaring, and the fire was so high it nearly touched the sky. Werewolves danced around in the glow of the flames, casting shadows across the forest.

Drinks were brought to us before we were both pulled out towards the other dancing bodies by the fire. Dean was stiff at first, watching to make sure I was comfortable with the personal contact, but I found it wasn't bothering me anymore. When he saw I was relaxed, he relaxed too, howling along with his pack.

I was passed between Cal, who fondly looked down at me as he twirled me effortlessly into Hamish's chest. His booming laugh echoed throughout the clearing as Hayley quickly stole me away with a mischievous grin. Her eyes nearly glowed in the light of the fire as we both swayed and twirled near the flames. She passed me to Miles, who picked me up by my waist and spun in a circle as I tipped my head back and laughed.

He finally put me down, the world spinning slightly as he smiled brightly down at me. "We missed you, little witch. Maybe stick around for a while." His words made my heart swell, and I gave him a quick hug.

I nodded. "Thank you for taking care of Sage while I couldn't."

Miles looked away from me then, and I followed his gaze to see Sage seated next to Valerie on the outskirts of the clearing, smiling as they talked. Warmth took over the expression on his face, and he dipped his head in response.

I added, "And if you hurt her, you know I'll cut your balls off, right?"

He laughed then, before looking me right in the eye and murmuring, "I have no doubt that you would, but she's safe with me."

I nodded before pushing him towards her. He resisted for a moment, trying to pull me back out to dance, but I nudged him again, and he relented, making his way over to her rather quickly. The way her face lit up when she heard him approach made me smile so wide my cheeks hurt.

Thick, muscled arms wrapped around me from behind, as the scent of leather and amber insnared my senses. A hard chest pressed against my back, and I leaned into it, letting my head fall back. Dean's scruffy beard brushed against my face as he leaned down and pressed a kiss to my temple.

I let my body melt into his as I hummed to the music, enjoying having him close. The warmth of the fire was nothing compared to the warmth I felt coming from him. The feeling of being home and cherished and loved. Something I thought was so rare—after being saved by Vivian, I never thought I would feel again.

Dean began pressing kisses down the side of my face, pausing at a spot near the end of my jaw, then continuing down to the curve of my neck. All thoughts emptied out of my head as his lips pressed on an especially sensitive spot, and I shivered at the sinful sensation.

He bit down on the spot, and I gasped, before he kissed the hurt away. I turned in his arms and peered up into his hungry gaze. A predator was looking down at me, his eyes more wolf than mortal, a blazing blue filled with liquid fire. The look alone brought a blush to my cheeks. The blush only increased as his large hands traveled down the small of my back and gripped my ass.

"You're a big, bad wolf, aren't you?" My voice was a husky purr as I lifted onto my toes to lick the tip of his nose. A feral growl left him, the noise so loud I felt it rattle in my chest. Heat pooled in my core, and I pressed my thighs together.

Dean leaned down and picked me up, wrapping my legs around him, grinding me into him as he growled, "I may be a big, bad wolf, but you'll be the one howling my name at the moon tonight."

Without another word, he began stalking away from the bonfire and up along the dirt path leading back to his house.

He kicked the kitchen door open, but before entering the threshold, he paused to look over his shoulder and growl, "Keep everyone away from the house for a while." I glanced past him to see Ophelia, her jade eyes flashing in the low light. She merely dipped her head in acknowledgement and turned around, standing guard.

Dean took the stairs two at a time, and instead of turning left towards my room, he went right, walking down a long hallway in a part of the house I had never been before. Once he reached the door, he kicked it open as well, and I let out a breathy chuckle as I rolled my eyes at his alpha-hole antics.

He reluctantly let me slide down his body, blushing at the hardness I felt pressing into me as I did so. I turned to see an enormous bed against the far wall, with a beautiful live edge headboard that expanded to reach both ends of the room. The walls were a rich green, reminding me of the trees that surrounded his territory. The ceiling had a beautiful skylight which gave the perfect view of the starry sky and nearly full moon, the silvery light raining down from the heavens.

The air became thick with anticipation, electrifying. I felt the lightning beneath my skin striking my nerve endings, making my skin sensitive. I turned to find wolfish, predatory eyes staring down at me, the blue nearly matching the silvery glow of the moon.

He stepped into me, bringing his hands up to cradle my face with such gentleness, it was so at odds with his werewolf nature. Dean brought his lips down to mine, adjusting my head slightly to give him better access, and I moaned, pulling him close. The kiss was soul-changing, all-consuming, and absolutely devastating.

I felt the bolts escape my skin, lighting me up as we gripped each other, and wrapped around him. Unable to wait any longer, I broke the kiss and pulled at his shirt, nearly ripping it as I rushed to get it off, needing to feel his skin on my own.

Dean chuckled, "So impatient." His hands trailed up my sides, teasing the skin there as he dragged my sweater up my body. "I want to take my time with you tonight, Blair."

He tossed my sweater to the floor before walking me back towards his bed, a move that was purely predatory, until the backs of my legs hit the footboard. I reached out to undo his pants, but he gave me his crooked smile and nudged my hands away.

Dean knelt down onto his knees before me and slipped me out of my shoes before gazing up at me. "Let me worship you tonight." His voice was deep and barely more than a rumble that caused my skin to pebble. I bit my lip and nodded.

He leaned in and kissed one of the many scars that littered my abdomen. His lips pressed into another and another, caressing the skin that had been marked with pain, like he was trying to give me new memories to look back on when I looked at them. His hands snaked around my back, unclasping my bra with a quick flick of his fingers. He quickly discarded the garment before running his thumbs over my already peaked nipples, and a shiver ran down my spine.

I let out a moan when he brought his mouth over the sensitive skin, and he nipped and sucked until I was nearly breathless. He turned his assault onto my other breast, his tongue rolling over the bud in a way that had me clawing at his back, trying to pull him up so I could feel him too.

"I'm not done with my worship yet," he growled as his fingers slipped underneath the band of my leggings, and he slowly pulled them down and off my legs. I pressed my thighs together as he growled, staring at the lacey underwear I had on. "While these are nice,"—his voice was like velvet, and his fingers danced along the edges of the thong—"they are in my way." He tore through the material before I could even process his words.

"Hey! I liked those." I laughed as he slowly pushed me into a seated position on the edge of the bed. He laughed with me, then spread my legs wide, baring everything to him.

Dean licked his lips before looking up at me, that damned dimple appearing with his cocky smile before he drawled, "I think you're going to like this much better."

Before I could even make a snarky comment back, he lifted my legs to rest on his shoulders, causing me to fall back into the plush bed. His mouth descended on me, his tongue going straight for the most sensitive flesh, and I cried out. Dean groaned and pulled me closer to him, which I hadn't thought possible. His tongue probed my entrance, and I moaned, the ache becoming nearly unbearable. And as if he knew what I needed, he moved back up to my clit while slipping a finger inside me.

He started at a leisurely pace, one that had me gripping the bedding and grinding into his face. *More.* I wanted more.

Then a second finger joined the first, stretching me, and he began to pump them faster, deeper, curling upward to hit that perfect spot. He was winding me up so tightly with each pump of his fingers, each pass of his tongue, the sensations building and building inside me.

The sensations were too much. My whole body vibrated with pleasure, aching for the release I was chasing. Each lick, each touch had my body nearly going into a frenzy, clawing at the sheets, burning with desire. He was relentless in his exploration of me.

"Come for me, Blair," Dean growled, just before he sucked my clit, the final sensation pushing me over the edge and into oblivion.

I screamed his name so loud I was sure the gods heard me across the realms. Lightning tore from my fingertips, the jagged bolts searing into the massive headboard above me, leaving silver embers glowing within the wood. Silver embers in the shape of wings.

My whole body glowed from the bliss of release, but Dean kept up his movements, slowing them as the aftershocks subsided.

His smile was pure male satisfaction as he finally raised his head from between my legs, pausing to suck the wetness from his fingers. Heat surged through my body as I watched him stand and slip off his jeans and underwear, his eyes never leaving mine. I bit my lower lip as I let my eyes travel down his muscular chest, following the dusting of dark hair to the long, hard length of him, nearly moaning at the sight of his arousal.

I wanted to taste him as he had tasted me, but as I sat up, reaching out to him, Dean's hands wrapped around my wrists, stopping me. I glared at him, and he flashed me a wolfish grin, his eyes predatorial as he pressed gentle kisses, with only a hint of bite, to each of my wrists before clasping them together in his hand.

His other hand grazed my hip, tracing idle circles in my skin that sent shivers down my spine. He playfully nipped at my fingers, quickly kissing away the bites. I arched a brow, his grin widening before he gave me a wink. In a move so fast I barely registered it, he had me pressed back into the bed with my arms pinned above my head and one leg wrapped around his body, his hard cock pressing against my core.

A rumble tore from Dean's chest as he ground his erection against me, causing me to arch into him. He released my wrists, and I immediately wrapped them around his massive shoulders as he slammed into me in one quick thrust. I cried out, rolling my hips in tune with his.

My body was already coiling up again, each touch electrifying every nerve ending in the most deliciously pleasurable way.

He kissed his way down the column of my throat as he pounded into me, drawing shivers all across my body. I raked my nails down his back, urging him on, pulling him closer, needing more.

Dean growled, and the sound alone almost pushed me over the edge. He hooked both of my legs over his shoulders, and the new angle in which he ravaged my body gave way to a whole new level of pleasure I hadn't thought possible.

In the midst of the lust-filled trance he had me in, I pulled him in close, our mouths brushing against one another as I gasped out, "You're mine."

Dean's eyes softened, the icy blue impossibly warm as he kissed me. The kiss alone could have left me dazed, but just before I was lost in him completely, he rumbled, "You are mine, and I am yours. In every realm. Every existence. Always."

I captured his lips in another earth-shattering kiss, feeling the words deep within our bond, like a vow etched into the very fabric of our beings. I saw stars as we came together, the sheer power of the orgasm tearing away all control of my grace as wind and lightning swirled around us.

But it wasn't just pleasure I felt; it was the unyielding feeling of our souls dancing with one another, merging into one impenetrable force of otherness. We were the push and pull of the moon and tides, the thunder and lightning of the storm. We were eternal.

Chapter Forty-Six

A slight tickling sensation roused me from sleep. Groaning, I brushed away the annoyance, only to feel blades of grass and not the stray strands of hair I assumed them to be. I cracked open an eye, my heart thumping with fear as I looked over my surroundings.

I was curled up at the base of a large willow tree, its branches gracefully brushing the plush grass beneath me. The light breeze rustling the leaves let in the silvery glow of the moon, and though the sight of it gave me comfort, I still had to work to keep my breathing slow.

Blair?

Relief thrummed through me as Ophelia's voice hummed through our bond. She was here with me. Wherever I was, I was not alone.

Slowly, I lifted to a seated position, and Ophelia creeped out from under a root of the tree, rubbing against my side. Her chartreuse eyes darted to our surroundings before she shifted to her larger form, her shadows swirling around her. "Where are we?" she murmured.

"Your guess is as good as mine," I grumbled, annoyed to find myself in a black slip dress that hugged my curves and fell just below the knee. "Do you feel that?" I asked, keenly aware of the presence of pure magic in the air. Powerful magic, unlike anything I had ever felt.

She dipped her head, and my unease only increased.

I silently stood, and we both crept towards the curtain of leaves, our footsteps silent on the plush grass beneath us. Ophelia's ears were pressed flat as she slowly peeked her head out in between the branches.

"What do you see?" I whispered.

Her tail twitched. "I don't believe we are in New Haven anymore."

I scoffed, "Fuck this." I pushed my way through the long branches of the willow tree, ignoring how the purple flowers seemed to glow beneath the night sky. The power in the air increased with each step we took, so strong it nearly vibrated my bones.

The surrounding forest was ethereal, with willow trees and glowing flowers surrounding us, all illuminated by the moon and the impossibly bright stars. The sky was swirls of lilac and indigo, and I couldn't help but marvel at the beauty. In front of us was a cottage covered in vines and plants, making it almost blend in with the vegetation.

Though the cottage was beautifully mystical, I was focused on the scene in front of the eclectic home.

A large bonfire was burning, flames so high they nearly licked the sky, and a woman twirled and danced around it.

When I looked at her, my vision seemed distorted, shifting between three separate women to one, her features hazy. From what I could see, she had dark hair tumbling well past her breasts, and she wore a silver crown with the three moon phases adorning the top.

I stopped dead in my tracks, and Ophelia mirrored my movements. I didn't think I was breathing. It couldn't be *her*.

The woman stopped her twirling, and as her three forms shifted to one, I could more clearly see her features. She was wearing a similar gown as me, with a beautiful midnight blue robe that glittered with small gems that looked like stars. Her plump lips curved into a smile as she regarded me, her impossibly violet eyes twinkling with amusement.

"Blessed be, Blair and Ophelia. Welcome to my home." Her voice was like silk, with a slight musical lilt to it.

I had to make a conscious effort to move towards her, and when I stood a mere few feet in front of her, I dropped down to one knee, bowing before her. Ophelia sat next to me and bowed her large head.

Hecate chuckled, "That is not necessary, especially from *you*, daughter of Azrael. Please rise, so we may speak."

I slowly rose to look upon the Goddess of Magic, unable to form words. She was breathtaking.

She appeared to be around the same age as I was, but ancient wisdom was stark in her gaze. Dark, arched eyebrows only made her violet eyes pop, and her high cheekbones exuded grace, appearing before me as the Maiden.

"Blessed be. To what do I owe the honor of being in your presence, Goddess of Magic?" I asked, though I was pretty sure I knew the answer. It had only been a few days since I had spoken with Nathara, and I could only hope I was here to get the answers I sought.

Before my eyes she shifted, her form swirling as her face aged, wrinkles surrounding her features, her hair dusted with a beautiful silver, and her gown flowing down to the ground. The Crone raised a now grayed eyebrow at me. "I am here to answer the questions you requested of me. And I will admit that I am slightly curious about you. The power in you is so close to ascension. The other gods feel it, too."

I stiffened at her words. "What do you mean ascension?"

The Crone's laugh was raspy. "Based on what I am feeling from you, it is close. It will not take much to tip over the edge." She took a step towards me. "You are the first and only of your kind, born of life and death, fire and lightning. They fear what you will become. What you will bring to the realms."

Her words sent a chill down my spine. "What will I bring?" I whispered.

She came forward to where she was only inches away from me. The Crone brought her hand up to my face, brushing her thumb across my brow.

"Balance." Her touch caused that ancient power I kept locked away to barrel into the door, the force almost bringing me to my knees. She laughed, as if she sensed the shift in my body. "Ask your questions. I will reveal what I can." She turned away, and with a flick of her hands, two piles of large cushions appeared near each other beside the fire.

She took a seat first, and I followed suit on shaky legs, tucking them beneath me as I made myself comfortable.

Ophelia crept along behind me and took her place at my side. The Crone shifted again, her wrinkles becoming less deep, the onyx color returning to her hair, she sat up straighter, not weighed down with brittle bones. The Mother now sat before me.

She regarded Ophelia with kind eyes before praising her, "You have done well, spirit guide."

At those words, Ophelia visibly relaxed, the tension rolling out of her muscular shoulders. I rested a hand on her soft fur, a silent agreement.

"Is my power borne from the gods?" I asked.

The Mother smiled at me and nodded her head, as if she had been expecting that question. She adjusted her robes before lazing onto her side, propping herself up on several cushions and twirled a stray strand of hair in front of her.

"I'm a little surprised you haven't figured it out. Or perhaps you have." She studied me before continuing, "True power borne from the gods can only exist if the child is *borne* from a god, not created." The breath was punched out of my lungs at her words, the truth of what she was saying settling in my bones.

"How?" I choked out, and Ophelia pressed in closer to me.

"Do you know who the first angel is?" she asked me.

I wrinkled my nose, trying to remember. "Michael?"

She shook her head. "That is the common belief, as Odenus has willed it. And in part, it is true. However, he was not the first angel, just the first angel *created*. The first angel was sired of two gods." My eyes widened at her words. "Odenus and Morana's child was your father Azrael, born of both light and shadow. The energy of the birth blasted through the realms, creating a whole new one: Purgatory.

"No god had borne a child with another god. It was forbidden, you see. The imbalance of power was usually too great, but the Fates intervened. Azrael's powers remained somewhere in the middle of the two, just a shade on the darker side. To keep their child a secret, for fear of retribution from other gods, they asked me to help create angels in his image and moved him to run Purgatory in their stead."

I opened and shut my mouth a few times before I was able to ask, "So the key is my father? As he is borne of two gods, his power could rival theirs?"

The Mother sighed as she shook her head. "He is not who the prophecy spoke of."

I stared at her expectantly, waiting for her to continue.

"A realm without a god. Forgotten soldiers, ancient powers, aimlessly wandering the in-between, a world of gray. Blurred lines of life and death, a child is born of flame and shadow, bound by lightning. Broken at the hands of man and claws of Hell, the deepest crack will be the beginning. She will be felt across realms, accompanied by the bloodline of the original howls and the fireborne. She will protect the balance of life and enforce the necessity of death. A gatekeeper, or harbinger, the result will be the same. War to achieve balance... or the all-ending." The Mother's voice was ethereal and deep as she relayed the prophecy, and chills swept across my skin with every word.

I replayed the words in my head over and over again as she regarded me quietly. I rubbed my palms on my thighs, a nervous sweat coating them as her words settled within me.

"The bloodline of the original howls, that's referencing the original Guardian Fenrir and Hellhound, Grem?" I asked her, needing this confirmation.

She nodded, her darks eyes sparkling with her power.

"Fenrir and Grem are among the original children of Lunae. But there was a third. One she went to great lengths to hide, after what Odenus and Morana did to them." Hecate's face twisted in disgust. "They tricked me, stole from me, all in the name of keeping the borders of their realms safe. But they stole Fenrir and Grem away from Lunae and bound them for their own purposes."

Was it possible Dean was a descendent of this third child of Lunae?

"What happened to Lunae's third child?" I asked, trying to keep my voice steady.

Hecate smiled at me before she winked. "I believe your fate is deeply intertwined with one of her descendants. Lunae kept her remaining daughter close and created the rest of the werewolf species in her image, however making a few adjustments to keep Odenus and Morana uninterested. Though, her child's genes leak through the ages, when extremely powerful wolves are born into her line."

Dean and Hayley were direct descendants of a child of a god. My mind was whirling from the information overload, but regardless of which line they came from, my next question remained the same.

"This Guardian spell, it was originally created to help guard the gates between realms?"

At this she tilted her head, and a slow smile spread across her face. She shifted then, becoming the Maiden I encountered first, her face full of mischief as she gave me a slight nod. I inhaled a deep breath, gathering all the courage I could from the air before I asked her my next question.

"Will you share the original spell with me?"

Ophelia slowly crept in front of me, making sure her body was in between me and the goddess. A move that did not slip past the

Maiden. Her eyes flicked to Ophelia, filling with pride before they shifted back to me.

"Now why would I do that?" she purred, twirling a piece of ebony hair around her finger.

"Because I think your spell has been twisted into something that shouldn't have been. Because I want to ensure the gates between realms are guarded, and the souls that reside on each side remain where they dwell. Because... because I want the balance my mother fought for, died for. And I vow to never alter your spell or share it with another. The Guardians of Purgatory will be what they were meant to always be: guardians, protectors."

I lifted my chin at the goddess, prepared to argue until my last breath. This is what I was meant for, what my mother died for. To fight for the souls that were at rest or had been taken too soon.

The Maiden nodded once before leaning towards me, one perfectly arched eyebrow lifting. "Nathara told me of one more question, but I will spare your breath. The answer is no. There is no spell to allow a vampire to walk in the sun. They were never able to walk beneath the sun, their bloodthirsty nature demanding that balance in their creation. Demons are notorious for lying, but the real question is, what does the demon have to gain from capturing you? What do *they* have to gain from your ascension?"

Now *that* was a question I had been asking myself since being captured. The manner in which Gadreel had acted, not allowing Alistair anywhere near me, offering up lame excuses as to why they could not proceed with this farce of a ritual. Whatever Gadreel's motivations were, they were not to the benefit of Alistair.

"I do hope that I have answered all of your questions, my child. Blessed be. I'm sure we will meet again very soon." The Maiden stood then and conjured a sparkling inky cloud of stardust in her hand before she strolled over to me, pressing a kiss to my forehead.

"Wait!" I protested. She paused, lifting a brow. "What was Lunae's third child's name?"

She smiled, though it did not reach her eyes. "Asenia. Her name *is* Asenia." The Goddess of Magic took a step away from me before murmuring, "Bring upon the storm, Protector of Souls. Your ascension will be a fearsome thing to behold." She brought her palm up to her face and blew the stardust over Ophelia and I, and everything went black.

Chapter Forty-Seven

Thick arms pulled me into a hard, warm chest. Soft light trickled into the room from behind the emerald curtains, just enough to illuminate Ophelia sitting up on the bedside table, staring intently at me with wide jade eyes.

You just met the Goddess of Magic.

Ophelia spoke to me through our connection, and I merely nodded in confirmation. The events replayed repeatedly in my mind, and I pressed myself harder into Dean, needing the contact for comfort. His arms tugged me in closer, his breath tickling my shoulder.

At least I'd received some answers. And I held hope she would grant me the spell I was seeking. Only Ophelia knew my intentions for the spell; I hadn't even broached the subject yet with Dean. But I knew it was the right move, and the ancient prophecy foretold by the Fates only confirmed it.

Sighing, I pinched the bridge of my nose. How was I even going to tell Dean all of this?

"You know, I can hear your mind turning. And it is far too early for anyone to be having that many thoughts," Dean grumbled behind me before he pressed a kiss into my shoulder. I shivered at the contact of his lips. He groaned, "Wiggle like that again and you'll get a glimpse of the *only* thought I'm having right now."

He pressed his arousal into my ass to further his point.

I chuckled, "Down, wolf. There are things we need to discuss." I paused as Dean began pressing kisses up my neck. "Hecate came to me last night in a dream."

He instantly stopped as his lips rested on my jawline.

I turned in his arms, so I was facing him. Worry swam in his eyes as he looked over my face for signs of harm. I rested my hand on his jaw, caressing his cheek with my thumb, and gave him a soft smile. He truly was the most handsome male I had ever seen, and he was mine.

I told him everything that Hecate relayed to me in the dream, his brows furrowing more and more with each word. He remained quiet as I told him, his hands tracing circles along my hip beneath the covers. Once finished, we merely stared at one another, letting him absorb the information, including the truth of his heritage and all that it meant.

"You want to create more Guardians." It wasn't a question, or even an accusation. Dean was stating what he had finally figured out. I silently nodded. "Why?"

"Someone is collecting souls not meant to be collected. One of the other gods. My mother knew, and it is what got her killed. I intend to put a stop to it."

His eyes flashed with pride at my fierce tone.

"I wonder if my father knew about our bloodline, where it origi- nated from. Perhaps that knowledge is what got him and my mother killed," he said quietly, and sorrow for his loss filled me. I had wondered about this myself and vowed I would find answers for him in Purgatory, so he could finally know the truth of their deaths.

Before he could say anything else, a knock sounded at the door.

Without waiting, Miles tore into the room, a wild look in his eyes. A room-trembling growl erupted out of Dean as he stared daggers at

Miles. Dean pulled the covers up to my neckline before slipping out of the bed to stalk up to him, totally nude, the muscles along his body rippling with rage. Miles smirked but leaned his head to the side, exposing his neck to Dean, a sign of submission to his alpha.

"Morning, little witch. I see you and Dean had fun last night," Miles quipped as he took in Dean's nudity. "But I wouldn't have interrupted if it wasn't important." Dean growled at him again, his head tilting with predatory intent. Miles turned his green eyes to me. "Nathara is here, and she wants to speak with you."

* * *

Dean and I followed Miles down the hallway leading to the stairs after we got dressed. Well, one of us did. Dean donned a pair of distracting gray sweatpants and decided to forgo a shirt. He claimed it was a precaution in case he needed to shift quickly. I think he was just trying to entice me into bed with him again.

It might have been working.

I managed to make myself slightly more presentable, with my fighting leathers, boots, and curved blades strapped to my thighs. Though I hadn't bothered with the tight leather tank that went with it; instead, I put on a vintage band t-shirt and tied it in the front. I briefly thought about strapping my blade to my back but decided that would be overkill and a possible insult to Nathara. After all, she had done us a favor and spoke with Hecate on our behalf. Best not to piss off a Basilisk.

Miles led us into the formal sitting room off of the kitchen, and we found Valerie there, leaning against the archway staring at Nathara.

The latter was perched on one of the leather armchairs, her dark hair pulled back into a sleek ponytail, which only enhanced her sharp features. Today she wore a blush-pink pantsuit, which made her pale skin nearly luminous. As we entered the room, she turned her bright yellow eyes onto us, but she remained silent.

"Leave us," I spoke to Valerie and Miles.

Both glared at me, but Valerie reluctantly stalked out of the room, her gaze never leaving Nathara. Dean growled at Miles, the command clear, and Miles reluctantly followed Valerie.

We took seats on the sofa across from her, and I flicked my hand, casting a silencing spell that would prevent others from listening to our conversation. Couldn't be too careful in a house full of werewolves.

"You may speak freely." I dipped my head at the ancient being before me. Her power slithered throughout the room, her aura a bright golden-green color.

"My goddess was very eager to meet you. You did not disappoint." She pulled a weathered scroll bound with a leather tie from her lime-green snakeskin bag and set it on the mahogany coffee table before us. "What is detailed on that scroll will be visible only to yours and your familiar's eyes only. No other will be able to look upon it. My goddess gifts this to you with only one warning: Wait until you ascend, otherwise, you will die."

Shivers tracked down my spine at her words, and I nodded again. She stood up then, smoothing out the wrinkles from her suit before grabbing her bag to leave.

"Thank you. I am in your debt," I told her just as she reached the threshold.

She paused, turning towards me, the slits in her eyes barely visible within the yellow.

"No debt is necessary. Let's call this an act of faith. I was around during the first wars, Nephilim. I saw the destruction the gods brought upon this earth. Those horrors, those screams and pain will forever be burned into my memory. No debt is necessary because I have faith that *you* will be different. You, born of two realms, you made of light and dark, you of fire and lightning, will fight to protect the realm you grew up in, as well as the realm you were destined for. Don't make me regret my faith."

Her voice was haunted as she stared at me, into my soul, allowing the horrors that lurked there to bleed into my mind, sharing with me the atrocities of war. I nodded in understanding, and with that she strode from the house, her heels clicking on the floor as she went.

Wordlessly, I disbanded the silencing spell and turned my gaze to the scroll on the table. I picked it up and opened the veil, just large enough to step through, and in an instant, I was up in Dean's bedroom once more. I strode to the closet, where I found a shoe box. Tossing out the pair of beautiful new motorcycle boots, I placed the scroll there for safe keeping and cast a locking spell that would only let the box open for me.

A creak of the door opening had me shoving other boots and shoes in front of the box, and I turned, expecting Dean, only to see Sage.

I sagged as I took in my best friend, her blonde hair hanging just below her shoulders, her blue-green eyes empathetic and knowing as she took me in. Without another word, she sank down next to me on the closet floor and pulled me into her small frame.

"So much has happened, Sage. So much is going to happen. And I'm scared. I can't... I can't lose anyone else," I whispered into her shoulder, gripping her tightly, thinking of Vivian and what she would think of all this. The guilt of her death ate away at me, and it was one of the only things I had thought of during my time in Gadreel's clutches. That I deserved it, because I couldn't save her.

Sage ran a hand through my hair, a soothing gesture that Vivian used to do. Sage was always in-tune with my emotions, or maybe that was just a bonus of being a Seer; I wasn't sure.

I pulled away to look at her as she spoke. "Sometimes I am immensely grateful for the gifts I possess. Like when I saw myself meeting you. Or how I saw that you leaving home would bring you here, to *him*."

She gave me a knowing look.

"But other times, I wished I didn't have this ability... It is so terrifying. I saw you give up, and I could do nothing to help other than let the others know that you were alive. But sometimes it's also a curse of what I *can't* see. Like when Vivian died. If I would have seen that, I would have gone to her, warned her..."

She took a steadying breath as tears welled up in her eyes.

"You are one of the strongest people I have ever met, Blair, and you have gone through so many things that would have broken most people, but you're still here, still fighting for what's right. You can't change what has already happened, like I can't change what I can't see. But it's how we react that changes the future. We are the masters of our own destiny."

Chapter Forty-Eight

The next night marked the Blood Moon, a rare occurrence the pack celebrated. In their culture, it represented total alignment, as the moon aligned with both the earth and the sun, as well as a time of great change. The pack was in a frenzy trying to prepare for their run.

While all those things were widely believed within the witch community as well, the Blood Moon also symbolized the possibility of something darker.

When the Blood Moon rises, blood will spill, and chaos will be unleashed during the eclipse. And even though I was trying to focus on the festivities and the excited faces of my new family, there was a pit deep in my stomach filled with dread. I was jumpy and unusually quiet, all of which Ophelia noticed. Our bond revealed she was feeling that same wariness, and she stuck close to my side throughout the day.

I helped Selene in the kitchen prepare a massive feast, and with the help of Sage and Valerie, we worked in unison. The delicious smells wafting from the massive amounts of food had my mouth watering, but the nerves turned any taste of food to ash in my mouth.

Dean and Hamish were gathering wood for the bonfire with a few of the other sentinels while Cal and Miles were helping with the decorations, stringing up vines and flowers, and lining the trails with beautiful moonstones from the mountains under Hayley's instruction.

Once we were finished preparing the monstrous feast of meats, potatoes, vegetables, and various deserts, I used my magic to bring the food out to the barn, much like I did for my first full moon with the pack. Dean was there waiting with a sultry smile and hunger in his eyes as he took me in.

Even though we were well into winter, and we were expecting snow any day now, most of the wolves were wearing jeans and shirts, not really affected by the cold. Dean stood before me in dark jeans and a Henley that hugged the curves of his muscles and allowed just a peek of his chest hair from the top.

Not having the benefit of shifter blood, I opted to wear my fighting leather leggings and boots, with a black long-sleeved tunic and a fur-lined coat. Hayley had provided the coat, and even though I hesitated, wanting to pay her for the garment, she refused, claiming she wanted to gift something to me for my return.

As I set the food down and pack members began to dig in, I felt Dean's strong arms wrap around me from behind. I shivered in delight as his warmth wrapped around me, and I inhaled his rich scent of leather and amber.

"You look like a wolf queen tonight, my Raven," Dean rumbled as he pressed a kiss to the column of my throat.

I turned in his arms so I was facing him and looked up at his beautiful ice-blue eyes.

"It's the coat. Not everyone is blessed with warm blood like you lot," I teased, and he laughed. A deep, rich laugh, one that had me laughing along with him.

After every one of the plates was nearly licked clean, and the moon was rising in the sky, we gathered near the bonfire, the wolves readying for their run. I stood next to Dean, with Ophelia curled around my shoulders, and Valerie and Sage off to my right. Hamish was lurking in a nearby tree, looking down at the whole scene.

"Tonight, we celebrate change! The Moon Goddess herself has blessed us with several new members to our pack, and my heart fills with pride at the grace you have all shown in accepting them. My love, Blair, being one of them." Dean paused, looking around at the wolves before him. "I'm not one for big speeches, as I'm not my father. But I do know one thing. I am proud to be your alpha. Let us run beneath the moon and howl her name!" He howled at the sky, and his pack joined him, baying at the moon in an eerie melody.

He turned to me and pressed a kiss to my mouth, all teeth and tongue and lust. It left me breathless when he finally pulled away and swaggered into the woods to shift. Around us, the werewolves began shedding their clothes and shifting into their wolf forms.

Sage leaned in close to me. "What's got her panties in a twist?" She jerked her head towards the fire, and as I peered through the flames, I saw Rose glaring at me, her whole body vibrating with fury. She met my stare and gave me a cruel, toothy smile before shifting into her reddish wolf from, tearing through the clothes on her body and slinking into the forest.

"Just stupid wolf jealousy. She'll get over it. She knows her place," Valerie murmured to Sage.

Hot breath rustled my hair that was hanging down my back, and I smiled.

Hello, handsome.

I turned around to see Dean's massive black wolf and stared at him, utterly in awe at his beautiful form. "Have fun." Dean chuffed in response before howling at the moon and tearing off down the moonstone-lined path, his pack trailing after him.

Hayley followed on two legs, howling as she went, and I smiled at the sight.

Hamish dropped down from the tree and sauntered over to the table lined with various bottles of alcohol, generously provided by Brodie, who assured us he would swing by for the after-party. He handed one to each of us, and we all gulped down a swig before turning to follow the moonstone path ourselves.

In minutes, we made it to the lake where the pack would end up after their run, the five of us drinking and laughing with one another. We lounged on the boulders there, listening to the symphony of howls and yips that kissed the night sky.

We were laughing at some ridiculous story Hamish was telling us of his youth when Sage went rigid next to me, her eyes filming over with a milky white as she was thrown into one of her visions. I immediately sat up, her discarded bottle shattering on the rocks as I knelt in front of her.

She began breathing heavily, her fingers twitching as we all waited with bated breath. Tears began streaming down her face as she screamed, and my own hands trembled as I reached out to hold hers. Sage came out of the vision then, fear contorting her features.

"They're going to breach the wards!" she exclaimed, scrambling off the boulder, still sobbing.

"Who, Sage?" I leapt after her and spun her around to face me. "Who?" I demanded, shaking her slightly, even though I already knew the answer.

She whimpered, "The demons and Alistair. They're coming."

I felt my blood run cold at her words, and just before I demanded what else she saw, I felt it.

The wards around the pack's territory shuddered under the dark magic before a red flash tore through the barrier completely, leaving a hole in the magic protecting us. I knew both Brodie and Dean would be alerted, and they would be on their way here now, but I needed to do something. I had to protect my family.

"Hamish, Valerie, get airborne and see if you can find out where the tear in the wards is; guard it until Brodie arrives and restores the magic. And take out any of those bastards you can." I turned to Sage. "You need to get to the house. There's a basement that is heavily warded, and the children know to go there to hide."

Sage shook her head at me, opening her mouth to argue when a deafening roar filled the clearing.

"What the fuck was that?" Hamish bellowed as he ripped off his button-up shirt, preparing to shift.

Ophelia sniffed the air and cursed. "Wendigos. Nasty fucking creatures created in the bowels of Hell. Silver to the heart and flames will kill them." She eyed Hamish just as he let out his own roar that shook the mountains and shifted.

Hamish was easily as big as one of the nearby cabins in his dragon form. His four powerful legs were armed with black talons that dug into the earth. His scales were a dazzling mixture of indigo hues and purples, matching the night sky. Horns and spikes adorned his head, and his eyes blazed a fiery gray.

Valerie wasted no time as she launched herself onto him, settling herself between two of the spikes on his back just before he beat his powerful wings and shot into the sky.

I spun to Sage. "You need to go!" I shoved her towards the house before summoning the leather chest piece, my twin curved blades, and my angelic sword, discarding the beautiful fur coat. Lightning blazed around me as they all appeared and strapped to my body.

"Blair, wait, there's more you need to know!" Sage shouted, and I turned to her. "This is all a trap. You know that." I nodded. My new family would not suffer because of me. "They have her. They have Hayley. You *alone* need to go after her. If the rest do..." She choked on a sob. "If anyone else goes to get her back, they will die. That much I can see."

Divulging too much of the future could change it, so I knew that whatever she was holding back, there must have been a reason. I pulled her in for a hug, squeezing her tight as she sobbed into my shoulder.

I let her go and turned to Ophelia. "You will take her to the house and protect her there. Until the others show up, you will remain there with her and guard her and the pups with your life." Ophelia snarled at my command, instantly shifting into her larger form, her shadows billowing out from her in anger.

"No!" she growled, shaking her large head as she paced in front of me, trying to ignore the command. "I will not leave you, Blair, not again!"

"Protect her life as if it was mine. Do not come for me until the pack arrives. I will be alright. I promise." I pleaded with my eyes, imploring her to listen to me, commanding her to go through our bond. Finally, she relented, ushering Sage off into the trees towards the house. Pure agony radiated down our bond, and tears threatened to roll down my cheeks, but I needed to focus.

I took a shaky breath before tearing off into the woods. Snow began to fall, dusting the trees around me in white, only adding to the chill I felt in my bones.

I was deep within the forest when a gargled wail filled the night and I slowed to a stop, hiding behind a tree. The stench of rotting flesh filled my nostrils, and I tried not to gag at the wendigos' rancid scent.

I peeked around the trunk to see a creature on spindly legs with too-long arms holding massive claws that dragged across the ground. The body was humanoid in shape, covered in brown and black fur, but bony with its flesh ripped and hanging off its sides. Its deer head was void of all fur and flesh, only a skull visible, with fangs dripping dark saliva, black soulless eyes, and antlers that would impale you in one swipe.

It screeched again, so loud I felt it vibrate in my bones. Silently, I unsheathed my sword from my back, gripping it tightly as I quietly made my way around the tree, careful not to step on any twigs. The smell was overwhelming, only getting stronger with each step I took towards the wendigo. It sniffed the air and whirled around with impossible speed.

A roar tore out of the beast, shaking the trees around me. My sword began to glow with grace as the creature rushed me, its steps shaking the earth beneath me.

I swiped out just as its claws reached for me. Black blood splashed onto the mossy forest floor as it screamed. It slashed out again with its other hand, and I barely rolled out of the way to escape its deadly talons. As I climbed to my feet, I charged the wendigo, thrusting upward with my sword, embedding it in the bony body, aiming for the heart.

I narrowly missed, and the creature bellowed, splattering me with its disgusting saliva.

I gagged, ripping my sword from its body, and ducked underneath its legs, slashing out as I went. More black blood fell, drenching me before I came up behind it.

The creature was slowing, but that wasn't saying much. This time when it swiped out, I was not quick enough. The acidic burn and horrible tearing I felt as it ripped its claws through my arm nearly brought me to my knees.

"You nasty fucker." I hissed. The wounds were not closing, and blood streaked down my arm.

I rushed the wendigo again, shredding my sword through its body as I went, not stopping even as I felt its claws tear through me. It was stumbling, losing too much blood. I took the opportunity and thrust my sword upward, this time piercing its heart.

Its screech was cut off as it fell in a heap. I summoned fire to my palm and let the flames engulf the carcass.

I was breathing heavily, shaking as I sheathed my sword.

Two more emerged from the trees, wailing at the site of their burning comrade. They wasted no time as they charged me, talons extended.

I sliced open the veil and popped out behind them. Their running paused in confusion as they searched the forest for me. I swept behind both, slicing through their legs with my curved blades as I went, their roars shaking the trees. They spun, arms arching to strike at me, but I was faster. It was a dance of death as I twirled and evaded each of their blows.

Finally having enough, I sliced their heads clean off and didn't hesitate to burn their now twitching bodies to a crisp. I was breathing heavily now, the deep cuts from their claws slowly healing as I called upon my grace.

Howls and the roar of a dragon shook me out of my exhaustion.

I needed to get to Hayley. As I whirled, I came face to face with a vampire I didn't recognize. His smile was pure evil, and as I reached for my curved blades to slice through him, he merely lifted his palm and blew a black dust in my face that reeked of sulfur and brimstone.

Everything went black.

Chapter Forty-Nine

Searing pain woke me, along with the excited chattering of voices I didn't recognize. The pounding in my head increased in intensity as I started to stir. At first, my memory was fuzzy, but then it all came crashing back as I tried to bring my hand to my face, only to find it shackled down by witch cuffs. The pounding only amplified as I opened my eyes to the scene before me.

Hayley was lying on the snow-covered ground, her shallow breath the only movement indicating she was still alive. She was shackled in similar chains on all four limbs, and a metal collar adorned her neck.

I immediately tried to reach out and go to her, fighting the cuffs that held me against a tree.

I tried to reach for my magic but found it muted, like it was trapped behind a door, and I didn't have access to the key, though it desperately thrashed against the barrier. A fire crackled in the center of the clearing between Hayley and I, at the base of the mountain, and lying near the blazing pit were my weapons and coat.

"Ahh, she's awake," Alistair purred, and pure rage burst from within me.

I turned my gaze onto him, scratching at the internal door keeping my powers at bay. I felt my power rising, trying to meet my grasp, only to be pushed away.

"Let her go," I growled, baring my teeth.

In a flash, Alistair was before me, sniffing my cheek and rubbing his face against my own. I craned my neck, trying to gain any measure of space between us back.

"Sorry, sweet Blair, I can't. She's a part of the deal," he murmured, pulling away and bringing his hand up to rip open my shirt, exposing my neck.

While he was distracted and looking at my throat, I reared back as much as I could and threw my head straight into his. He screeched in pain, pulling away and holding his bleeding nose. I let out a manic chuckle, relishing in the pain I caused him.

His cries of pain roused Hayley, and she looked around frantically, sitting up and immediately trying to remove the chains from her wrists.

"Try anything like that with me again, and the girl will suffer." Alistair pointed to Hayley. I glanced at Hayley behind him, seeing her pause for a second before she continued trying to break the cuffs. "Or I'll go and make a delicious meal out of Dean."

"Fuck you," I snarled at him, but I remained still.

No matter what happened to me, Hayley and Dean needed to make it out of this. I only hoped that Ophelia was keeping Sage safe, and Dean made it here with enough time to rescue Hayley. I knew I didn't have much time left. The full moon was reaching its apex, nearly entirely crimson. Whatever Gadreel had planned for me would begin soon.

"You will not touch him. That was not a part of our arrangement!" My eyes widened in shock as I took in the small figure making her way into the clearing.

Rose.

Hayley let out a fearsome growl as her packmate strolled right up to Alistair with her hands on her hips. Rose flipped her red hair over her shoulder with a smirk, and I began fighting hard against my chains again. She had led Alistair and those vile creatures onto pack territory, betraying us all. Pure blinding fury and disgust rose within me at the sheer selfishness of her actions.

She had damned her pack, her home, the entire city of New Haven all in the name of jealousy.

"You will die for this." I spoke low, my voice full of venom and promise. I felt the silver angel energy give way to black death magic as rage boiled through my body.

She chuckled, "No Blair, the only one dying tonight will be you. See, I'll be the first on the scene, acting as though I tried to help save you and Hayley, but unfortunately, Alistair and his men overpowered me. You'll be dead, and Hayley will be gone. Leaving me alone with Dean."

I burst out laughing at her ridiculous plan. "Dean sees right through you, Rose. And by the time he's done with you, you'll wish it had been me to deal the killing blow." I flashed a vicious smile and she snarled, her body shimmering with the change as her anger took over.

I shifted my gaze to Hayley to see her vibrating with the same energy, her wolf clawing to get free.

"Enough. Alistair, silence the wolf so we can get on with the ritual. The moon will move out of its position soon." Dread filled my stomach as I took in the demon strolling out from the darkness.

Gadreel emerged out of the shadows of the trees and made a beeline for Hayley. His awful stench of sulfur filled the air as I watched the demon who had tortured me for weeks approach her. She shuffled back as far as her chain would allow, her body still fighting the change. Rose stalked back to lean back on a tree, an eager look on her face.

"Not yet, little wolf. Your ritual will be next, your full potential unlocked this night." He reached out a hand to graze her cheek, and she snapped at him with her teeth, which were now lengthening into long canines.

I furrowed my brow. Her full potential? What ritual?

Hecate's story of the Guardians and the Moon Goddess whispered to me on a phantom wind. Shock clanged through me, and a cold dread sat like a leaden weight in my stomach.

Dean and Hayley were descendants of Lunae's third child.

They wanted to make her into a Hellhound.

"What do you mean my full potential?" she snarled at him. She kept her teeth bared, and I struggled even harder to get free. A scream of pain left her as her bones snapped and twisted, beginning the process of her first shift.

Gadreel smiled at her and beckoned something out of the darkness.

A massive wolf with singed fur and scars littering its body and face stalked out of the tree line. The wolf was all black in the spots where it still had fur. His eyes were a blazing crimson, and he smelled like fire and brimstone.

The menacing energy pulsing off the creature only confirmed what I knew upon it entering the clearing: This beast was a Hellhound.

Hayley's eyes widened and then lined with tears. "Dad?" she whispered.

I swung my gaze back to the burnt wolf, not understanding how it was possible. He showed no recognition towards his daughter; he only looked to Gadreel for commands. Horror rolled through me, and I realized Dean's father had never been killed at all but instead bound to Morana by the Guardian spell, made into a Hellhound.

"Hellhounds are hard to come by, and it takes a very special werewolf gene to make them, you see. And your family line is one of the last lines with this gene left. I have two other males in my kennel in addition to your father. Just need a bitch to continue the line." He reached out and *petted* her hair, but she was too stunned to move, staring at her father. "The descendants of Lunae's children can be made into Hellhounds, and for a long time we feared that the gene would die out with both her children already bound to Elysia and

Hell. But somehow, the gene showed up again, and we had to wonder, where had it come from? Perhaps Lunae is much more cunning than we all realized."

Azrael—Father, please, I'm begging you! For fuck's sake, get down here and do something!

I sent out my silent prayers, hoping it would reach my father before it was too late for her, even though I knew in my gut he would not make it here in time. Hayley was trembling even harder now as silent tears streamed down her cheeks. Her father bared his teeth and let out a growl that shook the forest floor. Gadreel silenced him with a firm look.

"You boys sure know how to keep a lady waiting!" I made my voice sound particularly bored as I leaned my head back up against the tree.

I had to give Dean enough time to get here and save Hayley with the hope that they would both make it out of here alive and not be made into Hellhounds. Ezekiel or even my father had to get here to save them from that fate. I had no hope left for me.

Three sets of eyes turned and landed on me. "Are you feeling neglected, love? Don't worry, we were just about to start," Alistair purred, his voice making my skin crawl.

"Ahh, yes. The *chaos witch*." Gadreel's smile widened. I raised a brow in confusion, knowing Gadreel was fully aware of what I was. "So glad we finally found one for you, Alistair. I know how long you have waited to feel sunshine on your skin again."

"Dude, I'm just saying, with your complexion, you might be better off in the dark." I chuckled, and though his mouth was curled into a smile, Alistair's eyes were blazing with fury.

"Get on with it and kill her already!" Rose yelled as she started pacing.

Gadreel silenced her with a glare, his awful power filling the clearing, and she came to a stop and glowered at him before slowly averting her eyes.

"But really, what are you waiting for, Alistair? Performance issues?" I smirked at Alistair, who hissed in response, trying to barge past Gadreel. "I'm sure that there is a spell to help fix that or an herbal tincture that you could take. Unfortunately, there isn't a spell that would allow your pasty ass to walk in the sun. And that comes from Hecate herself, you know, *the Goddess of Magic.*" Alistair lunged at me, his fangs bared. "You are a fool for believing the lies Gadreel has been weaving. You are merely a pawn in a much bigger game you know nothing about!"

He was sent flying back by a blast of dark magic that made my stomach roll. He landed close to Hayley, who was still fighting against the change, her screams echoing throughout the forest.

Her hands were now shifted somewhere between paw and hand, and claws protruded out from her fingertips. She slashed out at Alistair, who was too slow to move, resulting in a lovely fresh gash along his cheek.

Alistair snarled but made no move to punish her. Gadreel clicked his tongue and pulled my attention back to him. I raised a brow expectantly, egging him on, pulling his attention back to me and away from Hayley. The memories of his torture nearly had me emptying the contents of my stomach, but I could do this.

For Dean, I could sacrifice myself if it meant he could live. Alistair worked to remove the lingering snow from his clothes as he began making his way back towards me.

"I heard you had quite a mouth on you, and that you are quite the fighter. I guess we have Vivian to thank for that. So sorry about her death, but she had become a nuisance. She would have been a wonderful addition to the witches in my collection." Gadreel continued to study me as I fought back tears. The pain and guilt of Vivian's death coiled within me, and I bit my cheek to stop myself from sobbing.

"I'll show you just how well she taught me to fight if you let me out of these chains." I flicked my eyes down to the chains wrapped around my body, and Gadreel's smile widened.

He stepped in close, so we were almost nose to nose. "As much as

I would love to see that, it will have to wait for another time." With that, he turned away to stand by the fire, throwing a red powder into it.

Crimson smoke plumed from the flames and slowly floated up into the beginnings of a dome. The demon magic made the air thick, and it coated my skin like oil, my hands itching to scrub it from my body. Howls erupted from the forest, as well as the roar of a jungle cat, and all heads turned to the direction it was coming from.

Alistair snarled at two of his henchmen, "Go slow them down!"

Two burly vampires lurking near the trees sped off into the night. Panic flared in my gut; they were too early. They needed to wait until I was gone. Then they could take Hayley while Gadreel and Alistair were distracted.

The smokey dome continued to roll down around us, slowly trapping us inside.

Hayley was howling, trying to claw herself out of the cuffs, and I winced. Blood pooled at her feet, the smell of it permeating the air, drawing Alistair closer to her.

"Get in position!" Gadreel bellowed at Alistair, who snapped out of his bloodlust and prowled towards me. Howls broke the silence again, joined by the screams of the two vampires, this time sounding close.

Gadreel summoned a large grimoire from thin air and flicked through the pages until he found the one he wanted. He stood behind Alistair and winked at me, then began speaking the ancient words of a spell.

The wind picked up around us, rustling my hair and the snow at our feet. Gadreel's voice boomed throughout the clearing, and I ground my teeth together in preparation for pain. Alistair's body began vibrating with anticipation, his pupils now fully dilated so no red was showing, only black.

How could the vampire be so blind to Gadreel's obvious treachery? How many signs did he need that this supposed ritual was fruitless? If there was such a spell to allow vampires in the sun, wouldn't another vampire have attempted this in the past centuries that they have existed?

And as for the demon, his motives were truly a mystery. The orchestration of this entire scenario still baffled me, and I feared for the aftermath of all this, of what would be unleashed across the realms.

I flicked my attention back to Gadreel, who wasn't even looking at the grimoire, instead peering at me with mirth in his eyes. The words he spoke were Latin in origin, sounding real enough to fool Alistair. But I knew the truth: There was no way for a vampire to walk in the sun. Alistair took two menacing steps towards me, stopping as he was nearly nose to nose with me, a slow grin curling up his lips.

"Alistair, wait, he's using you. The spell, it's not real. He's only making you think something is happening. There is no spell that can allow a vampire to walk in the sunlight. Hecate told me herself," I blurted, hoping he'd at least question what was happening. To give Dean more time to free Hayley. "Gadreel is the one who let me out of the dungeon. I didn't escape, *he let me go!*"

At that his steps faltered slightly, as he turned slightly to look over at Gadreel.

"Lies. She'll say anything to get out of this. Hurry and complete the ritual, and soon you will see sunshine again. This is a grimoire stolen straight from Hecate's library." Gadreel paused his nonsensical rambling to reassure Alistair, who nodded and turned towards me again, pure hunger in his eyes.

"Demons lie, Alistair, but if I can't convince you, then I have one last thing to say. I'll see you in Hell, asshole," I growled at Alistair, giving him a dark smile of my own, and his malicious grin faltered a bit.

The last-ditch effort didn't work, and I resigned myself to my fate. I sent out one more silent plea to my father and then Zeke. Then one to my familiar.

Ophelia, words cannot describe how thankful I am that Hecate sent you to me. I don't know what I did in a past life to earn you as a familiar, but I will be forever grateful for all that you have done and taught me.

Her roars of fury sounded in my head, trying to interrupt me, but I continued.

I couldn't let you die along with me. Please, just help Dean get Hayley away from here. Stay with him, as he will keep you safe. And please tell him something for me? Tell him I wish we'd had more time. And that I'm sorry I was so damn stubborn and didn't see what was right in front of me. Tell him I would do it all again, just to have these last few days with him. That I am so grateful that he saw all of me, and he was never afraid.

She tried to shout at me through our bond, but I shut her out. She didn't need to feel what was coming next.

"Drink from her," Gadreel commanded.

I braced myself for the pain, shutting everything else out and looking up at the moon and stars, praying to Lunae to watch over the pack.

Alistair opened his mouth and leaned in, his hot breath making my stomach roll with disgust.

His fangs pierced my skin, but I refused to let out a grunt of pain. I felt my blood being pulled into his mouth, and he let out a moan as he drank from me. He gripped my hair tighter, and I bared my teeth at the sensation, but I did not make any move to get away. Over Alistair's shoulder, I could see Gadreel with a smug grin on his face, looking off into the distance.

As my eyes began to flutter, and my body became too weak to hold itself up, a growl erupted in the clearing as a hulking black form slid under the lowering shield spell just before it met the forest floor.

Chapter Fifty

Dean leapt onto all fours immediately and slashed at the chains trapping Hayley with his claws. The chains shattered, and Hayley scrambled to her feet just as the change overtook her. Her screams filled the clearing, her body trembling, the bright light of the shift glowing over her skin.

Dean rounded onto Alistair and launched himself at his back. I was unable to move as Alistair's fangs ripped my skin further when he whirled around and met Dean's attack. They rolled across the snowy forest floor, with Dean snapping his jaws furiously at Alistair's neck. I could only watch, my body still limp and chained to the tree, blood flowing from the wound.

They fought viciously, Dean's alpha nature fully unleashed as he tore into Alistair with his teeth and claws. The air was thick with demonic energy and the ancient power of Dean's bloodline. Snarls shook the trees around us, casting snow down from their limbs like we were in a fucked-up snow globe.

I noticed Rose slinking towards Hayley, screams tearing from her mouth as her bones cracked and elongated, trying to take shape into a wolf.

Gadreel stood back and watched with interest but did nothing to intervene, his Hellhound remaining at his side, shifting his weight from foot to foot, bloodthirsty to join in the fray. The rest of Alistair's henchmen were anxiously watching the fight between their master and Dean, waiting to jump in.

I pulled my arms against the chains as my strength slowly returned, trying to get one out and maybe wiggle free. The wound slowly closed on my neck; the blood already spilled dried up on my skin. I heard Ophelia's roar and looked to my right to see her pounding against the smokey shield with her giant paws, her eyes trained on me. She was soon joined by Miles, Calian, and Selene all in their wolf forms, knocking against the barrier.

A yelp turned my attention back to Hayley struggling to fight off Rose, who was swiping out towards Hayley's throat with her half-shifted claws. Hayley was still trying to finish the shift and was desperately trying to throw Rose off her body.

"Don't touch her!" I screamed.

Grace beat against the internal door so hard that a little crack formed. I eagerly began willing the celestial power to push against the weakness, hoping to bring the whole thing down, consequences be damned.

Dean flung Alistair away from us both and ran towards his sister to come to her aide. I saw Alistair jump to his feet and tackle Dean to the ground in the next instant. Dean barely had time to register his surprise as Alistair hopped onto his back, his arms wrapping around his neck. Dean began thrashing and bucking, trying to throw him off, but Alistair's grip only tightened, his face set in a deadly determined snarl.

Whispers laced with magic filled my mind, the Fates' prophecy repeated over and over.

A realm without a god. Forgotten soldiers, ancient powers, aimlessly wandering the in-between, a world of gray. Blurred lines of life and death, a child is born of flame and shadow, bound by lightning. Broken at the hands of man, and claws of Hell, the deepest crack will be the beginning. She will be felt across realms, accompanied by the bloodline of the original howls and the fireborne. She will protect the balance of life and enforce the necessity of death. A gatekeeper, or harbinger, the result will be the same. War to achieve balance... or the all-ending.

Alistair's arms squeezed and twisted, and Dean's eyes widened as he looked at me, nothing but rage and love boiling in their blue depths. I screamed, and his neck snapped at an unnatural angle, his body crumpling to the ground.

Dean's head dropped onto the snowy floor with a sickening thud, and his body laid in a black heap, like a shadow cast across the snow. I watched in horror as the light died from his eyes. Hayley's screams echoed in the clearing, and Rose stopped her assault to stare at Dean's body motionless on the ground.

Everything faded away except the echo of the sound of his neck snapping as I stared. His chest did not rise or fall, he was so still. A wispy form rose from deep within his chest and floated to the edge of the clearing: Dean's soul leaving his body. Light shimmered over him as his body shifted back into his human form, and Dean lay naked on his side, his lightless eyes staring up at me.

More screams filled the clearing. Or were they my own?

I felt twin cracks within me. The first was my heart ripping itself in two at the sight of Dean lying dead before me. My soul was on fire from the pain of Dean's being ripped away, the bond burning away to ash.

The second was the door holding my grace back bursting apart. I felt my power break down its barrier and explode within me, filling every part of my body, both silver streaks of lightning and the black smoke of my parentage tangling in a vengeful harmony.

And just before I let it fill me completely, I heard my father's voice whisper, *"Show them Death."*

A ringing blared in my head, and fury in its purest form boiled my blood; I was a supernova preparing to explode. All I could see was Dean's body lying in the snow.

He was dead. Dean was dead.

That bond between Dean and I, whatever it was, or what it could have been, was gone, like smoke curling away from the destruction of my soul.

Every fiber of my being erupted, burning through my body, ripping away all that I was. In that emptiness, in that roaring silence, I imploded, the darkness swallowing the void within me with glee, making room for the scorching light of creation, reshaping me into something entirely new.

I saw everything, even as I was rising from the ashes of my unmaking. Alistair began stalking towards me again, Gadreel behind him, watching with a delighted smirk. Hayley was screaming, screaming for her brother, who remained unmoving on the snowy ground.

I saw every being, living and dead across this world, and every other realm.

I could take them—I felt the power to do so, each soul dusting across my fingertips, but I stopped, focusing my rage on those who deserved it, the ones who took him away from me.

Raw power exploded from my body, both light and dark, as I broke free of my chains, the metal shards flying out around me, the tree I was bound to tearing out of the ground as a scream ripped from my throat. Silver flames danced around my body, and even time stilled to watch as I ascended into my true form.

Witch cuffs would not work on me any longer, as my godly powers rammed through me at full force, taking over. I summoned my blade to me, and as it warmed my waiting hand, a sweet pain burst out of my back between my shoulders. Light erupted from me, and I felt raw power leaving a gift in its wake.

An iridescent glow filled the entire clearing, matching the power of my scream as the ground shook. That celestial light expanded and took shape, shifting into two long planes that were so large they nearly touched the ground. Light gave way to dark, and as my guttural scream ended, the pain subsided.

I shifted forward on my feet, adjusting to the weight of the black feathered wings kissed by flames and lightning that were flared out behind me. Alistair paled even further, if that were possible, and stumbled back a step.

Death magic gifted to me by my father poured out of me, mixing with my mother's gift of resurrection, finding the dead buried throughout the land and binding them to my will.

"You're not a witch... you're a—" Alistair didn't move fast enough as I grabbed him by the throat and lifted him high above my head. The other vampires came running to their master's aid. I threw them back with a blast of lightning, the smell of burnt flesh filling the clearing as they shrieked in pain.

The earth shook as black magic poured from me and into the snow-covered ground, and mist swirled to life, curling over the ground, obscuring anything below the knees. I commanded skeletons of varying decomposition resting in the forest to rise from their unmarked graves to hold down the vampires, to keep them still and waiting for their punishment.

Spirits and ghosts joined in, only adding to their terror. I felt the dead latching onto the vampires, feeding on their fear.

Their screams turned from ones of pain to ones of unbridled terror, and I smiled darkly at the sound.

"I am the daughter of Azrael, the Angel of Death, and of the great resurrector Yvaine. I am the dealer of death, a giver of resurrection, the protector of souls." I slammed Alistair's body into the ground, and the earth quaked beneath me.

He screamed in pain as bones in his body snapped on impact. His eyes shot to Gadreel, who stood leaning on a nearby tree with a smug expression.

"Aren't you going to help me?" Alistair managed to bite out before I gripped his throat tighter.

He thrashed against me, fighting to get up, but I didn't feel any of his blows. Black tendrils flowed from my hands and swirled into his veins, spreading the dark magic throughout his body until his veins turned black too, and he started convulsing from both pain and the intensity of my power.

"Why would I do that? I got what I wanted. The Nephilim has awakened to her power. Her ascension is complete. I don't need anything more from you." He waved his hand, dismissing him, and I looked between the two of them.

Alistair's eyes widened at the treachery and then stared up at me in horror. "Please, I didn't know this was his plan. Have mercy. All I wanted was for my kind to walk in the sun!" He screamed in pain as the death magic wrapped around his heart, betrayal and agony shining in his crimson eyes.

I leaned in and hissed in his ear, "Did you have mercy when you killed Vivian? When you ripped out her throat and left her for dead?" I punched him several times, breaking his nose, letting his blood splatter my face before I snarled, "Did you have mercy as you snapped Dean's neck right in front of me? I am *Death*, and I have no mercy."

I thrust my blade upward, piercing his heart. My power erupted in a silver-lined black glow, removing his soul from his body and instantly turning him to ash. I flicked my other wrist, cutting the veil open.

The ground fell away beneath my hand, opening a chasm that glowed of fire. The smell of brimstone filled the air, and the heat from the Underworld melted the nearby snow. His soul let out horrific shrieks of pain as I cast it into the deepest pits of Hell.

Valerie had told me the extraction of a soul from an evil being was the most excruciating pain imaginable, only next to the torture one endured in Hell.

I hoped she was right.

I turned towards the other vampires. Their screeches of fury and pain at their master's death fell upon deaf ears as I stalked towards them to bring them theirs. I released the hold on the undead one vampire at a time, giving them a glimmer of hope before tearing into them with my blade. I cut them down easily, not even bothering to use my magic, wanting to feel each blow until I drove my blade through their hearts.

I reveled in their pain. As the last of the screams cut off with the final vampire's death, I released the skeletons back to their graves, and the spirits floated away into the night. With another flick of my wrist, I closed the veil to Hell, the ground closing beneath me, taking the fiery pits and mountains of brimstone with it.

I turned to Rose next, who was curled up next to a tree, shrinking away from a huge white wolf that was snarling in her face.

Hayley's wolf form was beautiful, her coat so white she nearly blended into the snow, a stark difference to her brothers. But those similar blue eyes flicked to me, in them mixture of rage and sorrow as she waited for my command.

"Please, please, don't kill me! I'll leave and never come back, I swear! I don't want to die," Rose wailed as I stalked towards her. Black smoke billowed out of me in anger, my lightning striking the ground from my fingers, thunder booming with each step I took.

"Did you offer me the same as Alistair had me strung up like an animal about to drink me dry? You sold out your own pack, let enemies onto pack territory, and endangered your pack members! And now look what has happened!" I pointed to Dean's motionless form. "Dean is dead because of *you*." My wings flared out behind me as my voice cracked with thunder, casting shadows across her face as she continued to sob.

I flicked my wrist, extending my palm upward, and the black tendrils of my magic curled towards her, eager to taste her flesh. They desperately licked her face, eager to wrap around her soul and rip it from her body. She shrieked wildly, pressing her body down into the tree. I held them back and I looked to Hayley, giving her a slight nod. I turned my back, pulling my magic with me, and Hayley began ripping into Rose, streaking her pristine white fur with red. I did not bother with opening the ground to Hell again.

I knew where her soul would be going.

Gadreel looked appraisingly at me, his Hellhound behind him, snarling at me in my true form. "Well, well, well, I was not expecting those." He motioned to my wings. "I didn't know what to expect, of course. The prophecy was a bit vague, as you know."

Lightning gathered in my hand, a magnificent bolt that held all my rage and thirst for vengeance, tinged with the darkness of my death magic. I twirled my sword and raised it to point at Gadreel.

"What's the saying? Death comes on swift wings." I spun, hurtling that bolt towards Gadreel with a scream of pure pain, only for it to hit a coupling of trees, the bark exploding and catching fire upon impact.

He chuckled, the noise coming from behind me, the scent of sulfur thick in the air.

I turned, seeing his body materializing out of black smoke, and slashed out towards him with my sword only to miss again.

"Come now, Blair. After all, I'm the one to thank for your wings, your power fully unleashed. You wouldn't have had all that rage to ascend without me. Where's my thank you?" Gadreel pouted, and I let out a screech and I continued attacking him again and again.

He was quick and agile with his lanky form, using his ability to travel through smoke and the veil to his advantage, evading my every strike.

I finally managed to land a cut, right on his left shoulder, and he hissed in anger.

Smoke plumed from the wound, and his Hellhound took a step towards me before he waved him off. "I can see we aren't going to have a rational conversation about our proposition for you right now. But when you've calmed down, I'll be in touch."

I raised my sword at him again, ready to strike the deadly blow, but he was gone in a puff of smoke, taking his Hellhound with him.

I breathed heavily and plunged my sword into the earth beneath me. I let out a scream, digging the sword deeper into the frozen ground. I couldn't turn to look at him, couldn't accept this fate. The smoke shield was slowly dissipating as the demon magic left with the

Gadreel, and a soft whine made me finally turn around to face my worst nightmare.

Hayley's white body was curled up next to Dean's, with her white head resting on his shoulder as her blue eyes looked up at me lined with tears. I inhaled sharply as the pain in my chest from his loss radiated through my bones, the echo of our bond breaking still rattling in my chest, the remnants of it like mist on the wind.

I shuffled through the snow towards them and dropped to my knees at his side, my wings dropping to the ground with me.

Howls sounded behind Hayley as Miles and Cal were finally able to cross over to us. They flanked Hayley and continued to howl, while she stayed silent, closing her eyes to blink away tears. More howls joined them from farther away, the sorrowful song of an alpha-less pack filling the night air.

I felt tears of my own begin falling down my cheeks. I reached out with a shaking hand and grabbed his. It was so cold. A scream filled with pure grief and anger shattered out of me as I sobbed, unable to look anywhere else but his face. I reached out to shut his eyes, as if it would help calm the storm in my heart.

Ophelia sat down beside me, leaning against me, caressing the walls I had erected during battle, to let her in.

They remained intact.

Zeke and Brodie appeared then, covered in blood and wounds of their own, shock and sorrow dominating their faces as they took in the scene before them. I looked up at Zeke and choked out, "Why didn't you help him? I *prayed* to you."

I barely heard his answer. Brodie knelt beside me and placed his arm around my shoulders, his soothing magic trying to breech my mental walls, like a kiss of the tide upon the sand. I let him hold me, but I denied his magic; I deserved this pain.

I kept sobbing and clutching Dean's hand in my own, as if that alone could bring him back. My magic leaked out of my hand into his, searching for his soul, desperate to find it.

The shadow of a dragon cast us in a momentary darkness, as

Hamish circled overhead. A lone figure leapt off his back and came barreling towards the earth. The figure landed in a crouch, and as she stood, the fading red light of the moon made her hair shine like rubies. Rage filled me again as I realized what she would do. I gripped his hand tighter and squeezed my eyes shut.

"Blair." I looked up to see Valerie standing before me, gore covering her body as well, with two translucent figures floating behind her.

"No!" I growled at her, scrambling to cover his body with my own. The two spirits behind her floated closer, and the features became clearer. The first was Dean's mother, and she was smiling sadly at me, taking in my broken soul, as well as her daughter's. To her left was Dean, his face pained as he looked between his pack and me.

"It's his time, Blair. Your father received the order. You know I must take him." She knelt in front of me with her hand outstretched, and I slapped it away, growling at her.

"I swear to the gods, Valerie, if you reap him, I will kill you. Neither you nor my father will take him away from me," I snarled in her face. Her golden eyes stared back at me sadly, unflinching.

It only infuriated me more.

Rage beat down the sorrow and tucked it away. She attempted to turn her back on me, walking towards Dean's spirit, but before she could cut the veil to take Dean to Purgatory for Judgement, I blasted her with grace, throwing her across the clearing.

She was up in an instant, her face flickering between anger and pity. I threw a shield around her for good measure, locking her in a bubble of my power, and she began beating against it and screaming for me to release her. My friends looked at me in shock and fear, cowering at my immense power raging throughout the clearing. Only Ophelia remained at my side, unfazed.

Hamish landed in front of the barrier I had placed in front of Valerie, her shrieks of rage muffled behind the magic. His large, spiked head swiveled between Valerie and me, until he rumbled and stood between me and everyone else in the clearing, his back to me. An impenetrable wall, protecting me for what I was about to do.

I covered Dean's chest with both of my hands and let my magic flow through me. Dark and light mixed, my whole body lighting up with grace and power I was born to wield as it flowed from me into his body. There was no barrier blocking the full extent of my abilities now; I had ascended into my true form, and an endless well of power danced at my fingertips.

Dean's spirit floated closer, being drawn back towards his body. Magic thrummed in the air, and bolts of lightning struck in a circle around his body and my own, illuminating the forest. The strikes rattled the ground, the sky, the clouds, and the realms.

I would not let them have him.

Wind whipped throughout the clearing, the scent of ether and storms filling the air. Vibrations from the small fraction of my abilities I was calling upon shook the earth beneath us. I let pure instinct guide me, following the tether of our bond, still a small wisp hanging between us, and wrapped my powers around it. Powers of life and death, of spirit, braiding around that lone strand of a soul bond, strengthening it, nurturing it, until it was an impenetrable cord that stretched between us.

You cannot have him, Goddess. His death has been called upon. You must let him go.

The Fates whispered through my head as I poured my magic into him, ignoring their hisses of warnings. I snarled at them through whatever connection they had made, willing to defy the very Fates themselves for him.

What would you give to change his fate? To save his soul?

The three voices chanted at me, calculating; the air around my body began to vibrate as I stared up into the sky, as if I would see the Fates themselves looking down at me. A sense of destiny washed over me, all other paths I may have had before me disappearing into shadows, leaving only one remaining.

"Anything. I would give anything," I breathed quietly, blinking away tears as the stars above seemed to shimmer at my declaration. The Fates laughed, and a sense of their satisfaction curled through my mind as my magic finally took hold.

And you will, Guardian of the Gray.

Dean's spirit was sucked back into his body violently as I let a scream tear out of me into the sky. The red faded from the moon, the whole forest no longer bathed in the color of blood, and all sound faded away as I focused wholly on him. His body lit up along with my own, rippling with the intensity of my power—the power of resurrection, of life.

The shimmering light covering his skin faded, and I stared down at his handsome face, waiting, willing him to wake up. The clearing was utterly silent and still, waiting on bated breath.

Warm tears leaked down my cheeks when I felt it.

Bones snapped back in place, repairing the fatal wound, and Dean's eyes opened, the icy blue radiant in the dark night as he sucked in a deep breath.

Chapter Fifty-One

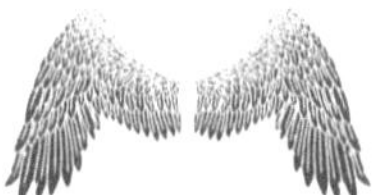

Hamish stepped to the side, his huge membranous wings tucking behind his back, revealing what I had done. Hayley let out an excited yip and howled at the moon. The other pack members joined her, and it was like music to my ears. I scrambled on top of him and wrapped my arms around his neck, needing to be as close as possible.

He was alive. Dean was *alive.*

Tears kept flowing as sobs wracked my body while he wrapped his arms around me, pulling me close. The warmth of his skin seeped into me, and our energies curled around each other, together once more. Our bond thrummed in my chest, and sweet relief spilled through my veins like a raging fire on an icy winter day.

He pressed kisses into my hair as I continued to sob against him. I slowly pulled away to look at his handsome face.

He smiled softly at me, and the emotion swimming in his eyes was nothing short of the love stories were written about. I gripped his face, reveling in the stubble of his facial hair and the warmth radiating from his cheeks, letting out a soft laugh.

"Did it hurt?" he asked, his eyes twinkling with mischief.

"Did what hurt?" I asked. He leaned in and kissed me lightly, and my entire body fired up in response.

"When you fell from Heaven?" His hand reached up and stroked the edge of my wings, and I shuddered at the touch. Our family groaned in response, and I let out a sound that was somewhere between a sob and a laugh.

"You just came back from the dead, and your first words back in the realm of the living are a cheesy pickup line?" I retorted, still cradling his face in my hands.

"What can I say? Resurrection can't keep me from being enamored by your ethereal beauty." He pressed his forehead to mine, and I breathed in his scent, letting it wash over me, comfort me. His hands curved around me, pulling me closer. "Hmm, it appears I chose my nickname for you wisely, Raven," he rumbled, gently touching my feathers, and I shivered at the sensation. I cursed softly, silently wishing those around us would disappear.

"I thought I lost you," I hoarsely whispered. I pressed my face into his neck, reassuring myself that he was here. "I would have destroyed all of the realms to get you back."

Dean gently pushed me back so he could look at my face, his eyes swirling with so many emotions. He wiped away the tears and said seriously, "Don't think I wouldn't have done the same if you had managed to sacrifice yourself, Blair. Wherever you go, I will follow."

Our family couldn't stand it anymore, and Dean and I were both rushed by the wolves, Hayley licking our faces wildly, still in her white wolf form, Brodie rustling Dean's shaggy hair, and the others bayed at the moon in celebration.

I finally released my hold on the shield keeping Valerie trapped and stood, making my way towards her and Zeke, allowing the wolves to have their moment with their alpha. Zeke threw a pair of leather trousers to Dean, despite werewolves being immune to the cold and not embarrassed of nudity, and I threw him a grateful glance. Valerie was still staring at Dean, unable to erase the look of shock on her face.

Zeke spoke first, "I got tied up in Elysia and came as soon as I could. I only managed to sneak away when you ascended and pure chaos broke out among Michael's legions. We all felt it, your power ripping across the realms. Odenus knows..." he trailed off, the implications of his statement letting me know that hard times were far from over.

I nodded, putting the worry on hold as I glanced back at Dean, alive and whole.

"You wouldn't have been able to take him, you know. Not unless I allowed it." I turned my head to look at Valerie, the usual golden gleam to her skin washed out, enhancing her dark freckles. Her mouth remained open as her eyes flicked between Dean and me.

I nearly saw the wheels turn in her mind as she grasped what I was saying, what she was feeling now radiating from my being.

Without a word, her jaw set, and she placed her right fist over her heart and bowed her head. Her chin tucked in towards her chest as she vowed, "Blair, reaper by birth, Protector of Souls, my dear friend." She paused, a flash of gold peeking up beneath her lashes. "I vow to shield your back, to aide in your reaping, and offer you family in the Realm of Gray. We are agents of the void, guides to the afterworlds, and warriors of balance and the natural order of life. We are yours, as you are ours. We are Death."

Silence followed her words; all sounds of the wolfy celebration behind us ceased. A ripple went through me at the ancient power of her words, and before I could respond, several cuts in the veil appeared behind her, and tall, leather-clad Valkyries and armored angels stepped out from the tears.

The air around us vibrated with energy, the little hairs along my arms standing up at the immense power filling the clearing. The moon seemed to shine brighter, the stars above twinkling. It felt like the entirety of the realm was hanging in the balance, waiting to tip in one direction or the other. In an instant, each of the reapers placed their hands over their hearts and recited the words Valerie had already spoken.

A connection flickered to life deep within my chest and webbed out to touch each of those who pledged the ancient words to me. I could feel them now, feel their loyalty to me and mine to them, to Purgatory, to the souls they reaped.

I placed my closed fist over my heart and bowed back, moving purely on instinct, my whole body seeming to vibrate with power, with the urge to claim Purgatory as my realm.

Shadows descended upon the clearing, and thunder boomed in the sky. A dark figure came hurtling towards the earth between me and the protectors of Purgatory. They drew their blades, but I waved them off as the familiar energy washed over me. They listened. Except Valerie, who kept her blade out and moved to stand at my side.

The dark figure slammed into the ground before us, the forest floor shaking from the impact. A chorus of growls erupted behind me, and Dean pressed himself close to my back. The shadows dissipated, and before us stood the Angel of Death himself.

"What have you done?" Azrael's voice was like the thunder booming above, with power behind each word. His dark wings were tucked in tightly behind him, his hands curled into fists.

"It was not his time to die." I lifted my chin defiantly and grabbed Dean's arm which was wrapped around my waist, needing to feel that he was still here with me.

"You do not know what you have started. This is the exact thing that got your mother killed. The gods do not take kindly to those who disrupt the natural order." At those words, power flared in my chest. Pure, white-hot fury filled me as I stepped up to him, leaving Dean and the pack behind me, snarling at Azrael.

I didn't stop until we were nearly nose to nose and I bared my teeth at him. "*They* are the ones disrupting the natural order, and you know it. Don't pretend you don't know what is going on here. Someone is taking souls that should not have been called beyond the veil, using them to fuel their own power. She knew those souls were not supposed to be taken; she was trying to restore order, *and they killed her for it."*

His nostrils flared with anger, but in his silvery gaze I saw the pain of her loss.

"I will do what she could not accomplish. I will restore order, protect the souls, guard the gates, and become the balance that the realms so desperately need. Either you are with me, or you are against me, and even though we share blood, *Father,"* I spit the last word out like a curse, "I will not hesitate to burn you to ash if you stand in my way."

Lightning skittered out from my body, the iridescent light shining through my chest, my unchecked power filling the clearing, shaking the earth, rattling the trees.

My next words were soft and hopeful as I looked up into his silver eyes.

"Together, we can reshape the realms, we can eradicate the corruption Odenus has created, we can get vengeance for what was done to her." I knew those words struck home, his eyes widening slightly as he took in my true form, my wings, and my now silver eyes.

My father's gaze was unwavering as he looked down at me, his brows furrowed as if for the first time, he felt the limitless power he held within him. The power of a god.

"You know that you are destined for more than this. You are the true ruler of Purgatory, a god born from the two gods of the afterworlds, with a legion of death behind you, and it is time for the realms to know the truth."

The crease between his brows disappeared, and his eyes were filled with pride and sorrow. I quickly pulled him into a hug, and his body shuddered before he squeezed me tightly.

I stepped away from his embrace and dropped to one knee, with my hand over my heart. "Azrael, God of the Purgatory, King of the Gates, Keeper of Souls, my father, please accept me into your service, to aid you in the protection of the in-between, the ruling of the Gray, to reap the souls whose time in this realm has come to an end, guiding them to their fair judgement, from this day until my last."

The Valkyries and reapers behind me bent the knee and repeated my words. Purgatory was a realm without a god no longer.

* * *

My father dismissed us to fix the damage in New Haven, and the rest of the angels and Valkyries under his service returned to Purgatory. I would follow soon enough to discuss the changes we would be making to the Realm of the Gray. My father warned me not to delay too long, as the other gods would have felt my ascension. But there were things here I needed to take care of before then. The other gods could wait.

We checked in with the rest of the pack, and relief flushed through my veins as we found that most were unscathed after the attack. Hamish had taken out most of the wendigos with his dragon fire, and the wolves took care of the vampires. No demons had been found on the territory, other than the awful wendigos and the demon who drugged me, and that fact puzzled me, along with Gadreel's parting words.

But I couldn't think of that now.

After healing the injured wolves, we left Miles and Cal to check the borders with Brodie and restore order to the pack. We could hear the beginnings of a party after everyone caught sight of Hayley in her wolf form, which she had refused to change back from since she shifted.

I pulled Dean into his bedroom silently, with Ophelia trailing behind us. I had his hand in mine, and I squeezed tightly, still needing to feel that he was here. That he was alive.

Dean pulled me close to him, turning me around, and I buried my face in his chest, breathing in his scent. He pressed a kiss into my hair and wrapped his arms around me, being mindful of my wings, as if he needed the closeness as well, the reassurance. The warmth of his body drove away the chill I felt deep in my bones.

He leaned back, tilting his head down to look into my newly silver eyes. The emotion that was held there was almost too much for me to bear. When he died—when I felt him die, my heart, my soul cleaved in two.

I never thought I could feel such pain. Never thought there could be a pain worse than growing up without a father, the abuse I suffered as a child, or the pain of losing the only mother figure I ever had. But the feeling, the sound, of Dean's bones breaking, of his soul leaving his body, it was like a black hole opened within me and inhaled my very being, my very soul, until there was nothing but darkness and pain in its wake.

"What are you looking at?" I asked, trying to muster a hint of sarcasm in my tone, needing to lighten this intensely intimate moment. Needing to bring back the light to my heart.

Dean's lips tilted up into a small smile. A smile I never thought I would see again.

"My heart." A lump formed in my throat, and tears stung my eyes. "Nothing and no one can break us apart, Blair. We are bound together by the Fates, and we will remain when everything across the realms has crumbled to dust. You and I, Blair, we are eternal."

Tears slid down my cheeks. The walls I had erected as we were taking care of the pack in the aftermath of the attack were collapsing. His words wrapped around my heart like a shield, coveting it, protecting it.

"I am utterly in awe of you." Dean reached a hand under my chin and lifted it up to have me look at him. Silent tears were running down my face as I gazed up at my mate, his azure eyes luminous as he looked down at me. "You already have my heart, my soul, my entire being. If I could offer you more for what you are preparing to do, I would. You have my teeth, my claws, until my last howl, and even in the next realm, the next life, I will worship you, Blair."

Dean pressed a kiss to my lips, soft and tender. It said things words could not express, but I still felt the unyielding devotion. As we both pulled away, he rested his forehead against mine, and we stood there for a few moments, drinking in the love between us.

Finally, I breathed. Flicking a silencing spell around us, I murmured, "Do you want to piss off the gods with me?"

His answering smile was purely wicked and wolfish as he purred, "It would be my pleasure, Raven."

Chapter Fifty-Two

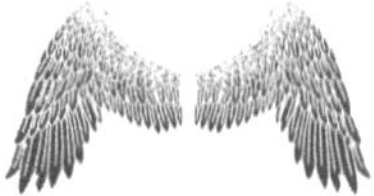

The hallways were quiet as we made our way towards the main chamber after entering Purgatory through a cut in the veil. To my right was Dean, clad in his usual jeans and dark shirt combination, but with the addition of a leather jacket. Ophelia padded silently in her larger form to my left, while Cal, Hamish, and Hayley trailed behind me. Miles had stayed with the rest of the pack and Sage in New Haven.

The massive wooden doors came into view and opened upon our approach. As we walked through them, the room was lined with Valkyries, Valerie included, and my father stood near the center, the dais behind him. Behind him was a throne, with black wings flaring out from the back. Intricate carvings detailing the wood, and the gilded scales of judgement were perched on the top. To my surprise, the throne had an adjusted back to accommodate wings.

My heart was hammering in my chest as I approached the dais, my boots rapping on the floor with each step, the only sound in the room. Finally in front of my father and the massive throne, I kneeled and rested my right fist over my heart. My father's boots filled my vision, and the bottom of his scythe hit the floor once, twice.

"It is my first decree as King of the Gray to appoint my replacement as Angel of Death, the one who will confer with the Fates, who will oversee the flow of souls into Purgatory for judgement and serve as a general for my legions." Azrael's voice carried throughout the throne room, laced with power as he surveyed everyone in attendance. "As it is her birthright as my daughter, a child of a god and witch, her power unmatched by any supernatural in any realm, I bestow this title unto her." He hit his scythe once more, the echo of it vibrating my very soul. "Rise Blair, as Guardian of Purgatory, the Angel of Death, and General to the legions of Purgatory."

I stood, my power bursting out of me like a wave, thrumming through the realm and alerting all to my presence. Magic thrummed in the air, and my body lit up with the iridescent light. My father's eyes were bright with pride as he looked at me, and together we made our way up the steps of the dais, turning only as we reached the throne. I stood to his right as he sat down, his true power blasting throughout the realm in a wave of an endless night.

A crown made of pure shadow and mist formed at the top of his head, each jagged edge more lethally beautiful than the next.

Everyone in the room, aside from Ophelia, dropped to their knee, with their right fist over their heart. My magic released from within me, spearing out to touch everything of this land, every being that resided here, and connected me to them. I breathed in that feeling, and it was as if some missing piece of myself had finally been restored.

A boom sounded beyond the doors. Swords were unsheathed, and Dean with his pack members took stances in front of the dais, leaving Ophelia and my father on the dais with me. I remained at my father's side, calling out a command for all to hold their ground.

Power pulsed, power that did not belong in this realm, and it crashed into the room, bursting the doors open.

Two angels entered first, one with white-blond hair cropped short, the other with sandy brown locks, and both with the golden eyes all angels shared. Their white wings were pulled back tight, and they were both wearing golden armor, but they had different symbols on the front. The insignia for Elysia and for Hell.

Behind them trailed their masters.

Morana wore a skin-tight red strapless dress, simple but it accentuated each curve of her body. Small rubies glinted on her brown skin, looking like drops of blood running down her neck. Her wild black hair was braided around her crown, which was made of what looked like charred bones. Her eyes were a brilliant crimson, with rings of orange just around her pupil. She was terrifyingly beautiful.

Odenus was a stark difference to the Goddess of Hell. His hair was a golden-blond which was styled to perfection, and his eyes were a deep blue that gradually faded to nearly white around his pupils. He was dressed in a cream suit with subtle golden embellishments, and a sky-blue button down, which was open enough to see his golden skin and dusting of chest hair. Odenus wore no crown but instead a circle of golden light floating just above his head, showcasing the strands of gold through his hair.

The angels stopped in the center of the room, their faces remaining impassive as they stepped to the sides, allowing the gods to step before them. The room was full of celestial magic, theirs pulsing towards me, feeling out my abilities after my ascension. The gods' attention was split between the image of my father sitting on his throne and of me as his side.

"Is that really necessary?" I drawled, leaning casually against my father's throne, arching a brow as I looked between our uninvited guests.

Morana's nostrils flared, her eyes blazing as she took in my laid-back appearance. I wore my normal threads, ripped jeans with my combat boots, a vintage band t-shirt adorned with my trusty leather jacket. The only addition I added were my curved blades strapped to my thighs and my sword resting against my back.

Odenus laughed, "My, my, what a spitfire you are. I have heard of your fiery personality. I just had not expected you to act that way in the presence of gods. After all, we have a right to be curious."

Although his tone was light, his eyes were hard, the threat abundantly clear.

Dean growled as he made his way to my side, the noise echoing throughout the room. I reached out a hand, lightly caressing his arm, and the noises ceased at my touch, though his posture remained rigid.

"What do you think you are doing sitting upon a throne in this realm, Azrael? Purgatory has no god." Morana nearly spat the words.

Before anyone could answer, Odenus crooned, "Now, now, Morana, we haven't even introduced ourselves. There will be plenty of time to get to the bottom of this. I am Odenus, the All-Father, the God of the Sun and Creation, King of Elysia. And this is Morana, Goddess of Hell, Master of Torture and Queen of the Damned. We have our archangel escorts with us, Michael with me, and Lucifer with Morana."

His eyes flicked to Azrael, burning with curiosity.

"It appears you have been *busy*, Azrael. I didn't think you would have risked your child ascending, especially after what happened to her mother, let alone steal the throne of Purgatory out from under its rightful rulers."

I stiffened and shifted my own gaze to my father, his face hard as stone as he glared at the gods.

"Her ascension wasn't my choice, nor was it hers. I left Blair on Earth, letting her be raised by humans. I had no knowledge of her whereabouts until recently. A demon forced it upon her. Perhaps you should be keeping a tighter leash on your pets, *Morana*." He sneered at her, and the room shook from Morana's rage, her face twisted in a snarl. "As for the throne, I stole nothing. This throne, this realm, is my birthright, or have you forgotten the details of my own making?" Azrael's voice was a cold death as he glared at his parents, his body posture stiff with a lethal stillness, a cobra ready to strike.

"My father speaks the truth." I waved my hand dismissively. "But none of that matters now. What matters is that there will be some changes made in this realm that are in effect as of now."

Odenus's gaze hardened. "And what authority do you have to make these changes, Nephilim?" he clipped out.

I gave him a wicked grin. "I have no authority, but the true God of Purgatory does, and as his General, I will see those changes are made by any means necessary."

Before Odenus could even utter a retort, Hecate emerged from the open doors with Nathara at her side. "You hold no authority over this realm now, Odenus. We all felt her ascension, as well as his claim to the realm. You *both* know whose blood flows in his veins as well as hers." Her face was that of The Mother, and she chose a deep purple gown that had sparkles embedded in the velvet fabric, making it look like the night sky, the color matching her eyes.

Eyes that flicked from me to the werewolves, one dark brow raised in a silent question. I gave her a subtle nod.

I strolled down the dais, weaved in between Cal and Hamish at the base of the stairs, with Ophelia and Dean at my heels, joined by Valerie. All eyes were on me as I swaggered to stand a mere few feet in front of Morana and Odenus. Michael and Lucifer let their palms rest on their blades, a warning that I had come close enough.

In the corner of my eye, I saw Hecate's features swirl, until The Maiden appeared, a mischievous grin on her face. Nathara's harsh features remained bored, but watchful.

"I am Blair, Guardian of Purgatory, the Angel of Death, and General to the legions of this realm. I am here to restore balance, to make sure no soul is called upon too early or taken to the wrong after-realm. I am here to bring the Realm of the Gray to the potential it was meant for under my father's rightful rule." I lifted my chin and smirked. "And we have the help to do it."

The air filled with magic, old magic, before the telltale light of werewolves shifting lit up the chamber. I saw the moment Morana and Odenus knew what they were seeing, the slight fear that flick-ered in their vision as they first took in Dean at my side. He pulled up the sleeve of his jacket to reveal a glowing silver symbol on the inside of his forearm, the same symbol that now marked the length of my spine.

A crescent moon glowed there, a sword resting atop the bottom crest of the moon, with wings bursting out of the hilt, and lightning wrapping around the blade. This mark, as promised, was given to those in the pack that wished to become a Guardian, to help protect the gates of this realm as well as their own. It just so happened that every adult wolf in Dean's pack asked for it.

I hadn't let anyone take the mark before I first performed the spell on myself, not willing to put anyone in any potential danger until I knew the spell was safe. Ophelia had reassured us both that the spell was formulated where free will would not be taken away, and that the bearer of the mark would only be duty bound to protect the realm.

Dean let the gods get a good long look at the new mark of the Guardians of Purgatory. Then he followed suit of his packmates behind him and shifted.

The spell allowed them to shift with their clothes on, no tearing required. His midnight body was even bigger than it had been previously, and there was no mistaking what he was now. What his whole pack had agreed to become. They were Guardians of the Gates now, all a part of Dean's pack, and all made the choice to help me protect this realm as well as their own.

Ancient power radiated off the three wolves, power that had never been present in Purgatory. And now it had a whole pack to protect it.

"What have you done?" Morana's eyes were wide as she took in the three Guardians with me, all standing taller than a horse, all with their teeth bared at the two gods.

"It appears someone has been sharing secrets," Odenus snapped, his head swiveling in The Maiden's direction. Her mischievous grin disappeared, and her features hardened.

"It was my spell to give, Odenus, and you'd do well to remember that." Pure magic radiated from her as all three of her forms manifested, her three faces all glaring at the God of the Sun.

Nathara let out a hiss, the sound sending chills down my spine. Her yellow eyes were wholly focused on the god, the slits so thin, they were nearly nonexistent.

Odenus straightened, a muscle flicking in his jaw as he straightened out his jacket before clearing his throat. "As our realms are connected, Azrael, I expect to be notified of all the changes you plan to make here. Though, I will implore you not to make too many. Things have been running quite smoothly for a long time, as you well know. You wouldn't want to disrupt another god's realm, would you?"

There was that threatening tone again, and my smirk only widened, an act that made a vein appear on his forehead.

"I will make whatever changes in my realm that I see fit, as I would expect you to make in yours. As for my changes affecting your realm, it seems like it would be your responsibility to adjust. After all, *my realm* is at the center," Azrael growled.

I turned to him, and he gave me a curt nod, giving me the approval to say what was surely going to piss them off even more.

"As for how it has been run, that is all a matter of opinion. My mother discovered that souls were being harvested before their time and being pulled through to one of your sides before judgement. That is unsanctioned and completely bypasses what Purgatory was created for. Furthermore, such acts could be seen as an act of war. I will find out who has been stealing souls and take necessary action." I shifted my gaze between the two, finding Morana regarding me quizzically.

As she caught my gaze, her face hardened before she reached out a hand to wrap around Odenus's arm. "Come now, Odenus. We have seen what we came here for." She flicked her wild eyes to me, then to my father. "We'll be in touch, God of Purgatory."

With one more hard look from Odenus, he turned with Morana, and they made their way out of the chamber, their archangels following silently behind. I let the door slam shut behind them and turned towards Hecate.

"I see you were able to get the spell to work for you. Very fine spellwork." The Crone faced me now, her indigo eyes regarding the three Guardians at my back.

"The spell was brilliant, and aside from that, I had a great teacher." I shrugged one shoulder, thinking of Vivian and all the days spent working on countless spells, always practicing various kinds of magic. I missed her deeply.

The Crone came closer and grasped my hands in hers. "You're still a witch at heart. Do pay me a visit in Strophalos, dear. I would love to teach you more about your heritage that hails from my realm." She let me go and glided towards the great doors, which opened at her approach.

Nathara dipped her head slightly with the hint of a smile on her lips before following The Crone out.

The Guardians shifted back, and I dismissed the Valkyries, letting only Valerie stay, before I took a seat on the stairs of the dais and let out a heavy breath.

"That went well," Hayley snarked as she sat next to me, stretching out her long legs in front of her.

"Could have been worse. They could have started a war right here." Valerie snorted, casting a look at me, her golden eyes swirling with amusement. "You surprised them. They underestimated your power and knowledge. They will not do so again."

I nodded my head in agreement.

My father stood from his throne and surveyed all of us, his jaw ticking and mouth set in a grim line. "This is far from over. Odenus and Morana will not forgive what happened here today, and there will be consequences. But we will be ready." He exhaled before he looked at me. "Your mother would be proud."

Tears filled my eyes as he gave me a sad smile before he strode out of the throne room.

I looked at everyone in front of me, my pack, my family. All of them offering to help me through all of this, laying their lives on the line to protect this realm and the passage of souls into the after-realms. My eyes finally landed on Dean, and my heart swelled at the pure devotion etched into his face as he stared down at me.

"You ready to bring on the storm?" I asked.

His lips curved into a cocky smile, his glacier eyes full of love and pride as he leaned in close and pressed a kiss to my forehead. "With you? Always."

He leaned away and let out a howl that shook the chamber, and it was answered by the Guardians at home in New Haven, and by the war-cries of the Valkyries and reapers of Purgatory.

Acknowledgments

There are not enough words to express the gratitude for those that have supported me on this journey, but I will try anyway.

To my husband, Alec, this book quite literally would not be here and completed without you. I like to think I would have eventually gotten the courage to write Blair's story, but the truth is, I'm not sure I would have.

I remember telling you about an incredibly vivid dream that I had, about a girl with nearly limitless power in her veins on the run from those who would use that power for their own gain. I remember feeling nervous to tell you that I thought it would be a good book, and that maybe I should try to write the story, wondering how you would feel or what you would think about the idea. I remember how you just smiled and shrugged as you said, "So write the book!"

So thank you, for giving me that final push that I desperately needed.

To my mom and dad, for always supporting me, and listening to me babble on about my characters, my ideas, and everything I have learned about publishing a book. I couldn't have done it without either of you. I love you both. Specifically to my mom—I will admit that you were right, I should have been doing this a long time ago.

To my absolute best friend Ashleigh, thank you for being there for me every step of the way. I'm still proud of myself for hooking you on the fantasy genre (and I will remind you of that fact until we are a couple of old ladies reading in our matching rocking chairs). Thank you for taking a chance and diving into a whole new genre for me, helping make my story better, and being the best hype woman and best friend I have ever had. I love you.

Thank you to my editor, Ashley Oliver at Enchanted Author Co for all the work and advice to make this story better. I know this was a big project, so I appreciate all of your hard work and dedication!

I will be forever grateful to you all for helping me bring this story into the world.

About the Author

Samantha Vance currently lives in Louisiana with her husband and four fur babies who are all integral members of her writing team. Mostly their job duties include listening to the ramblings of a madwoman hell bent on figuring out the plot hole in her story at 2am, cuddles and a steady stream of both coffee and Old Fashions. Yes, her pets are extremely talented bartenders.

She did not follow the traditional road to becoming an author. Though she often dreamed of witches, werewolves and grand battles, she thought becoming an adult was leaving those things in fiction and chose a career path in the healthcare field to help people.

It took a few years after college for her to realize that the real world can be cruel and boring, and providing readers with worlds to escape and dive into was her true calling.

Lightning Bound is her first published work and is Book 1 in the Lightning Bound Series. Check out her social media pages for future releases, announcements, and videos that (*hopefully*) make you laugh.

tiktok.com/@authorsamvance6
instagram.com/@authorsamvance

www.ingramcontent.com/pod-product-compliance
Lightning Source LLC
Chambersburg PA
CBHW031953150726
47990CB00005B/1682